Cinderolda

By Janet Periat

Awards

2008 Silicon Valley Romance Writers of America
   Gotcha! Contest
2009 Missouri RWA *Gateway to the Best* Contest
2009 Valley of the Sun RWA *Hot Prospects* Contest
2009 East Texas RWA *Southern Heat* Contest

Cinderolda

Copyright © 2012 Janet Periat

Published 2012 by Madison Avenue Press

www.janetperiat.com

First Edition: 2012

ISBN 978-1-937813-01-7

Cover Art: © 2012 Randy Cleveland

Book Design: Frank Higgins

For All My Gay BFFs, especially Curtis Caudill and David Yanez

Acknowledgments

I wrote Cinderolda during 2008 and 2009 and the dog ate my notes on all my research sources. So if I talked to you about something and you gave me answers and I don't mention you here, I owe you a beer and a free copy of the book.

I know I talked to my niece, Camile Periat-Steinmetz, and her husband Carl Steinmetz. Carl's a firefighter and gave me great EMT advice. And I picked the brain of a neighbor and good friend, Marissa Parsons, who is an RN and advised me on all the nursey stuff Cynthia was supposed to know.

Most of my research was done on the Internet, mainly through Google. I found out where drag queens shopped in San Francisco and what materials rich people used to decorate their homes. I researched online child adoption websites and other resources for adopted children in search of their birth parents. And I spent quality time on The San Francisco Fairmont's website, for menus and wedding ideas.

I'd like to thank to the judges of the Romance Writers of America contests for giving me such great critiques. And thanks for giving *Cinderolda* all those awards!

A huge mega thanks to my agent, Laurie McLean, for loving *Cinderolda* enough to sign me. Thanks for seeing the potential in me that other agents seemed to think was mental illness. And thanks for all the advice on *Cinderolda* and my writing in general. You've helped make me a much better writer.

I'd like to thank all the editors at the publishing houses for encouraging me to get this book out there. Thanks for your compliments and advice.

But the people who helped me the most and deserve the most credit for the book—and my writing—are my critique group, The Armadillos: Ann Fischer, Anne Maragoni, Teri Bradburn, Linda Baxter, and Linda Hill. I'd also like to mention Claudia Levin who was part of our group at the time I wrote this book. You ladies rock! Thanks for your continued encouragement, support and cheerleading. Not only did you keep me afloat during those bleak old days when the rejection letters seemed to come in avalanches, you continue to be a wonderful influence on my work.

And last, but not least, here's a giant shoutout to my best friend and husband, Frank, who restored my faith in men and made me believe in true love. Thanks for the last twenty-four years of fun, and here's to fifty more. Love you, big guy!

I love hearing from my readers. I can be contacted through my website: **www.janetperiat.com**. And if you are on Facebook—and can tear yourself away from Farmville for two seconds—you can "Like" my fan page called *Janet Periat's Fan Page, (Official, Authorized and Fully Licensed)*.

Preface

A few years ago, I watched Drew Barrymore in *Ever After*. While I enjoyed it, I wondered why every Cinderella story involved young people. I wanted a Cinderella story for adults. I have lots of friends who've found love at forty and fifty. And at sixty, seventy, eighty and ninety. The experience is just as intense and powerful as when we were young. The heart never ages.

So please enjoy *Cinderolda*, a timeless tale about timeless love.

—Janet Periat, September 2011

Chapter One

A street performer in a ten-foot-tall electric-pink giraffe costume appeared directly in Cynthia's path. She darted to the right, narrowly avoiding the freak and continued her jog through Golden Gate Park. While she normally enjoyed the human circus that comprised much of the population of San Francisco, today was not one of those days. Today she wanted to pop Mr. Giraffe.

Grumbling to herself, she ran past the Botanical Gardens, heading for the 9th Avenue entrance to the park. And then she saw him. Mr. Perfect. Jogging right towards her. Her heart beat faster and her palms began to sweat.

Tall, blue-eyed, brown-haired and beautiful, Mr. Perfect had become her favorite crush since she'd moved to the City. He'd caught her attention on her first jog through the park. Legs that went on forever, a nice tight little butt, buff arms and gorgeous running form. He had to be in his late forties, but he ran like a twenty-year-old. Yummy.

Not that he'd ever noticed her. Miss Invisible. Of course, considering her current circumstances, it was fine. No way did she want to bring anyone into her horror movie of a life.

As he neared her, she pretended to be self-confident and paid close attention to her feet. She'd already tripped twice when encountering him, no way could she handle doing a full face plant in front of the guy.

Right as he reached her, she averted her gaze. He ran by.

You idiot! You could have smiled.

Yeah, and what would that have done? Nothing.

When she reached the crossing at 9th Avenue and Lincoln Way, the light was red. She didn't feel like stopping, so she continued jogging along Lincoln. She'd cross the street further down the road.

Tires screeched loudly behind her followed by a sickly thud.

She swung around and her heart stopped. Mr. Perfect was lying in the street in front of a car! He'd been hit!

Racing to his side, she dropped to her knees to help him.

Blood gushed from a wound on his upper thigh. Cynthia pressed down on the injury with both hands, but the warm liquid poured through her fingers. Adrenaline slammed her system. Her heart pounded hard against her ribs. Where was her training? *Come on, Nurse Mode! Kick in!*

"Call 911!" she shouted over the din of the San Francisco traffic.

Ignoring the complaints of her bare knees on the rough asphalt, she got into a better position and moved her hands. His femoral artery spurted like a geyser. Screaming inwardly, she clamped down on his steely thigh. The bleeding slowed.

This was so hard! If the guy were a total stranger, her reactions would be automatic.

Dazed from the impact with the car, the wounded hunk groaned "Kelly," and moved to get up. Blood shot out of his leg.

Her body tensed and her pulse jumped. She pressed down hard on his upper thigh and gently blocked him with a shoulder. "Stay down! Don't move or you could hurt yourself more! We don't know all your injuries yet! And I have to stop this bleeding and I can't do it if you keep trying to get up!"

He stopped moving. She focused on his leg, approximating where to put the pressure to stop the bleeding entirely. In a quick move, she adjusted her hands upwards an inch or so and put all her weight on his thigh. The flow went to a bare trickle. She took a deep breath. Thank God.

Wait. Kelly, did he say? Was he married? No ring on his finger.

Focus! Dating him will be a moot point if he's dead!

What to do? ABC's of CPR. What were they? Airways, breathing, circulation. Airways? Unblocked, check. Breathing? Steady. Check. Circulation? Strong pulse in his leg. Good. What else?

He rubbed his forehead and smeared a swath of blood down his carved cheek.

"You're doing fine, just stay still."

She assessed his damage carefully from head to toe. Man, what a big guy. Had to be six five or six. Blood flowed freely from the cut on his forehead, but it didn't look deep. Facial wounds always bled a lot. The car had hit him hard, but his rebound into the curbside reflector had inflicted the most damage: it sliced open his upper right thigh. If she hadn't been within a few yards of him, he would have bled to death.

Still, he'd lost a lot of blood. His blue running shorts were now bright red, her own white trunks, splattered with polka dots. The warm sun enhanced the familiar metallic scent, sending her back to those wild days in the ER.

A crowd formed around them. Two small kids with scooters jostled for position.

She searched the onlookers' faces for help, but their blank expressions made her gut twist. "This isn't TV, people! Someone call 911, *now*! And get those kids out of here!"

"I called, ambulance is coming!" a black lady yelled beside her.

Relief flooded her and her shoulders relaxed a tad. "Thank you." She got into the runner's line of sight. "You're gonna be okay. Ambulance is on its way. Just stay with me, I'll get you through this. And don't move your head."

One move with a broken neck and he'd be paralyzed for life.

She scanned the crowd. "Could someone please help me here? I need someone to hold his head."

People turned away, looked down at their feet or pretended they'd gotten an important call. A tall older guy in a tweed jacket turned and walked away.

Rage fired through her veins. She wanted to kick them all in their collective asses. "Really, people, I need help!"

The black lady who'd called for the ambulance put a hand on her shoulder. "I would, but my daughter died from AIDS and I just can't take the chance, not with all that blood. I have a grandson who depends on me."

Cynthia sighed heavily. "I get it. I probably shouldn't be doing this, either, but I can't let him die."

"God's smilin' down on you, sugar," the woman replied, patting her. "Planet needs more people like you."

A bus roared by, spewing a cloud of noxious smoke. Cynthia coughed, tasting the diesel fumes. Great. Hopefully the guy wouldn't asphyxiate before the ambulance arrived.

More blood escaped the wound. She closed her fingers more tightly together and put all her weight on his thigh. He groaned and shifted sideways.

"Stay still, buddy!"

He grunted, rolled his shoulders, then stopped moving. Did that mean he understood her?

A flood of CPR techniques and emergency procedures flashed through her mind. Praise the Lord, her training was coming back to her. Seven years out of the loop had made her rusty. She checked to see if he was diaphoretic. Well, duh, sweat was all over his brow from running. How was she supposed to tell bad sweat from good sweat?

Think back to that guy who died on that horrible Christmas Eve shift. That horrific bleed out.

No, this guy didn't feel clammy. His color was better. In shock, but probably not on the verge of dying. "What's your name, honey? Can you tell me your name?"

"Rex…Rex Du Charmante."

"Perfect, Rex. Can you feel my hands on your thigh? I'm pressing down hard here, can you feel me?"

"Y-yes."

Excellent, not paralyzed. She sighed. "Great. Rex, you're doing fabulous. Now can you wiggle your toes on your right leg? Wiggle them for me."

His right foot twitched. A surge of hope rushed through her. Thank the Lord. This man was far too awesome to go through the rest of his life paralyzed. Plus it would ruin all her honeymoon plans.

Cynthia! Snap the hell out of it! He's a patient! And he's in love with some lucky woman named Kelly. Damn it.

"Wonderful, Rex. Now just relax and stay still for me, okay? It's really important that you don't move your neck or anything, okay?"

"O…kay."

Thank God, he was a runner and clearly had a strong constitution. She checked his color again. His cheeks were pinkish. She had to watch him carefully for sudden loss of color and a change in his breathing, indicators of internal bleeding. But if that happened…

Don't think that way! He can't die! Why wasn't there a doctor in the crowd?

A bit of fresh blood trickled out, she edged closer to his groin and pressed the wound even harder. "I swear, I'm not getting fresh with you. I have to keep the pressure on the wound."

Through his pained expression, a fleeting smile. "Didn't… think…that."

He opened his eyes and their gazes met. Intelligence and strength radiated from his brilliant blue depths. A zing went through her body and her pulse jumped a notch. Wow, what a hottie! Despite his injuries, he looked even better close up.

This was so freaky. Not ten minutes before she'd been having sex with him in her mind. And now, here she was touching him, right near his package—

Not the time! Nurse Mode, please!

His gaze went unfocused and he whispered, "Kelly."

Damn it. Kelly again. She wished someone loved her like this. "Stay awake, now."

He closed his eyes and his body stilled.

A wallop of fear powered through her and her shoulders tensed so much they burned. "Rex, you have to stay awake for me!"

Gasping for a breath, his lids flew open and he coughed a bit. "Need my daughter," he rasped. He took in a large lungful of air and finally settled down.

Her nerves rattled, her limbs shaky, she searched the street. Where was that ambulance? She couldn't do anything more for him until help arrived. He'd better not die on her or she'd spontaneously combust. God, she'd never been this fragile. How many freakin' traumatic situations had she endured lately? Her emotional toolbox only held fear, doubt and exhaustion. Pandora's Toolbox.

"Kelly, I can't leave her," he moaned.

"You're not leaving her. Stay with me and you'll be fine, Rex." She wished she could rub his shoulder or comfort him in some way other than verbally.

"Trying."

"Good job. Just keep trying." She let out a long breath and pulled her neck to one side to stretch it.

He gazed up at her, his mouth formed words but none came out. He swallowed and tried again. "Who…who are you?" His voice trailed off, sounding raspy and weak.

Cynthia didn't like the way he kept slipping in and out of consciousness nor the way his eyes looked: rolling and unfocused. She needed help and she needed it now.

"I'm a nurse. Lie still, you'll be fine. Where's the pain? Can you tell me where your pain is? How's your head?"

Lids fluttering, he groaned loudly and his breathing hitched. A shudder went through his body.

She saw her father convulsing in his hospital bed, his eyes rolling back in his head. Pain ripped through her gut and her throat constricted. Tears welled in her eyes.

"Rex, answer me," she demanded in a louder tone, her voice cracking. She cleared her throat. "How's your head?"

"Hurts. Did I get hit by a car?" He sounded much more coherent.

A small ray of hope pierced her gloom. "Yes, you did. But you're gonna make it." She took a deep breath, counted to ten and managed to center herself.

Reaching out for her, he fought to make eye contact. "You can't let me die. My daughter. Kelly needs me."

His daughter, Kelly? Not his wife? A rush of joy swept through her. Finally, some good news in all this hell. Whoo-hoo!

He grabbed her leg in a surprisingly strong grip. "Can't leave her. I'm all she has…I hope…left her enough money."

"You aren't dying on my watch, Rex, get that out of your head. You're fine. You'll see your daughter shortly, I promise."

What an awesome guy. His first thoughts were of his daughter? Being a caring father said a lot about his character.

A twinge of jealousy followed by a stab of grief tweaked her insides. What would it be like to have a father who loved you this much? Her father's last words were about his stupid insurance policy.

Rex's breathing grew labored. Sunlight glinted off the sweat on his brow. He speared his hair with his fingers and held his head. "Owww, this...feels like…blasted herd of elephants…stampeding on my head."

Cynthia laughed with relief. Thank God, he was coherent enough to joke. "It was a freakin' Prius. Didn't you see the red light?"

"No…was…looking at you."

Her heart leapt into her throat so fast, she choked. Oh, God, she'd been right, he had been looking at her! Two days ago they'd shared a smile that had made her heart—and other body parts—sing.

The ever-hopeful optimist inside her did a little happy dance. She immediately fired the choreographer. In her life, no good deed went unpunished. Watch, somehow this guy would sue her for saving him. That was her story. Give others all she had to give and get a stake driven through her heart for the effort.

A dreamy grin played across his handsome face. "You have the most perfect ass…I've ever seen…" His head lolled.

"Damn you, Rex! Stay awake and you can grab it!"

Several bystanders laughed. She hadn't meant that as a joke. Damn it, this was no time for levity!

He cracked a smile and made a weak grabbing gesture towards her rear. "Can't reach it…"

She busted up and worked hard to keep her weight and focus on his wound. It was a rare man who could make her laugh. And his quick comeback meant that his head was clearing. "You're cute, Rex, but please don't move, even for a joke."

"You're…cute one. Saw you…for three weeks…running… beautiful…you… have class…and taste…perfect woman. Perfect for me."

Her heart soared at his compliments, then she threw an imaginary bucket of cold water over her head. "Class and taste, *right*. Rex, you are beyond head injured, you're delusional. But keep talking, I'll take any compliment I can get, even if it's coming from a guy who just got hit by a car."

The crowd erupted in laughter again. She cringed. Why couldn't she keep her big mouth shut? How many times had she been reprimanded by her superiors for her "inappropriately timed humor"? Even if her patient enjoyed it, she didn't want anyone there to think this wasn't a serious situation.

"Sorry, Rex. I make bad jokes at super inopportune times. It's part of my charm. So ignore me. Well, not the part about staying awake and listening to me. Just ignore my inappropriate humor. My filters aren't working the way they once did."

"Like it. You're funny."

"Well, thank you, but I have to learn how to hold my tongue."

Sirens echoed from blocks away. Relief flooded her system and the knot in her stomach loosened. "Hear that? Paramedics will be here in a jiffy. How old's your daughter, Rex? Tell me about her."

"Kelly's...great." He gasped, his body stiffened. "Oh, no, the meeting."

"Calm down, Rex. Gotta keep calm for me, okay?"

He sighed and groaned, his face contorted with pain. "So important. Need a cell phone...have to talk to Marx..."

"Work is not something you should be worrying about. Think about something happy. Hawaii. Yeah, Hawaii. Picture this: you're on a beach." *I'm next to you.* "A lovely ocean breeze wafts over you, you're sipping on a nice cold Mai Tai." *I'm rubbing suntan lotion over your finely developed muscles, your lean belly.* "Now isn't that better?"

He grabbed her leg and looked her dead in the eye. "Won't forget this...take you sailing." He let go, his arm dropped to his side, his gaze drifted. "My...yacht...we'll go on my yacht..." His voice dropped to a whisper.

Her body knotted in fear. Damn it, why wouldn't he just stay coherent and alert? She checked his breathing, his skin color. Both seemed stable. "Right and I'm Cinderella and the pumpkin's just about to pick you up," she said under her breath.

Sirens whined louder. She looked down the street, a fire engine raced towards them.

Her mood skyrocketed. Medical equipment! Professionals! They were saved! "Thank bloody God, here come the mice now."

The fire truck pulled up in front of her. A tall blond thirty-something firefighter with a square jaw leapt out and rushed to her side. She didn't know if it was the relief, the situation or her wonky emotions, but the firefighter looked like a superhero to her. Like he flew out of his truck wearing a cape to save her man.

Two other firefighters—a man and a woman—joined Super Fireman. Cynthia gave them a quick update on her patient's status.

The blond firefighter knelt beside her and set a red plastic toolbox on the asphalt. He opened it and rummaged around. "You had medical training?"

"I was an ER nurse for a million years."

Her adrenaline on the wane, sharp shooting pains rocked her body. A pea-sized chunk of gravel felt like it had penetrated her kneecap. Searing daggers stabbed her back from her prolonged crouched position, and the vertebrae in her neck felt like they'd fused together. She straightened her spine and fought back a grunt.

The firefighter nodded towards Rex. "Guy was lucky as hell you were here. Wound like that, he would have bled to death in under two minutes," he said, sitting back on his heels. He gave Rex a once over and checked the positioning of her hands on the wound. "Just keep doing what you're doing, keep the pressure there, I'm going to put a tourniquet on it and get you out of here."

She couldn't wait to stand and stretch out her cramping limbs.

The firefighter moved closer to her, shoulder-to-shoulder. Slipping up Rex's shorts, he tied a rubber hose around his thigh, above the wound. "Okay, you can let go. Thanks. Hang around, police will need a report from you."

Her heart skipped a beat and she stopped breathing. Police? *No bloody way!* She had to get out of there. She had to run.

The firefighter sent her a questioning look.

Forcing a passive look on her face, she looked down at her hands on Rex's thigh. "Sorry, you can't believe how badly this guy bled. I'm having trouble letting go."

The blond firefighter smiled. "It's okay, we're on it. He'll be fine."

Reluctantly, she moved her hands, expecting Ol' Faithful to erupt again. Not even a drop came out. Her entire body loosened and she breathed a giant sigh of relief.

Her hands dripped with blood. Holding them away from her body, she moved to get up. Her knees, back and legs screamed in agony. Stiff as hell, she groaned loudly as she forced her body to stand. She hobbled a couple steps back and gradually straightened out as little jabs of pain jolted her.

She indicated Rex with a sharp nod of her head. "Where will they take him?"

"Injury like this? SF General Trauma Center," the firefighter answered, slipping an oxygen mask over Rex's nose and mouth.

"Okay, thanks."

Gravel clung to her pitted knees, but she couldn't knock it off because of her blood-soaked hands. Hopefully, Rex didn't have HIV. By the way he talked about her butt, he had to be straight. But she knew enough not to make generalizations. She had to get this blood off and right away.

Three police cars with lights flashing had blocked off the scene. Several cops were milling around and a few watched her. An ambulance with sirens blaring pulled up next to the fire engine.

She gazed down at her patient and bit her lip. No way did she want to leave the guy. She was tempted to insist on riding in the ambulance to make sure he'd be okay. But she couldn't afford to take the chance. The police would question her and that couldn't happen. No way was she giving them her name.

As if her worst fears summoned them, two uniformed cops approached her, a guy and a woman.

The female said, "Ma'am, we'll need your report. What's your name and do you know the victim?"

Cynthia's stomach wrenched, her chest tightened, she could barely force air into her lungs. She silenced her inner scream and concentrated on relaxing her face. "You know what? I need to get this blood off. I have no idea who this guy is. I'll go wash in the bathroom over there and be right back." She pointed at a public restroom off in the distance.

The woman followed her line of sight, then gave a brief nod. "Okay, then come straight back here," the cop said, pointing to the ground in front of her.

As Cynthia backed away, Rex reached for her. "Don't leave… need your name."

Not with the cops standing right there. She hoped the police didn't notice her reluctance. She smiled down at him. "No worries, honey. You'll be fine," she said in a chipper—hopefully innocent— tone.

She quickly evaluated the care Mr. Hunk was receiving. They'd put a hard collar on him, covered him with a blanket and had the slide board at the ready. Good. With one last long look at the beautiful man, she headed to the bathroom, praying he'd be okay.

Damn her stepsisters! If it wasn't for them, she could go with the guy and allay her fears. Christ, would the fall out from their screw- over never end?

As soon as she got back home to Jon's, she'd call the hospital to make sure Rex had made it through. It was the best she could do.

After washing off as much of the blood as she could, she slipped around the back of the cement block building, then took off running across the park towards home.

As worried as she was, Cynthia couldn't help but smile as she left the park. Her feet buzzed and hot energy warmed her body. Although Jon would kill her for getting blood all over his t-shirt, million dollar running shorts and shoes, she'd saved a life that day. The life of one of the most gorgeous men she'd ever seen.

Maybe things were turning around. Maybe things would get better. Maybe this was a sign of good things to come.

She hoped she'd run into Rex again. Talk about a great reason to strike up a conversation. Probably the best first impression she'd ever made on a guy. She'd ask him out for a drink or coffee. Better yet, manipulate him into doing it. A couple drinks at the Cliff House, a nice sunset and…

Oh, *right*. And a money tree would sprout out of the top of her head and shower her with cash. Romantic crap only worked for other people. Not for her, Cynthia Rella, the Human Apocalypse.

She silenced the happy voices in her head and wiped away an image of the two of them standing at the altar (he in a dark grey tux, she in a peach silk number from the thirties holding a bouquet of matching lilies). Gloom sucked the joy straight out of her soul. Shoulders slumped, she crossed an intersection and kicked an empty soda can out of her way. She had to get past all this optimism. Where had her positive attitude gotten her so far? Nowhere. She'd lost seven years of her life, a house, all her artwork and money because of her stupid cheerful outlook.

But wouldn't it be nice if she were wrong about being wrong this time?

*   *   *   *

Rex Du Charmante's head pounded like someone had smashed it with a steel bar. Beeping noises sounded near him. Disinfectant assaulted his nostrils. *Oh, right. Hospital.*

"Dad! Dad! Please be okay! Damn, Mother told me to take care of you and look what happens. Dad? Are you awake?"

He opened his eyes to the sweet face of his only daughter. Warmth spread through him and he managed a weak smile. "I'm here, Katydid."

He reached for her. She took his hand and pressed it to her wet cheek.

Kelly's vibrant hazel eyes were filled with tears; a few rolled down her perfect oval face. "Is it too much to ask that you stay alive? Huh?"

"No. And I'm so glad you're here. Feel better already."

God, he loved this girl. Relief washed over him. He wouldn't die. He'd be fine and he'd be there for her. Thank God. He couldn't stand the thought of her being alone. Even though she was now a responsible adult, she would always be his little girl.

"So is it true? Some woman saved your life?"

"I think…yes. Yes, she did. The Amazon Goddess."

Kelly's dark brow wrinkled. "Who?"

He coughed, sending a fresh wave of pain coursing through his skull. He waved a hand, flapping the IVs attached to the back. "Never mind."

"Amazon Goddess?"

"Think it was her."

"Her who?"

"A woman runner in Golden Gate Park."

The Amazon Goddess's lovely rounded behind was a work of art. Ever since he'd seen her, all he'd thought about was taking those lovely globes in each hand and squeezing. Then he'd slip one hand around to touch that inviting place between her thighs…

Good God, man, do not get an erection in front of your daughter!

Even though he was addled from his injuries and surgery, he managed a quick math problem that instantly deflated his half-shaft.

"Dad," Kelly began in a reproachful tone, "they said you ran out on a red light and some guy in a Prius hit you. Is this true?"

"Probably. Don't really remember." He'd already revealed too much, no way was he admitting his folly.

"The doctor said you'll be fine, but you have to stay here a week and then you're going to be in a wheelchair for up to a month. If you move too much, you could open that artery up and then—" Tears filled her eyes again.

"Kelly, don't cry, I'm fine."

"No, you're not, you almost died. That metal sign sliced your main artery."

He took her by the hand and squeezed it. "Didn't I promise you I wouldn't leave you? When your mother passed, I made you that promise and I'm keeping it. I'm not leaving 'til you're old and gray."

She smiled. He nearly burst with pride. Ever since she'd come into his life, she'd been the center of his existence.

Kelly rubbed his shoulder. "You did promise me and I'm holding you to it. Thank God my wedding isn't for another month. That'll give you some time to heal. I'm just glad we're not getting married in that church where you and Mom got married. With all those stairs? At the Fairmont, if need be, we can make sure there's enough room for your wheelchair."

"No way. I'm walking you down that aisle and not in a blasted wheelchair."

She laughed. "Good." Reaching up to push some hair off his brow, she twisted her mouth to one side. "I suppose this is actually good for you. The only way you'd put down that darn CrackBerry. Probably the longest you've rested in years."

The bulldoggish face of Greg Marx popped into his mind. "Speaking of work, do you know if Marx called? I missed an important meeting this afternoon."

Kelly made a little grimace. "I called Jess and told her what happened. What was her direct quote? 'Tell your idiot father not to worry about Marx or any of the other investors and to just concentrate on healing and getting back here to the office.' She knows you too well, Dad. She sounded pretty freaked out. I expect her to show up here at any moment."

He chuckled, which hurt. "So how's your office getting along without you?"

She rolled her eyes and sighed. "Mary called me a hundred times for details. Turns out this really isn't the best time for a wedding. There's a bill going before Congress about adoption records—a whole new Federal law that would really help adoptees." She bit her lip and looked away.

She'd had that pensive look on her face a lot lately. He knew what she was thinking about. Ever since she was twelve, she'd been on a search for her birth parents. The quest had shaped her whole life and why she'd become an adoption rights lawyer.

As much as he wanted her happy, he hoped she never found those idiots. All he knew was that she was the product of a nasty divorce and he and Elizabeth got her a month after she'd been born. Didn't want to know anything else. Even though he'd benefited, what kind of weak ne'er-do-well gives up a treasure like Kel?

"Dad, I have to go, I have to meet Vance at the dressmakers. Now he wants my gown altered. So annoying. I don't know what's wrong with him lately. You know he wanted to come with me here to see if you'd read that stupid prospectus? Here you are nearly dead—sorry—I mean, here you are in the hospital and all he's thinking about is money and controlling every detail of the wedding."

Sounded like Vance. Always working an angle, but Kelly would never want for anything.

He still couldn't believe his little baby was getting married. Here she was, an adult. When had all this happened? Far too quickly. But what a great woman she'd become.

Luckily, aided by the drugs, the image faded quickly and he saw his little girl in braces and pigtails again. He took her by the hand. "You're too good to me."

"Love you, Dad. I'll be back with some real food later." She leaned in for a kiss and then she was gone.

Rex relaxed against the pillows. A stab of pain seared his back, he jerked, tensing, then eased himself back down again. Damn it. The light had been green the last time he looked. He'd only taken a glance to see that wonderful butt of hers one last time before running across the street. The next thing he knew, he was barely conscious with her above him, pressing down on his thigh. On some level, he'd wondered if he'd slipped into some weird fantasy world where his deepest desire had been fulfilled. Only she hadn't been touching him exactly where he'd wanted.

He shifted in the bed and harrowing pain shot up his leg. "Ow, blasted leg." He managed to get comfortable without moving too much. He let out a huge sigh.

"Hey buddy!" came James Miller's gravelly voice from the doorway. "Okay if I come in?"

"Thank God. What did Marx say?"

Wearing an expensive suit, James sauntered into the room like he'd arrived for a cocktail party, smelling like cologne and beauty products. He must have come directly from the spa. His blond brows were plucked perfectly, his too-youthful haircut was packed full of gel, and his face had been smoothed of emotion by Botox.

James took off his hip, square frames, placed them in his coat pocket and leaned on the railing of Rex's bed. "Dunno if it was the deal or the fact that you got hit by a car, but he's on board." He beamed a huge tooth-whitened grin.

Rex melted into the hospital bed and let out a huge sigh. "Thank bloody hell."

James rubbed his manicured fingernails on his lapel. "Do I have it, or do I have it?"

"You have it. Thank God."

James chuckled in his wannabe aristocratic way.

Odd duck. The only man Rex knew who'd studied wealthy people's mannerisms and adopted them to appear richer and more sophisticated. Of course, because he was James, he'd gone overboard with his transformation. Over the years he'd become almost a parody of himself.

James pointed out the window. "Just saw my future daughter-in-law in the parking lot. Kelly seemed happy, so I knew you were doing okay. Wedding's coming right up. Should be a great party. Talked to Vance, he's very glad that his future father-in-law didn't just die in Golden Gate Park."

"Jesus. Yeah. Stupid car."

"So what happened? Kelly told me that you were checking out some chick's ass? And then this same chick saved your life?"

Rex's face went so hot, it felt radioactive. "I didn't tell Kelly that. Or I could have told her, I'm so blasted out-of-it on these stupid drugs."

James burst into hearty laughter. Grabbing a chair, he slid it up close to Rex's bed and leaned in. "And you can start telling me the story, now. Who is she? What does she look like and please, please, please describe her ass for me?"

His face warmed again and he laughed. His head throbbed with pain. "Owww. I'll tell you, but don't make me laugh."

"It only hurts when I laugh," James joked.

"Or move. Okay, so The Amazon Goddess—"

James chuckled and raised a brow. "That's what you call her?"

"Yeah. Didn't get her name, damn it. But, wow. The first time I saw her...God, what a sight. Long golden legs, high rounded, perfect buns." Rex held up his hands and made a slow grabbing motion. "Kind you want to take in your hands, get a good feel for them, then go in for the kill." He gripped her imaginary behind.

"Stop, I got somethin' goin' on down here," James said, checking below his waist. He shifted, then looked back up at Rex, eager.

A spike of shame flamed his insides and Rex frowned. "I shouldn't be talking about her like this, she deserves better. Blasted head injury. So, anyway, we were running in the Park. I'd come up on her from behind—doing a sprint interval—her beauty stopped me in my tracks. And height. She has to be six foot. A tall, muscled goddess. And the way she moves, man. Such perfect form. Kind of girl who runs like it sets her free."

James whistled and gave an appreciative nod. "Go on. What color's her hair?"

"Dark, short, cute on her. Lovely shoulders, amazing curves. But really, it's the tall thing. I always dreamed of marrying an Amazon and producing my own basketball team. She's around our age, too. Late forties, early fifties."

James grimaced. "That old?"

Rex made an exasperated noise. "She's beautiful. I don't want a kid, I told you. I want someone my age who remembers *Journey* and dial telephones and bell bottoms when they first came out."

"All over-rated. Go on, so she's on a walker and you passed her in your wheelchair—"

"Stop. And it's not just her looks, there's something about her. The way she smiles. A look in her eye. There's almost something regal about her. Classy and sure of herself."

"Classy, how? As in business classy? Trustafarian classy? Soccer Mom?"

"Don't know, don't care. But she was wearing top-of-the-line running shorts and shoes. Plus she's tan. No one sunbathes in Fog City, that means tanning bed. Which all adds up to money."

"What if she's penniless and wants a Sugar Daddy?"

Rex grinned. "Then I'm just the man to give her something sweet."

"Seriously. Think about it," James said, standing up. He moved the chair back to its place in the corner. "Got a lot to protect, my friend. Watch out for sharks. They can bleed you dry before you even catch on. People you'd never suspect in a million years." He cracked a wicked smile. "Sure she didn't push you in front of the car?"

Rex pointed at the door. "Okay, you can leave now. I want to be alone with my drug-induced fantasies."

"I was leaving anyway." He got a smug look on his face and puffed up his chest.

Here it comes. The Brag. James never left a conversation without revealing some new purchase or accomplishment.

James did a little smarmy tilt with his head. "Got some celebrating to do. Some Dom Perignon, caviar and lobster. Oh, sorry," he said with a mock sympathetic look. "Don't want to rub it in. I'm sure your broth, Jello and lukewarm tea will taste just as good."

"Out."

With a wink and a snap of his fingers, James exited, leaving only his cologne behind.

Rex carefully settled down in bed. While he wished he'd never introduced Marx to James, at least the deal had gone through. One thing off his mind. Five hundred things left.

The Amazon Goddess, however, was the only thing he really wanted to think about.

Damn it. Didn't get her name or her number.

Well, no matter. He'd track her down. And he'd better find her unmarried and straight. If so, he'd pursue her until she relented.

Just like he'd pursued Elizabeth.

Elizabeth. A pang of guilt wrenched his insides. It had been three years. High time he moved on. But it was still so hard. Here their daughter had finally agreed to marry someone worthy, someone they knew, someone both her mother and he approved of and Elizabeth wouldn't be there to watch their only daughter walk down the aisle. Every bride deserved to have her mother at her wedding.

At least he'd be there. Thanks to The Amazon Goddess.

Maybe someday he'd even get his hands on that wonderful derriere of hers.

Forget maybe. He'd find her.

He wouldn't stop until he did.

Chapter Two

"Oh my God, she's beautiful!" Cynthia stopped gazing at the girl to wipe the tears. Her hands shook so badly, she almost dropped the binoculars. Impatient, she focused in on the slim beauty again.

She flashed on the memory of handing the bundle to the nurse. *Take care of her, she's the most special girl in the world.* The binoculars dropped to her lap, she sobbed quietly.

Jon reached across the car to rub her shoulder. "You okay?"

"No." She gave her head a good shake and focused in on the girl across the street. Standing in front of a restaurant, the dark-haired young woman kept checking her watch.

"She is stunning, isn't she?" Jon said. "She's got your hazel eyes and brown hair."

"And your high cheekbones. And nearly perfect nose. Damn, this is unreal. It's so hard to believe. I mean, she's a real person. Last time I saw her she was tiny and red and squished." This was her daughter. *Hers.*

Jon sighed. "Wish I'd been there."

Cynthia's gut twisted at the memory. She turned to lock gazes with her ex. "Catching you in bed with Reverend Gary two minutes before I went into labor didn't exactly make me want you in the delivery room."

Jon's handsome face fell and a haunted look passed behind his green eyes. "That was so dumb. I wish I'd been, uh, had a brain." He shrugged and picked at a thread on his jeans.

Cynthia patted his buff shoulder and ran her hand down his back. "Jon, stop. We're both over that now. It's been twenty-six years. And look what we created. She's just beautiful. Perfect."

Alice Guinevere Wagner. The name still fit. She looked like a fairytale princess.

He sent her a soulful glance. "Don't you wish it would have turned out differently?"

She bit her lower lip and sighed. "Yes, but you aren't straight and you never could be. Besides, I think Alice is doing better than she would have if…" She gestured towards her daughter. "I mean, look at her. We gave her this shot. We could have never given her the Ivy League schooling or so many other things."

"No, we couldn't have."

Cynthia took in every line of Alice's gorgeous face. "She looks so familiar. She looks…" A two-ton anvil of recognition dropped on her head. "My *mother.*"

"Oh, honey." Jon ran a hand over her hair and gripped her shoulder.

She swallowed a few boulder-sized sobs. "Great, now I'm grieving for two people, my baby and my mother. Quite the fun-filled afternoon." She blew her nose, wiped the tears and looked at her daughter once more. "Okay, now I'm better. Jeez, this is intense. Damn, I want to meet her. Just to hear her voice."

"We could."

She put the binocs down and looked him straight in the eye. "No. We decided. The records stay sealed. That's all Alice would need. Forget it."

Jon's green gaze intensified. "She filed a Consent For Contact form. She wants to meet us."

"No way. She wants to meet her fantasy birth parents, not us. I mean, how would we fit into that whole picture, huh?" she said, jerking her head towards her daughter.

"We don't."

"I wouldn't ruin that girl's life for anything. God, can you imagine the press? I can see the headlines now: Rich San Francisco Socialite Discovers Secret Drag Queen Birth Father and Homeless Destitute Birth Mother."

"I know…" Jon didn't seem convinced.

"You wish we'd kept her and shared her?" A sudden burning yearning for those lost years seared her interior. She wished she hadn't asked the question aloud.

He shrugged and gestured vaguely. "I don't know—oh, of course, I wish we'd done that. But I had to go through my slutbag phase and no child should have to be witness to that. And I really had no idea what kind of a father I'd be. Butch turned out okay, didn't he?"

"Better than okay, you and Malcolm raised a conscientious, caring, amazing boy."

"It was you, too. I don't know what we would have done without you."

She flashed on the three of them sitting around her kitchen table, exhausted and shell-shocked, trying to eat pizza amid Butch and Jon's moving boxes. Malcolm's funeral had been gut wrenching. The boys' eviction two days afterwards had compounded the nightmare. "God, we were all so wounded."

Jon's green gaze hardened and his jaw twitched. "Cyn…"

"What?"

He twisted his mouth to one side. "I know I'm forbidden to talk about it."

"Go ahead, I'm already an emotional basket case."

"Never mind, I don't want to think about the Gorgon sisters, either. I still can't believe they wouldn't let you take your own stuff out of the house. Your father's body wasn't even cold. Why is it illegal to kill people, anyway?"

Darkness clouded her mind. Her fists clenched, still itching to punch the bitches' nasty sneering faces. "I don't know. I did sort of make a half-hearted attempt."

He grinned an evil grin. "Wish I'd seen that."

"You saw the aftermath. Still, I wish I'd just left. Getting arrested…what a terrible day. Without you, I'd probably still be in jail."

"Oh, honey, I wish you hadn't gotten caught up in all that."

"Dad needed me."

Jon snorted and sent her a disgusted look. "Yeah, when was he ever there for you? He should have known they'd cheat you out of all your money. And for God's sake, you took care of *their* mother. The stepmonster from hell."

Cynthia twisted around to face him. "Me staying there was about me—who I am—not about them. The Gruesome Twosome sure wouldn't have gotten their hands dirty." She had to get off this subject. Too much pain lately. Her stomach hadn't stopped hurting once since her father's funeral. "Who's Alice waiting for? She's been standing there for ten minutes."

"The fiancé?"

"Do you know anything about him?"

"He's cute, rich and graduated from Stanford."

A tall thin brown-haired man in a wheelchair pushed by a Filipino male nurse rolled past Jon's window and stopped just in front of their car. Since they were near the top of the hill, the nurse had to hold onto the chair to keep it from rolling backwards. The tanned man turned back and looked down the street from where he'd come. The chiseled features, the nose broken at one time, the distinctive jaw—she knew this guy. He wore sunglasses so she couldn't see his eyes, but she knew him. But from where?

Raw scar on his brow. Must have been in an accident recently.

The truth hit her like she'd run full steam into a concrete wall. It was Rex! The Roman God from Golden Gate Park! Right there in front of her!

Jon screamed in her ear, terrifying her. "Oh, God, she's headed right for us! Quick, do something!"

Before Cynthia could get out a word, Jon leapt across the seat and laid a liplock on her. It was like kissing her brother. Felt like an abomination against God.

She tried to push him away, but he grabbed her head and stayed with her.

Finally, he let go, she wiped her mouth and had to stop herself from spitting. Glaring at him, she demanded, "What the hell was *that*?"

"Shut up, she's right there," he hissed, pointing towards the front of the car.

She turned and there was Alice, no more than six feet away. She was even more beautiful close-up. So tall! Perfect skin, and so much like Mom.

"Don't stare," Jon whispered. "Pretend you're in love with me for God's sake."

Cynthia forced herself to look away. She sent Jon a goofy smile and checked out the scene from her peripheral vision.

Her daughter walked up to Rex in the wheelchair. He lit up like a million-watt bulb. She bent down and kissed him on the cheek.

The car tilted, her head swam, her stomach did a pukey dance. "Our daughter is engaged to The Roman God? Damn, he's old enough to be her father. This is horrible. The man I planned to marry is going to marry my daughter? What kind of screwed up games is the Universe playing with me?"

Jon looked at her like she had six heads. "What are you talking about? Who's The Roman God? Wait, the runner in Golden Gate Park?"

"Yeah, Rex. He's right there and is engaged to my daughter. This sucks."

He looked out the window at Alice and Mr. Hunk. "No, he's not. That's the Rex you saved? That's The Roman God? Are you sure?"

She gestured towards the window. "Sure, I'm sure, I stared at him for three weeks, then saved his life." She turned to Jon. "What do you mean, he's not? She kissed him. He's looking at her like she's a goddess descended from the heavens."

"She kissed him on the cheek, not the mouth. That's her father, not her fiancé."

The information was so overwhelming, it didn't compute. "Her *what*?"

"Her father. That is Rex Du Charmante, founding partner of Vector Venture Capital."

Her mind rocked with a series of startling epiphanies, each one felt like slamming open a solid steel door with her head. "*The Roman God adopted our daughter?*"

"Apparently."

"Holy God, these things don't happen, you don't save the life of your adopted—oh, shit, they're looking at us—don't kiss me!" she ordered, stopping Jon with a hand to his chest as he reached for her.

Jon waved his hands, exasperated. "Well, what are we supposed to do?"

"Not kiss, ewwww. I mean, I love you, but dude, that is not right."

Cynthia raced to catch up to the news. Rex adopted her daughter. Which meant that he must be married.

"Wait, where's the Hunk's wife?"

"Didn't I tell you? She died three years ago from cancer."

Her attention snapped to Jon so fast, a muscle caught in her neck. "Ow. Really?" She massaged the side of her neck, rubbing out the pain.

"Uh-huh."

So he was single! No wonder he said all that stuff about him being the only one his daughter had left. Too bad about the tragedy, but hot damn! And now that Mr. Hunk and her daughter's attention was away from them, Cynthia was free to devour every square inch of the man. Oh, what a sight. The cords of his ropy neck, that smile, those long legs. A nerve she thought long since dead roared back to life and she squirmed on the seat. *Wow, that felt good.* How long had it been since she'd felt this way about a man? Centuries.

Rex pushed himself out of the wheelchair and stood, much to the dismay and surprise of her daughter. Alice waved her arms, motioning for him to sit again. He sat.

Cynthia tingled all over. "Holy hell, he's a tall drink of water I'd like to imbibe. Man, it's been too long for me."

"How long?"

She wanted to look at Jon to make her comeback, but she couldn't tear her eyes off the father. "None of your business, Mr. Nosy Pants."

"Come on."

"Oh, Christ. Five years."

"Five years?" Jon shrieked, making her ears buzz.

She stuck a finger in her ear and winced. "Ow. Yes. Anytime I met a guy, he'd come by the house and Endora the Witch would charm him and then slip in something about how inferior I was. Just a nuance from her and the guy would start lookin' at me funny. She —"

"Was good. I fell for it."

"Oh, for crying out loud, here I was all excited about Rex being single, I completely forgot about poor Alice losing her mom. That must have been so hard on her. Poor little Alice. Wait, I keep calling her that, I know she has a different name."

"Kelly. Kelly Eileen Du Charmante."

Kelly! Of course! That's what Rex called his daughter.

Kelly Du Charmante, what a great name.

Rex Du Charmante. Cynthia Du Charmante. Had a nice ring to it. *Wait.*

The picture of her at the altar with Rex burst into flames and her happy mood chilled like she'd gotten tossed into a vat of liquid nitrogen. "This sucks. Now I can't date the guy. I swear, God has put me on this Earth just to torture me."

Jon turned to her, his brow furrowed. "Why can't you date him?"

"Hello? He's the father of my daughter? I can't let Alice, I mean, Kelly, know I even exist."

"I don't know, seems to me the world is conspiring to get us all together."

She jabbed a finger in his face. "Not happening. Can you imagine if the Gruesome Twosome knew she existed? And that she had been adopted into a rich family? They'd be all over her like stink on politicians. Besides, I told everyone that Alice died from SIDS."

Jon's stubbly jaw dropped and his eyes widened. He coughed, then cleared his throat. "You did *what?*"

She shrugged. "Dad would have never forgiven me for giving away his only grandchild. I had to lie."

Sending her an incredulous stare, he shook his head. "You have the most screwed up family."

"No spit."

A tall, blond metrosexual boy dressed in a dapper dark suit joined Kelly and Mr. Injured Hunk.

Cynthia pointed at him. "Wait, who is that? Wow, he's cute for a child. Oh! That's the fiancé?"

"Yes, that's him. Hot, isn't he?"

"What a looker. He almost looks gay he's so pretty."

"Tell me about it. She looks happy with him, though, doesn't she?" Jon asked, a dreamy look in his eye.

Kelly and her fiancé kissed quickly. Her father grinned affectionately at the two.

"Yes, she does. Well, good, she got a hunk, that satisfies me."

"You are so shallow," Jon drawled.

"That's me, deep as a wading pool. Damn, they are going to make some pretty children." Darkness swirled around her heart. Her belly hollowed. Her arms fell to her sides and she stared straight ahead. "Why did I think of that? Now I'm even more depressed. Grandchildren I won't ever see. Well, I guess if I stalk them, I will."

"I do feel like a stalker."

"Me, too. This is creepy, spying on them like this. Okay, they're leaving and I've seen enough, anyway. I need alcohol."

"I have to perform tonight."

"I didn't say *you* had to drink, I said *I* had to drink." She took the binoculars from her lap, handed them to Jon and started up his old Bug, eager to get away from the scene.

The Bug coughed, sputtered, then died.

Jon shrieked, "Oh, God, they're coming back! Quick, get us out of here!"

Her heart pounding, Cynthia turned the key and pressed the gas. Didn't catch. "I can't, this antique won't start!"

"Flutter the gas pedal, flutter the gas pedal!"

Rex, Kelly and her fiancé approached the car and stood in front, staring at them.

"They're looking at us!" Jon yelled.

"I see that!" She tapped out a fast rhythm on the accelerator. The engine almost caught.

Out of the corner of her eye, she noticed a building pass them. Wait. Buildings didn't move on their own.

He screamed, "We're rolling backwards!"

Adrenaline shocked her system and her heart jumped into overdrive. She slammed on the brakes, but the pedal wouldn't depress. She kicked it as hard as she could. The pedal gave, went to the floor and stayed there. The car kept going.

"Oh, shit!"

"What?" Jon demanded.

"I think I just broke the brakes."

"You *what*?"

"I'll stick it in gear!" Cynthia slammed down on the clutch and pulled on the stick. She let go of the clutch and nothing happened. She pushed in, then let go again. "Oh, shit, it's stuck in neutral!"

"Pedro told me he fixed it! Watch out for the car behind us!"

Cynthia looked in the rear view mirror and only saw grill. She yanked the steering wheel towards Jon, the car swung out into the street, narrowly missing the sedan parked behind them.

A black SUV appeared in their path, then dove out of the way, popping up on the curb to escape them, revealing a red compact directly behind.

Cynthia pulled the steering wheel hard to the left, just missing the front of the compact. Her pulse crazy, her hands shaking, she didn't have any time to think, she could only react.

Now heading straight for a parked Cadillac Escalade, she jammed the wheel the other way and overcorrected, sending them towards the parked cars on the other side of the street.

"You're going to kill us!"

Blood rushed in her ears. "No, I'm not!"

She jerked the wheel back towards the center of the street. A yellow cab skidded out of her way.

Jon opened the window and waved his arms. "Get out of the way!"

The sides of the street went by in a blurry flash: horrified faces, storefronts, parked cars.

A white Ford was right in her path. At the last second, the driver veered into a driveway, the Bug missed the back of the car by inches.

Thankfully, after the Ford, there were no more cars in their path and they had almost reached the bottom of the hill.

Unfortunately, at the bottom was an intersection with a red light.

And they were *flying*.

She laid on the horn and fought the shaking steering wheel. The Bug rocked and rattled and felt like it was going to come apart.

"We're going to die!" Jon cried.

"Shut up!"

The intersection was coming up fast. People on the street corners waved their arms and pointed at her.

A large truck began to cross the intersection. They were going to hit it full on!

"Oh, shit!" Jon and Cynthia screamed in unison.

Bye, Alice, I love you!

At the last second, she made eye contact with the truck driver. The guy slammed on his brakes, she gently pushed the steering wheel to the left and they flew by, missing the front of the truck by no more than a foot. The car climbed the next hill.

Near the top, the car slowed, then stopped. Had they made it?

Jon gestured wildly. "I can't believe we made it through that without hitting anyone. Pull the emergency brake!"

"I already did, that's busted, too! Don't worry!"

The car began to roll back down the hill towards the intersection. She slammed down on the clutch pedal, jammed on the stick, then released the clutch.

The engine caught, the car jumped forward, sideswiping a parked gold sedan.

"Oh, shit!" Jon yelled.

They bounced into the middle of the street. Cynthia yanked the steering wheel back and caught the front fender on a light pole. They scraped along the pole, slowing them. She kept the tires tight against the curb until the car finally stopped.

They both let out huge sighs of relief. Sweat ran down her neck. Her hands and body trembled. Her heart pounded so hard it hurt.

Jon wiped some sweat from his brow and slumped in his seat. He fanned his face. "I spoke too soon about not hitting a car, but at least you only hit one. I hope the damage isn't—"

"You ruined my car! I'm a lawyer and you are dead! You hear me? Dead!" came a thunderous voice from somewhere behind them.

She turned to look behind the car. A very large, very angry man stormed towards them. Bald with biceps the size of logs, his teeth bared, the man looked angry enough to commit murder.

They looked at each other in horror.

Jon lost all the color in his face. "Um, I don't know how to tell you this, but I just remembered that my insurance kind of lapsed this past week."

Without thinking, Cynthia stuck the car in gear and pulled it away from the curb.

The man's roar nearly deafened them.

She slammed on the gas.

"He's chasing us!" Jon yelled.

She checked her rearview mirror, all she saw were teeth framed by a very red face. She floored it, bombing down the hill. The now purple-faced man grew smaller in her mirror.

As she approached the intersection, the light turned green and, praise be to God, no one was ahead of her. She downshifted, hung a right and kept going.

Cynthia checked her rear view mirror, but she couldn't see Angry Man. "We lost him."

Five blocks later, she rolled into a parking lot and slid into a spot. The car hit the cement wall lining the lot, jolting to a stop. She turned off the engine and put the car into first. She melted into her seat with relief.

After a moment, Jon turned to her. "So did you take a Drama Pill this morning or what?"

She swung on him, incredulous. "Me? Mr. Oh-By-The-Way-My-Insurance-Lapsed? I think you crushed up a whole jar of Drama Pills and put them in the coffee pot this morning." She leaned into him and sent him a glare. "How did your insurance *kind of* lapse?"

Jon rolled his eyes and gestured, as if trying to find words to explain, but finally threw up his hands. "Long story."

Cynthia sat back with a sigh and rubbed her temples. "Christ. Forget the alcohol, I need a morphine drip."

He looked around the area outside the car. "One of my favorite bars is right around the corner." He turned to her, a hopeful look in his eye. "They make killer Bloody Marys."

"It's only one o'clock, I should wait. I mean, what will I do at five?"

"It's a known fact that car accidents reset all clocks to five."

She opened her door and stepped out. "Two Bloody Marys comin' right up."

*   *   *   *   *

Rex Du Charmante slammed down the receiver onto the cradle. Pens rattled in their steel mesh holder on his glass-topped mahogany desk. "How blasted hard is it to find a woman in this town?!"

His secretary Jessica came flying into his office, her eyes extra wide behind her coke-bottle-thick glasses. A tornado in a midget costume, Jessica was the tiniest person he'd ever met and the most powerful. Everyone was afraid of her, even he. She wore a severe black suit with a unicorn pin on the lapel and her giant red coiffure didn't budge despite her furious pace. He always figured she tried to compensate for her stature with her huge, outdated hairdo. She needn't have bothered. Although she stood no more than four feet ten, she might as well have been six-foot-four for the intimidation she caused when entering a room. Formidable.

"Are you all right? Did the wound open?" After a quick check, her huge eyes narrowed behind her frames. She put her hands on her hips, her nostrils flared and her wrinkled mouth drew tight. "What is wrong with you, hollering like that? You nearly gave me a heart attack. It's that woman, isn't it? No, couldn't be about Angel Island or Greenly, couldn't be about the thousand other things you should have your mind on. No, it's all about your penis. Will you please get your mind off your sex life for one second and get back to those darned figures I asked you about this morning? I swear, I wish that accident had knocked more sense into you instead of less."

Rex couldn't help but grin at his precious secretary. "Why don't you retire, old woman?" he playfully countered.

"And wouldn't you just love that? No, I'm stuck here and you'd better be grateful that I am. No one else would put up with your nonsense." She sighed and relaxed her tiny shoulders. "Did you try Lexington Investigations?"

"Yes."

A slight wrinkle of her brow. "What about Nightingale?"

His heart lightened and a trickle of hope seeped in. "No, no, I haven't."

"Do I have to draw a map for you? What's wrong with you, Rex? Is it the wedding?"

He sighed and looked out the picture windows of his thirtieth floor corner office. Tendrils of fog snaked around and through the Golden Gate Bridge, sailing ships and tankers passed underneath, but not even his spectacular view could cheer him. Kelly was moving out that weekend. Sorrow shrouded him like dark coat of ice. He shook off the emotion. If Elizabeth hadn't gotten sick, she'd have moved out years before. No, this was a good thing. She loved the boy and he loved her. At twenty-six, it was high time she moved on with her life. Even if it left him feeling more alone than a straight man at a lesbian bar.

He grunted.

"I knew it. That's why you've honed in on this Mystery Savior of yours. The Amazon with the perfect ass."

He swung his gaze back to his secretary. A slight smile played on her orange lips. Why she wore orange lipstick he'd never know, but she'd worn it ever since he'd met her. "What?"

Her grin burst into a large, toothy smile. "I overheard you talking to Bob."

His face warmed. She laughed in a high trill.

"You're terrible to me, just terrible," he said, grinning.

"Oh, honey, I'm just glad you're interested in a female again. It's past time you started dating."

"Been trying to. The only women I seem to meet are either vultures or young enough to be my daughter. They're in love with my money, my name, my business, my house, the society pages, anything but me. I finally meet a woman who doesn't know who I am—an honest, straightforward, good person— she saves my life and disappears. Spent the last five afternoons sitting around that blasted park being accosted by homeless people, but haven't seen her once. Not once. She's got me wondering if she's a fugitive or something. You know she disappeared before she could give her report to the police?"

Jess cocked her head to one side and crossed her doll-sized arms across her chest. "Maybe it's better you don't find her."

Rex picked up the hand exerciser from his desk and squeezed it several times, making it squeak. "No, even if she's in trouble, her actions spoke to her character. No one saves a stranger's life unless they're a good person. I've got a damned hoard of private detectives out there. I've taken out ads in all the papers and nothing. Damned frustrating." He compressed the exerciser in a fast short burst and tossed it back on the desk.

Jess's face softened, she sighed. Stepping forward, she placed her hands on top of his desk and leaned in a bit. "You'll find a good woman."

He shook his head. "I hope so."

She turned away and headed to the door, but stopped abruptly and returned to him. "Oh, one more thing. I put in that call to James Miller—I'm getting the runaround."

More bad news. "His secretary put you off?"

"Yeah."

His stomach tightened. Not good. He had far too much riding on this deal.

Jess appeared cool, but by the intensity of her gaze it was clear she knew what was at stake. "You'd think with the wedding and him being the father of your future son-in-law, he'd make sure to get his payment here on time."

He grabbed the hand exerciser and squeezed it violently. "Never missed one before. And he seemed really upbeat the last time I saw him. Plus I know he got a huge sum from Marx." He pointed the exerciser at her. "Tell you what, call Danny in their office. He'll know what's going on."

"Yes, but will he tell me?"

Rex sat back and grinned at her. "When has anyone ever said no to you?"

"George Clooney, said I was too young for him."

Flawless timing, as usual. He broke out in a belly laugh. "You should go into stand up."

"Great, more work, no thanks. No worry on that check, I'll get the dirt. Finish that report before you leave. You hear me?"

"Ma'am, yes, ma'am." He saluted her.

Jess made a face, then turned and made her usual flamboyant exit, complete with a flourish of her right arm.

Rex swung his chair back to the view. Damn, he hated this deal. He should have said no. But how do you do that with a new relative? He could afford the loss financially, but he couldn't afford the loss of face. Not with Marx and this new group of investors.

He shouldn't have taken the risk. He'd blown it.

Stupid kids' engagement party. After umpteen toasts, he'd spilled the names of some new investors, including Greg Marx, to James before he could stop himself. Powerhouses he'd been courting for five years. At the mention of Marx, James' eyes had bugged out and he'd started salivating. From that moment on, he wouldn't leave Rex alone until he finally agreed to introduce him to Marx and the group. Bad decision.

While James had never faltered on any of his investments and his returns were always higher than everyone else's, there had been something wrong with this last deal. And something different in James' demeanor. A desperation behind his eyes Rex had never seen before.

Still, he'd taken all the right precautions, did his due diligence. Had two sets of lawyers scour the documents. Everything looked good.

But his gut had warned him. And he'd ignored it. Because of Kelly. Her future.

Worst case scenario, Vector took a big hit and he lost the new contacts.

How terrible would that be? Might give him an out.

Lately he'd been entertaining ideas that had once seemed unthinkable. Getting off the money train. Devoting himself to his art. Finding a new woman—that Amazonian beauty would do nicely. Starting a new life.

But how would he do that? He didn't have near the money he wanted. He had enough to take care of himself and Kelly for life, but he wanted more. Needed more. Much more. Enough to protect his family from any scenario.

Elizabeth's voice rang in his head. *How much money do we really need? Will anything ever be enough? Keep going this way and you'll die a rich, but very lonely old man.*

"Elizabeth, we just weren't right for each other," he said aloud. He shook off the doubt. Jess was right. Everything would work out fine, like it always did. "James will come through and I'll find that woman."

With a firm nod, he reached for the phone and punched in a number. "Nightingale? Got a job for you. I need you to find a woman for me. I'll pay you double your normal fee if you find her in the next 24 hours. Yes, you heard me, *double*."

Chapter Three

Her mind groggy from one too many Bloody Marys, Cynthia sipped her morning coffee and flipped through the paper at Jon's chrome and red kitchen table.

A rare flash of sun beamed through a break in the fog, illuminating the retro fifties kitchen. The glare from the paper zapped her eyes. Pain shot through her head. She squinted and averted her gaze. Sun hurt like hell, but it sure made the kitchen look pretty. She loved the glass-fronted cabinets and the authentic red and yellow linoleum flooring. Not to mention his killer collection of vintage cookie jars. As always, Jon had been meticulous in his attention to detail. Very homey, very comfy and soothing.

Since it was early June, the Style section of the *Chronicle* featured weddings. Alice/Kelly must be knee-deep in her own arrangements.

Pain cut through the fog of her hangover. Her only daughter was getting married and she wasn't a part of it.

Oh, please, Cynthia, you idiot, you haven't been a part of her life for twenty-six years. She had a total of ten months with the girl that ended soon after her birth. She had no right to even want to see Kelly get married. She'd given her up.

"Oh, hell, that doesn't stop me from wanting to see her walk down the aisle."

Cynthia's mind clicked into high gear. Wait a minute. Why couldn't she go to the wedding?

Right. How the hell would she manage that one?

Gloomy, Cynthia gazed at the various pictures of San Francisco society's brides to be. A face popped out at her. Alice! Kelly! Despite her hangover, she bounced in place on her chair.

Kelly's wedding was in two weeks. The ceremony and the reception would be held at the famous and lavishly expensive hotel, The San Francisco Fairmont. There were a hundred and fifty guests invited, a literal Who's Who of San Francisco society. Even the mayor would be there.

Damn. She had as much luck getting an invitation as a homeless person.

Jon was right. She did wish he was straight and they'd kept the girl. Kelly was so beautiful. Cynthia couldn't imagine how her own life would have turned out. Much more fulfilling and a lot less horrible.

Just then, Jon came shuffling into the kitchen wearing his cowboys-and-Indians flannel pajamas, rubbing his eyes and yawning. He had a whole collection of weirdly printed nightwear, from pink poodles to Superman to vintage kitchen appliances. "So what's new? Who did we bomb today? How much did the Dow fall?"

"I don't know, but our daughter is in the paper."

His dark eyes popped open wide and he rushed to the table. "Kelly, where?"

Cynthia grinned at his enthusiasm and handed him the paper. "Here, look." She pointed to the picture and the column.

Jon pulled out a chair and sat. He read a bit, then stopped and stared into space. "No."

"No, what?"

"No, this is the wedding Michael was talking about!" he squealed loudly.

Her ears buzzed and pain ricocheted through her skull. Wincing, she covered her ears. "Ow, that was loud."

"Sorry." Jon's eyes glittered with excitement and his white grin flashed with unpleasant brightness. "I know the wedding planner, she mentions him and everything."

The heavens parted and the choir sung. Here was her ticket to the wedding! "I want to go," Cynthia announced.

He froze and stared at her. "Really?"

Suddenly imbued with a sense of urgency, she nodded. "Really, I have to see her get married. If you have an in, I have to take advantage of it."

Jon's thick dark brow furrowed and he ran a hand over his thick salt-and-pepper buzz cut. "Huh…are you sure?"

"Positive."

He thought for a moment. "Well, I'll bet I can get you a job, working the event."

"I don't want to work it, I want to be invited. I want to be a guest. I want to be able to talk to her and congratulate her and sit there and be served. I'm the mother of the bride, for God's sake."

Brightening, Jon scooted towards her in his chair. "If we just told her, she might—"

Her stomach wrenched at the thought. She held up her hand firmly. "No, God, no, I don't want her knowing. I haven't changed my opinion on that. I just…I have to go, Jon. I have to. I'll crash it if I have to."

He looked heavenwards and threw up his hands. "Here we go again. I swear, girl, at times I was convinced I married Lucy."

"I wasn't that bad."

"Yes, you were—are."

"This isn't like sneaking into political fundraisers to disrupt them or impersonating a cop to scare a landlord or sneaking a deep-fried cockroach into a fancy restaurant to avoid paying the bill. This is different."

Jon rolled his eyes and made an exaggerated "weary" face at her. "I could list twenty other crazy things you've done. And those freakin' cockroaches stunk up the kitchen for a week."

"That is not what this is about. This is about being at my daughter's wedding."

"Why do women get so sentimental about this crap? Those ceremonies are just designed to suck money out of people."

"I have heard this speech before," she said, pursing her lips at him. "From you. Right before you took over the entire thing and wouldn't let me help with anything."

"You loved me doing that. Besides, you had no overall theme. It was like you'd shopped at a garage sale and bought stuff from six different decades. Freakin' fine for some weirdo Dr. Who time-travel super fans, but not for a wedding. I was forced by good taste to take over the whole thing. Did a great job, too, if I do say so myself," he said with a smug grin as he held himself taller in his chair.

"You did. That should have been my wake-up call."

"No, it should have been mine," he said, breaking his pose. "I remember lying awake, worried about matching the colors of toile on the wedding favors to the groomsmen's corsages. Now that's a freakin' wake-up call."

She laughed, reached over and squeezed his sinewy arm. "God, I'm glad that's all behind us. And I'm glad that while you were straight, you were my husband. You were a really good husband. You even picked up after yourself."

On that line, they looked at each other. "Wake-up call!" they both said in unison and then burst out laughing and hugged.

They pulled away and Cynthia took a sip of her coffee. "Did you call about the car insurance?"

Jon sighed, his shoulders slumping. "No. I'm dumping the car. Don't need it anyway. The reason I let the insurance lapse was because I wasn't using it. That was before you moved in. But obviously, it was absolutely stupid to let that lapse."

Cynthia rubbed the back of her neck, focusing on a sore spot. Too much stress lately had her muscles in knots. "I still feel bad about running away. Never done anything like that before."

"Honey, if we hadn't, I would have lost the condo and we would have been homeless. We'll do a good deed and make up for the bad karma. Thank God, the license plates had fallen off the week before. And for some reason, no one got a really good look at us."

"Except for the bald gorilla."

"Yeah…him," Jon said, paling and biting his lip. "The Creature From The Steroid Lagoon. Thankfully crazy people don't make great witnesses. Hopefully, we'll never see him again."

"What are the odds? Even though, San Francisco is the smallest big town I've ever been in. I run into the same people all the time."

Jon sent her an alarmed stare.

"But that won't happen to us," she said quickly. She shifted in her seat and straightened her spine. "Okay, back to the wedding. I need a new identity and a good costume. I have to make sure Rex doesn't recognize his savior. That's all I'd need."

"She can't just go as a waitress, she needs to be a guest."

"Damn straight." She leaned back in her chair and stroked her chin. "I need a list of famous last names. We Google high society, figure out the family trees, pick a likely party—someone who is on some other continent or died as a toddler or something—and I will impersonate her. Don't need the persona for more than one night. I can pull off a couple hours of acting rich and snooty. Okay, so when can you call Michael?"

Jon stood and stretched, exposing his trim belly. "I'll try when I wake up more. He may not have time to talk. He hates to be disturbed when he's dealing with Bridezillas." He twisted from side to side. "Of course, that term is so over-used and I actually like Godzilla. I hate Ghidra, but Bride-Ghidras doesn't sound right. We need a new term," he said, touching his toes. Thirty-five years of dance had kept him limber and in great shape.

"Bri-demons?"

"Sounds like a 60's horror flick." He rolled his shoulders. "Elizabeth Montgomery is Bri-Demon! Eating the souls of the guests, drinking the blood of her groom."

The phone rang.

Jon looked over at the telephone on the kitchen sideboard, but headed for the coffeemaker on the opposite side of the room. "Let's let the machine pick up. I need coffee."

"Good plan. By the way, we're almost out of half and half."

He reached into the glassed-in cupboard and grabbed a Chippendale's mug featuring a Greek Adonis wearing a g-string. "You and your bloody half and half," he said, turning to make a face at her.

"Coffee is all about the half and half."

"Bad coffee." He turned away and grabbed the steaming carafe from his Mr. Coffee machine.

The female voice of a heavy smoker came over the machine. "Hey there Cindy, this is your sister Belinda checkin' on ya..."

Cynthia's blood froze and her stomach twisted tight as a hangman's noose. All the hair stood up on her arms and the back of her neck. Jon's attention jerked towards the answering machine and his expression turned to granite.

"Hope all is goin' good. We're all good here. Hey, when you get a chance, could you give me a call? We have a pesky little detail about some legal papers we need you—what? Don't tell me what to say, I didn't say anything. Shut up and let me leave this stupid message, I'm the one on the phone— uh, sorry, Cindy. You know how Sissy likes to control everything everyone says, *even if they weren't going to say anything stupid,*" she said in an exaggerated tone. "Anyway, give me a call and we can clear up this little mess. Okay? Uh, the number is the same. Can't wait to hear from you." *Beep.*

Every muscle knotted. Her body went rigid and her ears went back.

Images flew at her. Sissy on top of her when she was a kid, pounding her. The smug sneers on their hideous faces just two weeks before as she walked out of the courtroom, defeated. *Garden Dream*, her most prized sculpture, in Belinda's fist, high in the air, then it was gone. Shattered into a thousand pieces on the terra cotta tiled kitchen floor. She could still hear their hysterical laughter at her tears.

An unending tunnel of gloom stretched out before her. Like she was on a conveyor belt headed straight to Hell.

Jon frowned and shot her a stare, his gaze troubled. "That doesn't sound good at all. Did you catch the 'sister' line?"

"Didn't miss anything. What the hell do they want to do to me now? I mean, aren't they done? They got everything."

Coffee pot still in hand, he brightened and stepped towards her. "Maybe they found the original will. Maybe the courts figured out the signature was a fake on the new will. Maybe this is good."

"If it's anything to do with Tweedle Dumb and Tweedle Dumber, it can't be good."

"Are you calling them back?"

"No. Let the estate lawyer call me. I swear Jon, if I even so much as see one of those gargoyles, I don't know what will happen. Last time, I ended up in the back of a cop car in handcuffs. Besides, how can I contact them when they have that restraining order against me?"

"Good question. Well, don't worry about them," he said, turning away and finally pouring his coffee. "Finish your coffee, let's think about Kelly's wedding."

"Yeah, yeah, good plan."

But inside her stomach churned like an industrial washing machine.

She stopped herself. Damn it, they hooked her. One phone call and she was right back to her powerless childhood. When would she learn?

Straightening her shoulders, Cynthia nodded. She'd received all the tools she needed to deal with this problem from her therapist. She could handle those two. Things were different now. She'd be fine.

Nice try.

Shut up, voice.

Chapter Four

Rex Du Charmante's daughter walked into the mahogany-paneled dining room. A burst of pride and love welled up through his body. The house would be like living in a tomb when she moved out. A dreary, windowless, colorless crypt.

"Hey, Dad." Kelly kissed him on the cheek and poured herself a cup of coffee. "Oh, you're already done."

"Sorry, got up early, had to make some phone calls." *And check up on the search for The Amazon Goddess.*

Kelly nearly emptied the silver pitcher of half-and-half into her coffee. After two heaping teaspoons of sugar, she tasted the brew and nodded.

Rex raised an eyebrow and nodded at her cup. "Is there actually any coffee in there?"

"Yes, Mr. Nasty Black Coffee Man. For those of us with refined tastes, coffee is all about the half-and-half."

"Refined?"

"Yes, very," she said sticking out her pinky and sipping delicately on her coffee. She made a pruney face at him. He smirked back. "Vance called, he'll be stopping by soon. He wants to control yet another detail of the dreaded event."

Rex laughed. "Why didn't you just insist on the elopement?"

"Vance. God, he wants this thing. I swear, I don't know anyone on the guest list. He's trying to increase his business and he thought all those important people would help."

Rex gave a sharp nod. "They will. We wealthy people love nothing more than a free meal and he knows that. Nothing lubes the check-writing hand more than champagne and a pretty bride. He'll get plenty of capital for his clients."

Harrison, a tall man in his late sixties who served as their butler/valet/house manager, walked into the dining room with a plate of eggs and toast and set it in front of Kelly.

"Morning, Harrison, thank you," Kelly said.

"You're welcome, Miss." He picked up Rex's empty plate and left the room.

Kelly sighed. "Not only has Vance been crazy about the guest list, he's been absolutely anal about every detail. He picked out my dress, the bridesmaid dresses, the flowers, the cake, the invitations, I don't know why he bothers taking me along."

"Sure he's straight?"

"Dad, you're so bad! Yes, and I can attest—"

Rex put his hands over his ears. "Stop! I don't want to know."

"He's metrosexual."

He sent her his best puzzled look. "So he likes to sleep with what? Subway trains?"

Kelly shook her head and rolled her eyes at him, then burst into a large smile that warmed him all the way to his bones. "Honestly, your jokes are so bad."

"Your mother hated them, too."

"I know, I remember. I never understood how you ended up with each other. You were such opposites."

"Yes, we were."

A wonder they made it twenty-five years. Epic fights. Thankfully, they managed to keep them from Kelly. They purposefully put Kelly's bedroom far away from theirs. Which helped with the make-up sessions as well. Though in later years, there was little of that. Even before Elizabeth was diagnosed with cancer, there had been little intimacy between them.

Kelly sent him a searching look. *Uh, oh. Here it comes again.* "So…I've been meaning to ask you, have you found a date for the wedding?"

He sighed heavily and relaxed into his stiff-backed chair. "No. And I told you, I don't need a date, I don't want a date."

"That's a big, fat lie."

"A small, thin lie."

She laughed. God, how he loved the sound of her laughter. He stood and limped over to the bronze abstract sculpture of two intertwined lovers standing in the corner. He absently ran his hand down the female side and over her swollen belly. The smooth, cool feel of the metal always soothed him. He'd worn the patina down over the years.

"Really, Dad, you need to get back on the horse again."

"The last three women I dated *were* nags."

"You're so bad. And you haven't been able to find The Amazon Goddess?"

He let out a long breath. "No. Even though I sent the whole cavalry out, still nothing." He ran a thumb down the jaw line of the bronze female.

"I swear you're going to take the surface off that thing. You know you only rub that sculpture when you're worried about something. After Mom died, I thought you'd wear it down to a nub."

He took his hand away as if the surface had burned him. He hadn't even realized what he was doing. "Yes. I don't know why I love this thing so much. It comforts me somehow."

"When did you get it?"

"Years ago. Before we stole you from those gypsies."

"Oh, Dad."

He grinned. "Got it the week I founded Vector. Just a couple weeks before we got you. Don't know why I was so drawn to it. Guess it sort of represents perfection to me. You know, whole cycle of life: man, woman, their baby growing inside her. Perfect love or some stupid thing like that."

"That's so sweet. I wonder why Mother hated it. Who did it?"

"Artist's name is Rella. Cynthia Rella."

"If you liked it so much, why didn't you buy more of her work?"

He stroked the head of the female and ran his hand down her back. "Tried to, but by the time I went back to the gallery, all her sculptures were all gone. Some tragedy happened to her. Young woman, too. Quite a prodigy in her day. Written up in a bunch of magazines. She just dropped out of sight. I never found out what happened to her."

"Too bad she's not around, I'll bet you'd date her."

He laughed and walked over and joined his daughter at the table. He reached over and clasped his big hand over her small one. "Don't worry about me, Katydid. That day is all about you, not me. Besides, I'll be busy being the father-of-the-bride, won't have much time to flirt."

And by the guest list, he was going to be very busy talking business.

"Hello future father-in-law!" came a booming voice from the entry hall.

Kelly's eyes brightened. "Speak of the devil."

Vance, sharply dressed as usual, came bouncing into the room, all white teeth and perfectly coiffed blond hair. Looked like he belonged on the cover of GQ. Not very manly. So much wasted energy devoted to primping. Just like his bloody father.

Vance walked up to Kelly. "And how's my favorite bride-to-be!"

Kelly jumped up and kissed him. It was obvious that Vance loved his daughter, of course, who could blame him? Vance clearly got the better end of the deal.

While almost no one met his standards, at least Vance came close. He had the upbringing, the education and the drive. A little too much drive, but in the end, his grandchildren would have a nice home and good educations. Kelly certainly wouldn't make much helping a bunch of blasted adoptees. But he'd had little influence over her chosen career. Thankfully, she'd listened to him about Vance.

Vance pulled away from Kelly and offered his hand to Rex. "Did you get a chance to look at my proposal?"

They shook hands and a cloud of expensive cologne attacked his nasal passages.

Kid may be a bit of a dandy, but he was all male when it came to business. A shark.

Kelly's smile vanished, she dropped her fork onto her plate, which clattered sharply. "Vance, I really don't want Dad bothered by this kind of stuff so early in the morning."

Vance sent her a slightly patronizing smile. "Yes, I know, sweetheart, but this is important," he said, patting her shoulder. "This could mean a better future for our children. So, sir, what did you think of those numbers? Damn good return, right?" he asked, sending Rex a dazzling smile.

"Haven't had a chance to look at it, Vance. But I will. By the way, have you seen your father? I haven't been able to get hold of him in the past couple days."

Vance clearly didn't like the change of topic, nor did he expect it. He probably thought Rex would roll over and play dead for him. Boy had a lot to learn.

After a second of regrouping, Vance said, "Really? I don't know, haven't seen him since last week."

"Well, if you do hear from him, have him call me, will you?"

"Yes, sir," he said, impatiently. "But about my proposal—"

"Kelly's right, I really would rather handle this kind of stuff at the office—"

Vance held up his slim hand. "I know it was rude to presume, but I'm afraid other investors are going to jump on this and you'll get cut out of the deal. I really want to make my new father-in-law some money."

Rex smiled inwardly. Boy could care less about making him any money. But he had to give him credit, Vance was good at the game. "Of course, first it will cost me some. Tell you what? I'll give it a look-see later on today."

"Good, I just happened to bring another copy, in case the other was misplaced." The blond boy set a new gleaming packet next to Rex.

Rex reached for his coffee.

Vance eyed the packet hungrily, anxious. "Uh, sure. Whenever you get to it." He tapped his long manicured fingers against his pant leg. He opened his mouth to speak when his Blackberry interrupted him with a dance tune. He checked it. "Oh, damn, I have to take this. Darling, I'll be in the formal living room." Pressing a key on the Blackberry, he held the phone up to his ear and hustled from the room. "Mike? What have you got for me?"

Kelly glowered at his retreating back. "Great. First I have a father who couldn't get through a simple dinner without jumping up to take calls, now I'll have a husband who does the same. I swear, if he takes that stupid Crackberry to Bora Bora, I'm throwing the damn thing in the ocean."

Rex laughed, reached over and tousled her hair.

She made a face at him and smoothed her hair. "Dad, I'm an adult. You don't tousle the hair of an adult."

"Until I give you away next weekend, you're still my little girl."

"Oh, Dad." There was a pause as she examined his face. "You're worried and not just about the wedding and me moving out. Something's wrong with work, isn't it? Does it involve Vance's father?"

Uncanny the way his daughter could read him. So much better than his wife ever could.

He turned his attention to his coffee. "Nothing to worry about, Katydid," he said, taking a sip and finding his brew had gone cold. He rose from the table and went to the buffet. He could feel Kelly's eyes on him.

"You look more preoccupied than normal. Deal must be a pretty important one."

Rex filled his cup and turned back to her. "It is. You haven't noticed anything different with James, have you?"

Kelly shrugged. "Seemed fine the last time I saw him. Last week he took us to Chez Panisse. He's going to Europe this week, right before the wedding."

Rex's body stiffened, his heart rate jumped and some of his coffee spilled on the Persian rug. Alarming news. He stepped back, swearing under his breath. Setting down his cup, he turned to his daughter and examined her face carefully. "Really? James hadn't mentioned the trip to me. When's he getting back?"

She frowned. "I don't know. And why are you so worried? And why didn't he tell you? I thought you two talked daily."

"Yes, we do. I mean, we have, just..." He forced his shoulders and face to relax. "Look, it's nothing for you to worry about, Katydid." He turned away, picked up a napkin from the buffet and bent down to blot the coffee from the rug, his injured leg twinging from the long stretch.

Something was wrong. He'd seen James the week before and he'd had no plans to go to Europe. Of course, he hadn't said anything about the funding problem, either. Maybe he should take all those private detectives off The Amazon Goddess and move them onto James Miller.

No. He'd give him another few days. Couldn't risk the backlash if James found out. He'd just hang tight.

"Dad, you look super worried. What is this deal you guys are working on?"

Rex waved off her concerns. "I'm over-reacting, Katydid. Project involves some big players and big money. Just has me a little nervous, that's all. It's a development in a new city," he tried to say in a casual tone. He sat down at the table. "Large groups of investors from Colorado are creating an entire city where there had only been a one-horse town before. Called Greenly. FutureSoft, California

Computer, Zeonics plus a bunch of other large firms are relocating there. Sure to be the next Austin. James did a fantastic presentation. Had the congresswoman of the district and several members of Colorado's government there. Deal looked good. I've never seen James so pumped."

"So why are you worried?"

"Must not have enough other stuff to worry about," he tossed off. "Everything will work out fine. These kinds of deals take superhuman effort to make happen." As he said the words, he began to believe them. His stomach calmed. With all the craziness associated with giant deals like that, it was no wonder James wasn't around and had missed a payment.

Vance came back into the room and he didn't look happy.

Kelly asked, "What's wrong, honey?"

He poured himself a cup of coffee and sat next to Rex, a dark look in his eye, his mouth a fixed line. "My Mercedes won't be ready for another week, some problem getting a new side panel. And they haven't been able to find that maniac who was driving the Volkswagen. What is wrong with the San Francisco police department? My father donates to all their little fundraisers, you'd think they'd maybe devote a few hours to finding that driver. That idiot nearly killed a bunch of people that day."

Kelly eyed her fiancé with a hint of disapproval, her lips tight. "There were also four murders in Hunter's Point that day and they didn't do anything about them, either."

Vance flipped a hand in the air, let out a huff and rolled his eyes. "Darling, there are always four murders in Hunter's Point, it's what those people do. This was in a good part of town, that cheap old wreck had no right even driving in the area," he spat. "It did nearly twenty thousand dollars damage to my car."

"That's because you paid too much for your car," she said in a pointedly imperious tone.

Vance glared at her. "I know you think image doesn't matter, but it does in my work. Right Rex?"

Rex coughed and laughed a bit to cover his discomfort. "Don't involve me in this. Besides, look what I drive."

"That dumb Bentley," Kelly said with a raised brow. "I think you're both overspending. Image schmimage. No way to help the planet."

"Miss Greenpeace, could you please pass the sugar?" Vance smirked at her.

She broke into a smile.

Vance beamed and shook his head. "Your daughter certainly keeps me on my toes."

Rex grinned, relieved the row had been settled so quickly. Unfortunately, he saw shades of his own relationship with Elizabeth in their banter.

Niggling doubts scratched at the back of his mind. Had he pushed Kelly too hard into marrying Vance? Was he sentencing her to the same loveless fate as he?

No, this was a completely different situation from his marriage. For one, Kelly adored Vance. She'd been mooning after the boy since she was four years old. He could still see her, teddy bear in hand, chasing after Vance and his friends.

And his marriage to Elizabeth had been a good one, a successful union. Elizabeth's father had been instrumental in helping him achieve his success. And he'd do the same for Vance.

Marriage was not just about love, it was about safety. About a safe financial future. For both families, the bride's and groom's.

His own mother should have figured that out before she married his alcoholic jerk of a father. If she'd married the right man, she might still be alive.

His uncle's voice rang in his mind. *Just think, kid, if you'd had the money, you'da been able to save your ma.*

Old pain fired through his gut. He took a deep breath. While it had been devastating at the time to hear those words, they became the rocket fuel that powered his money-making engines. With every dollar he made, it put him that much further ahead of that awful, powerless time of his life. Money was protection, plain and simple.

Which was why he was so worried about this deal with Vance's father. What would happen to Kelly and Vance if things blew up between he and James? A terrible strain.

Not only a family strain, a public strain. James and he had many ties. They were in the same social circle and belonged to many of the same clubs.

He had to stop this. James had never flaked on a deal. Ever. There had to be some reason he hadn't made a payment and wasn't returning his calls.

Probably a good reason. He felt a stab of guilt for doubting James' integrity. What kind of a friend was he? Doubting James. Crazy. He must just be tired.

Once Kelly got married and the deal went through, everything would be fine.

And if he found The Amazon Goddess, that would be one hell of a bonus.

Chapter Five

"It's going to work! It's going to work!" Cynthia cried, dancing down Market Street in the midst of a throng of pedestrians. She almost careened into an executive on his Bluetooth and had to jump over a homeless guy with a coin jar in his hand to avoid smashing into him. But she didn't care, she was going to Kelly's wedding!

Jon raced to catch up with her. "Calm down, we still have to come up with names and occupations! And outfits, hello?"

She gasped and stopped dead in her tracks. Black rain clouds of doom drenched her happy mood.

An elderly Chinese woman slammed into her and began chiding her in rapid-fire Mandarin. Several more people bumped into the Chinese woman, a huge pile-up ensued.

Cynthia jumped out of the way and into a red-haired guy with a beard. "Sorry!" she said to them both.

The Chinese woman continued on, chattering and shaking her head. The red-haired guy laughed, a black guy in a suit behind him glared at her while a group of Mexican ladies with several children pushed past her on all sides.

Jon grabbed her by the arm and pulled her out of the surging river of people, towards the front of Walgreens. "What's wrong?"

Waving her arms, she yelled, "The dress! I have no money! You have no money! What the hell am I going to do? And my feet! Holy

God, I'm screwed! I can't go naked and barefoot to my daughter's wedding!" she shouted over a vintage trolley car that careened by, loaded with tourists.

Jon grabbed her by the shoulders. "Calm down. We'll think of something."

"What? Where am I going to get a gorgeous ball gown?" Cynthia demanded, pulling out of his grip to gesture dramatically, just missing the jaw of a tall, pierced college girl wearing an iPod. "These are high society type people! I'm screwed!" She had a quick mental picture of herself in torn jeans and a dirty t-shirt with bare feet surrounded by rich people dressed in glittering expensive attire.

Jon took her by the arm and led her down the street and across a busy intersection. "Look, let's get a cup of coffee and calm down. No, wait, I'll get a cup of coffee and try to get to your level of freaked-out-ness," he said, yanking her out of the way of a blue-haired street kid on a skateboard.

She regarded him, arching an eyebrow. "Freaked-out-ness is not a word."

He snorted and rolled his eyes. "You knew what I meant."

He stopped in front of a corner coffee shop with a covered angled doorway and floor to ceiling windows. Five minutes later, they were seated in the window of the coffee shop, Cynthia lost in a sea of gloom, Jon lost in the *San Francisco Chronicle*.

"We'll figure this out, don't worry," he said absently, more focused on the paper than on the conversation.

"I can't help it. I can't go without a good dress and I can't afford one, not in my size. And my feet, why did God have to give me size freakin' fourteen feet?" She pointed at her flipper-sized feet. "The only dress and fancy shoes I've ever fit in were your drag queen outfits."

Jon dropped his paper and stared at her. His mouth dropped open, then an awed smile overtook his handsome features. He leapt to his feet and shrieked, "That's it!"

Cynthia clutched her chest. "Jeez, that was loud. I swear, your mother must have had an affair with a foghorn. What's 'it'?"

"You fit in my clothes exactly," he said with an expectant look on his face. As if that explained his whole idea.

She stared at him. "Great, so I can wear your jeans and a t-shirt to the wedding, what?"

He sat. "Duh, what? Carol Channing? Hello?"

"What…" Like a frying pan in the face, his plan walloped her good. "You have to be kidding me."

"That dress cost over ten grand. Silver sparkles, tasteful cut, slit up the side and the shoes. Voila!" he pronounced with a grand gesture. "Secret Mother of the Bride—wow, if that isn't a Harlequin romance title, I don't know what is."

Cynthia pictured herself in Jon's costume. Crazy and outrageous as it may sound, his wild idea might just work. She did fit in his clothes, the two were nearly the exact same height, weight and size, albeit with different proportions.

He was right. This could work.

Her heart lifted and her mood soared. She pictured herself wearing the silver gown with little birds flying around her holding red ribbons in their mouths like in a Disney film, a cloud of cartoon hearts over her head.

"Oh, my God!" She leapt out of her chair, knocked into the table and barely caught her tea before it spilled. Luckily, Jon had been holding his coffee. Waving her arms, she pointed down at him. "This will work! You're a genius—wait." Jon's tight-ass boss, David, came to mind. A flash of the gown flying off her body went through her head. "Wait, wait, wait." She plopped down in her seat. "There is no way David is going to let us borrow a ten thousand dollar dress. That man is more uptight than Miss Manners. In fact, I think he is Miss Manners."

Jon cocked his head and twisted his mouth. "Wow, what if he is? Would fit." He dismissed the idea with a wave of his hand. "Oh, hell, David's never backstage anymore. He doesn't have to know."

"But it's a night wedding. We won't get out of there until late."

He seemed confident. "I don't go on until after midnight. No sweat. That time of night, it's nothing to get from the Fairmont to the Castro. We'll trade clothes in the cab. Easy."

She sat back down slowly, lost in thought. "Damn, it is a beautiful dress. The most tasteful one in the entire show. Where will you get your tux? And please don't get one from your Chippendales' friends. That's all we'd need. You go to take something out of your pocket and accidentally yank off your tear-away pants."

His eyes lighting up, Jon put a hand to his mouth and giggled. "Wouldn't that be funny?"

"No. Not at our daughter's wedding." She leaned back in her chair and rubbed her chin. "Damn, we might actually pull this off."

"Not might, will. We've got it in the bag, honey."

His nasty old Carmen Miranda dress popped into her head. Stunk up the whole closet until she insisted he send it out to get cleaned. "So how often do you clean that thing?"

"Don't worry, I'll make sure it's dry cleaned before it touches your precious female skin."

"I just don't want to go there smelling like man."

"You won't." Jon returned to his paper.

She finally realized that all obstacles barring her from the wedding were gone. The dress, the invitation. Everything. She squealed, startling him. "This is so killer! That outfit is perfect. All sparkly and form fitting and tasteful."

His eyes widened from her volume, then he relaxed and continued reading. "Yes, my dear, you'll be the toast of the town, only we will—" Something in the paper caught his attention. His face went blank. "Holy God. No."

"What?"

"This can't be. Of course, it is. Get this, honey." He looked up at her, his eyes shining as if he were about to feast on the most delicious nugget of gossip ever. *"To The Female Runner Who Saved My Life In Golden Gate Park On June 5th at 3:30 PM."*

Her chest tightened, she couldn't breathe. Finally, she got enough breath back in her lungs to respond. "No!"

His green eyes sparkling with excitement, Jon pointed at her. "Yes. Wait, listen to this: *I need to meet you to thank you. Please call as soon as you can*—oh, my God, he has an 800 number here."

Her heart thumped at a crazy beat. "He does not. Let me look at that," she said grabbing away the paper from him. "Oh, my God, he didn't take out a personal ad, this sucker is a quarter page!"

Jon grinned so hard, his face nearly split in two. "He wants to meet you!" he teased in a singsong voice.

She fanned herself with a hand. "This is too much. How the hell am I going to get to that wedding with this guy searching for me and putting out stupid ads in the paper? This is crazy," she said, gesturing so violently she knocked her hand on the window making a loud *pank*. "Ow!" She rubbed her hand. "Nothing like this has ever happened to me. And now that it has, I can't even jump on it or him. Why did he have to be Alice's father?"

He sent her a covetous smile. "You are so lucky, no man has ever put a quarter page ad looking for me before. When you hook 'em, you really hook 'em, honey."

"And I can't do a damn thing about it. This is too weird. Man, what other weird things are going to happen to me today?"

Out of the corner of her eye, she noticed two people on the other side of the glass standing very near to the window. They were so close they blocked the light.

Probably homeless people looking for a handout. She pretended not to notice and took a sip of tea.

A rapping on the window next to her head made her jump. Damn aggressive street people.

She set her face to Death Stare and glowered at the two. She found herself staring into her worst nightmare. The Gruesome Twosome, live in downtown San Francisco. All the air left her lungs, her heart stopped, but every nerve ignited. A wave of ice-cold hatred chilled her to the bone.

Her stepsister Belinda's ski-jump blond bangs shot off the top of her head so high, it looked like she was falling from a skyscraper. Underneath the hairsprayed gravity-defying wonder, furrowed penciled-in eyebrows sat atop vacant dark eyes. Her turned up nose wrinkled as though she smelled something foul and her corpulent cheeks pouched like a cow with a mouthful of cud. And this was her pleasant face.

Sissy stood next to Belinda, her beady dark eyes boring into Cynthia like a cat preying upon a mouse. Her gaunt and skeletal face, ashen and lined, was a roadmap of her bad lifestyle choices. At forty-two, she looked sixty-two.

Sissy attempted a smile, showing off yellowing teeth with one missing. The effect was as menacing as the evil clown's in the Stephen King novel, *It*. Sissy didn't do kind. She only did manipulation. She wanted something. Something big.

Cynthia's tea crept up her throat. "Oh, God," was all she could get out.

Jon turned to look at what she was staring at. He screamed and clutched his chest in horror. "What the hell do they want?"

"Shit. Probably something to do with those legal papers they mentioned on the phone."

Sissy started to walk inside, but Belinda, staring at Jon, didn't notice and Sissy ran right into her. They heard the yell through the glass.

"Move your ass, bitch, you're in my way!" Sissy shouted, pushing Belinda hard.

Reeling back, Belinda snarled, "Shut up!"

They shoved each other a bit, then Sissy walked around her, pushed the door open and rushed up to Cynthia's table with Belinda right on her heels.

They stunk of cigarettes, weed and yesterday's booze. White powder clung around the underneath of Sissy's nostrils. Still on drugs, what a shocker.

Sissy attempted a bigger smile. Even more frightening. She speared her greasy, spiky black hair with her fingers. "Hi, Cynthia, how are you? And you, Jon, how are you doing?" Sounded like the pleasantries burned her tongue.

"Yeah, how are you guys? Or should we say *girls*?" Belinda snorted with laughter, sounding like a hoard of pigs snuffling in the mud.

Sissy backhanded her across the shoulder. "Shut up! We need something—I mean, we need to talk to her. So be nice." Another fake smile. "Sorry about Belinda, we don't let her go out much. You know how she gets."

Pouting, Belinda stared briefly at the floor. "Yeah, I didn't mean nothin' by it. Jon gets my sense of humor, don't you, Jon?" she asked with an empty smile.

Jon coughed. "Uh, sure, Belinda."

Sissy made a cutting motion across her throat. "Okay, enough with the chit chat. Here's the deal." She placed her weathered hands on her scrawny hips and her small dark eyes narrowed. "We found out about the insurance policy," she said in an accusatory tone.

"Yeah." Belinda crossed her arms across her formidable chest and frowned. "We found out about the insurance policy."

Cynthia glared up at them. "What insurance policy?"

Sissy pointed a bony finger at her, her inch-long, fake black fingernail coming dangerously close to her face. "Don't play dumb with me, sister, we're onto you, so stop the stupid act. Look, here's the deal. You sign that over to us and you get your artwork back and your real mom's photos and all her little mementos. I know, you thought you'd go collect the five hundred grand and we'd be none the wiser, but we're onto you," she said, sniffling and wiping her nose on her scrawny arm. "That's why you let us bully you and con you out of the house, you knew there was bigger fish to fry."

Belinda nodded. "Yeah, bigger fish to eat."

Sissy swung on her sister. "Shut up. Did I tell you to speak?"

Belinda's thin brow drew into an exaggerated V. "No, but you shut up, you don't get to say what I say. I'm in on this, too."

Sissy got in her face. "No, you're not. We split this sixty-forty because I found the policy."

Belinda stood her ground and tried to pull herself up taller, but gravity wouldn't allow her three hundred and fifty pounds to move much. She ended up jiggling in place. "No, I get half because Mom always said I get half even though you always got more."

Sissy crossed her skinny arms across her chest and stood on her tiptoes to glare down at her sister. "Mom is dead so now I'm in charge and I say you shut up and let me deal with this." She abruptly turned back to Cynthia. "So here's the deal. You come to the house this week and sign that over to me and I'll give you all your stupid crappy artwork and all your real mom's shit. If you don't, I'll burn everything and send you a videotape of it. Got me? Sister?"

Cynthia's blood turned to magma and her jaw set. She had a quick flash of ramming Sissy's head into the cement floor of the coffee shop.

She grabbed hold of her fantasies with both hands. *This has to stop. Now.*

She concentrated on channeling her therapist, because if she tried to speak as herself it would be a solid stream of expletives. "Sissy, I understand you suffered extensive emotional damage in your childhood which has made you incapable of distinguishing fact from fantasy. I will try to make this simple so even you can understand. I know nothing about a policy. I reviewed every piece of paper in that household before I was kicked out. There is no insurance policy."

Sissy sneered. "Oh, yes there was, it just came in the mail last week. I called and checked and everything. Your father left you— God knows why, you probably drugged him and forced him to do it just like you did with the will—your father left you five hundred grand. All you gotta do is go pick it up. Then give it to me."

Cynthia's heart raced and dollar signs danced in front of her eyes. Her father's dying words about an insurance policy, here it was! She gave her head a good shake. She'd had access to all the paperwork, she'd run her parents' finances for the previous three years, there were no amounts of money missing. She'd controlled it all. Mostly because it was hers.

Aside from that, her father simply hadn't loved her enough to do something like that. He didn't care about her.

Another huge factor: Sissy lived in a fantasy world. This was a woman who sent money to the Nigerian email scammers. This was a woman who believed every advertising mailer that touted "You've Won!" She even went out on a spending spree once because she'd received the *entry form* for the Publisher's Clearing House Sweepstakes and mistook it for the actual award. Cynthia couldn't count the astounding amount of get-rich-quick schemes Sissy had bought into. A bona fide idiot.

"You. Are. High. Get lost."

Sissy's dark stare sharpened. Her anger lines deepened. "Did you hear me?"

"I'm not supposed to engage with you and here I am talking to you. Jon?" She jerked her head towards the door.

Jon gave a sharp nod. "Gladly."

Sissy's sallow face screwed up so tightly she almost looked like an apple doll. She jabbed a talon at her. "You can't get rid of me that easy. You owe me money! You didn't even pay rent for that whole seven years you were there—"

"Because I was taking care of *your* sick mother and my sick father."

"Bullshit! You cheated us!"

"Yeah," Belinda chimed in. "You cheated us!"

Cynthia sighed, her therapist's voice ringing in her mind. *Listening to crazy people makes you crazy. Don't expect crazy people to make sense. Run away from the crazy people and stay away from them.*

She turned to Jon. "Let's split. Now."

Jon did a full body shudder. "Please, this is a double-feature horror movie I need to walk out on," he said, quickly folding his newspaper and tucking it under his arm.

They got up. The Nasty Twins blocked their exit.

Cynthia's temper at the boiling point, she had visions of being locked up, blood all over her hands.

Behind the gargoyles, two beat cops walked by the glassed-in front doors of the coffee house. A perfect out.

She somehow calmed herself and sent the two an evil grin. "Since I've been here, I've made some new friends. I wonder what Roy and Cory would think of this little shake down." She nodded towards the cops.

Her stepsisters turned, Belinda yipped and Sissy gasped so hard, she choked on her spit and had a coughing fit.

Cynthia waved to the two cops as they passed by the window. They smiled and waved back. Out of the corner of her mouth, she said, "By that reaction, I'll just venture there's a load of meth in your purse, Sissy. Wonder what they'd think of that. Aren't you on parole?"

Sissy's face went from white to crimson. Her eyes crazy, she pointed a shaking finger up at Cynthia. "Don't think you're getting away with that money! That's my money," she said, jabbing her chest so violently it was surprising she didn't slice herself. "I got the house, I got all your stuff, I won, not you. And I'm gettin' that money or I'm burning your mom's stuff and smashing all your retarded sculptures. You'd better come sign that over or I'll make your life a living hell."

Cynthia narrowed her eyes at the anemic troll. "Too late."

Sissy's dark gaze filled with fire, her wrinkled mouth twisted. "Come on, Belinda. Let's get away from these assholes." She glared up at Cynthia. "Have fun with your fag husband, bitch!" She turned and stalked out the door.

Belinda sneered at the two. "Yeah, bitch," she spat, then turned and waddled out, her two-ton buns bouncing behind her.

Cynthia didn't breathe until they'd disappeared from sight. Then she slipped back into her seat, put her head in her hands and let out a heavy sigh. "I should have walked. When they came in here, I should have pushed past them and left. *Shit*. I bit the hook. I swallowed the mother."

Jon reached over and rubbed her shoulder, then patted it. "Oh, give yourself a break, I'm proud of you. You did really well. Last time you beat them up. I'm surprised they had the balls to come in here and push you around."

"How did they find us here?"

"We are only a block from the condo."

Cynthia rubbed her temples. "Remind me to hang out in coffee shops that are more than a block away from home." She took a large swig of tea.

"Maybe you oughta find out what's going on. You don't want 'em destroying any more of your sculptures or your Mom's stuff."

"Look, I've had to let go of all that. Yes, it breaks my heart like you can't believe, but I can't let them have any hold over me. I can create more sculptures, buy more tools. Besides, if by some wild, million-to-one chance they're right, they won't destroy that stuff, it's their only trump card. But if Dad took out a policy, why didn't he tell me?"

"His last words were about an insurance policy."

"No. I told you, that was about his auto insurance policy. The premium came due the week he went into the hospital. I know that's what he meant because he'd been pestering me about it daily, hourly, for two days before. Besides, I went through every single piece of paper in the goddamned place. No, they have to be high."

"Still, five hundred grand might be worth a look."

Cynthia chewed on her lower lip. "I do not want to get my hopes up," she said with a long, drawn out sigh. "But I can call the lawyer. He'd be the one who'd really know."

Jon sent her a sympathetic smile and put his hand over hers, squeezing it. "You poor thing. I wish you hadn't gotten stuck in that hellhole. For seven years."

"Look, I know why I was there, okay?" she said, pulling away to tap the table. "I walked into that. I stuck myself there. I was trying to get what I needed from my father. I thought if I took care of him, maybe he'd finally accept me. Love me. And of course, seven years later, no. He never really liked me. Not my fault—not because I'm defective—because he was too emotionally damaged. Which is how he ended up with the Step-Monster. He was a jerk. Truly. But the bottom line, I have to take responsibility for what's happened to me or I'll never stop being a victim."

Jon's eyes widened and he seemed awed. "Wow, you've been doing some serious thinking, girlfriend. Frightening." He reached over and touched her hand. "Tell me I can get enlightenment without looking too deeply inside myself and my past."

She stared at him and blinked.

He withdrew his hand and gestured towards her with a bright smile. "Okay, back to you. Honestly, you have no idea how proud I am of you. It was your total right to kill those imbeciles. I hate them."

"Me, too."

He ran a hand through her hair in an affectionate gesture. "You'll be fine, you always are. And I hope you end up with Rex."

"Me, too. Not a chance, but me, too."

He stopped and stared into space. Eyes narrowed, his brows slightly raised, he crossed his arms high across his chest. "Zoltan sees the future."

She sighed and reluctantly smiled. "Not this."

He squinted and nodded to himself, dead serious, still in character. "Zoltan predicts much sex with the tall gimp."

She smacked him on the arm. "He is not a gimp."

Jon broke out of his pose. "He is now."

"That is not politically correct. You should be ashamed of yourself."

"You're laughing."

"That's beside the point."

"So did you know those cops who just walked by?"

"No," she said with a giggle.

Jon broke into a wide grin. "Jeez, I even believed you."

"Good. Damn, I want to stop thinking about those horrible bitches. Let's plan our attack for the wedding. We need names that will fit our fancy outfits."

"Prince and Princess Outtaluck from the Kingdom of Debt."

"Funny."

Jon gave his hand a flip. "Oh, don't worry. We're theater majors —well, you switched degrees, but you took enough drama. We'll fit right in."

Chapter Six

As they walked into the lobby of the Fairmont, Jon's gaze went wide. "Oh, my God, we so don't fit here," he said out of the side of his mouth.

Cynthia tried to play like she belonged, but she'd forgotten how ostentatious the hotel was. The lobby was big as a football field. Cream-colored, gold-trimmed Corinthian columns rose from the marble floors to the high, domed ceiling. The expansive ornate room had been created to welcome real kings and queens, not drag queens and penniless paupers. Cynthia had never felt poorer nor more out of place.

Even though, she had to admit, she and Jon looked the part. Her sparkling silver gown, form-fitting and tasteful looked perfect next to Jon's borrowed tux. Together, they made a striking couple. Of course, they always had. Even though they were going as brother and sister to this event, they could have easily passed for married. Especially because of the shared mannerisms from all the time they had spent together.

They followed the signs to the elevator that would take them to the wedding ceremony in the Crown Room. The reception was to be held downstairs in the Gold Room. Sounded like yet another place she'd feel insecure.

They stepped into the elevator with two old ladies wearing furs. Neither Jon nor Cynthia uttered a word, they settled for exchanging alarmed glances. Outclassed at every turn.

When they walked in the Crown Room, she gasped. Windows lining the walls of the ornate room afforded magnificent views of the San Francisco nighttime skyline. The Bay Bridge was lit up and the tall buildings twinkled. The sky was unusually clear, showing off an array of stars and a sliver of a moon. An amazing backdrop.

An arch of pink orchids stood where the ceremony would take place. Pink, white and red rose petals were strewn over the chairs and maroon carpet. About half the chairs were filled on either side of the aisle.

They were escorted to their seats by a very nice-looking young man. No one seemed to take notice of them as they got settled. She got the idea most of the people at the wedding didn't know each other. Except for the in-crowd from the Who's Who of San Francisco society.

Jon pointed up ahead of them. "Is that Bob McCahon, the famous fashion designer? Of course, who else would wear a purple suit to a wedding?" He gasped. "Oh, my God, there's the mayor!" he shrieked loudly. Two older ladies seated directly in front of them turned to glare at him. He improvised, "We played golf last week and he beat the pants off me." Quieter, he said, "Oh, God, now I just started some gay rumors about him."

Cynthia stifled a laugh.

The rows filled with people. Since it was an evening wedding, the wealthy were displaying all their crown jewels. Cynthia contemplated a new career as a jewel thief.

Jon seemed to forget all his acting training. He stared bug-eyed at the circus parade of eccentric have-mores. "Whoa, is this the Plastic Surgery Reunion Tour or what?"

"Keep your voice down. And yes."

"Space aliens. They're Bentley-driving space aliens from Planet Bloomingdale's."

"Ssshhh."

"I can't help myself, you dragged me here."

"Your daughter is getting married."

Everyone around them stood and faced the back.

Jon stood. "Well, when you put it that way."

She joined him. "Shhh, it's about to start."

When Cynthia turned around and saw Kelly standing there in her cream-colored, beaded wedding dress, she couldn't breathe. Then her waterworks blew a gasket. Rivers of tears, oceans of sobs.

Not very convenient for trying to remain unnoticed. Jon had to physically hold her up.

"You. Are. Blowing. It," he hissed in her ear. "I love you, but get it together."

His words shook her. She centered. This shouldn't mean this much. Kelly was in actuality a stranger. Someone who looked like her mother. But someone she didn't know at all.

Her emotions let loose again. All that she'd lost. This beautiful person. She'd missed Kelly's whole life. And for what? To hurt Jon the way he'd hurt her? Oh, God, she'd been so naïve! Could she ever forgive herself?

But if she'd kept her, the girl would have been raised in a split household. It took Cynthia a good five years to forgive Jon. The arguments had been terrible. Sharing custody would have been a war. Kelly would have been raised in turmoil and derision. She'd never be this happy.

Or would she? Cynthia would have loved her with her whole heart, like she did right then. Kelly certainly wouldn't be this rich, but would she have been happier being raised by her own parents?

That was a question no one could answer. Cynthia wished she hadn't thought of it.

Jon whispered, "Cynth, you thought I was blowing it—"

"I'm here." Finally, with a visual of taking all her pain, wrapping it in a ball and tossing it away, she stopped crying. And just in time.

Kelly was right there, Rex on her other side. He still had a hell of a limp.

Cynthia couldn't tell who affected her more, the Hunk or her daughter.

Kelly turned and looked straight at her. Cynthia froze. There she was, in all her radiance, a mere few feet away. It was one thing to look at her through the windshield of a car and another to be in her presence. Poise, self-confidence and strength shone clear in her sparkling hazel gaze. She had been loved and respected, it was all over her face. *The father.* What a great job he and his wife had done.

The father! He'd recognize her!

Just as Rex turned towards them, she dropped her purse, bending down quickly to pick it up. She stayed down until they passed.

"Whew," she whispered as she stood.

Jon was strangely silent, save for some gurgling noises. She turned to him and tears were streaming down his face.

He reached for her and fell into her arms. "Our baby! Did you see our baby?"

She chuckled through her tears. "Welcome to the club."

An old biddy seated in front of them turned around. Wearing diamonds the size of ice cubes, she looked like she'd just sucked on a lemon. "Will you please keep your voices down?"

Before Cynthia could apologize, Jon leapt in with, "I'm sorry if expressing myself emotionally bothers you, but unlike your generation, I have no issues with my emotions."

Cynthia looked down, pinched the bridge of her nose and couldn't stop a chuckle. Freakin' Jon. Never took any guff from strangers.

The old woman sputtered for a moment, then said, "Well, at least my generation has good manners!"

Jon snorted. "Yeah, being nasty to strangers is totally considered *good manners.*"

"Humph!" The woman made a big display of turning around.

"Is 'humph' a word?" Jon asked Cynthia in a low tone.

"It is now."

The ceremony was blessedly short. By the time Kelly walked back down the aisle with her handsome prince, Cynthia had her emotions in check. And so did Jon.

Kelly and Vance were a beautiful couple. So perfect, like wedding cake toppers.

And just as Rex passed by, she turned to gaze out the window. Perfect timing. Now if only her luck would hold through the reception.

They followed the rest of the guests downstairs to the Gold Room. Cynthia immediately figured out why they called it the Gold Room, because you'd have to own a mountain of gold to rent the place.

When they walked into the French Provincial ballroom, it was like stepping back in time. Ornate gold leaf bas-reliefs adorned the walls and high columns, crystal chandeliers hung overhead. A series of balconies overlooked the ballroom. Gorgeous sconces and amazing, hand-painted murals covered the gold damask walls. Crazy beautiful.

They so didn't belong there.

Instead of heading to the open bar like most of the guests, Jon and Cynthia searched for their places at the tables so they could hide. The guests' names were hand printed in perfect calligraphy on small, cream-colored place cards.

The first eight tables yielded nothing. No Tony or Abigail Maxim.

"Where are we seated?" Jon whispered, his eyes darting from card to card.

"I don't know, but let's not get nervous. Keep acting like we belong here."

"No worries, no one's really looking at us. Besides, I don't think we're anywhere near as weird as these Botoxed, cut and pasted Prada freaks—oh, thank God, here we are."

Breathing a sigh of relief, Cynthia and Jon grabbed their seats and tried to assume authoritative yet unobtrusive postures. She thought her performance was coming off well, but her stomach was twisted so tightly, it threatened to implode.

"Thank God, we're the first ones seated here," Jon said. "Gives us a chance to get our heads together. Remember your character and her story?"

"You bet. Oh, thank you," Cynthia said as a waiter poured some champagne in her glass. "This should help," she said under her breath.

Jon put his hand on her arm. "Not too much, dearie."

"No worries, I won't blow it," she whispered back.

Someone sat next to her. She turned to greet them. She stared. Every muscle went rigid.

She was going to kill Michael. He'd seated her directly next to the mayor of San Francisco, Calvin Newman. Mr. Movie Star. Mr. Cover Of The Freakin' Paper.

Great, this is all she needed, her face plastered all over the newspaper with her fake name underneath. *Son-of-a-bitch.*

Heart pounding, she turned to Jon with an intense stare. When he saw who was next to her, his jaw dropped, his pupils went to pinpricks. After blinking rapidly a few times, his shoulders relaxed. He shrugged. Snapped right into his character. Good for him.

If only she could do the same thing. Cynthia was so flustered, she couldn't remember what her damn name was supposed to be, what her occupation was supposed to be, nothing. So she did the only thing she could think to do: she reached for her champagne. After a couple glasses—along with a yummy marinated mussels appetizer—she relaxed and decided to introduce herself.

She waited until he turned to her. She offered her hand. "Mr. Newman, great job, sir. Thanks for all your hard work."

His white-toothed smile nearly blinded her. She thought he'd looked hot on TV, up close, the man was on fire. Her heart went into triple time.

He shook her hand. Nice grip. "Thank you. And you are?"

"Abigail Maxim."

His dark eyebrows shot up, recognition clear in his sparkling chocolate gaze. "Of *the* Maxims?"

Perfect.

Cynthia nodded slightly. "I'm a cousin. We're not the most fabulous Maxims, but we're much more fun than the others."

He laughed. Warmth radiated through her. She'd made the Mayor laugh! This was so fun!

That broke the ice. Confidence filled her, she relaxed. Completely committed to her character, Cynthia let loose like the entire table was full of her long lost friends. Once she got going, it was hard for her to stop. Thankfully, the crowd got her sense of humor. While she was playing a character, it was more or less based upon herself. Only richer. Still, it worked.

"…and I said, but Senator, how can I vote from the backseat of a limousine?"

Her audience roared.

"And he said, 'baby, don't leave my chad hanging'—he actually said that—"

Calvin—they were on a first name basis now—pushed on her shoulder and said, "He did not."

She held up her right hand and placed her left on her glass. "I swear a solemn oath on this flute of champagne."

Calvin threw up his hands. "Well, then, it's gotta be true."

The entire table laughed. Probably more to do with the alcohol rather than the quality of the humor. Champagne had a wonderful effect on jokes.

Calvin's fiancée waved a hand at her. "Okay, I've been dying to ask this, where did you find that beautiful silver gown? I've been admiring it since you walked in. I'm looking for a wedding gown and I love that cut. It fits you like glove. Who did it? Where did you get it?"

Cynthia blinked, her mind flying for an answer. She turned to Jon. He had a barely hidden grin on his face, obviously fully enjoying her predicament. He raised his eyebrows and leaned in, as if he were very interested in her answer. The jerk.

Two can play at that game. With a triumphant little half smile, Cynthia replied smoothly, "My brother found it for me. Where did you get it again, Tony?"

His brows went flat and his mouth became a grim line. Ha! Score two points for Cynthia!

Kicking her under the table, he replied, "I have a friend who designs these types of gowns for Las Vegas shows. I thought it might be a kick," he said, kicking her again, "if he did one for my dear sister. His name is Jerry Galliano, I'll get you his number if you want it. Very creative man."

Calvin's fiancée beamed. "I'd love it, thank you." She gestured towards Cynthia with her glass. "And how wonderful you have a brother with such great taste. You're so lucky to have him."

"I tell him that every day," Cynthia said, then sent Jon a fake smile. He returned the favor.

Dinner was served. Deeee-lish. Salad was heirloom tomatoes, Mission figs and Brie over baby greens with a Port vinaigrette. For the main entrée, beef tenderloins with a Cabernet reduction, potatoes au gratin and asparagus with walnuts.

Since their table was one of the last to be served, the wedding party had finished eating and was making the rounds.

Cynthia spotted Rex across the room, working the tables. She had to avoid him, but she couldn't risk attracting his attention. Luckily, she had Mr. Movie Star Mayor next to her. Great distraction. While Rex greeted the local dignitary, she'd slip away to the bathroom.

Jon was onboard, he would signal her at the appropriate time so she wouldn't have to turn around.

Her ex stared over her shoulder. Only his eyes moved. After a minute or two, he looked at her and gave a quick nod.

Right as she stood, Calvin started choking. Badly. Jon pulled on her arm and she ripped out of his grip, her focus on the mayor. Calvin turned red, then purple. He grabbed his throat and began trying to get the attention of the table.

Cynthia put her hand on his shoulder. "I know CPR. Do I have your permission to help you?"

He nodded vigorously. She thumped him on the back five times. Nothing.

"Okay, I'm going to do the Heimlich maneuver, stand up!"

Calvin stood, his face a deep purple. He was about to lose consciousness.

She got behind him, knotted her fist, shoved it up under his sternum, then placed her other hand over her fist and pulled hard with both hands. A chunk of beef flew out of the mayor's mouth and sailed across the table, narrowly missing the centerpiece. He coughed and worked hard to get air back into his lungs.

She checked his color, it had returned to normal. She patted him on the back gently. "You okay?"

He nodded, cleared his throat and turned to her, his face full of emotion. "Oh, my God, how can I thank you? You saved my life."

She grinned and waved a hand. "No worries, my dear. What would our fair town do without you?"

He grabbed her hand and pumped her arm, then embraced her. Hard bodied, the man was a hunk. He released her with a grateful smile on his handsome face.

His fiancée got up and shook her hand, too. "That was such quick thinking. Did you take a CPR class?"

Cynthia nodded, flailing for a plausible excuse. "Uh, yeah. Yes, one of our villas is so remote, I felt it was necessary to, you know, make sure I could, uh, take care of the family's needs in an emergency."

Crisis averted, she suddenly became aware of her surroundings. Holy crap, great job of trying to go unnoticed. The whole table stared at her, then began clapping. Two tables near them also broke out in applause.

Her face went hot.

Someone tall stood right beside her.

She looked up into the riveting blue gaze of none other than Rex Du Charmante.

Chapter Seven

Rex's azure eyes dilated, his mouth fell open and then widened into a huge smile. "It's you!"

Oh, shit.

Cynthia couldn't get anything out. Completely dumbfounded.

He continued on in a rush. "God, woman, what I've gone through trying to find you!" He turned to the table and gestured towards her. "Everyone, this woman saved my life." He turned back to her, an overjoyed and awed expression on his chiseled face. "And now you save the mayor's life?"

"She saved your life? In the park?" Calvin demanded, looking between the two.

Rex nodded enthusiastically. "Yes, she did." He blasted her with his white-hot energy. The man was a fireball. "I never forget a beautiful face."

"Uh." Suddenly unable to lie, she nodded. "Yeah, that would be me."

Rex crushed her in a bear hug. Energy shot from her feet all the way out through the top of her head. His scent, the strength of his arms, his warmth, his hard chest—wow!

He was so tall! She rarely hugged a man who made her feel small. Who made her feel like such a woman. All she wanted was to be naked in his arms, that firm chest pressed against her, skin to skin. Her sex cried out with joy. *Mate with him!*

He pushed away and kissed her on the cheek. Hot electricity blasted her skin. The room took a spin. His soft, but strong lips sent shockwaves of pleasure rioting through her body. She had to forcibly center herself.

The man annihilated her resolve with one hug and a kiss. This was a very dangerous person. He was a human nuclear bomb and she was his Hiroshima. No man ever had this effect on her.

He pulled back with a giant grin. "My God, you, here at my daughter's wedding. What's your name? Where did you go? Didn't you see my ads? How did you learn to save someone's life? Wait, you have to meet my daughter."

He turned and searched for Kelly.

"Uh, you don't—"

He spotted the bride and his eyes lit up. "There she is." He took Cynthia by the arm and pulled her across the room. "You have to come with me."

She sent one helpless look towards Jon who shrugged and laughed.

As she was pulled by table after table of fabulous rich people, she couldn't help but chuckle. This guy was a dynamo. She pitied anyone who got in his way.

Kelly was a few tables away. She looked up when she saw her father coming. Her smile lit up the room.

Cynthia suddenly realized that she was about to meet her daughter. This was too dangerous! She shouldn't be doing this! This was wrong!

And then, it was too late. There she was, her baby, right in front of her.

She couldn't move, couldn't think. Even the hunk didn't register for a moment. All she saw was her Kelly. The intelligent, kind hazel gaze. She looked like everyone Cynthia had ever loved. She saw her mother, Jon, Jon's mother, her grandmother, even her father in the girl's beautiful face. It was like Kelly got the best of all the physical attributes of the family. Amazing.

Her heart beat so fast, she hoped she wasn't having a heart attack.

"Kelly, this is the woman who saved my life in the Park. This is The Aah—uh." He looked down at Cynthia, his smile vanished, a look of alarm crossed his sweet face, then he abruptly burst out laughing and turned back to Kelly. "This is the woman who saved my life."

Kelly stifled a laugh, she and her father shared some silent communication, then both laughed. Some private joke.

She turned to Cynthia and sent her a very genuine smile. "So this is the mystery Amazon. Wow, you are tall."

"Uh—"

One arm around her, Rex gestured towards her with his other. "She also just saved the Mayor's life. I was right there, I saw her. He was choking on a piece of tenderloin, she performed the Heimlich maneuver and saved him. She saved my life and the Mayor's. All in the same month."

Kelly's mouth dropped open and her eyes went wide. "Wow, really? How cool! I'm so glad you're here and I can't thank you enough for saving my father and the mayor. You're too much, girlfriend! High five on that one!" She held up her hand.

She laughed and slapped her daughter's palm. The gratitude in Kelly's warm gaze, the radiant smile, her playfulness, Cynthia's heart swelled to the point she thought she'd bust an aorta. *My daughter. My baby.* It was all she could do to stop from throwing her arms around the girl.

"You're very welcome," she finally managed to say.

Kelly touched her arm. "I'm sorry, I'm Kelly. I can't believe I didn't ask your name right off the bat. You are?"

"Cyn—I mean, Abigail Maxim." She immediately felt like one big rat for lying to her daughter.

"Well, Abigail, I'm pleased to meet you. You have no idea the lengths Dad's gone to find you. So how do you know us? Are you a friend of Vance's?"

"Uh…yes. He may not remember me, I'm an old friend of the family."

Kelly scanned the ballroom quickly, then turned back to Cynthia. "Have you seen him yet? I'm sure he'd be pretty surprised to find out the woman who saved his father-in-law's life was a friend of his family."

"Oh, I'd bet he'd be surprised. But really, it was nothing. Anyone —"

"Not in this town," Rex said, squeezing her. "They let people die out there. Didn't you see my ads?"

Kelly nodded with enthusiasm. "Dad put ads in all the papers looking for you."

Cynthia coughed and stifled a panic attack. "Uh, no. How sweet. Actually, right after I saved you, I had to hop a plane for, uh, Milan. I've been in Milan."

"Oh," Rex said, relaxing. "I thought you were avoiding me. So why didn't you stay and give the police your report?"

Cynthia attempted a light-hearted laugh and gave a little flippant toss of her head. "Sounds dumb, but I really didn't want the publicity. The family tries to keep a low profile and I was covered in your blood and really wanted to clean up better than in a public restroom. You know the police, they make you wait forever and I had a plane to catch," she said with a wave of her hand.

For some reason, both Kelly and Rex bought the story. Thank the Lord. Their gratitude must be clouding their judgment. She'd never lied so poorly in her life.

Pulled in two different directions, she didn't know which was more overwhelming, meeting her daughter or being in the Hunk's embrace. Physically, it was difficult to ignore Rex. She could feel his body heat and the hardness of his chest and arm. She was on the verge of swooning. And right there in front of her was her baby, smiling at her. All too much.

Kelly looked over her shoulder, off at Cynthia's table. "So are you here with your husband?"

Before she could think, she replied, "No, my brother. I'm not married." She regretted the words the moment they left her tongue.

Kelly sent a sly smile to her father. Cynthia was afraid of Rex's reaction but she couldn't stop herself from checking up at him.

He glowed like he'd just won Olympic gold.

Bummer. She was *sunk*.

She tried for aloof, but was so emotional, she had no control over herself. She beamed back at him.

Mayday! Mayday! Hit the escape pod! Hit the ejector seat!

Cynthia came to her senses. "Look, I hate to keep you two, you have guests to attend to, I'll just—"

She tried to break out of his grip, but Rex would not let go.

He grinned down at her. "Oh, no. Not after what I went through to find you. First, your number and address. I'm afraid if I lose sight of you, you'll disappear like you did before." He reached into his jacket pocket and pulled out a pen and his card. "Here," he said, shoving both into her hands. "I'm not letting you go until I get information."

Dude was a freight train. Pen in hand, Cynthia froze. "I don't have a permanent address, I'm only here to see my brother."

Rex raised an eyebrow. "You don't have a cell phone?"

"I hate phones. Never carry them."

Her cell phone rang loudly in her small shoulder bag.

Shit.

At their quizzical expressions, she forced a laugh. "Even as kids, my brother made me look bad. This is his phone I'm carrying for him. I'll just let it ring. Tell you what? I'll give you his number, that's where I'm staying." She wrote down part of Jon's phone number, then realized she was giving Rex actual information that could be traced. She quickly wrote down a made-up number.

Consumed with guilt and shame, she handed him the card. "Uh, here."

He took it like she was handing him a pile of diamonds.

Could her life get any worse?

After reading the card, Rex's brow furrowed. "You didn't write your name." He handed back the card.

Her face flaming, she wrote: *Abigail Maxim.* She'd never felt more rotten in her life. This situation was completely intolerable. Why the hell had she decided to come?

She gave him the card and attempted a confident smile. She was so conflicted, she prayed her expression didn't come off as deranged. "Rex, you have to get back to your duties here, I've kept you too long."

He laughed. "You? I haven't let go of you once. And I'm not likely to. But I do have to make the rounds. Please, you saved my life, you owe me a dance. There's a rule somewhere about that."

She giggled to cover up her exasperation. "You just made that up."

He grinned a full-wattage grin that made her toes curl. She'd never met anyone more handsome or more charming.

"Damn right I made it up. I was starting to think I'd hallucinated you. But here you are, all six feet of beauty."

Her face burned hot.

He laughed delightedly. "And she can still blush. I don't think I've ever met anyone more adorable."

Cynthia cooled her face with her hands. "Will you stop? I'm feeling like Rudolph here, my face is so red. Okay, you two go do your work, I'm going to go finish my dinner."

"You owe me a dance," Rex reminded her, his hand still on her arm.

"You should not be dancing with that leg. It's only been a month."

"I have to dance at my daughter's wedding. But you're right, I'll take it easy. I'll save myself for you and my lovely daughter."

She shook her head and laughed. "You're too much."

Their gazes caught. She couldn't breathe. Kindness, strength and confidence shone from his soul. She wanted to fall into his arms and never leave.

After a long moment, he looked down at where he held her arm and smiled. "I guess I'll have to let you go." He shot her a smoldering, heavy-lidded look that paralyzed her. "But I don't want to."

Caught in his power and warmth, she could only stare back, lost in a fog of want. If a bomb had gone off in the room, there's no way she would have heard it.

Move your ass!

Since Cynthia obviously wasn't home—she'd been transported to Dreamland— some robot answering machine in her head replied for her. "Well, then, I'll see you later."

Another robot took her by the shoulders and turned her away from him. She inwardly shouted at her legs to move.

Thankfully, her body obeyed. She concentrated on getting back to her chair without her knees giving way. The man had just redefined the word *hot* in her head. He was the pinnacle. The Hottest Man on the Planet.

She wouldn't allow herself to turn back to see if he was looking at her. She knew he was.

Not only Rex, nearly every eye in the place was on her as she made her way back to the table. Several people stopped her along the way to thank her. The savior story had made the rounds like lightning. So much for being discreet.

Calvin rose and pulled out her chair.

"Thank you," was all she could think to say.

She couldn't even look at Jon.

Now what the hell was she going to do? There was no way out. All roads led to more contact with the Hunk and her daughter. Coming to the wedding was such a dumb idea.

Maybe she'd spontaneously combust. Get abducted by aliens in the ladies room. Short of a miracle, Cynthia was doomed.

Damn it! When would her bloody luck change?

Chapter Eight

Soon after Cynthia returned to her seat, dinner was over. People left their tables and mingled up in front of the band and around the open bar.

When all of their tablemates were gone, Jon leaned over to her. "Should we just slip out?"

"No. I mean…oh, God. Yes."

Jon examined her face carefully. "You're falling for him. You already fell. I know that look. Your eyes are all goofy. Oh, speaking of goofy eyes, get this: while you were off with Rex, the waiter slipped me his number. He knows the show and loves it, but never had the courage to approach me. Well, I got his number and oh, my God, am I in for some fun after the show." He waggled his eyebrows at her. "Maybe we'll both get laid tonight."

She nearly jumped out of her skin. "I am not sleeping with my daughter's father!" she announced to everyone in hearing distance.

Several people turned around to stare at her.

Cynthia finally heard what she said and burst out laughing. "Sorry folks, too much champagne," she said, holding up her glass.

She received polite nods and some fake tittering, only because she was The Savior. In any other circumstances, these people would have called the Society Police on her.

When the guests turned away again, she groaned and downed a huge gulp of bubbly. "Oh, my God, I've lost my mind. This was a stupid idea."

Above them came a deep voice. "May I have this dance?"

She looked up into the super-charged blue gaze of Rex Du Charmante.

"I'd love to," every atom of her body answered.

In a dream, she rose and took his proffered hand.

Only ten percent of her brain registered Jon's remark as she walked away. "Told you so."

Rex smiled down at her, the picture of courtly manners. She felt like she had transported into a fantasy realm where all her dreams had come true.

He was in his grey tux and she desperately wanted to be in that peach silk number.

They reached the dance floor and his arms were around her. With a deep sigh, she lost herself in his gaze. Soon, the music faded, the people faded and it was only the two of them.

At first he said nothing, just looked down at her as if she were the most precious treasure in the universe, turning her insides into fire-hot goo.

"My God, you're beautiful," he finally said.

She responded without thinking. "If you were the last man on earth, I'd kill every other woman just to have this dance with you."

His eyes dilated and he took in a breath. "Oh, lordy."

So much for the cooling-off period.

Neither spoke for a few moments.

His eyes cleared a bit. "When can I see you again? Tell me soon."

"Soon."

He grinned. "No, really. I have to see you. Away from here."

"I'm not very busy right now."

"Tomorrow. Let me take you out tomorrow."

"You bet."

What the hell are you thinking, woman?

She smiled nervously. "Wait. I'm sorry. You've got me all flustered here."

His grin grew predatory. "I intend to get you much more flustered."

A Lust Attack annihilated her. She could only think about ripping off his clothes and throwing him to the floor. She took in a deep breath and closed her eyes for a moment. "Oh, man. Okay, give me a second here." She fought for sanity.

Lie, damn you, lie!

Breathing out fast, she opened her eyes and sharpened her focus. "Look, I have to work. Well, it's not really work, I, uh, not tomorrow. Let me call you."

His dark gaze didn't waver. "No way. You got away from me once. I'll call you tomorrow morning and you give me a time."

This guy was too much! "You're moving fast."

His smile faded, all she saw was the hunter going in for the kill. "When I want something, I see no reason to wait."

Her sex throbbed and her knees nearly gave way.

Wait a minute. He couldn't like her this much this fast. The man was richer than Trump and had the pick of all the best of San Francisco's single women. Why her? "Is this some savior thing? Are you sure you're not confusing gratitude with interest?"

His head jerked away slightly. "No. Well, yes, partly. Damn, woman, you saved my blasted life. And no, it was before. When we were running."

That was true. She hadn't known he was rich back then. That exchange had been real. "Yes. I did notice you."

The corners of his mouth twitched. "I noticed you noticing me." His attention dropped briefly to her mouth.

Oh, God, don't kiss me! I couldn't take it!

She smiled. "At least I didn't run out in front of a moving vehicle. I suppose I should be flattered."

He gave a sharp nod of his head. "You should. Never gone to the hospital for a woman before."

She laughed.

He tilted his head and a dreamy expression played across his handsome face. "You've got a lovely laugh."

"You're the most gorgeous man I've ever seen in my life. Oh, damn it. That should have stayed in my head."

His grin stretched wide and his blue eyes sparkled. "No, I'm loving hearing it."

She took a deep breath, then laughed at herself. Hopeless. The man rendered her hopeless.

He pulled away and twirled her. She giggled like a schoolgirl.

After gazing at the length of her, he pulled her in tight. She inhaled his cologne and reveled in his taut body next to hers. A wave of heat rushed through her, centering on her sex. Had she died? Was this Heaven?

He leaned in a bit. "How long have you been running?"

His lips kept distracting her. He had the most kissable mouth. "Uh, forever. Since I was a kid. I found it clears my head."

"Me, too. So you come from the Maxim clan, but you were a nurse in the ER?"

Startled, she averted her gaze and nearly tripped over her feet. Alarms went off in her head. How did he know that?

His smile faded and his gaze intensified. "You told the fireman you were a nurse in the ER for a million years."

Ulk. This was exactly where she didn't want to be. Why did this guy have to be Kelly's father?

She coughed. "I was. My life has been, uh, rather complicated. Fell out of disfavor with the family and I wanted to, uh, well, I was good at it. Long story. I'll tell you on our date."

Sudden sadness tore at her. She had no intention of dating the man. She was rotten for lying. But she simply couldn't stop herself from dancing with him. It was like she had no will. The man obliterated her self-control.

He examined her closely, seeming to almost peer into her brain. "Are you all right?"

This guy was no fool. He knew something was up.

She squashed her doubts and concentrated on the moment. It was the only one she'd have with him. She wanted to relish it. She allowed joy to surge through her again. "I haven't been this fine in a long time."

Sunshine lit in his eyes. A much younger man appeared before her. She fell harder.

This was bad.

The song ended about a minute before they realized it. Rex finally looked at the band in surprise, then back at her and laughed. Then his attention went to the room. His smile disappeared, his eyebrows shot up and his face reddened. When Cynthia checked to see what he was looking at, she froze. The entire crowd in the ballroom was staring at them.

They looked at each other and burst out laughing.

"This is gonna be in the society pages, Rex."

"Don't I know it."

But he didn't look upset about it. *Shit.* Could she be more screwed?

A boy of about twelve rushed up to them. "Uncle Rex! She's about to throw her bouquet!" He pointed towards a corner of the ballroom and jumped up and down.

Rex looked off and nodded, then turned to her. "Don't go anywhere," he stated simply. Then he rushed off after the boy.

Off in the distance, Kelly stood on a balcony overlooking the ballroom, holding a bouquet high in her hand.

Oh, my God, she'd almost forgotten about her daughter! What was wrong with her? The whole reason she came was to see her, and here she'd spent all her time drooling over the father.

Jon appeared at her side. "Are you quite through making love on the dance floor? My God, you guys were like a laser light-show, beaming your proclamations of love all over the walls and ceiling. I thought you two were gonna do it right in front of everybody."

She sputtered then finally got out, "You are exaggerating."

Her ex snorted. "I couldn't exaggerate. Everyone was staring. It was like you sent up this flare, this arc light for a Hollywood preview. *Our New Love* by Cynthia—I mean, Abigail—"

"Will you stop? I am fully aware of how screwed I am."

Jon grinned. "Looks like you're gonna get plenty screwed."

"I am not sleeping with him!"

He burst out laughing. "I love you when you're deluded." He hugged her, then pulled away to grin at her. "God, a train is coming right at you and you're all, 'no, there's no train I can see'. So freakin' blind."

She pushed him away. "Denial is the word."

"Oh, yeah and plenty of that." He looked off after Rex, then back at her. "That's some heavy-duty chemistry."

She rubbed her temples. "Too much chemistry. It's annihilating my brain cells and affecting my judgment."

In the distance, Kelly threw the bouquet. A huge cheer went up.

Jon's cute waiter approached them with a tray of glasses filled with champagne. A tall young man with a flawless olive complexion, his dark eyes were alive with mischief and fun. And he had a square jaw to die for.

Jon's eyes went lazy-lidded with lust. "Isn't this a nice picture? I want the whole thing, the champagne and the boy."

The waiter tossed his head and pursed his lips. "Big flirt. I should have played hard-to-get."

Cynthia cracked up.

Jon made a face at her, then swung his hungry gaze back to the waiter. "Oh, Colin? I'd like you to meet my sister, Cynthia. I mean, Abigail. I mean, oh, God, I'll tell you later."

Colin sent them an incredulous stare. Then blinked. "You don't know her name?"

Jon nodded, not the least put off by his faux pas. "Mom used to call her 'the Brat'. I didn't find out her real name until high school."

Cynthia backhanded him across the shoulder. "And what she called you was unprintable. So we called him Censored for years."

Colin chuckled. They both served themselves glasses off the boy's tray.

"Well, Censored and The Brat, I'll see you both later." With a wink, Colin left to go serve the other guests.

Jon took in the length of him as he walked away. "Nice assets."

She rolled her eyes. "You're incorrigible."

"I'm very corrigible. Mega-corrigible. Man, I hope he corriges me. What does corrige mean, anyway?"

"There is no corrige. I don't know." She spotted Rex talking to a group of men near the stage. He kept glancing over at her. "Can we go soon? I can't take much more of this."

Jon nudged her with an elbow. "So did you give him your number?"

"No. Well, yeah, a fake number."

Jon gasped and his eyes went wide with shock. "You're so mean!"

Ugly, but true. "No, I'm not. I'm a chicken-shit. That's why there's a chicken-shit way out of things, because it's a valid choice."

He shook his head and put down his glass, apparently so he could gesture more dramatically. "I can't believe you're just gonna walk away from all this."

"Believe it."

Jon's expression softened, he reached out and took hold of her arm. "Why don't you just tell him the truth, honey? Right up front. That will either get rid of him or keep him. Hell of a test, but with guys, it's better to be straightforward. If his lust survives the news about you being Kelly's mother, well, then it was meant to be."

She pulled out of his grip. "No way. I can't do that. God, I can't imagine his reaction."

Jon took hold of her arm once more. "Well, how do you think he'll feel when you ditch him with no explanation? He may look like an Alpha Male, but he's still a vulnerable person. Be straight with him. It's the kindest thing to do and the only way I can see out of this hormonal mess you're in."

She yanked her arm away. "I can't. I can't ruin that girl's life."

Jon reached for her, but she stepped back. He exhaled in frustration. "How would you ruin her life?"

"I wouldn't, but I've got a huge target on my chest and the Gruesome Twosome would do anything to hurt me. Therefore, they'd do anything to hurt Kelly."

"Rex is rich, he'll protect her."

"He can't. No one knows how evil they are."

He put his hands on his hips. "Money protects everyone."

"I'm not arguing with you, I'm getting out of here. Besides, dude, look at the time," she said, showing him her silver watch. "Do you want to make your show or not?"

Jon's eyes popped open. "Is it that late? Damn, I can't believe I had an okay time here. This is so weird."

"I got one word for you—actually two: cute waiter."

A huge grin dwarfed his face. "Aaah, yes. Colin. Okay, you go say good-bye to Rex, I'll go make some quick plans with Mr. Cupcake and then we'll go."

"No, you go, I'll stay, then we're slipping out unnoticed." She scanned the room for Rex, but didn't see him anywhere. "I cannot take any good-byes with that man. My heart is breaking." She nodded off towards the kitchen.

A deep voice came from right next to her. "Don't tell me you're leaving? Didn't I tell you to stay put?"

Rex, with a teasing grin, right there.

She gasped and held her chest. "You'd think a guy as big as you would make more noise when approaching someone."

Rex smiled, his blue eyes shining, warming her entire being. "Should I carry my trumpet everywhere I go then?"

She chuckled. "Might help. Rex Du Charmante, I'd like you to meet my brother, uh…" Blank. Total utter blank.

Mayday! Mayday!

Jon saved her by sticking out his hand. "Tony. Tony Maxim, pleased to meet you."

Rex shot a quick glance between the two, then took Jon's hand. "Sister doesn't know your name?"

"I think you've knocked all the sense out of her." Jon winked.

Rex laughed. "Well, she's certainly had the same effect on me. And if you don't mind, I'm just going to borrow her for a bit here."

Without waiting for a reply, he took her by the arm and guided her away.

Fight him! Fight this! Run!

She worked hard to clear her head. To little effect. All she could do was float along with him.

He led her out the ballroom doors, down a hall and into a little alcove.

Rex took her hands in his and beamed down at her. "Tell me you're not going away to Milan or anywhere else anytime soon."

Paralyzed by his intense gaze, she probably sent him some goofy grin. She really had no control over herself. A first. "Had no plans."

Lie! Tell him you're off to Antarctica for the next twenty-five years on an expedition!

His smile widened, as if that was possible. A massive amount of energy bubbled within him. His crow's feet, brown and silver hair and the deep creases in his rugged cheekbones were a luscious contrast to the teenage energy and excitement he exuded. Best of both worlds. Youth inside, yummy adult exterior. And it was clear he really liked her. So cool!

No, it's not. It's the biggest tragedy you've ever faced.

He tilted his head playfully and dropped his gaze to her lips.

Oh, shit, no! You'll be doomed if you kiss him!

As he leaned in, she blurted, "So what kind of music do you like?"

He stopped, a bit startled, then smiled. "Uh, well…"

God, how childish! How virginal! Wrong in so many ways, but at least it stopped him. She had to get out of there!

"Ranges. Symphony, the classics to Radiohead to seventies metal." His attention went to her mouth.

"Uh…wow. Me, too."

Rex leaned in again.

Quick! What will make him stop kissing you! Think of a subject!

"God, I love your daughter, Kelly. She's amazing."

He stopped abruptly, blinked a few times, and sent her a questioning look.

Cynthia pretended not to notice that he'd noticed. "I just love her. You've done such a good job raising her," she said in her most bubbly tone.

His shoulders relaxed, he smiled, and lit up like a sun going nova. "She's the best thing in my life." He looked away briefly. "She's…I'm going to miss her so much. She stayed with me, uh, well, you know my wife passed away—"

"I'm so sorry for your loss."

A haunted look passed behind his eyes. "Yes, it's been difficult. But Kelly made all the difference in the world," he said, brightening again. "Couldn't love her anymore even if she was my own. Well, she is mine. I raised her. But she's adopted."

"How wonderful the two of you found each other. Just because a child is born to another family doesn't mean they belong there. Kelly clearly belonged with you." She realized the truth of her words as they left her mouth. A harsh truth, but one that felt right to say in the moment.

His grin widened. "Love the way you put that. I feel like she belonged with us. Not that I know anything about her birth parents." A quick flash of anger burned in his gaze. "Don't really want to know. But it's important to Kel. It's why she became an adoption rights lawyer."

The news hit her like a fire hose turned full on. Her daughter wanted to find her so badly, she'd dedicated her life to the cause. *Shit.* Intense pain seared her gut. She'd feared the kid would be hurt by the adoption, but figured with a good set of parents the child would forget all about her. Apparently not.

Rex leaned in, concerned. "You all right? You went pale."

Coughing, Cynthia groped for a lie. "I'm fine. I lost my daughter, too. I mean, you didn't lose one, I lost one. A long time ago. She'd be about Kelly's age now."

His features softened, he reached out and ran a hand down her arm. "That's a tremendous loss."

His touch went beyond her skin, to her heart. It had been so long since someone comforted her like this. Her pain subsided, replaced by love for this wonderful man. Which quickly turned back to pain. This was all so confusing!

She sighed and looked away. "By the time you get to our age, you acquire some battle scars. Makes us who we are."

His touch turned lighter, igniting her skin. Her feet tingled and her heart fluttered.

"Said that right. Dinner tomorrow? A show? There's a great play at the Curran."

Oh, Christ! How can I resist this guy? But she had to.

Staring at his shoulder, she tried to stay calm. "That sounds wonderful. But I have to beg off for the next three days, my nephew is coming home and I haven't seen him in three years and we made all these plans."

He seemed to buy her lie. Of course, why wouldn't he?

"Certainly. I'll call you and we'll make arrangements." He smiled warmly. "I'm so glad I found you."

"I'm glad you found me, too," she responded automatically.

Damn it! Shut up! Stop leading him on!

He pulled her close, looked at her mouth and before she could stop him, he kissed her.

Her brain exploded like a hydrogen bomb. All thoughts blew up in a giant mushroom cloud. The only thing grounding her was his supple, yet firm lips.

He gently took her face in both hands. His cologne and intoxicating and unique male scent filled her senses. Her knees went rubbery.

His kiss deepened. It was like she'd grabbed the third rail on the subway. Thunderbolts, fireworks, cymbal crashes. White-hot magma erupted from inside her.

His expert tongue manipulated her own. Playing, teasing, then conquering.

She groaned deep her in throat and kissed him back, hard. He slipped a hand behind her neck and drew her closer. His other hand traveled down her back to cup her ass. He squeezed and drew in a sharp breath.

She instinctively pressed herself against him, loving the feel of his hard body against hers. The floor tilted. She gripped him harder.

From far away, she heard a cell phone ringing.

He took her rear in both hands, seemingly worshipping it with his talented caresses.

Her clit ached and her sex was so wet, all she wanted was for him to be inside her.

Nearer now, a cell phone announced there was a caller.

She ran her hands through his soft hair and he drove his tongue deeper into her. Sliding his hand up her side, he cupped a breast. His touch was so sweet, so caring. This guy wasn't a masher, he was a gentleman. They were both clearly on the verge of tearing each other's clothes off, but he still had enough self-control to hold himself back and concentrate on giving her pleasure.

Rex was a diamond.

Cell phone ringing.

They pulled away. His gaze was dark with lust. "Wow, lady. I need one more of those before I can let you go."

"Oh, God," she moaned as she opened her lips to him.

Commandeering her mouth, he caressed her back and she melted into him. He took her rear in both hands and squeezed, sending a super-charged lightning strike to her clit. Her head swam. *Why were they still clothed?*

"The dress!" came a scream from right near her ear.

She and Rex jumped and pulled apart, blinking in confusion.

Jon. Frantic. Waving his arms, he shouted again. "Midnight, Cynth—sister! The dress! The dress! It's bloody midnight! Sorry to ruin your little moment, Rex, but my sister and I are LATE!" Grabbing her by the wrist, he pulled her out of Rex's embrace and dragged her down the hallway. "Run! Run! The cab is waiting! Run!"

Coming to her senses, she yanked out of Jon's grip, ran back to a stunned Rex and kissed him quickly on the mouth.

She pulled away and looked deep into his eyes. "Thank you so much, this was the best night of my life."

Jon latched onto her wrist with an iron grip and pulled her away.

As she was being yanked down the hallway, she called out, "Thanks for raising such a wonderful daughter! You did a great job!"

"Run!" Jon screamed.

She turned and ran. As she neared the lobby, she glanced back over her shoulder. Rex was at the far end of the hallway, limping after her.

"Wait!" he cried.

Struck by his need, Cynthia slowed. But Jon had an inexorable hold on her wrist and wasn't about to slow down.

He yanked harder. "I go on in fifteen bloody minutes! I looked everywhere for you! Didn't you hear your cell ringing?"

"No." She reluctantly turned to lope alongside him.

As they flew through the lobby, Jon finally released his grip on her.

Everyone, guests and hotel staff alike, turned to stare at the "rich people" running through the lobby, but no one stopped them. They burst out the doors and ran down the steps. The cab was waiting at the curb with the backdoor open. The cab driver—a fifty-something swarthy Sikh guy in a turban—stood beside it.

"Cabbie, get in the car!" Jon screamed loud enough for the entire neighborhood to hear. "I'll pay you an extra fifty if you get us there in ten minutes!"

The cab driver raced around and jumped in the car.

Jon tore off ahead of her, Cynthia on his heels.

From far behind her, she heard Rex call out. "Abigail! Wait! Abigail!"

"Sorry, buddy," she said under her breath.

A step later, she tripped, lost a shoe, and headed down.

Save the dress! It cost ten thousand dollars!

With some fancy footwork she caught herself at the last second, narrowly avoiding doing a face plant into the sidewalk. She skidded to a halt and turned around to retrieve the shoe. The pavement froze her shoeless foot.

"No!" Jon screamed.

"I have to get the shoe!"

She was within five feet of the shoe when Jon latched his strong arms around her middle, picked her up and ran for the car, jostling her.

"The shoe! Don't you need it?!" she cried.

They reached the cab.

"No, I got three more pairs back at the show!" He tossed her in the back of the car like a large sack of cat food and leapt in beside her.

"Drive!" he shouted in her ear.

The driver stepped on it and the two were slammed back against the seat.

She looked through the back window. Rex stood at the curb with her shoe in his hand. He held it up and waved it in the air. After a few seconds, his shoulders drooped and his arm dropped to his side. He threw up his hands.

What a horrible, pathetic picture. Cynthia turned around and burst into tears.

"We don't have time for emotion!" Jon yelled. "Cry later—get that goddamned dress off now!"

Cynthia fumbled behind herself. "I can't reach the zipper!"

"Turn around!"

Jon wrestled with the zipper and finally got it undone. The damn thing fit so tightly, she had to squirm to get her shoulders out. Pushing it down, she slammed against the car door as the driver took a corner.

"Ow!"

"Keep going!" Jon urged.

She frowned at him. "Oh, yeah, Mr. Hurry Up, there's no bloody room here. Let's see how you do, getting your stupid pants off."

Jon sent her an evil grin, grabbed the crotch of his tux pants, lifted his ass off the seat and pulled. In one swift movement, they were in his hand.

Slack-jawed, she gasped. "Tear-away pants!" She slapped at him. He held up his hands for protection. "You wore tear-away pants to our daughter's high-class wedding? I told you not to borrow a tux from one of your Chippendale friends!"

Jon laughed, pushing her hands away. "Well, you didn't know, did you? No one did. Besides, I knew I'd have to do a quick change in the back of a cab with another giant person, so I decided to take your suggestion."

She tried not to, but she laughed. "It wasn't a suggestion, I told you not to."

"Too late. Cabbie, the light is green, hello?"

Cynthia checked the rear view mirror. The driver's eyeballs were popped out like ping-pong balls. "Do you mind?"

Startled, the driver turned his attention back to the road.

Cynthia carefully lifted up her butt and pushed the dress off. Sitting back down, she pulled up her knees so far she was eating them. She pushed the dress the rest of the way off and gave it to Jon. He handed her the tear-away pants in a large heap.

She took the tangle of long strips of black cloth and pulled them every which way but couldn't figure them out. And the pieces kept sticking to each other. "What am I supposed to do with this cloth puzzle? How the hell do you put 'em back together?"

"Velcro, Velcro!" Jon hissed, wrestling the dress over his head.

"Oh, that's helpful. Velcro! Velcro!" she mocked. She held the pants up, they went around another corner and she slammed against the door again. "Damn it!"

"Sorry, lady," the driver said.

Jon twisted his large body, jamming himself inside the dress. Grunting, he pulled on it, squirming and wiggling on the seat. His elbow came flying at her, she ducked and he grazed her ear.

"Watch it!"

"I'm trying!"

Cynthia frantically pulled at the cloth strips, flipping them, ripping them apart, turning them, folding and unfolding, but couldn't straighten them out.

"Zip me, zip me!" Jon ordered.

Setting aside the heap of cloth, she grabbed the zipper and wrestled it up. "Damn, Jon, you need to stop working out, you almost don't fit in this thing."

"I know." He turned back to her and seemed alarmed. "For God's sake, at least put on the shirt. No wonder the cabbie's staring, you're just sitting there in your underwear."

"I can't put the damn pants together!"

"Here, give them to me." He yanked them out of her grip. "Driver, the light is green!"

The cabbie cleared his throat. "Sorry, sir."

She put on the white tux shirt, buttoned it and Jon handed her the pants. She pushed her feet through, caught her toe on the leg and ripped them apart.

Jon made an exasperated noise. "You are hopeless!"

"Shut up and help me!"

The car stopped.

Jon looked outside the window. "Oh, God, we're here. Sorry, babe, you're on your own." He leapt out of the cab. "Pay him, will you?" Before she could yell at him, he'd vanished inside the club.

As she wrestled with the pants, she fought back the tears. What a horrible night!

The turbaned driver looked at her in his rear view mirror. "He promised me an extra fifty dollars if I got him here on time."

"Oh, shut up, you'll get your money."

"No reason to cry, lady. I know you are shamed to have shown your body to me, but it's very beautiful, I did not mind."

Cynthia's blood turned to molten steel, so mad she couldn't speak. All she could do was growl.

Wide-eyed and ashen, the cabbie turned around and put both hands on the steering wheel.

Thankfully, anger forced the tears away. With as much dignity as she could muster, she Velcroed the pants back together. After putting them on, she grabbed her purse, fished out her emergency hundred-dollar-bill (her last) and threw it at the driver. Jon's shoes in one hand, her purse in another, she stepped out of the cab and slammed the door behind her.

As the cab drove away, she realized she was supposed to stay inside. She'd been so eager to get away from the driver, she'd jumped out without thinking. She had no way home and no money. Jon was on stage by now, his wallet safe in his locker. She could ask one of the performers backstage for cab fare, but no way did she want to face them when she was on the verge of an emotional breakdown.

She dug through her little purse. She found three dollars and eighty cents in change and a fuzzy stick of gum with no wrapper. Pathetic, but enough for bus fare. Cynthia slipped on Jon's shoes and headed off towards the nearest bus stop, a half a block away.

The foggy drizzle soaked her coat. Jon had forgotten to give her his socks. Her right heel hurt like the dickens with every step, blistered for sure.

This night would go down as the best and worst of her life. She wished she hadn't had that dance with Rex. Hadn't felt his steely arms around her. Hadn't lost herself in his magnificent kisses.

This trek home said it all about her miserable life. Alone, waiting for a bus in a wet, tear-away tux. She tried to think of a time where she'd felt lower. Malcolm's funeral, Dad's funeral and Mom's.

But her other tragedies had not been of her own making. This Rex Thing, she'd done this to herself. This was pure Cynthia Idiocy.

Her body wracking with sobs, she didn't care what the passersby thought of her.

All she could see was that last look on Rex's face.

Chapter Nine

Rex pounded his desk with his fist so hard his pen cup fell to the floor, spilling the contents everywhere. "I don't understand it. Abigail liked me! Why did she give me a goddamned made-up number? She was not lying. I know people. Something went wrong."

Jess walked into the office in the middle of his rant, but Rex was too wound up to stop.

He got up and paced. "This makes no sense. She said it was the best night of her life and I believed her. I know she meant what she said. Am I stupid? Desperate? I know people, but for the life of me, I cannot figure out this woman."

"Rex, you're going to rupture that wound in your leg."

He threw up his hands and continued pacing. "How can I relax? You weren't there!"

Jess watched him, the picture of calm. Her eyes large behind her thick glasses, she pursed her wrinkled orange lips. "Of course I was there. We were all there and there was no missing the two of you. Did Leah Garfield talk about anything else in her society column? I'm not sure she even mentioned Kelly's name. With publicity like that, she'll turn up."

"But why would she give me a crazy number?"

His miniature secretary shrugged. "You had her flustered. People change their cell numbers all the time. She could have given you her old one. Are you sure she has your number?"

His throat closed up. His world went dark. "Didn't even think of that. Maybe she thinks she gave me the right number. Shit, she could think I'm not interested."

Jess snorted and rolled her eyes. "I don't know how anyone could think that after your little display at that wedding. Don't worry, Rex. Besides, you've got more pressing problems. James Miller has disappeared."

Reeling, Rex spun on her. "He *what*? Why didn't you tell me? We have an investors meeting tomorrow."

"I tried to tell you, but you've been ranting non-stop since I walked in here. Look, I've been trying to reach James all morning to confirm the meeting. One of his flunkies finally squealed. Well, with some persuasion. James left for Europe this morning."

Rex pounded his desk with his fist. "What the hell? He just got back from Europe! We planned to meet before the big meeting."

"That's not the worst of it. You're the only one he's paid in two months. He hasn't sent a dime to any of the other investors and they're not happy."

His pulse whooshed in his ears. "When did all this surface?"

"Just now. Put the screws to one of James' minions, he spilled way more than he meant to. I think you'd better track James down." She pointed at his phone.

"I will. Goddamn, what's wrong with him? Even if he had a shortfall, you'd think he'd come to me to cover it. He knows I went out on a limb. They'd never invested with him before. They took the deal on my word. If this crashes..." His gut tight, he rubbed his forehead. "I can't think that way."

"There's probably a valid explanation. Call him to find out what it is." She indicated the phone again.

Damn it, Abigail disappears again and now this? Darkness claimed his mind. "Just when I thought everything was going to work out…"

Jess waved her small hand in the air. "It will. Don't get maudlin."

"You're right," he said, taking a deep breath. "I don't know what's wrong with me."

"Uh, your dream woman disappeared, James is acting suspiciously and Kelly moved out. I'd say that's enough to dampen anyone's mood."

"True." He smiled and relaxed a bit. "You always know what to say to make me feel better. I mean, I don't—"

"I get you," Jess said, noticing the spilled pens by his desk. She walked over and began picking them up. "Trust me, everything always works out for you, Rex. You get a hold of James and find that mystery woman and I'll bet in another few weeks, all your troubles will be over." She placed the pen cup back on his desk.

Hope replaced his gloom. He grinned at his faithful secretary. "You're a doll."

"That's what all the boys say. Call James."

Rex walked around his desk and sat down. He hit speed dial for James' private cell number. "Stay here and stay quiet. I want your take on him."

Jess took the seat in front of his desk.

After two rings, James answered. "Rex? What can I do for you?"

Rex pressed the button for the speakerphone. "Why the hell are you in Europe? Don't we have a meeting tomorrow?"

"Rex, never one to chitchat," came James' voice out of the speaker. "No worries, old friend. I'm on a plane in three hours. I'll make the meeting. What's wrong? You sound upset. Never missed a meeting yet."

"Why haven't you paid the other investors?"

"Oh, that. Stupid bank. Clerk made a transposition error, screwed up the whole account and they put a freeze on it. Bank assures me the issue will be solved by this afternoon. I'm bringing certified checks to the meeting, along with a bit of extra interest to smooth things over."

He reminded Rex of a politician making campaign promises. His gut tightened. Something didn't ring true, but nothing he could call James on.

"Well, good. But you should have let me know the payments would be late. I could have advanced whatever you needed. I don't like worrying those guys. I brought them in the deal on my word. This was all on my reputation and yours. They're nervous and these are not guys you want to make nervous. Not if you want money from them in the future."

"I'll convince them tomorrow, don't you worry about a thing," James said in a glib tone. "And in two weeks, this will all be behind us and we'll all be rollin' in the dough. When they see their return, they'll be happy. This is a big one, Rex. More than I expected."

Rex leaned back in his chair. "Good. So tomorrow around eleven? Meeting's on for two. I thought we'd have lunch first."

"Perfect. I'll be at your office on the dot. Have you heard from the kids?"

"No, and I don't expect to. There's no cell reception where they are in Bora Bora and only one landline. Kelly picked it out specifically so your son had to pay attention to her and not his Blackberry."

James deep resonant laughter filled the speaker. "I'll bet. Good girl. She's a thinker. She'll keep my boy in line. Good for her."

"See you tomorrow."

"You bet."

Rex pressed the button to hang up and looked at the phone. "Why am I not reassured? He said all the right things, is doing all the right things, why am I still bothered?"

Jess narrowed her eyes. "I don't know. I'm not reassured, either. Too rehearsed. Nervous, too, if I'm not mistaken. Overlaying that, a deep weariness."

He nodded slowly and rubbed the back of his neck. "James has seemed off recently. Tired. He looked older at the wedding. Bags under his eyes. I've known the man for twenty-five years and haven't ever seen him this down. Maybe some health issues."

"Could be jet lag. He'd just returned from Europe two days before the wedding." Jess picked off a green thread from her tight, outdated wool suit. "But my intuition says something is up. And from the buzz at his office, something's going on. But you'll find out."

"Yes, I will. Can't worry about it now. But this is the last time I'm bringing anyone else into James' deals."

"Do you think he took advantage of you because of the wedding?" Jess asked with a twist of her orange lips.

His jaw twitched. "Crossed my mind."

Jess got up, staying the same height. "Well, don't worry. See what happens after tomorrow's meeting. You'll be able to tell what's going on."

"Right."

Two of the other investors were close friends of his and neither had mentioned the missed payment. Was their confidence in him shaken?

He had to stop worrying. Nothing he could do about it now, anyway.

Jess smiled at him and straightened a stack of papers on his desk. "And now that you got that out of the way, you can resume your search for the missing Amazon."

"Yes, Abigail." His mood soured once more. "I Googled her after I couldn't reach her and the only Abigail Maxim I found, died as a toddler. And Anthony Maxim is a hundred years old in a retirement home in Italy. Weird, huh?"

The line between Jess's large dark eyes deepened. "And exactly why did a Maxim ever become a nurse? Not a normal occupation for someone wealthy."

Rex stroked his chin. "Puzzling and troubling. She ran from the police that day, too, at my accident," he said more to himself.

"Talk about some red flags. Maybe it's better you let this one go. She sounds like a whole load of trouble to me."

"But she saved my life and, oh, God, I have to find her, Jess," he said, surprised by the emotion in his voice.

She examined his face carefully, then sighed and smiled. "Well, then, let me do what I can to help."

His heart warmed at her sympathetic grin. Something was clearly wrong with Abigail, but it couldn't be anything serious. His instincts kept telling him that she was the one. That everything would be all right. All he had to do was find her.

He walked over to a bookcase and picked up Abigail's silver shoe. "Only thing I have of Abby's is this." He held it up for Jess to see.

"Oh, it's Abby now, is it?"

He grinned and his face heated. "If the city wasn't so big, I'd pull a Prince Charming and wander around looking for the woman who fit this shoe."

"Did you find out where they were bought?"

"No, how would I do that?"

"Well, look at that thing," she said gesturing towards the shoe. "That is not a shoe you can find just anywhere. Here, hand it to me."

Rex crossed the room and gave her the shoe.

Jess examined it closely, turning it over and checking inside. "Hmmm, I thought this was big. This is a damn size fourteen, Rex. She really is an Amazon. Where the hell would you find a size fourteen woman's shoe that's covered in silver sparkles—well, of course, the Haight. I mean, this is large enough for a man to wear."

His skin prickled. "The Haight?" *Please don't make me go there.*

Jess nodded and set the shoe on his desk. "Yes, several costume shops there sell unusual women's shoes in large sizes. They sell them to the drag queens."

Rex gave a short laugh. "How do you know that?"

She sent him a smug grin and gave her head a little toss. "There are lots of things you don't know about me, Rex."

"Guess so."

"My next-door neighbors started the Trannyshack shows. You spend anytime around drag queens, you find out every minute detail about their lives. Where they buy their clothes, everything." She raised her painted-on eyebrows. "More than you'd want to know, believe me."

He shot her a quick grin. "I'll have to take your word for that. The Haight, you say?"

"So we've got your day all planned."

"Thanks, Jess. I don't know what I'd do without you."

"Oh, you'd muddle through somehow." She winked at him and left the office, closing the door behind her.

Haight Street, huh? In his mind it was Hate Street, because he *hated* it there. Blast it. But for Abigail, he'd suffer through almost anything. Walking on broken glass, getting a root canal without anesthesia, going to The Haight. All about on the same par.

But what if Abigail was trying to lose him? What if she didn't like him as much as he liked her? What if she'd just given him the big shove off?

He couldn't believe it, not after that kiss.

However, it would fit with his current pattern. Ever since Elizabeth died—and for some time before—things had not gone well. Work deals that had been a breeze just five years before had become much more labor-intensive. Businesses he picked to develop weren't getting the returns they should. While he still made a lot of money, it wasn't the avalanche of cash he'd come to expect.

Probably because his interest in the game was on the wane. Now he did the job more because others depended on him rather than because he enjoyed it.

At first he believed his lack of interest was due to Elizabeth's battle with cancer. But after she died, he had a devil of a time getting back to work. He kept thinking it was the grieving process, but lately, he'd realized the problem went deeper.

Basically, he was sick of the grind. Sick of being tethered to his Blackberry and computer. And since his passion for the job was lessening, his deals were suffering.

Which was why he'd started to do more outside investing with his income. James had been really helping with that. Soon his investments should pay enough for him to retire.

At this point, he wanted to travel, indulge in his passion for history and work on his paintings.

And find a good woman.

He decided to send a quick prayer to God, someone he'd been ignoring of late. Ever since his prayers hadn't saved Elizabeth, he'd lost interest in The Big Guy.

But now? Certainly worth a try.

Please God, I want her.

And I need her.

Please let me find her and let her love me the way I love her.

Amen.

Chapter Ten

An hour later, Rex drove his Bentley along the Bohemian cesspool of Haight Street, looking for a parking place, wishing he were driving a cheaper car. Transients strolled the block with hippies in their twenties and sixties, along with a few business people on their lunch hour.

He'd only journeyed to Haight/Ashbury once and it had been enough. He shuddered at the memory. A friend had a gallery opening there. Within ten minutes of arriving, a woman in a shiny snake costume tried to get into his pants with his wife standing right beside him. (*"Sssssnakey Girl wants a sssssnake."*)

When they left, a homeless man grabbed Elizabeth's purse and Rex had to chase him two blocks. When he returned with the purse, Elizabeth was pale and shaking, standing in a cloud of pot smoke, flanked by two street artists who were trying to get her stoned and sell her a nude painting of Bill Clinton. While it had given them a great story to tell at cocktail parties, neither ever returned.

And he wouldn't have either, if it weren't for Abigail. He'd just arrived on the block and he already wanted to take a shower.

After parking, he checked his car three times to make sure it was locked. Taking a deep breath, he steeled himself, put on his "hard" face to ward off the beggars and headed for the first of the two places Jess had told him about.

Unfortunately, he'd forgotten to dress down. Two toothless homeless men eyed his suit like it was made of gold. He tightened his jaw and his fists and avoided eye contact.

He found the first place easily. Nice little boutique with some costumes and vintage clothing. But no big shoes. Disheartened, he continued on. Probably all a waste of time.

Ahead of him above a store, two fake women's legs clothed in fishnets and stilettos protruded out through a second story window. Speakers nearby sounded with female laughter and moaning: simulated sex sounds.

Please, God, not this place.

Of course, it was.

As if the legs weren't enough of a deterrent, semi-nude mannequins wearing chain-mail bathing suits engaged in questionable activity in the window display.

Saying a silent prayer that no one he knew would notice him, he opened the door and slipped inside the shop.

Thankfully, the interior looked more like a costume shop. But as he examined the wares, his spine stiffened and his palms began to sweat. The type of costumes were at the far range of acceptable. Mainly fetish gear for a wide range of sexual activities. From rubber suits to leather corsets to mini-skirts that wouldn't cover any normal-sized female rear end. The piece de resistance? A crotchless gorilla costume. His lunch threatened to return. He prided himself on being open-minded, but places like this made him realize his limitations.

He desperately wished he could transport himself back to the safety of his car.

He approached what appeared to be the saleswoman, a young woman with bright blue hair and no less than thirty piercings in her face. Covered in tattoos, she wore a red and black corset, a black ruffled mini-skirt, fishnets and thigh-high black boots. She stood beside the counter, setting up a display of penis-shaped lighters.

He wanted to run.

But when she turned around and sent him a brilliant, sweet smile, he relaxed. *Don't judge a book by its cover.*

"Can I help you?" she asked.

He held up Abby's silver shoe. "Yes, I was wondering about this shoe," he said, his voice cracking. He cleared his throat and stood taller. "Do you people sell this kind of thing?"

Her grin spread wide. "Oh, yeah and much more. Let me see," she said, reaching for the shoe. "Yeah, we do, I'm not sure about this specific shoe, but we definitely carry this size and bigger. Let me get the shoe person." She turned towards the back of the store. "Maybelline? Could you help this guy?"

From far end of the store came a very large and very tall woman with a huge candy-apple red beehive hairdo. As she got closer— from her square jaw and deep-set eyes—it became clear that this was not any ordinary woman. This was a man. A drag queen.

Sweat broke out on his forehead and his legs got twitchy. All instincts told him to bolt.

He forced his shoulders to relax. Why was he worried? He was bigger than the guy. He could take him if he had to. And he wasn't wearing high heels.

She gave him an up and down appraisal. Her smile widened hungrily. "Help him? I'd love to," she purred.

Oh, God, no.

His worst fear realized, the large man-woman sashayed up and attached herself to his side. He had to force himself not to fling her away, willing his arms to stay relaxed. *Play it cool, man. Play it cool.*

Good thing he chose the relaxed route. Built like a tank, the drag queen was much bigger than he originally thought, nearly as large as he. Intimidating in or out of the black and red polka dot dress.

Heart pounding, sweat trickling down the back of his neck, Rex pretended not to care and allowed the drag queen to lead him towards the back of the store. He came up with a quick plan to immobilize the girl-man if he had to.

Maybelline grinned at him and batted her long, fake eyelashes. They were so long, he could almost feel the wind coming off them. "Honey, you came to the right place today. Maybelline will take good care of you."

"I've got a rag to clean up your drool, Maybelline," the young woman called out. "Be gentle with him, it doesn't look like he hangs out in places like this very often."

"Oooo, a virgin!" the drag queen squealed.

Startled, his heart thumped painfully.

She winked at him. "My favorite. Come on now, darling, and let me help you discover the inner you."

Horror shocked his limbs into immobility. Him? A drag queen wannabe? How could the woman/man possibly think that? Eager to correct the misunderstanding, he stammered, "But these aren't for me, I—"

Maybelline nodded and smiled knowingly. "Right, *your friend*. I get it. Not quite ready to embrace the urge." She patted him on the arm. "No worries, your secret is safe with me."

The young saleswoman laughed. "It is not. Don't tell her anything you don't want blabbed all over the City."

Maybelline swung on her coworker. "Irridia, is it your period? Stop scaring him. Even if he's looking for shoes for his girl, he may get tired of her. I never meet any nice guys anymore, don't ruin it for me." She turned back to Rex, smiled up at him coyly and led him away. "Don't pay attention to her, she's just jealous. Come on now and let's get away from that nasty little girl."

Irridia laughed. She sang, "Nasty, nasty, I'm nasty, nasty. Doin' the nasty!"

Maybelline giggled. "You wish you were doing the nasty," she called out over her shoulder. She turned back to Rex and squeezed his arm. "Irridia's a big talker, but I get laid far more often than she does. With all that metal in her face? Who wants to fuck a cyborg?"

"I am not a cyborg!"

Maybelline winked up at him and nodded. "She is such a cyborg, she poops bolts and machine parts. Now let's find you some shoes."

"I heard that!"

Rex realized that he wasn't about to be attacked. Maybelline and the girl were playing. These were nice people, albeit very eccentric. And what did it matter if a drag queen mistook him for another drag queen? Why was he so freaked out? Was his hold on his masculinity this tenuous? No. He got a grip on himself and relaxed.

Laughing, he said, "They aren't for me, really, they're—"

"Of course, they're not." Maybelline led him up to a rack of large, glitzy women's shoes. Platforms and stilettos. "Okay, here we are." She let go of his arm, took the shoe out of his hand and examined it. "We don't have anymore of these, we sold out last spring, but look at this pair," she said, grabbing a blue shiny platform with six-inch heels, "these would be darling on you. I mean, *your friend.*"

Finally centered, he chuckled at the absurdity of the situation. "No, look, I need to know if you sold this pair. And to who. I'm looking for the person who bought this shoe."

Maybelline stared at him, seeming perplexed. Then she gasped in mock horror and clutched her formidable fake chest. "What? You had a one-night-stand and she left her shoe but not her number? What a *bitch*. Honey, I'd never do that to you."

"No, she was a woman. A real one."

Maybelline jerked her head back in surprise, her giant red hairdo wiggled a bit. "A woman in this? What? Was she Godzilla? Like some huge Amazon? Freakin' Xena?"

"Well, yes. Six feet of ravishing—I mean, uh…"

Her features softened. "Oh, God, you're in love." She beamed at him and pushed him lightly on the shoulder. "Well, aren't you cute? I love you, here you are tracking down this wench who dumped you. Irridia? This guy isn't shopping for shoes, he's looking for whoever bought this pair. He's looking for his true love! I love him, don't you love him? So romantic! Darling, I'd love to help, but I don't remember all the people who come in here."

"Do you really have that many people buying these?"

She nodded and raised her penciled-in black eyebrows. "You'd be surprised. That's why I thought you wanted them. So many straight-looking guys, so few shoes in their size. Especially a giant like you. Oh, my God, you would look sooo cute in these."

"Maybelline, really, if you could help me, I'd be…"

The drag queen smiled warmly and touched his arm. "Okay, well, let Maybelline think." She squinted her eyes and stroked her chin with her long, blood red fingernails.

Irridia asked, "You think it was the Trannyshack girls?"

Maybelline worked her bright red mouth, thinking. The movement made the beauty spot on the corner of her mouth dance on her slightly stubbly face. "Maybe. But no, they don't have that kind of money, these are pricey. Let me look at it again." Maybelline carefully inspected the silver shoe. "Hmmm. Yeah, let me think. We had these in spring, I know that. I almost bought myself a pair. But darling, women don't buy these. I haven't had a woman come in here to buy this size in years. Only men."

"Could she have borrowed them from someone?"

"Well, sure. We used to get the big-footed girls, but ever since the Internet came online, they don't want anyone to know they have huge feet, so they buy online. So stupid. So really, you're looking at a man who bought these. She either borrowed them from the guy or, uh, honey, you were fooled."

For a split second, Rex panicked. His throat constricted. Sweat broke out all over his body. He grabbed hold of his runaway thoughts with both hands. *Think, man, think. Abigail, sweet Abigail.* Her taste. The feel of her breasts in his hands. No, she was all woman. "I was not fooled."

Maybelline grimaced and shrugged. "Never know."

Rex gave a definitive nod. "I do. She's just a big girl. Who could have bought them somewhere else. I don't even know if she bought them here in the City."

"More than likely. Either here or New York or Seattle. That's it. It's not like there's this huge demand for Drag Queen Wear. Wait. I think David's costume designer came in and did that big order, right at the end of spring. He might have bought them. I mean, these are really show shoes, fabulous shoes. A bit too much for just lazing around the neighborhood. So you've got the Trannyshack, but they've been on the road forever now. These say David's show to me."

Rex's head snapped towards her. "David's show? David who?"

Maybelline smiled broadly. "You are so cute. David Leigh, honey, his show is called *Vamps and Tramps*, at the Tuxedo Club. They play Thursday through Sunday. Do this special nun show matinee on Sundays. They're really good. Best in town, do all the celebrity impersonations. If I were you? I'd go down there, watch the show and see if your girl shows up. Normally, they buy these pairs in threes or fours, you know, because of the wear. So maybe you'll see the match in the show and that will lead you to your girl."

A surge of hope rushed through him. He might find Abigail! "Great, I can't believe it. Came in here on a whim, but this may actually pay off."

Maybelline smiled, showing off a set of very white teeth. "Good for you, honey. So are you going to have her try it on? Watch out, you're so cute, the boys will be chopping off their toes to fit in that puppy."

Rex laughed. "Thanks for the advice. I think I'll remember her face just fine."

"I'll bet you will." She touched his arm briefly. "Say, do me a favor? If you find her, drop me a line and let me know. I love love stories."

"You bet."

"I want to know, too!" Irridia said.

He turned and smiled at the pierced girl. "Thank you, I will."

He hurried to the door, past a tattooed man with a green Mohawk wearing a leather skirt examining a display of latex whips.

"Darling?" Maybelline called out. "You forgot your shoe," she said, holding it up.

Laughing, Rex went and retrieved the shoe.

His heart singing, a bounce in his step, he headed for his car.

Abigail! I'm on my way!

Chapter Eleven

Cynthia stood back and admired the Tuxedo Club stage. With more effort than she'd wanted to put out, she'd managed to sweep most of the glitter off the black surface. Good. Perhaps the manager would keep her on as a stagehand for another couple weeks. Long enough for her to pass the registered nurses exam.

Even though her license might not help her get a job. She'd sent out feelers to some old colleagues. For women approaching fifty, nursing jobs were scarce. Hospitals couldn't afford the health insurance for their older workers, so they were mostly hiring twenty-somethings straight out of school.

Having been out of the game for seven years worked against her as well. But she'd figure out something. Hell, she had to.

Damn. She didn't even want to go back into nursing. All she wanted to do was sculpt. Hopefully, when she got some money together, she could start again. Her body tingled, her heart sang at the thought of pulling art out of some clay. She missed the emotional release, the power of creation. She had so many ideas, once she got started, she'd have enough for a gallery opening in no time. That was if she could find a gallery. Heavy sigh.

She headed backstage to the main dressing room. The long room was full of men in various stages of undress, applying make-up and adjusting wigs. Most sat in front of lighted mirrors lining the room and some stood, wrestling with their elaborate costumes.

Glittery dresses hung on racks along the back of the large room. Feather boas and other accessories were draped over mirrors and the backs of chairs. Scents of pancake make-up, cologne and male sweat overshadowed the heavy musty smell of the old building.

Cynthia picked up a large chip of peeling paint from the cement floor and tossed it in an ancient rusty and dented garbage can. "Hey girls. Does anybody need anything? Water? Coffee?"

"How about a Percoset and a shot of tequila?" Mark said, carefully applying his long eyelashes. He portrayed Joan Rivers, Cher and Dolly Parton.

Jon tilted his head back to apply makeup to his square jaw. "I'd like a tall hunky god with serious pecs—"

"And a huge bank account," Randy finished, patting his large red bubble wig. He'd nearly completed his transformation to Lucille Ball.

Mark waved a tube of lipstick her way. "I'm so glad Jon brought you in here, Cynthia. Can we keep you? Shit, the last stage hand—"

Jon interjected, "Gave great hand jobs, but couldn't clean the stage for crap."

Mark turned, mouth agape. "Joey gave you a hand job? Where was I?"

"In the next stall," Jon quipped. "Watching."

Mark smirked at him and turned to the group, smoothing his long black wig. "I wish the house hadn't been dark last week. I got lazy. All I want to do is curl up on the couch and watch TV."

Jon messed around in his make-up case, looking for something. "Yeah, heard David's new moneyman—what's-his-name—advised he paint the place, then freaked out when he found out the house would be closed for two weeks. A-ha!" With a triumphant smile, he withdrew a case of eyeshadow.

Cynthia grabbed a program from a makeup counter and fanned herself. Felt like a sauna in the room from all the lights and bodies.

Tim, a black guy dressed as Queen Latifah, stared at his reflection and ran his hands over his fake boobs. "Have you seen Mr. Money? Gor-geee-ous! Man, I'd like to get my hands on his—"

"Money," Jon finished.

Tim laughed. "No. Well, of course, but no, he's beautiful," he said, pursing his large red lips in the mirror. "Looks like a model, like Jude Law. Heard he just got married to a woman."

Mark flipped his long "Cher Hair" over his shoulder. "Married? What about that bald guy?" He gestured vaguely towards the front of the house.

Randy examined his profile in the mirror. "Baldy is his side job. Bet wifey doesn't know a thing," he said, adjusting his hemline.

Tim plumped up the padding around his hips. "I'd bet Wifey would flip out if she knew where all his money was going."

Randy waved a gloved hand in the air. "I heard he comes from money. His dad is some huge investment guy, travels the world." He stood, grabbed his prop purse and hung it over his buff arm.

Cynthia said, "Wish I came from money. But at this point, I'm glad I have a job. Any job."

"Here, here," Mark said. He turned around and checked out his ass in the mirror, shaking it a bit. He gave a satisfied nod.

She picked up a stray boa on the floor and hung it over a clothes rack. "Well, since you girls don't need anything, I'll go help set up the stage. Randy, twenty minutes."

"Oh, joy," Randy as Lucy muttered. He bent over and looked in the mirror, then patted an eyelash in place. "Someday I'm gonna get a real job."

"This is as real as it gets, girlie," Jon said, pursing his lips to apply lipstick.

During the break between shows, Cynthia went outside with Randy to the nasty little alley off the stage door to watch him smoke and to cool off. By the second show, not only the dressing room, but the backstage was frying from all the stage lighting.

As the foggy cool air bit into her skin, she shivered. "Feels good, but God, it's freakin' cold tonight."

A plume of steam poured out from a vent high atop the tall old brick-faced building, bringing with it the welcome scent of French fries from the club's kitchen. Still didn't do much to mask the noxious days-old garbage and heavy car exhaust odors. Even Randy's cigarette smoke was like a wonderful spring breeze compared to the normal scent of the dingy little alley.

Randy still dressed as Lucy, raised a pencil-thin eyebrow. "This is warm, honey. Where's your jacket?"

"Gilroy."

He did a double-take. "You don't have one here?"

Cynthia laughed and rubbed her arms to warm them. "Nope. Forgot the one Jon lent me."

Randy gave her an up and down appraisal and blew out some smoke. "So why are you working here, anyway? I mean, I know you're waiting for your license, but Jon said you might have a life insurance policy coming to you?"

Cynthia's stomach twisted. "No. Called the lawyer for my father's estate, there ain't nothin' there."

"Those bitches sure screwed you."

Her fists and jaw tight, she nodded. "Tell me about it."

Randy grabbed her arm. "Oh, talking about getting screwed, my boyfriend moved out last week." He let go to gesture broadly. "What a slut!"

As Randy embarked on a long diatribe about the jerk who dumped him, Cynthia rocked back and forth on her heels to stay warm and scanned the traffic out on Polk which ran perpendicular to the alley. A large van passed by. On the other side of Polk, a tall dark-haired guy in a black leather jacket leaned against a black sedan and stared at her.

Like an arrow between the eyes, recognition smacked her. Her limbs froze and her stomach went cold. All the hair stood up on the back of her neck.

Troy Slaughter, Sissy's son.

He turned away and got into the car.

What the hell was that sociopathic creep doing there? With a last glance at her, he sped off in his car.

This was not good. He was spying on her.

Sissy clearly wasn't going to stop her quest for the imaginary insurance policy. She'd deployed her rotten son to see if he could dredge up anything to blackmail Cynthia with.

Kelly.

Holy God, did that little thug follow her to the wedding? Even if he had, would he and his slimy mother make the connection between her and Kelly? No, how could they? The entire family believed that Alice/Kelly died from SIDS.

Still, she had to stay on guard. Sissy wasn't stupid. Jesus, talk about yet another reason to steer clear of Rex and Kelly. She shuddered from her toes to the top of her head.

Randy finally noticed she wasn't paying attention to him. "You know that guy? You don't look happy."

"Yeah, unfortunately. My nephew, Troy. My stepsister Sissy's son. What a creep that kid is."

"Creep, why?"

"Remember those killings in Golden Gate Park in the early eighties? The Rope Killer?"

Randy shuddered. "Oh, God, those were horrible. All those nice girls. Yeah, I was a teenager and just starting to experiment with women's clothes. Let me tell you, girlfriend, I stopped wearing dresses after that. Wore all these butch clothes until that freak was caught. Rocky Slaughter, wasn't that the guy's super appropriate name? Wait, what the hell does that have to do with that boy?"

"That kid," she said, jerking her head towards the street, "is the man's son. Troy Slaughter."

Randy's eyes popped out nearly beyond his inch-long fake eyelashes. "What?"

"Yeah. Nice, huh?"

He waved his hands in the air. "What?!"

"Yeah. Crack Whore Sissy's son. Spawn of Satan." She kicked an empty Coke can across the alley.

"I've heard a few of the stories, how'd I miss this one? Wait, how did she screw the guy without getting killed?"

She rubbed her arms vigorously and jumped in place, careful to avoid a puddle of dubious liquid near her feet. "Met him in jail. She was being processed out when he was being booked. Apparently, they met in the hallway and it was lust at first sight. Troy was conceived during a conjugal visit after Sissy forged a marriage license."

Randy blew out a giant cloud of smoke. "Ewwwwww!"

"Tell me about it."

"Is he like his father?"

"I think so. Creeps me out. Kind of kid who liked to torture small animals. I avoid him."

"Oh, that's so horrible!" Randy shook dramatically. "So where does he live? And why is he following you?"

The muscles in the back of her head and neck were so tight, they ached. She tried to rub away the pain. "His mother is after that imaginary life insurance policy. She's the one who deluded herself into thinking it was real, so she's sicced her kid on me. Troy lives here in the City, he's going to UCSF to—get this—become a doctor. Either Jekyll or Frankenstein, I'm sure."

Randy's eyes widened. "Creepy! Aren't you afraid of him?"

"Not really. Kid knows I hate him. Caught him choking my cat at Christmas once and I beat him up for it when no one was looking. Told him I'd cut his pecker off if he went near my pets or if he told on me. He respected me after that and never touched my animals again. Now that he's grown, he avoids me mostly. I'd better warn Jon. If—"

Beyond Randy, deeper in the alley, two men exploded in a heated argument, startling her. It was so dark, she hadn't noticed them before. She could just make out the features of the two.

A very large bald man had a smaller light-haired man pinned against the wall and was railing at him. "You owe me more time, goddamn it! You're off chasing that bitch, leaving me alone most of the time! I didn't see you for a month! A month!"

While the large man's posture seemed threatening, the short man didn't seem fazed by it. "I told you this wasn't going to be easy! And I was on my honeymoon, stupid! I told you things would be different after I got married!"

"You were supposed to marry me, not her!"

"Do you want the money or not?!"

Cynthia recognized the voice of the smaller guy. But from where? Probably a friend of Jon's.

The little one pushed on the bald one's chest and stalked towards Randy and her, making a motion for the big one to stay.

"Don't walk away from me!" Baldy cried.

The smaller guy came into the light and Cynthia gasped and gaped.

Vance. Kelly's new husband.

He stopped and stared at her, his brow furrowed. "What are you staring at?"

Cynthia couldn't speak. Then her blood turned to fire. Her body coiled for war. She got into Vance's face. "You married Kelly Du Charmante and you're gay? How dare you hurt her like that? You slime bag!"

Vance's eyes and face blank, he coughed and sputtered.

His boyfriend came up next to him and glared at her. "Is there some problem here?"

"Yeah," Cynthia bit out. "Your boyfriend here married Kelly Du Charmante and is taking her and her father for a big fat ride and I don't appreciate it. So look, you freakin' monster, you'd better go home and tell her the truth or—"

Vance's blue gaze sharpened and a deadly cold look overtook his handsome features. "I don't know who you are, lady, but you'd better back the fuck off."

"She's our new stage hand. Why? Is there a problem, Vance?" came a new voice.

David, the owner of the show. A sixty-something guy with no chin who looked like an accountant, complete with bifocals.

She was so hyped up, she couldn't restrain herself. "You think I'm afraid of you?" she demanded, pointing at Vance. "You got way more to lose than I do, buddy. And you're gonna lose it. I'm gonna see to that. And you'll be really lucky if you don't get your ass kicked soundly in the process."

"Cynthia, back off there or I'll have to fire you." David stepped down, closer to them. "Sorry, Vance, I don't know what's wrong with her."

She swung on David. "What do you mean, fire me?"

David seemed torn. His attention vacillated between Vance and her. "He's bankrolling the show right now."

The realization hit her like an oncoming commuter train.

Vance's grin spread. A superior edge came over the look in his eye. "You are so fired. Now go back in whatever hole you crawled out of, bitch. And if I hear that Kelly catches wind any of this, I will spend the rest of my days ruining your miserable life."

Trumped. If she pushed too hard, Jon would lose his job as well. Cynthia's interior exploded in a cloud of anger and frustration. Her vision shifted.

Vance's boyfriend suddenly pointed at her. "You! You hit my car! I mean, Vance's car! This is the bitch in the Volkswagon!"

The gold sedan she side-swiped was Vance's!

Thankfully, Cynthia was lost in fury, processing her horrible predicament. It gave her that extra second to think before she reacted. She immediately recognized the bald guy. Mr. Anger himself from the day of the accident. How had her recognized her?

Damn it, she was wearing the same orange Moxie t-shirt.

She blinked and forced a bewildered look on her face. "Uh. What the hell? Hit your car? I don't even own a car." Her stomach flip-flopping, she turned to David. "I'm sorry. I, in no way, meant to complicate your life. I won't cause any more trouble. I'll go. Besides, Pretty Boy here will destroy his own life all by himself. I just hope I'm there when it happens."

Vance sneered. "How would you be there? How do you know me?" His eyes widened, he pointed at her. "You were at my wedding! You saved the mayor's life! Wait, David just called you Cynthia, but you said your name was Abigail Maxim. You're not any Abigail Maxim. Who the hell are you?"

Holy God, no! This wasn't happening to her!

Cynthia snorted, thankful her anger covered any evasiveness. Her heart slammed her rib cage and she stuck her trembling hands in her pockets. "Cynthia is my name and I don't know what the hell you're talking about. I know Kelly from childhood. I was her babysitter. I know the family. I wasn't at the wedding. But I saw the pictures of you. I know who you are."

Vance nodded to himself and smirked. "You were at the wedding, I remember you. You upstaged us. I never forget a face. Especially not the savior of the Mayor and my father-in-law. You saved Rex's life in the Park and then danced with him at our wedding—it's all bloody Leah Garfield could talk about." Vance turned to David and Randy. "David, don't worry, I'll handle this. But I would look for a new stage hand."

David sent a harsh glance her way. "Uh, thanks, Vance." He nodded at Randy. "Come on, Lucy, let's go back inside." He turned and took a step, but Randy didn't move. His attention ping-ponged between Vance and Cynthia, riveted to the drama.

David grabbed Randy by the arm and dragged him inside.

Vance examined her, head to foot. His intense blue gaze met hers. "What's your game, lady? Why the lie? And I'll just bet you're no Maxim. What's your angle here? Ahhh, you want Rex's money. You're a con artist after Rex's big bank account. I see."

Hate poured from her belly. She blazed him with a glower. "You see me through your own eyes. You don't know my motivations. Someone like you couldn't possibly understand someone like me."

He laughed and gave his head a haughty toss. "Money. It's as plain as the greedy look in your eye. You want to feed from the Du Charmante trough and figured a way in. You probably pushed Rex in front of that car. And what? Did you shove a piece of meat down Calvin's throat just so you could save him?"

Flames of rage billowed inside her. Her fists itched to punch his smug face. "You're insane," she spat.

He narrowed his eyes, studying her. He gave her an up and down appraisal. "I don't think so. I think I just saved my wife's family a whole lot of cash."

"So you can suck it all up yourself. Look, I only care about what you're doing to Kelly. How could you hurt her like that? She loves you, you idiot. How could you do this to her?"

Vance snorted. "Oh, Christ, hurt her. She's built like a battleship. Besides, there's only one man in her life and that's her father. I barely have anything to do with her. And she likes it that way. I swear, if it weren't illegal, those two would marry each other."

She gasped. His boyfriend laughed.

"Oh, don't look so shocked," Vance said with a smirk. "I mean, she is *adopted*. I'm sure they could get a waiver."

She slapped him so hard, his head jerked back.

Cynthia pointed at Vance, her arm shaking. "You hurt her, I will fucking strangle you until your pretty eyes pop out of your head," she seethed.

His boyfriend lunged at her. Vance held him back, his focus intent on her. "What the hell is your game, lady?" He rubbed his face where she'd hit him. "This isn't about Rex or the money, is it? You're after the daughter. What? Are you some cougar lesbian after my girl? Is Kelly bi?"

She got queasy, held her stomach and took a step back. "Jesus Christ, no."

"Okay, that's not it. But you love her. And I know she doesn't know you. What's your stake in all this?"

The kid was a shark. Cynthia averted her eyes and turned her body away. "I have no stake. Look, you got what you wanted. I'll shut up and go away." She took a step towards Polk Street and glanced back at him.

His intense blue gaze bored into her. "Now you're retreating. You're hiding something. One second you're a pitbull, the next you're running away. Why? Why wouldn't you want me knowing who you are?"

Cynthia stepped up on the curb to avoid a pile of dog crap. "I told you, I used to baby-sit her. I love her and want to protect her, that's all."

"No, you didn't," Vance said, pursuing her, careful to step around the doggy land mine. "I've met everyone Kelly has ever known. I grew up with her and we had the same sitters. You didn't know that, did you? You haven't done your homework and your lies are abysmal. You're acting just like her personal guard dog or mother…" He stopped and stared at her. "Oh, I am so stupid. It's right here in front of me." He gestured towards her. "The age is right. I see the resemblance. You're her mother, aren't you? You're her goddamned birth mother."

Cynthia's belly hollowed, the street wobbled and her body tensed so much it hurt. She tried to respond but nothing came out. How the hell had he guessed? This kid was way too smart for her own good.

His eyes dilated, he stepped back from her. "My God, I was right."

Emergency! You are blowing it! Save your ass!

She stepped towards him, her hands up in a defensive posture. "I don't know where the hell you're getting this weird idea—"

Vance stared at her as if she were a ghost. "The resemblance is so strong. But why the deception? You accuse me of hurting her, you know she's spent her whole life looking for you? What are you hiding?"

Cynthia couldn't stand his x-ray vision any longer and looked down. There was no way she could talk her way out of this, she just had to beat it. She took another step away. They were almost at the corner. "I'm not hiding anything and I'm not her mother. You're crazy. Besides, I don't have any kids."

He followed her, anger lines creasing his perfect face. "Stop lying. It's obvious, your reaction, the look in your eye. My God, your face. At least Kelly won't be a hag when she gets to your age, but I need to know what your intentions are. You don't want her knowing who you are, that's clear. Why not? You're a criminal, aren't you?"

"No." Cynthia stopped. She rubbed her forehead and ran a hand through her hair. She had no idea how to handle this situation. Pitbull Boy clearly wasn't leaving her alone until he got answers. Intolerable! "No, I'm a nurse. And I *was* a stagehand."

Vance nodded to himself. "You are her mother, aren't you?"

"Oh, for crying out loud. Okay, what the hell? Yes, I'm Kelly's mother. But I don't want her knowing that. Look, man, don't do this to her. She loves you and you're going to decimate her heart. The truth will come out. I won't say anything, but I won't have to, you'll blow it. I know, I married a gay guy myself. Kelly's father is gay."

His head jerked back. "You're kidding."

"No, came home and found him in bed with the pastor."

Vance burst out laughing and his boyfriend joined him. "You're kidding."

"No, and it wasn't funny. My water broke, that was Kelly. And in a fit of stupidity I gave her up. A decision I have regretted ever since."

"Oh, poor you," he said with mock sympathy.

She had to grab her arm to stop herself from popping him one.

He narrowed his eyes and frowned. "But why come back now?"

As angry as she was at the man, she saw no reason to lie to him any longer. "I wanted to go to her wedding. The whole Rex thing was a fluke. I had no idea he was Kelly's father when I saved his life. Then when I finally tracked down Kelly and found out that he was her father, I gave up on him. I need to keep my life separate from Kelly's. But now I find out that you're an imposter and it just breaks my heart."

Vance blinked rapidly a few times, pursed his lips and looked down. After a second, he met her gaze. "So what are you going to do?"

"I'm going to walk away. But that doesn't mean I don't want to kill you for doing this to her."

"I love her," he said simply, his eyes clear.

His boyfriend pushed him on the shoulder. "You told me you didn't."

"Shut up," Vance replied, then turned back to Cynthia. "I've loved her my whole life. But…" He nodded towards the bald man. "I also love him. Even though he's a total lunkhead." He looked at his boyfriend and gestured back towards the stage door. "Darling, go have a drink and we'll work this all out later. Let me talk to— whatever her name is."

"Cynthia," she said.

"Cynthia, then."

The large bald man—she still didn't know his name—pouted, his shoulders drooped and he ambled down the alley and into the club.

Vance regarded her and pulled his mouth to one side. "Look, I may be a bit of an opportunist, but I do love her. I won't hurt her."

Cynthia crossed her arms. "You already are."

"I won't be sleeping with the pastor in our bedroom," he said, squaring his slim shoulders. "I'm not in denial. I'm bi. And this is how I've chosen to live my life."

"But she didn't choose. You chose for her."

"She won't ever know. I have a bunch of friends doing the same thing. There are still certain glass ceilings for gay men. I can't operate in the social arena I want to without a wife and children. And I need Kelly. She keeps my head on straight."

Cynthia didn't budge and kept her arms locked tight across her front. "You're betraying her."

"No, I'm not. Only if she finds out and she never will. I won't let that happen."

There was no use in arguing with the man. "Okay, whatever, after I found out about my husband, I got over it. Just don't get her pregnant. Don't bring a baby into this."

He snorted and made a disgusted face. "What nerve you've got. The woman who abandoned my wife. Forget it, I want children and I intend to have them. With Kelly. And I'm going to keep mine," he added pointedly.

Hot fury poured out of her so powerfully it made her head hurt. "Whatever, I don't know why I'm having this conversation, all I want to do is strangle you. I just hope before this goes too far, you'll tell Kelly and find a woman who will be okay with your needs. I don't fault you for who you are, I fault you for the way you're approaching this."

Vance examined her face carefully. "So you're not going to try to contact her? She wants to meet you."

She shook her head. "Unlike you, I care about her enough to put her needs ahead of mine. And I need to protect her." Sissy would destroy Kelly. Blackmail her, beat her, hurt her. All Sissy would see was a huge walking pile of money. She'd never leave her alone. "Don't worry, your secret is safe with me." She sighed and looked down. "All I want to do is protect her. She's going to be so hurt."

Cynthia turned to leave.

"I won't hurt her."

She didn't even turn around. "Yes, you will. And I won't be there to pick up the pieces."

Her vision obscured by tears, she stepped onto Polk. Roiling emotions thundered through her and she punched her fist.

What a horrible night! The only positives were that Jon had stayed inside and out of the fight, and she found out the gold sedan she'd hit belonged to Vance. Which was totally funny—not to mention ironic—but tonight, she couldn't even muster up a giggle over it.

Poor Kelly. Marrying a gay guy. How weird was that? Was there something screwed up in their DNA that made them attracted to gay men? Some strange homing device that picked out homosexual men that pretended to be straight?

She wiped the tears from her eyes and searched for a cab. Up ahead of her, a man in a black leather jacket stepped out onto the sidewalk from a doorway. He was young and had short dark wavy hair. It couldn't be.

"Troy!"

He turned around, his mouth dropped open and his large green eyes widened. He took off running up the block.

Fear slapped her brain and jolted her nerves. Had he overheard the conversation? Jesus Christ! She had to stop him! She had to find out what he knew!

"Goddamned you! Stop, you little creep!" She gave chase.

It was late and all the clubs along Polk were hopping. Couples strolled along the street, intertwined. Cynthia ran around and through them, keeping Troy in her sights.

He led her down two blocks. Mid-way through the next block, he looked over his shoulder at her, then leapt out into the middle of the street in front of a bus. The bus driver honked and kept going. After the bus passed, there was no sign of Troy anywhere.

She ran along the sidewalk—dodging small groups of people—looking for a break in the traffic to cross the street. He had to be somewhere on the other side.

"Abigail!" a man shouted from a vehicle in the middle of the street.

Focused on searching for Troy, she didn't pay any attention.

"Abigail Maxim!" The voice was louder now.

Why did the voice and the name—*oh, God*. No.

Cynthia finally looked at the driver and choked.

Rex.

Chapter Twelve

Waving at her from a black, expensive-looking car, Rex shot her a radiant smile. "Abigail! It's me, Rex! I've been looking everywhere for you!"

Oh, God, if Vance saw them together, he might think she ratted him out and then he'd tell Rex who she was and everything would go to hell. She had to get Rex out of there. And tell him a story to make him stay away without hurting his feelings. She'd utilize as much truth as she could.

"Rex!" She checked the traffic. There was a break. She dashed across the street, went around the back of his car and got in the passenger side.

A heavenly smell met her upon sitting, a mixture of cologne and leather. The warmth of the car and the luxurious plush leather seats enveloped her. Such a contrast to the hard, worn seats and stinky gasoline smell of Jon's car.

He pulled the car over and parked, but left the engine running. She glanced at him, but couldn't hold eye contact. Pain wrenched her stomach. She wanted him so badly, but needed to protect him, Kelly and herself.

She took a deep breath and turned to him to speak, but his beauty stunned her into silence. Dressed in a sleek brown leather jacket and jeans, his commanding blue gaze immobilized her. With his cut cheekbones and a light stubble on his chiseled jaw, he looked like a ready-made Cynthia treat. She flashed on their kiss. His taste. The feel of his strong arms around her. A deep hunger roared from within her.

She had to get rid of him and fast or she'd be on top of him before she knew it.

His smile faded. "Damn, woman, you gave me the wrong number for your cell. You know what I've gone through to find you?"

Her breath caught. Overwhelming news. "How *did* you find me?"

He arched a brow. "Wasn't easy. Luckily, you left me this." He grabbed Jon's silver shoe from between the seats and handed it to her.

The picture of him standing at the curb with the shoe in his hand popped into her mind. Acid filled her gut. "Oh, Christ. But wait, how the hell did you find me with this?"

"Went to a costume shop on the Haight and luckily, the lady—well, man—drag queen—who works at the shop remembered they'd been sold to a performer who worked at the Tuxedo club." He took the shoe and put it back between the seats. His expression sharpened. "Did you purposefully leave me a wrong number?"

She rolled her eyes and sighed. "Oh, God. We need to talk. After what I've got to tell you, you won't want me in your car."

His brow went into a deep V, his gaze went hot and his mouth hardened. Clearly not the answer he wanted. Wasn't the answer she wanted to give him, either.

Even upset, he looked so good. Such kissable lips. She longed to run her hands through his soft hair. Feel that hard taut chest pressed against her, his strong hands caressing her ass.

Not helpful!

He turned off the motor and turned to her. "Okay." Wary, wounded. She'd already hurt him. Wonderful.

She found she couldn't take his laser-sighted gaze. She looked down at her lap. Her stomach flipped and flopped like she'd swallowed a school of fish. "Oh, God, this isn't easy."

"You're married."

She had to look at him on that line. "No. Well, I was, but he, uh, left. I'm single, I didn't lie about that."

"You lied about other things."

She stared at the polished wood glove compartment door and rubbed her forehead, her face burning with shame. "Yes."

"Why?"

She stole a quick glance at him, then gazed down at her fingers, wrapped tightly around her wrist. "Because I was trying to protect you. When I saved you in the park, I had every intention of finding you and asking you out. Or conning you into asking me out. I had many elaborate plans. Then I found out who you are. The whole rich, society thing and I just couldn't do that to you."

"Do what to me?"

"Get involved," she said, gesturing sharply. She pinched the bridge of her nose and took a deep breath. "Look, Rex, my life is in complete chaos right now. And I didn't want you to get hit with the fallout." She finally met his gaze full on, which wasn't easy. All she wanted to do was throw her arms around him and make that hurt look on his face go away. "You're obviously a super nice guy and our connection is very intense. I haven't felt this way about a man since Jon, my husband. Which is why I ran."

He chuckled, but wasn't amused. "You're making no sense, you do realize that?"

She held up a hand. "Stay with me, I will. I have no idea how to say this." She checked out the passersby on the sidewalk and tried to get her head together. She needed a plausible lie. A slight muddling of the truth might work. But she had to play this cool. She had to watch every word that slipped out of her mouth.

A one-legged homeless woman hopped by pushing a grocery cart with a giant stuffed bear inside. Up a half a block or so, a dark-haired man stood behind a car and stared at her.

Troy.

Her heart kicked into high gear. "Oh, shit. Um, excuse me, don't leave. I'll be right back."

She opened the door, leapt out and ran after Troy. The boy dashed around the dark sedan and jumped inside. As she reached it, he started it up.

Fury searing her veins, she pounded the top of the car. "Tell your mother to leave me the hell alone!" He pulled away from the curb and sped off. She pointed at him. "Stay away from me!"

He turned the corner and disappeared. Damn it. He must have seen her get into Rex's car. For sure, he got the license plate number. Great, now he'd find out who owned the car. Probably heard Rex call her Abigail.

She let out an exasperated yell and stomped her foot. What a mess! Shaking her head, she turned and jogged back to Rex's car.

He stood outside, leaning on his car door, no color in his face, his eyes dilated as if he'd just witnessed a murder. She couldn't help but laugh, even though the situation was not funny.

Rex's gaze went hard and his brow became a flat line. Great, now he thought she was laughing at him. Sighing, she opened the car door and got in.

He hesitated, then joined her, but it looked like he was considering jumping back out and running. "What was all that about?"

"Oh, God, Rex. My life is so crazy right now, I can barely explain it."

The line between his eyes deepened. "Make an attempt, will you?"

She chuckled and rubbed her arms vigorously. "I'm not laughing at you, I'm laughing at the absurdity of my life. What a night! Let's see, I've been fired, followed and spied upon, and now you've found me. I should go buy some Lottery tickets, I'm at some weird nexus of luck. Okay, let me begin at the beginning. No, where was I?" *Where was her bloody story? Think!*

Rex gave a nod towards the front of his car. "Who was that you were chasing? That's my first question."

"That was my stepsister's illegitimate son, Troy. I should stop saying that, it wasn't his fault. Even if he is a total sociopathic creep."

"He was following you? Why?"

"Because his mother thinks I have money I don't. And she's trying to blackmail me for it. So she's having her son follow me around to try to dig up dirt on me. She's the reason I can't get involved with you—she's dangerous and I can't let you get hurt. And you would—you look really worried and like you aren't believing any of this."

"Do you blame me?"

"No. I don't. My life doesn't make much sense to me, either." She rubbed her eyes and took a deep breath. Time to mix some more truth into her story. "Look, okay, let me back up some. First of all, my name is not Abigail Maxim and that was not my brother at the wedding. That was my gay drag queen ex-husband."

Rex did a double take. "*What?*"

"My gay drag queen ex husband," she pronounced more carefully.

He squinted at her, confusion twisting his gorgeous features. "You married a gay man?"

"Didn't know it at the time. Neither did he."

His expression softened. "Oh, that's whose shoes you were wearing."

"Yes, Jon's. And I wore his dress. His Carol Channing outfit." She thumbed behind herself, towards the club. "Jon's in that *Tramps and Vamps* show at the Tuxedo club."

"That's where I was headed when I saw you on the street."

Rex had all his senses tuned into her. The way he held his head to hear her, the way his penetrating gaze took in her face and hands, each of her words and motions was being evaluated and processed in a nanosecond. He didn't miss a thing. His shoulders were tight, his expression, stony.

She had to dance and dance fast. She concocted twenty stories and rejected them. Alien from another planet. In the witness protection program. Transsexual ("My real name is Bob!"). Serial murderer.

Say something! "You went there because you traced the shoe to a performer at the club. Right?"

"Yeah." His gaze darted to his cell phone in a holder on the dash like he was trying to determine whether or not to call 911 and report a mental patient on the loose.

All at once, a story came to her. "Okay, running into you at that wedding was just weird luck. Jon and I had just seen *Wedding Crashers* and have never been to a fancy wedding before. Your wedding planner happens to be Jon's sometime lover. So Jon coerced —blackmail is such an ugly word—coerced Michael into getting us on the guest list. He said you didn't know most of the guests, anyway."

Rex looked at her like she had squirrels doing the can-can on top of her head. "Why would you want to go to someone's wedding when you didn't know anyone there?"

She forced a flippant shrug. "Free fancy food. We're both super poor right now and wanted to go to a fancy event. Yes, weird, I know. But you don't get it. I hadn't had restaurant food in months. Anyway, I'm sorry. I had no idea that it was your daughter's wedding. Not until you walked down the aisle with Kelly. I was so shocked, I think I inhaled my necklace. Then I didn't know what to do, but I didn't leave because I wanted the food. Sorry. So I planned on eating and running and then you made your rounds at the tables and I was getting up to run when Calvin choked on that stupid piece of meat and then you saw me and I should have told you what was

going on, but I didn't have the guts," she said in such a rush she had
to gasp for air. "And then we had that dance and I got lost in you. I
was telling you the truth when I said that was the best night of my
life, Rex. It was."

Rex sat back, his brow wrinkled, his mouth twisted. "You
crashed my daughter's wedding because you wanted the free food,"
he stated, rather than asked, sounding like he was trying on the
excuse for size because it didn't fit.

She had to admit it was THE lamest excuse she'd ever come up
with. The aliens story would have been more plausible.

She began gesturing dramatically, normally a sure sign she was
lying. But he wouldn't know that. "I know it sounds dumb, but that
movie made it look so fun. Jon and I have done all sorts of crazy
things—we're terrible instigators for each other. Look, I'll pay you
for our meals. I feel bad about that. Once I got there, I felt like such
a creep. Sounded like such innocent fun until I realized that actual
people were getting married."

He chuckled and shook his head. He angled a glance at her. "Are
you really a nurse?"

"Yes. Well, I will be again hopefully, I'm in the process of
getting recertified. And boy do I need the money. I had a part-time
job at Jon's club until I got fired tonight because I inadvertently, uh,
had issues with the financial backer of the show. I was on my way
home when I caught Troy spying on me. I was chasing him when
you found me."

Rex waved a hand and frowned. "Wait, Troy is your nephew?
Who wants to get something on you so his mother can blackmail
you? Even though you don't have any money?"

Her stomach was so tight, she wanted to puke. "Yes. I didn't say
they were smart. They're stupid and ruthless. But I'm not worried
about me right now, Rex, I'm worried about you. They'd destroy
you. Sissy and Belinda would find out you were rich and come after
you with everything they've got. They're soulless monsters. Their

whole lives are about destroying me. They attack anyone I get involved with. I won't put you at risk like that."

Rex shifted in his seat, turning towards her a bit more. His expression grew more intense. "So you ran because you're afraid your stepsisters will hurt me?"

"No. I ran because *I know* they'll hurt you."

He didn't look convinced. He continued to examine her. Shit!

"Look, Rex, you obviously don't believe me, but I'm telling you the truth. Run. Run as far away from me as you can get and forget you ever met me. You deserve better. Kelly deserves better. I can't let either of you get hurt. So I apologize for leading you on. I apologize for lying to you. I apologize for attending that wedding, I had no right to be there."

He relaxed back in his seat and rubbed the back of his neck. "Mayor would be dead if you hadn't been there. No, I'm glad you were there, more than glad, actually. But I only have one question for you..." He sighed, then leaned towards her again. His dark gaze burned into her, making her stomach and feet feel funny. "Do you like me? Was that real? You just said it was, but when people make up elaborate stories like you just did, they're usually trying to blow someone off. If you don't like me, you can just say that."

She looked him dead in the eye. "Rex, I didn't make up that story. I know it sounds ludicrous, but I'm telling you the truth." *Partly.* "But since I've already admitted to lying to you, I don't have much credibility here. And I more than like you. I've never felt what I feel for you. This is not easy for me. All I want to do is to attack you. Carry you off into the sunset. But it wouldn't work. You're rich, I'm a disaster. I won't do that to you."

He cogitated a few moments, tracing the steering wheel with a long finger. He turned to her, thought lines etched deep into his symmetrical face. "So my money is the obstacle here?"

"Yes."

"So if I was poor, you'd want me?" he asked like it was craziest thing he'd ever heard.

"If you were poor, I'd have you pinned to the backseat right now."

He chuckled, shaking his head to himself. "You are crazy. Funny, adorable, hot, and very crazy."

She pointed at him. "Yes. Now you're getting the picture."

His wide shoulders relaxing, he eased back into his seat and absently ran his fingers over the stitching in the leather cover on the gearshift. "Well, I appreciate you wanting to protect me, but I don't see the difference in our incomes as any kind of a deal-breaker here." He turned to her, his gaze sharp. "I mean, what the hell does my money have to do with anything? I am not my money. I'm just a man. Who thinks you're very attractive. A bit scary around the edges, but very attractive. And I want to see you."

A surge of joy rushed through her immediately followed by an icy jab of pain to her gut. She was doing a lousy job of getting rid of him. Her muscles tensed with frustration. She tapped her foot and regarded him. "You aren't easily put off, are you?"

"Not when I find something I want. And I want you."

She threw up her hands. "But you don't even know who I am. Well, you do. I'm a liar. You do not want to get involved with a liar."

Completely unaffected, a smile twitched at the corners of his mouth. He'd clearly dismissed his worries about her. "You're obviously more than that. You just explained why you lied. Most people lie, especially in business. I judge people only by their actions. And your actions do not line up with this disaster assessment of yourself. Besides, I knew you lied about your name after I Googled you."

"Oh." Of course, he'd do that. So he really didn't care that she lied?

His took in the length of her, then met her gaze. "I pursued you because I knew there was nothing intrinsically wrong with you. Well, other than some flaws in your decision-making processes—bit impetuous and unorthodox. But that just makes you more interesting."

This guy was not to be dissuaded. What was wrong with him? She waved her hands, exasperated. "I don't get you, Rex," she said, her voice rising. "You seem like a level-headed guy. If I were in your position, I wouldn't want someone who lied to me. I could be a con artist, trying to get money out of you."

Eyes twinkling, his crow's feet deepened and a sexy smile played on his lips. "You had a perfect opportunity to bleed me for money after saving my life and you didn't. All you've been doing since I met you is run from me. Con artists don't run before they get their money. I figured there had to be a good reason why you lied, but it clearly had nothing to do with your character. I know people, Abi— just what the hell is your real blasted name, woman?"

"Cynthia—" She stopped. "Wait, here, we'll start over. Rex Du Charmante, my name is Cynthia Rella." She offered her hand to him.

He blinked several times, then stared at her, ignoring her hand. "Cynthia Rella, did you say? You can't be! The sculptor? You sculpt? Was some of your work in local galleries, maybe twenty-five years ago?"

She stopped tapping her foot, her arms fell to her sides, she could only stare back. Did she just step into an episode of the Twilight Zone? How the hell could he know that? "How did you…uh, yeah."

His mouth dropped open, then he broke into a gigantic smile. "No way! I can't believe it!" His happy expression broke and he eyed her suspiciously. "Wait, you aren't lying about this, are you?"

"No. Here, I'll prove it." She pulled out her wallet and handed him her driver's license. "And no, it's not a fake."

He read it. His gaze went wide and his face transformed into pure joy. A blinding smile on his face, he stared at her, seeming awed. "I can't believe this. God, I have to show you something." He handed her back her license, started up the car and took off.

She'd completely lost control over the situation. What the hell happened? "Wait, where are we going?"

He shot her a cute grin. "It's a surprise."

"But wait, this is the part where you order me out of your car."

He turned to her, startled. "What? Why?"

"Well, I lied about who I am. I'm penniless and destitute and you don't want to be around me."

He rolled his eyes. "What crap. Granted, I've always been a snob —oh, God, I just admitted that. Anyway, now that I find out who you are, none of that matters. We all lie at one time or another. And change our names. For God's sake, I wasn't born Rex Du Charmante, you know."

This stopped her. "You weren't?"

"No. Was born Melvin Stanley Schmelzenbach."

She burst out laughing. "*Melvin Stanley what?*"

He signaled for a right and turned onto the next street. "Schmelzenbach. Can you see it on the side of a building? Neither could I. 'Course, I picked Rex Du Charmante when I was fourteen. Sounds like a blasted fairy tale. But it worked. A lot better than Schmelzenbach would have. Cynthia, you don't get to our age without some skeletons in our closets, without history."

"I suppose. I just never lied about who I was before."

He stopped at a red light. "Wait. This makes no sense. You didn't know who I was when you saved my life. Why did you run then?"

"Uh, I, didn't want to get involved with the police. Don't worry, I'm not a felon. But I recently went to jail for—oh, God, this sounds so bad. Uh, assault."

He spun on her, slack-jawed. "Assault?"

"Yeah." She sighed. "This goes back to the war with the stepsisters."

A car honked behind him, the light had changed. His attention snapped back to the intersection and he hit the gas. "You never finished that story, go on."

"Okay, Reader's Digest Version," she said, settling into her seat. "Five years ago, I sold my house and was going to buy a condo here in the City, but then my dad got sick. I was supposed to move in and take care of him for three months and that stretched to seven years."

"Seven years?"

"Yeah." She let out a long breath. "Dad was on death's door nearly the whole time."

"Christ."

"So, in return for my caretaking—and the outlay of all my cash to help take care of them and the house—Dad was going to sign over the property to me so I'd get it when he died. But when the stepmonster died, followed shortly by Dad, this new will surfaced which left me with nothing. Four hours after he died, while I was at the funeral home picking out a casket, my stepsisters changed the locks on the house. When I got back, they showed me the legal papers, ordered me out and I lost my mind."

He shot her a serious look. "I can see why you assaulted them."

"No. Yes. Well, I didn't, not then. I pushed past them and we had this huge fight in the middle of the living room."

He gave a sharp nod. "And that's when you hit them."

"No. It was when Belinda—the youngest and the most stupid— picked up—I can barely even think about this—picked up my favorite—shit, I'm going to cry. Sorry, this…" She rubbed her eyes. "…didn't happen that long ago. Belinda picked up my favorite sculpture from the mantle—the one I won a huge award for—it was really beautiful—and she smashed it into a million pieces."

Rex gasped, the color left his face. "No!" His attention bounced between her and the road.

"Oh, yes. It gets better. Not that I remember much of the day. Then Sissy, the other one, grabbed a framed picture of my mother and lit it on fire. When Belinda picked up another sculpture to break it, I tackled her, saved the piece and then I don't remember much except for being on top of her and pounding her. I think Sissy pulled me off, then I went for her, the cops showed up and the next thing I knew I was in handcuffs in the back of a police car."

He stopped at another light and turned to her, his expression full of sympathy. "Terrible."

She averted her eyes and toed the plush floor mat, trying desperately to avoid getting sucked closer to him. "Yeah. And thank

God for my ex-husband, Jon. He saved me. He bailed me out of jail and took me in. Because I have *nothing*. I mean, nothing but two pairs of jeans and a few t-shirts. I don't even have a bloody coat. I have a court order, allowing me to pick up my belongings, but every time we arrange it, the gargoyles figure out a way to screw it up. A family friend told me that they threw out most of my stuff, whatever they didn't want. I'm not sure anything of mine is left in the house," she said, rubbing her hands together so hard they hurt.

A horrible ache throbbed deep in her belly. "Forty-eight years of pictures, my artwork, my favorite sculpting tools, all my school mementos, all gone. Because they hate me that much." She shook off the pain. They would not win. She was in charge and she was fine. "So, that's why when the cops wanted my name and to talk to me after your accident, I freaked out. Then I found out you were rich and ran from you because I couldn't stand the thought of them hurting you. I won't let it happen, Rex."

He glanced over at her. "That's crazy. You need people on your team. I'm not afraid of idiots like that."

"You would be if you met them."

He gave a slight shrug and sent her a sweet grin that went straight to her sex. She had a quick mental flash of leaping across the car and attacking him with kisses. He'd pull over, she'd reach down and unzip him—*hello!*

She mentally smacked herself on the head. *Wake up! Stop, I repeat, STOP thinking about him naked and inside you! You will be leaving him shortly!*

Well, whenever he let her out of his bloody car.

Where the hell was he taking her?

Chapter Thirteen

Rex reached the top of a hill, turned into a short driveway and stopped in front of a very large and fancy wrought iron gate. He hit a button on a square device attached to the visor and the gate slid open.

He gestured out the car window. "Here we are."

All she could see on her right was an ornate art deco wall. She couldn't see the top of it. "Holy Christ, where is here?"

"My house."

He drove inside and followed the driveway, skirting the edge of the building. On his side, the headlights shone on a row of perfectly trimmed hedges.

She couldn't tell the exact size of the house, but it seemed immense. "House? This is a mansion, Rex."

"Just a house."

They came to the end of the wall and turned the corner, revealing a huge circular driveway that wrapped around an enormous fountain. Directly ahead was a covered area, supported by large columns.

"See, this is crazy, Rex. You can't be with someone like me, your friends will think I'm a gold-digger. And damn it, I take care of myself. I have pride. I don't want people thinking I'm some suckerfish, only after you because of your money."

He parked under the covered area and turned to her. "Why are you worried about what other people will think of you?"

She opened her mouth to answer, but had no good reply. "Uh. I don't know."

He laughed. "Lame argument, woman. Look, I understand your concern about my money. I used to think the way you do, before I got wealthy. Money is just money. Doesn't make the person who they are. Just gives you more security. And this place. Yes, it's large and grand, blah, blah, blah, it's just a big house. Elizabeth wanted— oh, hell, I did too—wanted this big thing. But as it turns out, the place is just a big pile of wood and stucco and brick. Filled with crap. Well, there's one thing that isn't crap and I want to show it to you. Come on."

He got out of the car and she followed. The cold night air chilled her.

Rex came around the back of the car and gestured towards an enormous set of carved dark wood double-doors.

She stopped him. "Wait, before you got all this wealth? You weren't born into this?"

"God, no. Cynthia, go in, you're freezing in that t-shirt."

She walked with him to the double doors and he opened one side for her.

She stepped into a vast, domed entry hall that had to be three stories high. A magnificent mahogany staircase circled upwards. A round stained-glass window in a fleur-de-lys pattern crowned the dome. Nice and warm inside. Her chill eased.

He followed her inside and closed the door. "My parents, well, mother, was dirt poor. After my father ran out on us, she worked herself to death cleaning houses. She died from cancer when I was ten. Had to go live with my asshole father. That was a touch of hell. My uncle always told me if I'd been rich, I could have saved my ma. So I got rich."

"Is that why you changed your name?" she asked, her voice echoing off the marble floor in the large hallway.

"Yes. I wanted to rid myself of anything to do with my father. And my past. Follow me."

He walked across the entry hall and through an arched doorway leading to a huge, mahogany-paneled room with giant picture windows that overlooked a patio and pool. Orange-tinted, brightly lit fog probably obscured a gorgeous view of the City.

The place made her feel so small and so poor. She'd never even met anyone with his kind of wealth before. Intimidating. She'd played up the disparity in their incomes as an excuse for why their relationship wouldn't work, but there was truth to her argument. This opulence was an ugly mirror. Compared to this man, she was a total loser.

Cynthia followed him across the intricately inlaid hardwood floor, past a polished runway-sized dinner table. Ahh, the formal dining room. Jeez, the whole of Jon's apartment would fit inside. Maybe even two of his apartments.

Place smelled of lemon furniture polish and lilies. A huge bouquet of fresh flowers sat on a buffet lining one wall. The room was so clean, you could probably eat off any surface.

Rex led her over to a corner of the room and stopped. "Ran away at sixteen, worked my way through college, met the right people and thankfully, had some good luck picking businesses. I started the venture capital thing when we got Kelly and did well. Right around then, I found this in a gallery."

Cynthia gasped. She hadn't even noticed the sculpture of intertwined lovers until that very moment. It was *Love Unlimited*, one of the best pieces she'd ever created. One of the few in bronze. When she could afford to work in bronze.

It was like seeing a long lost friend. A family member. Tears stung her eyes. Longing welled in her heart and constricted her throat. She sighed and moved forward to touch it. The female was pregnant. The male kissed her passionately while resting a loving hand on her swollen belly.

Rex grinned at her reaction. "I fell in love with it on sight. I wanted to buy more of your sculptures, but by the time I went back, they were all gone. What happened to you? Is that when you found out your husband was gay?"

She swallowed a sob. "Yeah. Sorry, getting emotional again. I— I've missed this piece," she said, running her hand along the back of the male figure. Cool to the touch, it brought back her past. The light coming in the high windows of her studio. Jon bringing her in a hot cup of tea. The feel of the baby moving inside her. "I never really wanted to sell it. I wondered who'd ended up with it. God, it's so wonderful to see this again."

The female's color looked different than the rest of the piece. The patina had worn off, especially on her belly, it was just down to the bronze. "What happened here?" she asked, inspecting the sculpture closely.

She looked to Rex for the answer.

He reddened and coughed. "Well, I, uh, kind of rubbed it off." He shrugged with an adorable smile on his rugged face.

She laughed. "No worries, you loved the patina off. That's fine. I made this to be pleasant to the touch. I love the tactile quality, too. God, I love this thing. This piece…oh, I'm glad you have it. I—I was feeling so good. I was pregnant, I was happy, fulfilled, my whole life in front of me. This represented pure joy. Me and Jon and our child and a future of artwork and joy."

"Didn't turn out that way, huh?"

"I was ten months pregnant, came home from the store and found Jon in bed with Reverend Gary."

Rex's mouth dropped open and his eyes dilated. "No, what did you do?"

"My water broke. And I rushed to the—"

What are you doing? You are about to tell him about your daughter! Shut up!

Cynthia was so caught up in the story and the emotion and seeing the sculpture and all it brought back to her, she couldn't change thought trains. She couldn't think of what to say.

Lie, damn you, lie!

Rex put his hand on her shoulder. "Did you raise your child alone then?"

The words tumbled out. "No, I lost her."

His face fell, he reached out and swept her up in his arms. "I'm so sorry, Cynthia."

The sudden comfort of his big strong arms, his warmth, kindness and caring, tipped her over the edge. Tears flowed down her cheeks and she sobbed quietly.

He tightened his grip on her and rocked her gently, kissing the side of her head. "It's all right, Cynthia. I'm here."

"I know, that's why I'm crying," she blubbered.

Oh, great, why don't you tell him everything, you idiot? You have to get out of here! Pull away! Run away! He's blasting past your defenses! Do you want to be in a relationship with your daughter's adopted father?

Well, if he never found out, would it matter? If Kelly never knew? She could keep a secret.

But Jon couldn't.

She'd glue his lips shut. With super glue.

She forced herself to calm and pulled away, but couldn't let go of him. When she looked up into his sympathetic gaze, she got caught in a force field. Hypnotized by the caring in his eyes, his sweet soft expression, his presence, she couldn't do anything but stare up at him, her mind a near blank.

He leaned in and kissed her. Ka-pow! Her brain went off-line. Pure emotion, pure power, pure exhilaration. Nirvana.

Her feet hummed with energy. Power zapped up and down her body. She wanted to eat him alive.

This couldn't continue, though. She couldn't do this to him. The truth would eventually come out, and then where would she be? All roads led to losing him.

She pulled away. He ran his hand down the side of her face in a tender gesture, sending shockwaves of conflicting emotions rocketing through her. "Don't be sad, Cynthia. Don't worry about hurting me. The only way you could do that would be to run away from me. We have something special here. And if you trust me, I can make sure nothing bad ever happens to you again."

His words twisted her heart. Pain tore through her chest. All she wanted was a guy like this. And if life had taught her one thing, it was that she'd never have this kind of man. She looked down and fumbled for a reply. "They will hurt you."

"No, they won't, I won't let them," he replied, confident.

She met his gaze. Warring emotions ravaged her. She had to get rid of him, but she was weakening. His rock solid stance, the proud way he held his shoulders, the surety of his gaze, assaulted her resolve. Her concrete foundation reduced to Swiss cheese.

She coughed to put some distance between them. Didn't work. "You can't understand the depth of their desperation, their greed. They will stop at nothing to hurt me." She pushed away from him, but Rex wouldn't let go of her hand. "I'm sure my nephew saw me get in your car. Hopefully, if I leave today and you never see me again, they won't come after you. Because if they even get a hint you like me, they'll sight in on you like some heat-seeking, money-extracting missiles and destroy your life."

He squeezed her hand and pulled her in tight. He ran his hand down her shoulder. She fought to keep from melting into him.

"I'm in a different world than you. Money buys a lot of power. You had no money to fight them."

She couldn't take his intensity and the truth of his words. She looked down at her sculpture. "You don't want to play with these people."

"You need someone powerful on your side, Cynthia." He took her by the hand, held it, and looked at it.

She checked his face. Complex emotions flitted across his carved countenance. So intense.

His gaze lifted to hers. "Are you going to let me be that person? Or are you going to run again?"

The vulnerability behind his eyes blasted her heart wide open. There was no pretense here. He was offering himself to her.

She gripped his hand, closed her eyes and took in a deep breath. She opened them and stared down at their clasped hands. "There isn't even one little part of me that wants to run, Rex. I'm in love with you—oh, shit, that was supposed to stay in my head." She looked up for his reaction in time to see him coming in for a kiss.

She should have pushed him and run. But she didn't. She tilted her head and accepted the kiss.

All thoughts were obliterated. Her heart swelled so much, it hurt. The room whirled. He held her tighter and his kiss deepened.

She collapsed into him. A hunger overtook her, a core deep hunger. She hadn't known she was starving until that moment. In his arms—his intense energy enveloping her—she fed on him, his caring, his love.

Asylum. Heavenly asylum. All those months and years of being alone. Having to be stoic. In the trenches, enduring blanketbomb after blanketbomb of demands and abuse from people who didn't love her.

Finally, in this man's arms, she wasn't alone any longer. Someone was there for her. Not just physically, but emotionally, mentally, psychically. He reached inside her with his kindness and touched her soul.

Her mind filled with him; this gentle, kind giant. She felt so protected, so cared for. Aside from the lust firing her sex into kiln-like temperatures, she wanted to be with him to be close to him. She wanted nothing between them. She wanted to feel his heart next to hers.

He ended the kiss. A few tears rolled down her cheeks. He brushed them aside. Sliding his fingers down her cheek, he kissed her again.

Something shifted inside her. Her past vanished. There was only Rex. *Hadn't he always been there?*

Gravity and other laws of nature no longer applied. She felt sixty pounds lighter. Her body buzzed, vibrating with intense energy. The room seemed to glow bright with yellow light.

He pulled away and took her hand in his. Without a word, he led her out of the dining room, through the entry hall and up the staircase.

Her vision foggy, her sex swelled with want, she couldn't wait to get her hands on him.

As she followed him down a long hallway towards a set of double-doors, some part of her realized that she was about to have sex. Her stomach fluttered wildly. Anticipation gripped her and her legs got shaky. She turned a bit more attention to her feet. No way did she want anything to ruin this moment. Especially not a face plant into the ivory-carpeted hallway.

It had been five years! Was he going to find a bunch of cobwebs? And what about birth control? She didn't need it for pregnancy protection, but they both had sexual histories. Hopefully, he had condoms.

He turned and looked at her, all her thoughts, except for thoughts of him, disappeared.

He opened one side of the double-doors and gestured for her to go inside. The master suite was magnificent, dark wood paneling, understated and refined. Simple furnishings in mahogany were upholstered in dark blue and cream satin.

The king sized bed was turned down, revealing cream-colored brocade satin sheets.

He stopped her at the foot of the bed and took her in his arms. He leaned down and gently kissed her. His heady male scent and the warmth of his lips made her clit and nipples buzz. He took her face in his large hands. The heat and energy from his palms flamed her skin.

All at once she attacked him. Frantically tearing at his clothes and her own, she had them both naked in seconds. He laughed at her exuberance. When she saw his proudly erect cock, she gasped. Beautiful. Ramrod straight, flesh-covered steel.

God, she wanted him inside her.

She pushed him down on the bed and kissed him briefly, then feasted upon his nakedness with her eyes and hands. The guy was in his fifties, but his body was in its early thirties. She stroked the silky skin of his bare chest, then bent down and took his nipple into her mouth and spun her tongue around the tip.

He yelped, laughed and pushed her back. Shifting places, he pressed her against the softness of his down comforter.

A huge grin on his lusty face, he said, "Man, that tickled."

She giggled. "No one's ever done that to you?"

He shook his head. Eying a breast like it was a chocolate éclair, he gently took it in one hand and pressed a light kiss on the tip of her nipple.

She squealed and writhed under his touch, reaching down to pleasure herself. Her clit throbbing, the hungry ache inside her grew stronger.

He suckled at her breast and massaged it gently. She arched her body, delighting in the feel of his dexterous tongue on her nipple and his smooth, supple fingers on her skin.

He brushed her hand away from her sex and his fingers gently explored her soft folds.

Groaning, her head swam. Biting the back of a knuckle, she thrust her other hand through his soft mane of hair, gripping his head. He made a deep sound from within his throat, heightening her lust. Covering his teeth with his lips, he bit down on her nipple while simultaneously easing a finger inside her.

She cried out and spread her legs for him. "Oh, my God, Rex that feels so good!"

"Feels good to me too," he said against her breast.

He slipped his finger in all the way to the hilt. Shivers of delight raced through her and she took in a deep breath. Sliding it back out, he went in again. She curled her toes and exhaled so fast she got lightheaded, fueling the ecstasy. She rode the wave of sensations, bringing her higher and closer to coming.

"You're fun," he said, his voice thick.

Kissing his way down her body, every place his lips touched her sent shockwaves through her, increasing the rapture. He removed his finger to stroke her inner thighs. She further opened to him, and he took his time running his hands over her hard muscles, his hungry gaze on her soft triangle of hair.

All at once, he moved down between her legs, parted her and flicked his tongue over her engorged clit.

"Oh!" she cried out, the intensity overwhelming her. She bucked against him, nearly throwing him off. "Sorry. It's been a long time."

He grinned from between her thighs. "Thrash away, baby. I can ride you."

Taking her hips in his hands, he held her to the mattress and lightly licked her swollen nub. Delicious sensations rocked her sex. She scissored his head and pounded the mattress with her fists. Almost too much to take.

"God, that's intense, but don't stop. Don't stop!"

Slowly, carefully, he teased a rhythm on her clit. She'd never felt anything so wonderful in her life.

Grabbing the bedsheets in both hands, she fought to stave off the orgasm. "Rex, oh, God what you're doing to me! So good. So amazing. Want to come. Want to *come*…Not going to let myself. Not going to give in. Oh, God!"

His rhythm increased. Circling her nexus with the tip of his tongue, he lightly licked just the very center. She writhed, wanting away from his tongue, but not being able to stand parting from it. The thirst for climax overtook her.

Her mind and clit exploded. Bright colors streaked her vision. Screaming and grinding her sex into his mouth while holding his head, she jerked and thrashed, the orgasm powering through her, lasting longer than anything she'd ever experienced. Wave after wave blasted her, making her sex spasm and contract. Feasting on the release, Cynthia delighted in her orgasm. Luxuriated in it. Rex stayed with her, reading her body and adjusting accordingly. He didn't miss his mark once.

Finally, as she began to come down, Rex moved from between her legs. Wrapping his long arms around her thighs, he kissed her belly below her navel. Nuzzling her, he moaned. "God, you're amazing."

She fought to get breath back in her lungs.

Releasing her, he sat up, turned and swung his legs off the bed. Opening a bedside drawer, he withdrew a small foil packet.

He glanced back at her body, a hungry, territorial edge to his dark gaze. He slipped on the condom. A commanding set to his strong jaw, he gave her a brief nod. "You're mine, woman."

Rendering her speechless with desire. Her starving need boomeranged back, her wet and ready sex cried out for him.

With a deadly serious expression, he climbed on top. His hard chest above her, his dark gaze penetrating hers, she gasped as he slid inside.

He took it slowly, examining her face carefully for her reaction. All at once, he found her g-spot. Spasms of wild joy echoed through her, launching her right back to the edge of orgasm.

Shocking her. It had never been this way before. With anyone. Magic. His dick was magic. A special passkey that opened the secret gates to her libido.

Three strokes in and she catapulted into a thunderous climax. Bellowing at the top of her lungs, she grabbed his ass, pulled him tightly to her and thrashed against him. She gloried in the feel of his cock inside her, joyfully crying out, "Feels so good! Yeah, yeah! God, Rex, yes!"

He growled, thrusting into her even harder.

She blasted into a series of hellacious orgasms, like a succession of cannons firing through her body. With every stroke, she came so hard, she screamed until her throat gave out. She went at him like a wild woman. Pounding on his chest and thrashing like a crazed animal, she wanted to eat him alive. Primal, bestial. She couldn't get enough of him.

He grabbed her flailing wrists, pinned them above her head and powered into her, sending her even further out into the stratosphere. Images flashed at her as her sex and clit throbbed: his face, his blue gaze, his cock, his pumped chest. She screamed, lost in one, long, momentous, world-shattering orgasm.

His pace grew frantic. She moaned louder and launched into a massive climax. Felt like her world blew apart. The rapture consumed her.

His body jerked, he threw his head back and yelled. Their two voices blended into one long deafening cry.

He continued to thrust into her, his pace slowing. Her body shuddered with its last throes. She squeezed around him, savoring every last bit of pleasure.

Breathing hard, he withdrew and collapsed next to her.

Her vision obscured by lack of oxygen, the room raced around her like she was on a merry-go-round. Slowly, her brain cleared. The warm afterglow of sex radiated through her loins.

She hadn't felt this satisfied in years. Come to think of it, maybe never. She relaxed against the bed, luxuriating in the heady buzz. Her body tingling, she stretched and sighed happily.

She started to laugh. "Holy God, that was—wow. Spectacular."

Chuckling, he rolled up on an elbow and kissed her. A nice, long, sweaty one. He tasted of her sex and his cologne, an intoxicating combination. His expert tongue teased hers, thoroughly exploring her mouth. She crossed her legs and moved her hips as little echoes of joy pulsated through her clit and womb.

He pulled away and gazed down her breasts and crotch. "That was the most fun and the best sex I've ever had." He shot her a quick grin and stroked her belly lazily. "Damn, woman. I knew you'd be hot, but not this scorching. This body…" He leaned down and lightly bit her stomach.

She giggled and pushed on his head.

Grinning, he said, "I love this body. I could fuck you all day and all night. And then eat you and fuck you some more. I can't get enough of you."

She pulled him up to embrace him. His slick skin next to hers felt delicious.

Pulling away, she nestled into his side and wrapped an arm around his lean belly.

"Ditto, bud. You rock. This…" she took hold of his flaccid member. It came back to life instantly. "Tool of yours is magic."

"Watch it, it could go off. God, that feels so good. I will do you again, lady. But I need a bit of a break."

"By all means, take your time. Doesn't mean I'm not gonna play with you until then."

He gave a low chuckle. "You keep doing that, I'll never let you leave here."

"Looks like I'm staying awhile."

She moved up onto an elbow and toyed with the hair around his base, then lightly cupped his balls. He curled his toes.

Unable to resist, she licked the head of his cock. He got stiffer. Taking him in her mouth, she tasted the salt of his cum, a bit of latex taste from the condom, but mostly she tasted him.

Spinning her tongue around the head, she deep-throated him a few times, locking her lips around his shaft.

Groaning, he ground his hips upwards. She gently massaged the softness of his balls.

Working him up and down, she breathed in his scent, felt the warmth of him in her mouth and under her touch. What a man.

With a gentle push on her forehead, he disengaged her. "I'm going to come again, which is mind-blowing, but I'm not wasting an orgasm on your mouth. My man wants to come inside you. Come here," he said, pulling her up into an embrace. "Plenty of time for that later."

He kissed her deeply, running his hands down her back to cup her ass. Groaning deep in his throat, he said into her mouth, "The most perfect ass in the universe."

She pulled away to grin down at him. "Since I'm lying on top of you, I can't grab yours. But I've thought the same thing since I met you. I thought your body looked like a Roman statue. I called you The Roman God."

He laughed and hugged her. "My name for you was The Amazon Goddess."

"Really?"

"Yes." His attention went to her mouth and he kissed her. Soft, sweet, lazy. He pulled away, his gaze sparkling with lust and admiration. "Amazing how much we have in common."

"Perfect asses and similar nicknames. It's a start." Thankfully, the comeback had come out first. She had to bite back her third addition to the list: *Kelly*.

He wrinkled his brow slightly at her fallen expression. He kissed her on the cheek and hugged her. "Don't worry, Cynthia. Nothing will drive us apart."

A mountain of ugly truths threatened to destroy the moment. She buried her face in his chest and willed the bad thoughts away.

She didn't have much time left. Her Shield of Denial had a time limit. And it was just about up.

Chapter Fourteen

Rex's entire body tingled. He nibbled on Cynthia's earlobe, she giggled and nuzzled back against him.

In his arms, Cynthia locked into place like she'd always been there. He felt whole again.

He'd never fallen for anyone so fast, so completely. So utterly.

He tried to remember if it had been this way with Elizabeth. With anyone.

Not this driving hunger, this blind passion. He wanted Cynthia in his arms, her nakedness pressed against him forever.

He kissed along her neck. She made soft pleasure noises, giving him goosebumps. Her scent made him crazy: a mixture of sex, flowers and something that was only hers.

He nuzzled behind her ear. She chuckled and kissed his shoulder. Such a perfect playmate.

He had to stop himself from proposing right there on the spot. Had to be careful not to scare her. She'd run from him plenty already. He needed to take things slow with her. She spooked easily. Been too hurt in the past. Or something.

She still had secrets she was keeping from him. It was clear in the car and just now. The pain in her hazel gaze. A haunted quality behind her eyes. The inability to look at him at times. All signs of evasion. Yeah, and that cock-and-bull story about those stepsisters.

Some of it seemed truthful. He just couldn't tell which parts. Didn't sound like anyone had been in her corner for years. He wanted to kill whoever had hurt her. Whoever made her this distrustful.

Still, to take care of her properly, he needed all the information on her. He'd have an investigation done on her, a thorough one. He'd never let her know it. He'd keep the information to himself and pretend to be surprised when she finally told him.

Eventually she'd come clean with him. She'd just met him, he didn't blame her for being cautious. Soon, she'd see how constant he was, how reliable, how trustworthy.

And in the process of winning her trust, he'd make love to her from one end of the house to the other.

She was the next Mrs. Du Charmante. He was sure of it. He sighed with ultimate satisfaction and happiness. He hadn't felt this good since he sold WatchMe.com to Microsoft.

She shifted in his arms so she could look at him.

His kissed her nose. "What?"

She chuckled. "Didn't you hear that?"

"No, what?"

"My stomach growling."

"No, my mind was on…" He cupped a breast and kissed her cheek. "Other things."

She rubbed her face into his and bit his neck lightly. "Oh, God, I can't get enough of you. No, wait. Before I jump you again, really, I need some food. I haven't eaten since, damn, four or five and it's eleven-thirty."

"Um, wow. Suppose we could call out for something. Servants are all gone for the evening."

Cynthia burst out in delighted laughter. "You are so funny." She sat up, made a serious face and assumed a straight-shouldered pose. "Well, there's no way to eat if the servants aren't around," she mocked in a deep tone. She giggled. "I assume you have raw ingredients in the kitchen."

He chuckled and pulled her into his arms. "Sorry. I sound helpless, don't I?"

"Incredibly."

"Well—and I hate to admit this—I am where food is concerned. Completely dependent on others to feed me. Cooked ramen in college, but mainly ate in the cafeteria or had girlfriends feed me. I've always been useless in the kitchen."

"Well, you're damn lucky I'm here." She nodded towards the door. "Let's go check out what's in the fridge."

He kissed the side of her head, breathing in the arousing aroma of her hair. "You got it. I could use a nice glass of wine and a snack."

"I need to fortify you so I can take advantage of you again." She sent him a wicked little grin.

He got hard fast, his cock pressing against her firm hip.

She reached down, grabbed him and shot him a hungry stare. "A hard man is good to find."

Her hand felt so amazing pressed around him, he wished they never had to leave that bed. "Oh, God, lady. I feel like a teenager. Can't remember the last time I made love more than once in an evening."

"Really? Not with your wife, even?"

A small storm of memories clouded his mind. Stinging pain. That familiar ache. Disappointment. Emasculation.

Elizabeth naked in bed. Not reacting at all like Cynthia. Had she ever? Not that he was angry with her, just sad. All that joy she denied herself. And him. Maybe they were just ill matched.

Not so with this one. Cynthia was pure dynamite. "No. Elizabeth…"

She stroked his arm. "I'm sorry, I didn't mean to bring up a painful subject."

"No, it's not painful, really. We just drifted apart over the last ten years of our relationship. Rarely had sex. Quick when we did. She didn't like to, uh, linger."

To put it mildly. Had she even come in recent years? Felt it was her duty, that's for sure. Early on, that part of their life had been good. But not this good. Ever. Elizabeth never let herself go. She always had polite orgasms. Not the feral mind-blowing variety that Cynthia enjoyed.

Hit the gold mine with this woman. He'd never let her go.

She hugged him hard. "I feel sorry for the both of you."

He sighed deeply and ran his hands down her body and squeezed her superior ass. His cock roared to life. "I'm just glad I found you."

Even though he wanted to climb on top and ram inside her, he forced himself to play the gentleman. *Food now, more sex later.*

He kissed her on the neck, then sat up. "Let's get some food."

Rex gave her his extra robe, which wasn't as ridiculously large as he thought it might be on her. A shorty robe on him, it went to her calves. Her luscious gorgeous naked calves. He hoped the food prep wouldn't take long, he had no idea how long he could hold himself back.

On the way to the kitchen, she gawked at everything and made enthusiastic observations about the architecture of the house, the artwork on the walls, and the furnishings. It was fun to see his house through new eyes. His friends were all richer or jaded, no one commented or gazed at his home with such awe.

When he turned on the light for the kitchen, she gasped. "Amazing! Look at this kitchen! It's a goddamned restaurant kitchen. Oooo, the stove, a bloody industrial Viking range. Looky at the fridges with the glassed in fronts, come on! My God, I feel like I'm in a grocery store. Uh, yeah, you have food. Damn, are you having a huge party or something? Who are they feeding?" She turned to him. "I thought you lived alone."

"I do. But I have businesspeople here frequently with little notice. And Kelly was living here until just two weeks ago. With the wedding and all—she had the shower here—I guess Helga likes to be prepared."

Cynthia laughed and turned back to the fridge, her eyes feasting on all the offerings behind the glass. "Yeah, she's prepared all right. For the Apocalypse. Doomsday. Well, I know where I want to stay in an earthquake. Damn, you'd ride out the disaster in style. I don't think Jon has had more than two things in his fridge at any one time. Mustard and champagne, pretty much. Well, since I moved in and we're broke, we've been cooking more. But this—wow. What a paradise. Brie. Okay, need some of that. Look at those strawberries!" A sudden sheepish look came over her face. "Am I just being a total dork or what? 'Ooo, look at the architecture, ooo, look at the food.' You probably think I'm an idiot."

Her bubbly energy warmed him to the cellular level. He smiled so hard, his face hurt. "No, I think you're adorable. Nice to be around someone who doesn't take this for granted. You make me realize how blessed I am. My friends have much more grand places. I always feel like their poor relation."

Her eyes widened and her head jerked back. "You're kidding me. This place?"

He gave a slight shrug and gestured towards the room. "You lose your objectivity when you get surrounded by luxury. And you have no cause to apologize. I love your spontaneity and exuberance. It's so natural and you're so much freer than I am. I don't know, I used to be a joker. I liked to play and have fun. Now I only do that on my boat."

She opened the doors to the fridge and grabbed the strawberries. "That's right. You said something about a yacht after you got hit by the car. You were going to take me for a ride on it." She put the strawberries on the granite-topped island, next to the double stainless steel sinks and returned to the fridge.

He took a seat on one of two leather-upholstered stools at end of the island. "I still am."

She fished around in the refrigerator. "Cool, I love boats."

"You'll love mine. Has this wonderful cabin." An image of her naked on the cabin's bed flashed in his mind. Her lips slightly parted. Her eyes, hungry and lazy-lidded.

He got up, walked over to her and shut the fridge door. Turning her towards him, he brought her close. He ran his hands down her firm body, her sexy curves felt delicious under his touch. His cock came to life again.

She moaned and pressed her length against him.

Her gaze, dark with desire, hypnotized him. "Yeah? What will you do to me there?"

A charge went through his body and his penis went diamond-hard. Took all his strength to resist the urge to fling her up on the island and enter her.

Calm down, man, you have all evening. Seduce her. Play with her. Tease her.

"First, I'll do this." He covered her lips with his and drove his tongue deep inside. She twisted hers around his playfully and ground her hips against him.

The pressure on his dick, the taste of her and her softness played riot with his resolve. Every neuron of his body wanted to be inside her. Pound into her until she threw her head back and screamed with delight.

He pushed off her robe and ran his hands greedily over her soft skin. She moaned deep in her throat and grabbed his ass, hard.

A charge of lust pulsed through his cock. Big and hungry, he began to ache.

Why the hell not?

He picked her up and set her on the tall counter at the end of the island, just the perfect height off the floor. She opened her legs and wrapped them around his waist, grabbing his shoulders for support.

With one easy thrust he was inside her welcoming wet softness. She gasped when he hit his target, then threw her head back and laughed with pure exhilaration—his fantasy becoming reality. He nearly swooned from lust.

Grabbing her ass with both hands, he ploughed into her, growling in a guttural snarl at the sensation of her tight, slick lips pressed around him.

Crying out in a loud moan, she dug her fingers into his shoulders and thrust her hips against him.

He couldn't fuck her hard enough or fast enough or deep enough. He took in her full breasts, her red mouth open in tortured pleasure, and her dark lashes against her cheeks.

"God, yeah! Deeper! Deeper!"

Her words whipped his need into a frenzy. Lifting her off the counter and high into his arms, he thrust up into her with everything he had. He wanted to own her, command her. Take the whole of her for himself. The feel of her. The sight of her. The taste of her. All for him. All his.

All at once, she screamed and her pussy throbbed around him. Thrusting hard and fast, he drove into her, his pulse pounding in his ears.

Adjusting her, he kept his pace fast and went even deeper. She screamed and contracted again, seeming like she came even harder. Her face flushed, her lips swollen, her mouth open wide in a yell, Cynthia was amazingly beautiful when she came. So hot. So fully committed to her pleasure, it made him horny just to watch her.

As much as he'd like to, he realized he wasn't going to come again, not right then. He eased off and she collapsed in his arms. Kissing the side of her face, he withdrew and set her gently on the floor. She wobbled a bit, but he held onto her fast. She seemed overcome. Made him feel like a superstar. A lovemaking superstar. Don Juan of Nob Hill. Like he could conquer the world.

She gazed up at him, her eyes dilated, and kissed him. Gently, sweetly, then hard. She moaned and ended the kiss. "Jeez, I'm ready to go again and I can barely stand up. My God, man, you are one hot number. Holy hell that was fun."

She shivered, he pulled her closer and hugged her. "More fun than I've had in years and years. We've got to get your robe or you'll freeze." He dipped down, picked up her robe off the floor and wrapped it around her. "We'll get you all warm."

"That's what I'm afraid of."

He laughed. Her hazel eyes sparkling, her hair slightly mussed, she felt so good against him. He wanted to carry her around in a specially built sling with a hole cut out so he could be inside her always.

She was so pretty! Her skin, lined appropriately for her age, glowed. She felt so soft to his touch. He kissed her perfectly straight nose and bestowed light kisses on her high cheekbones. Nibbling on the ridge of her square-ish jaw, he moved to a cute little mole next to her mouth and licked it. His cock surged.

She giggled and moved some dark hair off her sweaty brow. "Jeez, I thought I was hungry before, now I'm starving."

He rubbed his dick against her. The feel of her bare skin sent a charge through him. He closed his eyes for a moment in pure bliss.

She pushed against his bare chest. "Okay, I'm going to make us some food."

Reluctantly, he let her go. "I'll open a bottle of wine. Yes, a Chardonnay. Wait, what are you going to fix?"

"Um, first starting off with some Brie, crackers and strawberries. Then I'm going to make an omelet."

"Champagne, then. That will be perfect."

Humming to himself, he went to the beverage refrigerator under the bar and chose a bottle of Cristal. "I've been waiting for an occasion to open this. Some investment group that was trying to court me a few months ago, gave it to me."

"I've never had Cristal. I'm gonna feel like Puff Daddy here."

"Sans the penis and recording contract."

She laughed.

Man, how he loved the sound of her laughter. She had the most adorable laugh. Not high and fake, it came from deep in her belly. She honestly enjoyed her life. She responded freely. Didn't take the time to think if the reaction was appropriate, didn't hold herself back, just let loose with what she felt. Like Kelly.

She bit the end off a strawberry and chewed. "So why does Cristal cost so much?"

Shrugging, he said, "God knows, tastes the same as some cheap stuff I've had. All about the bottle, I guess, and the brand." He searched through the drawers of the bar for a proper towel. "See, the problem is, you have all this money and once you get the basics—the house, the food, the car—you don't really need anything else. It's a real letdown. You want to spend your money, but you can't eat that much or drink that much. So, you progressively buy more expensive crap."

Rex withdrew a towel and shut the drawer with his hip.

"Never had that problem." She gave a nod at the bowl of strawberries, and headed back to the fridge.

That was a stupid thing to say, you idiot. Money was a sore spot with her. "Sorry."

She waved her hand dismissively. "Don't be. I'm not actually jealous. There's been this weird freedom aspect to my misfortune. I don't have any debt. And I don't have any assets. I have nothing. Kinda frees you. When I had my house, damn, what a time sink. I spent so much time taking care of it, I didn't spend a lot of time enjoying it."

He relaxed. She was so understanding. How could he not love this woman?

He placed the bottle of champagne on the Spanish-tiled bar and draped the towel over his arm. "I hear you. Just sold a jet, three boats and five houses because I was spending more time managing the assets rather than enjoying them. Besides, it's all shite." He worked on untwisting the wires holding the cork in place. "I'd give it all up for a good woman and a nice home and a dog and a fireplace with some logs burning in it. You laughed when you saw this house, well, that's because it's too much house."

Hovering over a plate with a wheel of Brie on it, she pointed at him with the knife. "No, it's not. Don't listen to me. I love this house. It's cool, it's you, Art Deco, fantastic architecture. You appreciate your good fortune. Nothing wrong with owning stuff. I just wouldn't want the hassle. Of course, all I want to do is my art. I'd give anything just to have my own studio, nice stereo, good lighting. Microwave and a beer fridge. I'd never leave," she said, slicing off a piece of cheese. "I could work and eat and drink and work and—oh, yeah, need a Lazyboy in there, too. To sit and ponder the work. Pondering is a big part of doing art."

"Yeah, I need to spend more time at it."

She ate a bite of cheese. "At what?"

"At painting. I paint."

"You do art?" she asked with a glance at him.

"Yeah, I paint."

Knife in mid-air, her mouth open, her eyes wide, she turned all the way towards him. "You *paint*?"

He laughed. "You look very shocked."

"Well, you just…" she said, gesturing towards him with the knife, "I had this idea of who you were and—yes, I am. What do you paint? What style? What medium?"

"Oils, expressionist abstracts, mainly."

She burst into a huge, happy smile. "Oh, my God, how cool is that? Wow, so you get it. You get me."

Such enthusiasm! With every word out of her mouth, he fell harder.

He grinned back at her. "You bet. Only my need for money came before my need for art. I think that's changing." With a tug on the cork, it popped off in his hand. Thankfully, the champagne didn't overflow.

She shot him a lovely grin. "Good for you. So where are your paintings? When can I see them?"

A warm glow started in his belly and quickly swept through him. She might actually appreciate his work. How great would that be? "Later, I'll show you my studio."

"I can't wait."

"I don't have the formal training you do. Took some classes. I mean, it's not that great."

She made a face at him. "Oh, pshaw. Rex, whatever you do, you do well."

"Reserve that opinion until after you've seen it."

"I'm sure it's great. That's so awesome. We're both artists. Man, I can't wait to get back to it. Necessity got in my way. I did some work while I took care of Dad and Endora, but not much. Too busy."

He withdrew two flutes from a cabinet over the bar. "Endora was not her name."

Fury flashed in her gaze and her jaw clenched. She grabbed a baguette and began slicing it with a bit too much vigor. "No, it's not. Her name was Agnes. Fucking bitch. Sorry, I need to let go of all that, but man, she roasted me. The gift that keeps on giving. Unforgivable leaving me with Sissy and Belinda. And the Spawn of Satan, Troy. I don't want to think about that. I am going to think about food."

He stopped pouring champagne to make eye contact. The pain on her face made him want to shoot her parents and stepsisters. "I want to help you get rid of them."

She grimaced. "Murder would be great, if I didn't have morals. No, Sissy's living in her own hell. I hate her, but I understand her, too. Not that it makes it any easier to take her crap. See, her father raped both her and her sister, went to jail for it, then got killed by the other inmates for being a pedophile. My father took in a very wounded woman and two damaged adolescents."

Rex stared at her, fighting the urge to shudder. "Yikes."

She continued slicing the bread. "Yeah. Well, I wasn't that damaged and I got this success early on—touted as some prodigy— and it just tweaked them. Endora was actually nice to me at first.

Loved my talent. Paraded me around as her daughter. That's when Dad insisted I stop calling her stepmother and made me call her Mom. Which she loved and I hated. And was also just more abuse to the Gruesome Twosome. Plus Endora was jealous of her girls because of the attention they got from their father, if you can believe that."

A wave of nausea roiled his gut. "Are you kidding?"

"I wish."

"Jesus. Horrible."

"Tell me about it. The whole reason Endora turned in her husband to the police was not to protect her girls, it was to separate them. She honestly thought the girls had seduced him. Oh, God, the screaming matches and what she said to those girls. So their whole lives became about destroying me and getting even with their mother. Hardcore, those girls are hardcore." She sighed and rubbed her forehead with the butt of her hand to avoid rubbing food on it.

And he thought his childhood was ugly. "Wait. I thought you said your step-mother hated you."

"Yeah." Her gaze clouded and Cynthia aged ten years. "Things changed when I was seventeen."

That look on her face said it all. His gut wrenched. He wished he'd kept his big trap shut. "Forget it, I didn't mean—"

"No, it's okay." She shrugged, but the pain lines on her face remained.

He'd give anything to wipe them away.

She took the sliced bread and began to arrange it on a plate. "See, I didn't make it into this very prestigious art college that would have launched my career and advanced my art. Horrible. That was my out. My way out. But anyway, when I got the rejection letter, everything went to hell. I was now a failure, so Endora turned on me —and I mean *turned on me*—and began fawning all over her girls. My senior year in high school was the worst of my life. Moved out on my eighteenth birthday. Got a job at a gas station and worked my way through college. That's when I met Jon." She put the bread plate on the counter at the end of the island.

Damn, this woman was strong. Unimaginable how she'd suffered. And throughout her trials, she kept her head held high. This was a worthy woman. Someone he could count on. Someone like him.

She turned back to grab a last piece of bread, her robe parted slightly and he got a great shot of her full rounded breasts. Milky white, smooth soft skin, pink nipples. Damn, he couldn't wait to be inside her again. What a perfect match for him.

She walked over the fridge and scanned the shelves. "Three years into our relationship, Jon helped me rebuild my studio and I got those new pieces done, including yours. Jon really encouraged me. Got me back on my feet. A gallery I'd sold to at sixteen accepted the new works. It was a miracle. I got another article, the buzz started again and then everything blew up." Her shoulders slumped, her gaze turned tired and she let out a long sigh. "I've gone back to it over the years. Did some woodcarving. Haven't touched clay in God-knows-how-long. I'm going to get back to it as soon as I get my license and have some cash. Well, once I get rid of the Gorgon Sisters. At this point, I'm ready to change my name and move to another state."

He squared his shoulders and stood tall. "You'll do neither. I'll protect you. I can and I will."

She turned to him, her eyes twinkled and a grin spread wide on her sweet face. "Ooo, you got me all turned on again. Forceful, aren't you?"

He wanted to leap across the counter, throw her to the floor and pump her into next week. He gave her a sharp nod. "Damn straight. Especially when I see an injustice. You need your sculptures and a studio. I'll make sure they never bother you again. Just give me the word."

"We'll talk. Right now, I'm laying low." She returned to the island, grabbed the strainer of strawberries and rinsed them under the tap.

He pictured her screaming her lungs out, pounding her fist on top of that black sedan. "Does laying low entail chasing people and yelling at them?"

Her face flushed and she chuckled, but her smile faded quickly. "Touché. I don't know. Let's just put it this way, I can't deal with it right now. I need to pass that test, get a nursing license, get a job and move out of Jon's. I need to be on my own. I'm used to taking care of myself. Being dependent on him is killing my ego, not to mention my love life. Haven't really wanted to bring guys back to my ex-husband's, know what I mean?"

"I can imagine how well that'd go over."

"For sure. Yeah, I need my savings back, need to build up a retirement account, buy property again. Besides, I've been living with people forever. People I don't want to live with. Well, except for Jon. He's cool."

He brought the two flutes over to the island and placed them on the counter. "What about your love life? Are you looking for a long-term relationship?"

She leaned across the island with a plate of strawberries and Brie, searching for a place to put them. "Oh, at some point."

He watched carefully for her reaction. "What about with me?"

She dropped the plate on the counter. It clattered loudly, but didn't break. All the color left her face. "*With you?*"

His body went on alert, tensing. Shit. Had he blown it? No, he just needed to take control. "Yes, don't look so scared. Are you ready for a relationship?"

Cynthia blinked rapidly and clutched the granite counter. "Uh…"

His stomach did a flip, then knotted. Damn it, he'd shot his mouth off too soon. "You're not."

She shook her head and her shoulders relaxed. But she didn't make eye contact. She busied herself with the plate of food. "No, I am. I just…this is happening fast. I don't want to put on the emotional brakes. I love you, but I have to take it slow because…I just do." She shrugged.

"I hear you. I'm not pushing. I just want to know if you have room in your future for me."

She met his gaze. Her eyes shone with love for him. She smiled, warming his center. "Yes."

He relaxed. He had her. No matter what, he had her. It might take time, but she was worth it.

She looked down at the plate of cheese and her smile faded into a small frown. The line between her eyes deepened.

His spine stiffened. Here it was again. That block. What was holding her back? "What aren't you telling me?"

She glanced up at him, then her attention returned to the cheese plate. She toyed with a strawberry and bit her lip.

Rex took a step towards her, but was careful not to crowd her. "See, it's right there. You want to tell me, but you can't. It's all right, I'm not pushing, but whatever you're keeping to yourself is hurting you. I only want you to tell me so you'll feel better."

A brief raise of her eyebrows, her gaze remained on the food. "This is not the time," she said, her voice cracking a bit. She cleared her throat.

"But there is something, isn't there?"

"Oh, yeah." She picked up the knife and placed it in the sink.

"Will you tell me?"

Still no eye contact. "Yes."

"But not now?"

"No." She finally glanced at him, her worry lines deep.

All he wanted to do was jump into her life and save her. Carry her off somewhere and make sure nothing bad ever happened to her.

Her mouth worked, her brow crinkled and she exhaled a long breath through her nose. "Is that okay?"

He reached over and clasped his hand over hers. "Very okay. I'm in this for the long haul. I'm not proposing, but I'm going to. I can tell you that right now. You are what I want. You and I and this place. Make it a home again. Good parties."

Her pensive expression broke. "I want that, too." She gave him a small smile.

"You tell me your secrets whenever you feel comfortable." He returned to his chair. "Whatever you've done, there's been a good reason for it. Don't worry. I'll be here. You'll trust me soon enough, trust this. Until then, let's just enjoy each other."

The rigidity in her body eased, she let out a long breath and her face relaxed. "Good plan."

What the hell could it be? What was she hiding from him?

It couldn't be that bad. Some problem that seemed insurmountable to her that would be easy for him to solve. Like that stepsister nonsense. Cynthia had no idea what money could buy.

He'd come into her life at the right time. Finally, they'd both have someone on their side.

Maybe he'd allow himself to paint more often.

Maybe quit the venture capital group. He had enough money to support the entire clan for three generations. He'd reached all his goals with his business and was actually bored with the routine nowadays. Maybe Cynthia would be the catalyst that helped him leave his empire behind.

A wallop of fear made his shoulders tense and stomach clench. God, how could he do that? He'd built it up from nothing and now it was a multi-billion dollar group. He *was* Vector Venture. It'd be like leaving his left arm behind. Painting all the time, would that satisfy him?

Money. That was the real issue. How the hell could he walk away from all that cash?

She sat next to him on a stool, nuzzled into him and kissed him on the neck. Heat radiated through him, centering on his dick.

An image of him painting and Cynthia coming up behind him and wrapping her arms around his waist went through his mind. Pulling off her top, he'd bury himself in her breasts, take her superior ass in both hands, then explore that wonderful place between her legs. Much better than going to some office.

It was time he took control. Walk away from the Money Trap. Instead of the game controlling him, he'd control the game. A surge of power welled up inside him. He could change. He wanted to change.

With Cynthia in his life, anything was possible.

Cynthia followed Rex back to his room. When they reached the upstairs landing, ahead of her was a wall of photos. She hadn't noticed them before. Of course, that was no shocker, considering she'd had on her Lust Blinders during that first trip to his bedroom.

As she got closer, she noticed the photos were of a little girl.

Kelly.

She locked onto a large photo in a silver frame. Kelly as a baby. Taken right after she'd given her up. The same image she'd had in her head all these years.

Suddenly, she was choking back the tears. Goddamn this!

She tried to avert her gaze, but all the photos popped off the wall at her.

There was all she lost. In Technicolor.

The first teeth, the first steps, the first smile, the first words. Skinned knees, Tinkertoys, Barbies and Saturday morning cartoons. Soccer games, prom, college graduation. All missed. All gone. Never to be retrieved again.

Her stomach hurt like there was a buzz saw ripping through it. This was why she didn't want to see her daughter. This unbearable pain. This unbearable loss. Unimaginable. So much buried so far within herself. Locked away in a secret chamber of pain.

And now she couldn't stop it. The floodgates had burst open and the pent-up agony was pouring out.

Arms were around her. Rex. The father. Too much to comprehend.

What had she done? Slept with him? Twice?

He would hate her. She knew he would.

Yes, he will. So enjoy yourself now. You know he's going to be taken away. You've lost everyone you've ever loved. Think about what Rex said. Enjoy him for the moment. Forget everything else. All you have is now. Hold onto him.

And just like that, the spigot of self-recrimination turned off. She got control.

He slid his hand down her back. "Are you all right?"

"I wasn't, but I am," she said, sighing and leaning into him.

He gestured towards the wall, seeming perplexed. "Why did these photos upset you?"

She wrapped the robe more tightly around herself. "Just seeing her life like that…" Tears choked her. She fanned her face. "Damn it, I'm not going to cry. I'm, uh, just emotional tonight. You, us, this. And…" She took a deep breath. "These photos remind me of the little girl I lost. And I'm a sap. Forgive me."

He took her in his arms and hugged her tightly to his hard chest. His cologne fading, she smelled his raw musky essence. Intoxicating. She buried her face in his chest, savoring everything about him: his scent, his heat and his ropy arms.

He stroked her back. "Don't apologize. No need," he said, kissing her on the side of the head. Pulling away, he took her by the hand. "Come on, let's go to bed. It's late, you've had a hard day."

"Had a hard night, too." She grinned up at him.

He burst out laughing, sunshine in his sweet blue gaze. He grabbed her and hugged her, then pulled away and kissed her on the nose. "You are bad, woman. Very bad. And very, very good." He moved to her mouth, and kissed her deeply.

Her world went warm and fuzzy, and her body turned into a puddle.

How could she ever let this man go?

Chapter Fifteen

Seven o'clock in the morning, Cynthia sat straight up in bed, her heart pounding. Jesus, she was naked! Holy Christ, where was she? An ostentatious bedroom? Oh, no, Rex was with her.

Thankfully, she hadn't woken him. He grunted and rolled over and promptly began snoring.

She wanted to barf. The cold reality of what's she'd done slapped her hard. How had she let it happen? Why didn't she tell him she was Kelly's mom? He could take it. She'd told Vance, for God's sake.

She was a rat. A horrible, rotten nasty rat.

Her face blazing with heat, she couldn't stop cringing. Her needs had outweighed everything and obliterated her rational thinking. Her morals, her logic, out the bloody window. Such an ugly mirror. Shit. Time to head back to the therapist.

Or tell Rex the truth.

Her throat tightened, her heart wrenched at the thought of his reaction. She couldn't handle that. She couldn't do it. *Run!*

She slipped out of bed, put on her clothes and stole out of the room. She'd write him a note, tell him she was sorry for bothering him and disappear again. Only this time, she was leaving town for good.

She would go back east. She had a really good friend who'd bugged her about moving out there. The rents were cheap and there was a good artist colony. She could get a nursing position and sculpt in her time off. A good life. A lonely one, but better than living here in lies and shame.

Getting home without another scene with him was her next challenge. She pulled out her cell phone to call a cab. Dead. Damn it! Where was a phone?

She remembered seeing one in the corner of the dining room and headed for the stairs.

As soon as she hit the entry hall, the scent of fresh coffee hit her nostrils. And food. Bacon.

Adrenaline jacked her system. Oh, God, the servants were up. She turned to run when the front door opened and Kelly walked inside.

Cynthia's heart stopped beating. She froze to the spot.

They stared at each other, dumbfounded.

Finally, for lack of anything else to do, Cynthia laughed. Kelly joined her.

Her face burning, she rubbed her brow and half hid behind her hand. "Well, this is awkward."

Kelly flipped a hand and made a dismissive noise. "Don't worry. I'm an adult. I can take it. Besides, I'm really glad you're here." She searched the area briefly, apparently for Rex, and turned back to her. "So you two are getting along well, then?"

Cynthia coughed and glanced at her feet. *If you call porking the hell out of your father getting along, then yes.* "Uh, you could say that."

"You want some coffee?" Kelly gestured towards the dining room.

"You got half and half?"

"Coffee is all about the half and half," Kelly replied matter-of-factly.

Cynthia gasped and clutched her fists to her chest. "That's my saying."

Kelly sent her a brilliant smile. "Well, then, I hope they've got a half gallon back there, because honey, we're gonna need it." Taking her by the arm, Kelly led her into the dining room. "Come on now and sit down and have breakers with me."

Reality shifted on its head. Breakfast with her daughter. A dream. A wonderful, amazing dream.

Just shy of Cynthia's height, Kelly smelled of soap and lavender. Cynthia resisted the urge to lean over and smell her hair. Instead, she delighted in every square inch of her sweet daughter. Her straight nose, her long dark lashes, perfectly shaped lips, her clear skin. The way she held her head, the way she moved. *Am I there? Where am I in her?* Glimpses of familiarity, her mother's eyes, her grandmother's high brow. Yet, still a stranger.

Bursts of volcanic love mixed with serious agony washed through her. How could she have given away this beautiful person?

All she remembered was the most harrowing pain. Unending black despair. Sobbing her guts out while holding this perfect little life. So traumatized, she'd almost depended on the newborn for emotional support. Talk about unstable.

Still, she wished she hadn't surrendered the baby.

Just as they reached the large buffet table along a wall with a coffee service set on top, Cynthia realized she had to bring Kelly up to speed. "Oh, wait, wait, wait. First, I have a confession to make. A couple. I already told your father and he didn't seem to care, but I do. My name isn't Abigail, it's Cynthia Rella."

Kelly snapped her head back in surprise and blinked rapidly. Her brow furrowed. "The artist?"

Cynthia pointed to *Unlimited Love*. "Yeah, that's my sculpture in the corner there."

"Wow." She tilted her head a bit to one side and frowned. "Wait. How did you end up at my wed—"

"My gay ex husband and I had just seen *Wedding Crashers* and
—"

Kelly took a step back away from her and examined her. "You
crashed my wedding?" Varying expressions flitted across her perfect
oval face.

Cynthia wanted to disappear inside herself. Her head hurt from
the heat flaming her cheeks and ears. She shrugged. "Uh, yeah. I
didn't know you were Rex's daughter until he walked you down the
aisle. When I saved him in the park, I had no idea who he was."

"So why did you crash the wedding? For dates?"

"No. Food. I'm broke, seemed like a good idea at the time."

After a moment, Kelly lit up like a neon sign and jumped up and
down, clapping her hands.

Startling Cynthia. This was not the reaction she expected.

Her daughter's eyes shining, she chirped, "This is so freaky! This
was meant to happen! Just like in those books I'm reading. This is
totally a Deepak Chopra moment here. You were supposed to be
there to save Calvin's life. This is so weird. Fate." She grabbed her
arm. "You could have crashed anyone's wedding, but fate brought
you to mine. This is so cool!"

Cynthia could only smile at her adorable daughter. What a cutie!
Could power the whole of the San Francisco peninsula with the
energy radiating off of her.

Was I ever this young? This effervescent? "Perhaps you're right."

"Well, you were meant to be there, look at all that happened
because of it." The girl let go of her arm to gesture broadly.

In that moment, she looked just like Jon. Frightening.

"...you met my father again, you saved Calvin's life AND you
got free food."

Cynthia laughed. "Well, when you put it *that* way. I felt like a
total rat when I saw you in your beautiful dress. It all became real. I
still feel bad about sneaking in."

Kelly waved her arms in another exaggerated gesture. "Don't
feel bad, look how great it worked out." She took Cynthia's arm

again, so excited, she vibrated. "You made my father so happy. I've never seen him like that before. He lit up like a fireworks display. And the way you two danced, I was actually jealous. Vance and I have known each other so long, there was no real mystery when we got together. No explosive chemistry like that. He's only looked at me the way Dad looked at you once or twice. And certainly not during our wedding. No, you and Dad made my wedding feel so magical. It was great."

Cynthia wanted to frown, but kept her smile. It was clear her daughter had settled for Vance. Why wouldn't Kelly think she deserved better? Was it a simple case of buying into a childhood dream or did the issue go deeper? Elizabeth sounded like she withheld emotion. Critical. Why would the kid settle for no passion?

Could be for the same reason she had. She'd loved Jon. They didn't have the chemistry sexually, not like she had with Rex, but she'd adored him. At the time, it was enough. Just to have someone be kind to her. Aside from his sexuality issues, Jon was the nicest man she'd ever met. Maybe Vance was there for Kelly emotionally.

Cynthia ran her hand over her head and realized that she still had bedhead: her short hair was sticking up in back. She smoothed it as nonchalantly as she could. "Yeah, the wedding. Felt like we upstaged you there. And sorry about the society column, they should have talked more about you."

"Don't apologize. Funny you should mention upstaging us, Vance used that very same word. Oh!" Kelly said, putting her hand to her mouth. "I'm sorry."

"No worries. We did. If I were Vance, I'd be upset, too."

"Oh, it was no big deal. I was just so happy for Dad. And now come to find out you did that sculpture?" She let go to gesture again. "See? Kismet. It's all Kismet."

Little more than that, kid. We stalked you. "So, what brings you to your father's house so early in the day?"

Kelly's face went dark. She looked down at her feet. Trouble in paradise. "Oh, nothing. Sometimes I have breakfast with him." She turned to the sideboard and busied herself with pouring a cup of coffee.

"That's nice."

Kelly snorted, gave her head a little shake and met Cynthia's gaze. "Yeah, I know you didn't believe that. Wouldn't get an Oscar for that performance. Have you been married?"

"Oh, yeah."

"I thought that when you got married, both parties stayed the night with each other. I mean, they didn't go out and stay out late. Not a few days after the honeymoon."

"Vance stayed out late?" Cynthia wanted to bash him—and his bald squeeze—over the head with the silver coffee pot.

Kelly bit her lip, her bright energy dimming. "Yes, last night. He called and said there was something wrong with a proposal and he had to work on it all night. But when I went to surprise him with a late night snack, he wasn't there." She grabbed a small pitcher filled with half and half and poured nearly the entire thing into her coffee cup. "And the doorman said he hadn't seen him. I can't believe it, but I think he has another girl." She checked Cynthia for her reaction, her sweet face pale.

Anger fired through her limbs, her jaw set. *Play it cool. Don't let anything slip.* Even though she wanted to strangle Vance, she couldn't let her emotions show. "No. Why would he marry you?"

Kelly snorted. "For the connections." She grabbed her cup. "Help yourself." She indicated the coffee service with a slight nod of her head.

"Thanks, I will."

Kelly took a place at one end of the long, dark, polished wood dining table, next to the head of the table. "And he loves me, I know that, but I feel like an old shoe, sometimes. He's more like my brother at times than my lover."

Cynthia poured a cup, her blood boiling as hot as the coffee. "I know the feeling," she said, emptying the small pitcher of half and half into her cup. Kid almost left her enough.

She sat opposite Kelly. Head of the table was Rex's place, indicated by a silver napkin ring engraved with the initials *RDC*.

"What would you do? I'm actually glad you're here. I mean, I don't want to talk about this with Dad, he'll kill Vance. I was going to lie to Dad this morning about why I was here. There was no way I wanted to be home, waiting there like a good little wife when the butthead returned." She leaned in and whispered, "Don't tell Dad, okay?"

Cynthia fought with the Mother Bear within. Anger raged inside her. She wanted to rush to Rex and tell him what she knew. Together they would tear Vance limb from limb.

She'd never been in such an untenable situation before. She would rather swallow a bowl of razor blades than see Kelly go through this. The secrets were killing her.

To make things even worse, rather than help her, she was aiding the girl's adulterous husband perpetuate their farce of a marriage.

But she couldn't blurt out the truth. If Sissy and Belinda found out about Kelly, they'd destroy her.

Great. If she told Kelly the truth, she was screwed. If she didn't tell her the truth, she was screwed. Everywhere she turned she saw despair.

Kelly waved a hand at her. "Cynthia? Are you all right? Are you okay with not telling Dad?"

"What?" She shielded part of her face with her hand. "Oh, God. No, I'm sorry, your life just sounds a lot like a really bad time of mine and I'm having flashbacks." She forced her hand to drop. "But no worries. I won't tell your Dad."

She had to get out of there. To save them all, she had to run.

Kelly twisted her mouth to one side. "So should I worry?"

Cynthia measured her response. What would she tell a young wife in Kelly's situation if she didn't know the truth? She ignored the voices screaming in her head, begging her to tell Kelly everything. "Well, of course, worrying is natural and appropriate. Vance lied. You just have to find out why. If I were you, I'd confront him and get it all out in the open. Tell him what you think and demand to know where he was. And if you don't like the answer, hire a private detective. Wish I'd done that."

"You had someone cheat on you?"

Yes, your bloody father. "Yes, my husband. Now my ex."

"How did you find out?"

"Walked in on them. In our bedroom."

Slack-jawed, Kelly gasped and waved her arms around in a large, wild motion. "*Your husband was making love to another woman on your bed?*"

"No, it was worse. A man. And it was the Reverend Gary, our pastor, of all people."

Kelly bounced in her chair, her arms flapping like a bird, her mouth wide open. "Oh, my God! A man? Your husband was gay?"

Why did she open this can of worms? "Apparently."

"Didn't he know?"

"No."

"What did you do?"

She intended to say she left him. "My water broke and I lost my baby," sprang out instead.

Stop this now!

Kelly's eyes were as big as moons. "Oh, my God, no! Cynthia! You were pregnant?"

Cynthia's gaze dropped briefly to her coffee. "Yep."

"Is this why you disappeared after you sold that sculpture to my father?"

"Yeah."

"Oh, that's terrible. God, I hope—" Kelly looked away and teared up.

Cynthia pointed at her firmly. "Don't think that way. I'm sure there's a perfectly good reason for Vance's disappearance. Don't go jumping to wild conclusions. And my husband didn't cheat on me right after the honeymoon. It was five years afterwards. You met him, he was with me at the wedding."

Kelly jerked sharply backwards in her chair. "Him? That's your ex? He was the one?"

"Yep."

"Damn, he was cute. I mean, for an old guy. But kind of flaming."

"Wasn't when I met him. He's able to be himself now. Besides, I've totally forgiven him and we're best friends. We always were. That was the problem. He loved me. He was just bi and in denial. Didn't really get he was gay until I caught him blowing the damn Reverend."

Kelly giggled and covered up her mouth with her slender hand. "Sorry, it just sounds funny."

"Agreed. Needless to say, I left that church."

"Wow, I'll bet."

Cynthia ran a finger around the edge of her porcelain coffee cup, trying to figure out a way to comfort the kid. "Besides, Vance might not have lied, the doormen don't see everyone. He could have left through the back door, minutes before you arrived. He figured you were asleep at home and went out to wind down at his club," she said, the lie leaving a nasty taste in her mouth.

Kelly's eyes sparkled and her face shined with hope. "You're right. That could be it. Oh, and here I am convicting him of a crime. I feel so terrible."

"Don't," Cynthia said a bit too forcefully. "You don't know the truth yet. Find it out, then deal with it. You'll make it through, either way. I did."

"Yeah, I guess," Kelly said, toying with a fingernail. "I just—I always wanted to marry Vance. Since I was four. He isn't exactly who I thought he was. Pretty controlling, really. A lot like my mother. God rest her soul."

Poor kid. "I'm so sorry for your loss." Cynthia heaved a big sigh and nodded. "I lost my mom when I was twelve."

"You poor thing," Kelly said, her expression turning sympathetic. "It's horrible, isn't it? I'm glad I was older. But twelve, that's so hard."

"Yeah, it was."

"Yes..." The girl looked away, pensive. She let out a huge, long sigh. "Oh, God, the whole death thing makes me wonder what happened to my real mother."

Cynthia choked on her coffee and went into a coughing fit. It took her awhile to get breath back in her lungs.

"Are you all right?"

"Sure. Just inhaled some coffee." She cleared her throat and forced herself to calm. "That's right, you're adopted."

"Yeah," Kelly replied, grimacing. "And damn, I wish I could find out who my real parents are."

"Your real parents are Rex and Elizabeth."

"You know what I mean."

"No, I wasn't adopted, I have no idea what's going on in your head. I mean, I understand you, I just can't imagine what it's like to be adopted."

Kelly checked the doorway to the entry hall. "I don't want Dad hearing me, but..." She leaned in and lowered her voice. "Look, I love those people with my whole heart, but I feel like something's missing. I need to find my birth parents. I want to know. Why did they do it? Why did they give me up? I was with my mother for a month, I know they were divorcing, but why didn't she just keep me?"

Cynthia's stomach twisted so badly, the coffee felt like it was re-percolating inside. She would have given anything to disappear from the face of the Earth at that moment. She swallowed hard. "She probably wanted you to have a better life. And look, you've done pretty damned well. Most people don't have this kind of money, these kinds of opportunities you've been offered. You would have come from a broken home. Pitted between two warring factions. When Jon and I split up, I was actually kind of glad I lost the baby—

I mean, not really. But she would have been torn in half. We hated each other."

"You would have set aside your differences for the child."

Cynthia crossed her arms over her chest and realized that she was assuming a defensive posture. She moved her arms, but became so aware of them, she held them awkwardly at her sides. "At the time I was very young, younger than you. By four years. And I wasn't as rational as I am now. God, if I'd had her with me…her life would have been hell. My life has been a marathon of horrific events. I can't imagine dragging a child through all that. I tried hard to have a good life, but I had to deal with some horrible people in my family. Demonic. Monstrous. People."

"Maybe so." Kelly frowned and looked down at her coffee.

Cynthia reached across the table and put her hand over Kelly's. "Honey, you'll find them and all your questions will be answered. I'm sure they loved you. They probably gave you up because they loved you so much."

Her brow wrinkled and her jaw tightened. "That makes no sense."

Cynthia pulled away. "It does when you're a parent. Well, I was only one for a brief period of time, but if I hadn't lost my kid, I would have been close to giving her up rather than let her get torn apart by Jon's and my stupidity."

Kelly gazed straight into her eyes. "No, you wouldn't have, Cynthia. I can tell. You would have kept her and loved her and done fine by her. You would have protected her to the best of your ability."

Cynthia couldn't take her penetrating stare and shifted her attention to the polished silver candlesticks. "Protecting her could entail giving her up. I'm just saying. Don't make any decisions about your birth parents before you meet them. And believe me, you'll probably be glad they gave you up."

"Maybe so."

"Kelly? What are you doing here?" came a deep voice from behind them. Shit, *Rex.* She'd meant to leave way before he got up. Damn this!

Kelly shot her a look like *keep your mouth shut.* She gave a slight nod. The girl's shoulders relaxed.

Cynthia turned to Rex and said in a bright tone, "Vance was gone early to work, so Kelly dropped by to have breakfast with you and look what she got instead!"

Rex laughed. "More than she bargained for. Darling, I didn't expect you, I—"

Kelly smiled and gave a tiny wave of her hand. "Dad, don't be embarrassed." She gestured towards Cynthia. "We were just getting to know each other. I don't care what you adults do in your spare time. I mean, we are all adults here, aren't we?"

His face a deep red, Rex choked and rubbed the back of his neck. "Yes. Er. Yes, we are."

Cynthia grinned. "I like that particular shade on him, don't you, Kelly?"

"Goes great with his robe."

He held himself straighter and put his hands on his hips. "Okay, you two. Great, now I have two foils. Goil foils."

Kelly raised an eyebrow. "Did you get that he's weird?"

"Picked that up right away. It's why he took to me." Cynthia leaned in and whispered loudly, "I got a secret for you, I'm weird, too."

Kelly beamed. "Then you two should make quite a couple. And Dad," she said, giving him the once over, "I haven't seen you this, uh, relaxed in years."

He gave her a hard face and pointed a finger at her. "Watch it, Missy. Treading on dangerous ground. I haven't even had my coffee yet." He came up to Cynthia and kissed her on the cheek. "Morning, gorgeous."

Her mind and body warred with conflicting emotions. Torn between wanting to run and wanting to run her hands over his body,

Cynthia's insides were in such knots, she hoped she wasn't bleeding. The scent of him and the warmth of his stubbly chin played havoc with her resolve. "Morning yourself, handsome," she choked out.

He gave her an extra glance. How could he not notice her reaction? She felt like she had a billboard on her forehead announcing all her private thoughts.

After a moment of hesitation, he walked over to his daughter and gave her a quick peck on the cheek. "Good morning, Katydid." He smoothed his hand over her hair.

The way the two looked at her each other wrenched her heart even more. They loved each other so deeply, she could feel the bond from across the table. All she'd wanted her entire life was a stable relationship with a good man and some kids. Sharing these moments with her family. Feeling that extraordinary love. That sense of belonging.

No love in the world could come close to it. These two were the epitome of a healthy relationship. And Cynthia would never experience it. She coughed and fought back the tears.

"Mornin' Dad." Kelly reached up and ran her hand down his cheek. "Wow, you're scratchy. I haven't seen you unshaved in years."

He gave a wry smile. "Wasn't expecting company this early."

Kelly's cheeks went pink and she giggled. "I'll call next time. I had no idea you'd be…" She looked at Cynthia. "Um, busy." She turned back to her father.

He relaxed and chuckled. Giving her a pat on the shoulder, he said, "Still, I'm glad to see you. I want you to get to know Cynthia."

He met Cynthia's gaze and sent her a wink that made her pulse jump.

Then he leaned down and whispered loudly in Kelly's ear. "I think I have her hooked."

"Line and sinker," Cynthia added without thinking.

A little more acid dripped into her gut. She was going to blow this whole happy picture into a million pieces. Why couldn't she just shut the hell up?

I'm a traitor! she wanted to scream at them. She wanted to bash herself over the head with the silver butter plate. Maybe that would knock some sense into her. Idiot. A blind idiot.

She quickly came up with several escape plans. She had to get away from these people and stay away.

All at once, a realization hit her like a tank of ice water dumping on her head. This was not her. She didn't do things like this. She didn't hurt people. She didn't lie.

Running without an explanation would only cause more pain. Rex didn't deserve that. He deserved the truth.

She had to tell Rex who she was. Warn him about her stepsisters and tell him about Vance. He needed all the information. He may hate her for it, but at least he could protect Kelly. If he didn't want her telling Kelly who she was, then she wouldn't. She'd let him make the decision. It was the least she could do.

She had to get him alone. She leaned over to touch his arm and opened her mouth to speak.

The phone rang.

Without noticing her outstretched arm or that she was about to say something, Rex got up and answered it. "Jess? What are you doing in the office so early? Oh, Jesus, that's today? I thought it was next Friday. No, keep them there, keep them happy. I'll be there in fifteen." He hung up and sent a sheepish look towards Cynthia. "This is not how I planned this morning. Not that I planned this morning, but I have to run."

The rocket of urgency Cynthia had been riding took a nosedive into the ground. She nearly crumpled from the impact. Damn it! Now that she'd made the decision, she couldn't stand the wait.

He walked over to her chair and put his hands on her shoulders. A thrill went through her at his touch and her thought train got momentarily derailed. Then a sledgehammer of guilt smashed her over the head.

Lightly rubbing her back, he said, "Sorry 'bout this, but I mixed up the dates on a very important meeting. Kelly? Could you drive Cynthia home?"

Oh, great. More bathing in the Lake of Shame. Cynthia made a dismissive gesture. "I'll take a cab."

He squeezed her shoulder. "You got fired last night."

"I can take you, Cynthia, no problem," Kelly said. "My first meeting's at nine-thirty today and it's only eight now."

"Great. I have to fly." He bent down, gave Cynthia a quick kiss on the lips and raced upstairs.

Cynthia could only stare after him. Shit! Now how was she supposed to tell him?

Kelly misunderstood her reaction and sent her a smirk. "That's something you'll have to get used to. Both Vance and Dad are like that. He's always been like that. You think you got him to yourself and poof! He disappears. I hope he gives up that stupid business and goes back into painting. I keep telling him he doesn't need that much money. Maybe with you in art, he'll follow your lead."

Since I'm leaving his life today, probably not. "We'll see. He's got to want to do it. And did you see the look in his eye? He's still loving his work. Whether or not he wants to admit it, he loves what he does."

Kelly made a little grimace. "Sad, but true."

As she rode home with her daughter, her stomach turned into a giant grinder. She longed to tell Kelly who she was. Apologize. Explain.

But all she did was smile and nod as Kelly chattered on about her work. She barely heard a word the kid said for all the voices screaming in her head, telling her what an asshole she was for hurting these lovely people.

There was no rectifying this madness. She'd blown it. And probably cost her the relationship with not only Rex, but with her daughter as well.

She thought her life had been miserable before. But apparently no one could screw up her life better than she could.

He'd hate her forever.

And boy, did she deserve it.

When she walked in the door of the apartment, Jon was in his small living room on a brown leather loveseat, having coffee and reading the paper.

He sent her a pissy look. "So you've decided to come back, how nice. Not even a call?" He folded up the paper and threw it onto the coffee table.

She shut the door and ambled over to him, but didn't make eye contact. "Sorry. I was…"

"Screwing Rex's brains out. Did you tell him first?"

She couldn't look at him. Her face burned so hot, her ears felt like they were engulfed in flames. "I'm going to throw up now."

His shoulders slumped. "Oh, God, no. Honey, why do you do this to yourself? You had a chance with him, a real chance."

Tears welled in her eyes and she held up her hand. "Please don't. I'm in hell."

"I'm sorry." He patted the couch next to him. "Let's have some coffee and you can sit down and tell me all about how big his dick is."

She gaped at him. "Jon!" She tried not to, but she cracked up. She had no idea why she was surprised by his audacity. This was a man who'd asked his mother if she was a virgin when she got married.

He smiled a little covetous grin. "Inquiring minds want to know."

"Bigger than yours."

He grimaced, looking wounded. "Ouch."

"You started it."

"Didn't I?" he admitted dryly.

She grabbed a cup of coffee, settled in next to him and downloaded the entire evening. Jon kept stopping her for more detail. Exhausting. She almost had to tell it in real time for all the information he wanted.

Finally seeming satisfied, he relaxed back against the couch and tucked his legs underneath him. "So now what are you going to do?"

"Kill myself."

He didn't blink an eye. "My property values will tank if there's a suicide in here. And Butch will be home soon from med school and he's sick of dead bodies."

"No problem. I'll off myself in Belinda and Sissy's house." She put her head in her hands, her gut burning like she'd had a habañero omelet for breakfast. "God, I'm dyin' here. I can't tell Rex on the phone, I have to see him in person. But with Vance knowing what's going on..."

Jon giggled. "I still can't get over the fact it was his car we hit. That is so funny. So karmic."

"So out there. This whole thing is out there. Well..." She got up and stretched. "I'm going to go take a shower, slice my wrists and bleed to death."

"Make sure the blood stays in the shower."

"No worries, mate."

She was joking, but there was a part of her that toyed with bringing a razor in the shower with her. No guilt when you're dead. No horrible pain in your stomach. Rex would find out after the fact. She wouldn't have to see that look on his face when she told him she was Kelly's mother.

She put on a neutral face for Jon, but she barely made it to the bathroom before she puked.

What a great morning after.

Idiot.

As she walked out of the bathroom, the phone rang.

"Let's let the machine pick up," Jon said. "Michael's been hounding me. Rex called him looking for Abigail Maxim's address and he's totally freaked out."

She decided not to tell him that she'd already confessed that info to Rex.

"But if it's Colin, I'm totally here."

She shot him a grin. "So it's going well?"

Jon did a little toss with his head and sent her a lascivious grin. "Oh, yeah. You just missed him."

"I thought it smelled like sex in here."

A deep voice came over the speaker. "Cynthia? I hope this is you."

Rex. Her interior wrenched so hard, it felt like all her internal organs had compressed into one painful lump.

"Speak of the devil. I'm gonna take this." Holding her stomach, she went to the phone.

"Be my guest. And stay in the room, please." Jon added with a smirk.

"No bloody way—Rex, I'm here," she said, quickly walking to her bedroom. She shut the door behind her.

"First of all I have to apologize for—" were the first words out of his mouth.

She cut him off. "No, you don't." She sat on the bed and hugged herself.

"Yes, I do. Here I abandoned you after that wonderful—"

"Rex, stop. I get it, I got it." *I'm actually grateful.* "What is that weird noise in the background?"

"I'm on a plane to Europe."

The room spun, all the air left her lungs and little multi-colored lights dotted her vision. Slumping over, she caught herself on the bed. When would her torture end? This was unreal. Unreal horribleness.

"Europe?" she asked, her voice cracking. She cleared her throat. "W-when are you coming back?"

"A week. Next Thursday. Big deal, happened faster than I thought. Can't really talk here, but I need to say this to you. Last night was—you are—well, you're incredible, woman."

Guilt and shame seared through her. A sob caught in her throat.

"Cynthia? You there?"

"Oh, I'm here," she said, choking up.

"You sound funny. Oh. Oh! You're. Oh. Well, sweetheart, no reason to cry. Wish I was there to hold you."

Her heart twisted so hard she thought it would snap in half. She put a hand to her chest. "I wish you were, too."

"There's something else, too, isn't there?"

"Could you not read my mind from a freakin' plane?"

He laughed. His resonant laughter tickled her ears and warmed her toes. Immediately following, a shroud of black gloom closed in around her. Her throat tightened, making it difficult to breathe. She'd taken the place of her evil stepmother and stepsisters as her Number One Enemy.

Beyond hurting herself, she'd taken advantage of a wonderful man. A man who'd loved her daughter as his own and raised her to be an outstanding human being. She was now scum just like her stepmother. Hurting someone with her sickness. She'd gone from victim straight to abuser.

Ye Gods, how has it come to this?

Rex said, "The guy next to me just left so I can say this. Wanted to last night and meant to, but fell asleep before I could. I love you."

A stab of agony blazed through her chest like he'd speared her heart with a red-hot pitchfork. She cried harder. "M-m-me, too."

He chuckled softly. "Don't cry."

"Okay," she sobbed.

"My food just arrived. Look, I'll call you when I get back. Set aside Friday for me, okay?"

"Okay."

"I'll call you later."

She hung up the phone and pulled her knees up to her chest. Holding herself, she wracked with sobs. A complete emotional purge.

She felt weight on the bed next to her.

Jon wrapped his big, strong arms around her. He smelled of cologne, bacon and coffee. "You'll be okay, Cyn. Don't worry. Things will turn around."

Even though she felt like she didn't deserve it, she allowed him to comfort her. After all they'd been through and done to each other, their bond still amazed her. He was her only family. In all the blackness, it was a mighty gift.

After a few moments, she pulled away and grabbed some tissues from her nightstand. "Couldn't get much worse." She blew her nose.

"No, it couldn't." He took her by the hand and pulled her up off her bed. "Come on and let's drink some mimosas."

"Got any heroin?"

"Fresh out."

Cynthia made a short stop at the bathroom to wash her face. She gazed at her pathetic, puffy hazel eyes and the haggard quality to her face. Looked like she was ninety.

All she wanted to do was blurt out the truth on the phone to him. Get it over with. But he deserved better. She'd tell him on their date. Let him do his worst to her.

Then she could move on.

To what, she didn't know.

But at this point, anything would be better than this.

Chapter Sixteen

Wednesday morning, Cynthia was in the middle of making breakfast when the doorbell rang. Butch, Jon's son, had just left. Probably forgot his keys.

"I'm cooking eggs, can you get that? Butch forgot something," she called out to Jon.

No answer. She strained and heard his shower running. Great.

She set the pan aside and went to go let Butch back inside.

As normal, she checked through the peephole. She gasped and a wave of fear slammed her.

Sissy, Belinda and Troy.

Sissy's dyed black hair stuck up off her head like she'd grabbed a high voltage line and her pallor was gray. She looked even worse than normal, like an embalmed version of Joan Jett. Must have been on a hell of a meth bender.

After a second of shock, Cynthia catapulted into a rage. Atomic hate blasted through her veins. Her vision tweaked and her body readied for battle. She growled, "Get the hell away from the door!"

Sissy's beady dark eyes narrowed and she crossed her arms over her bony chest. "Kelly Du Charmante is your daughter and I have proof!" she said with her lip curled. Her eyes shone with victory.

Belinda nodded so hard, her blond ski-jump bangs actually moved a tad. "Yeah! We have proof!"

Cynthia couldn't process the horror. Seeing the bitches, the news about Kelly, it was all too much. Her mind overwhelmed with fear and anger, she stepped back away from the door, stammering some nonsense.

"Open up, bitch! We gotta talk!" Sissy demanded.

Cynthia's vision twisted further and her entire body shook with rage. "Get the hell away before I open this door and kill you," she snarled. "And if you go near Kelly, I will fucking rip your lungs out." She checked through the peephole for Sissy's reaction.

Sissy raised one eyebrow. That was it. Completely unaffected. "Since you're a total psychopathic idiot, I'll ignore your threats. Here." She shoved a large manila envelope under the door.

Cynthia shoved the envelope back. "Whatever it is, I don't want it."

"Unless you want me going to your daughter and telling her everything, you'll look at these." She slid the large envelope back again.

Cynthia kicked the envelope back to Sissy. "Get the hell away from the door, now! Jon! Call the police!"

The lines on Sissy's face deepened into crevasses. Her washed-out pallor went red. She pointed at the peephole. "Listen, sister, you're gonna sign over that life insurance policy to me. All I want is my money. You owe me that money. Left me with a rundown house —you know I can only get four hundred thousand for that piece of shit? You sign the papers or I'll go after your daughter with both barrels loaded. I'll—"

A loud whooshing in her ears and Cynthia hurled herself at the door and pounded on it. Fury possessed her limbs like a demon.

Jon came rushing into the room, his hair wet, dressed in a bathrobe, his eyes as large as volleyballs. "What the hell is going on? Cynthia! Are you all right?"

He snapped her out of her fit. Thankfully. She gave her head a shake. "Sissy and Belinda are out there trying to blackmail me."

As if on cue, the envelope came flying back under the door.

At that moment, Jon's son, Butch, yelled out in the corridor.

Cynthia looked through the peephole. Butch faced the nasty threesome, all bared teeth and bulging muscles. "What the hell are you guys doing here?" he demanded, his pale blue eyes blazing.

"Butch!" Cynthia yelled. "Escort them to the elevator! We're calling the police!"

Troy made a large gesture like a referee at a baseball game calling a player out. "Wait! All of you wait just a goddamned minute!"

Sissy snarled and pointed at him. "You tell them, Troy!"

He turned on his mother. "You, too, Mother, shut up. I told you I'd handle this." His voice dripped with icy contempt.

Slack-jawed, Sissy glared at her son. "Don't you talk to me like that!"

He narrowed his gaze at her and his jaw twitched. "I'll talk to you any way I want. Now shut up. You got me involved when I specifically told you I wanted nothing more to do with your stupid dramas, so shut the hell up and let me handle this."

Sissy stammered and sputtered, then finally shut up.

Troy turned to the door, the normal coldness returning to his green gaze. "If you could please just open the door, we can settle this fast and be on our way. You can keep the chain secured."

They clearly weren't leaving until they had their say. And Butch needed to come inside at some point. Cynthia slipped on the chain, then opened the door.

"I'm sorry for coming by like this," Troy drawled. He turned and gave a nearly imperceptible nod at Butch. "Butch, my apologies. But you know my mother. Is it possible we can start over without the screaming and threats?" he asked his mother in a tired, bored tone. Then he turned to Cynthia.

As angry as Cynthia was, Troy's lack of emotion threw her off and she lost some of her fire. "Please leave, Troy."

He held up his long, manicured hand. "I will, we will. But first, please allow my mother to blackmail you or she'll never stop bothering you. Or me."

Sissy was apoplectic. Her eyes wild, she shook so much Cynthia thought her rickety little body would fly apart. "I resent that! It is not blackmail! She owes me that money! That's my money!"

Troy's only reaction was to give a small snort. It was clear the seat of power had shifted in the family. He was king now. Hard to get her head around it.

The features of his too-handsome Greek face sharpened. "The hell it isn't blackmail, mother. Now I would appreciate it if we could conduct our unseemly business without anymore unnecessary outbursts. I have a class in an hour and it's all the way across town." His oily, emotionless gaze rested on Cynthia. "Here's the deal. You sign over that life insurance policy to my mother and she'll keep her nasty trap shut about your daughter and leave you both alone."

Sissy gasped and clutched her Harley-Davidson t-shirt. "How dare you insult me! I'm your mother!"

Troy rolled his eyes. "Please stop reminding me," he replied dryly.

Sissy pointed a shaking chipped black fingernail at him. "You—"

He held up his hand to quiet her, his dead eyes filled with contempt, his dark brow in a deep V. "Shut it, mother. Now. Or I walk. And I mean it this time. Out of your life. You're lucky I'm here and you know it."

So many conflicting emotions passed over Sissy's face, so fast and so exaggerated, she almost looked like a cartoon. Rage, despair, desperate need, frustration and finally back to rage. But she kept quiet.

Despite the tiny rays of glee from Sissy's humiliation, Cynthia still had to work hard to keep from reaching through the gap in the door and throttling the desiccated deadling.

Troy turned to Cynthia. "These papers…" he said, handing the large manila envelope through the crack in the door.

Cynthia didn't make a move to take them.

Troy gave a slight eye roll and flung them past her into the room. "…are life insurance policy papers that were delivered recently to the house. Had your name and your father's name on them, so, of course, my mother opened them. Apparently—unbeknownst to Grandma or my mother—your father had a life insurance policy that named only you as the beneficiary. He wasn't as dumb as we thought. He knew my grandmother would double-cross you along with my esteemed mother here—I said, shut it, mother."

Sissy, red-faced, made a strangled gurgling sound.

"I checked, there is no policy," Cynthia spat.

"You checked with Cheney who handled the estate," he continued in his lifeless drawl. "The lawyer my mother and grandmother bought. The policy is legitimate. Your father hired a lawyer my grandmother didn't know and paid for the policy in cash. The lawyer had instructions to contact you and only you after his death. Problem was, the lawyer didn't check to see if you actually still lived at the house and sent the paperwork there. You have two days to make up your mind or my mother will go to your daughter. Of course, you could go and tell Kelly yourself making this all a moot point, but I gather from your recent actions that you don't want her knowing who you are. You can call me and I'll handle the transaction so you don't have to see my mother."

Sissy glared up at her son. "You went too far, boy," she hissed.

Troy didn't react. He sighed and looked at his trim, perfect fingernails. "Shut up, Mother. God, you make me sick," he said in a freezing tone.

All the color drained from Sissy's face. Her shoulders drooped and the whites of her eyes showed as she stared at the floor. Lost. It was a sight to behold. The son hating the mother as much as Cynthia did. Wow.

Troy turned to his aunt. "Belinda, we're leaving. Mother, the elevator. And spare us any parting shots and threats. Cynthia, the

papers are self-explanatory. All you need to do is sign them over to
my mother."

Cynthia jerked her head towards the elevators. "Get out."

Troy chuckled, amused. "With pleasure." He turned to Sissy.
"We're leaving."

Sissy rebounded from her son's attack and was back to furious.
Shaking, her nostrils flared, all the veins popped out on her gaunt
neck. She started to say something but Troy sent her a deadly cold
glare. She forced her mouth shut. With obvious great effort, she
turned around and walked past Butch without a glance up at him.

Belinda looked like she'd just witnessed an assassination. Her
eyes wide, her lower lip quivering, her attention darted between
Troy, Cynthia and Sissy. She finally shook her blond head, threw up
her chubby hands and followed her sister.

With an ice-cold stare in his reptilian green gaze, Troy gave
Cynthia a little bow. Then he turned and followed his mother and
aunt. Cynthia closed the door, removed the chain and let Butch
inside.

Cynthia closed the door and turned to Jon. They stared at each
other in stunned silence.

Butch's pale blue eyes wide, he demanded, "What the hell was
that? What daughter? Cynthia, what the—"

Jon put a hand to his son's broad chest. "Give her a minute,
Butchie."

"Sorry," Butch said, holding up his mitt-sized hands. He backed
off.

Cynthia was so confused, so angry, so crazed, so frustrated, she
felt like she was about to pop. "Okay, things just got worse."

"Damn, and you haven't even had coffee yet," Jon said.

"I don't think I've ever wanted to kill anyone more," she said,
chuckling even though she wasn't happy or amused. Light-headed,
her stomach was tight as a fist.

Cynthia's adrenaline on the wane, the floor beneath her feet felt
unstable. She sighed and collapsed on the couch, putting her head in

her hands. "Shit, this is terrible. Why the hell is Rex in Europe? I just want to get this over with. Fuck, how long do I have? How long did Troy say?"

"Two days," Butch said. Kid was near to jumping out of his skin he wanted the story so badly.

Cynthia ignored his searching gaze. "Rex will be back then. And I know them, they'll wait a bit longer than that. They want the imaginary money. They are so high. Dad wouldn't have done that."

Jon grabbed the envelope, withdrew the papers and examined them. "Hmmmm. They look legal. This looks like the letter explaining the whole thing," he said, handing her a piece of paper.

Cynthia took it.

"Is someone going to explain what's going on?"

Jon grabbed Butch's beefy arm. "In a minute. Please, this is huge."

"Which is why I'm dyin' here."

"Shhhh."

Cynthia read:

Dear Miss Rella:

My name is Edward Higgins, an attorney hired by your father several years ago. As per his written orders, enclosed is a copy of his life insurance policy naming you as the sole beneficiary. He took this out when you were born, but a few years ago was pressured to discontinue the payments. He made arrangements with me to continue the payments until his death. He believed that certain parties in the family would prevent you from your rightful inheritance. He wanted to ensure you were repaid for all your sacrifice, both financially and emotionally, over the previous years.

Also enclosed please find a sealed letter from your father.

I look forward to hearing from you.

Cynthia looked up from the letter. "What letter? Jon, is there a letter from my father in the papers? Probably isn't sealed any longer. It would be in longhand. My dad's writing."

Jon shuffled through the papers while Butch stood back and watched. "Here it is. Yes, it's opened." He handed it to her.

Her hands shaking, her heart beating hard, she took the letter.

Cinderella,

If you're reading this then it means I'm dead. I wanted to say some things to you that I couldn't when your mother was around. I couldn't hurt your mother that way. I know she was a tough cookie, but she was fragile, much more fragile than you.

This is hard for me to say, but Agnes is not an honest person. If you knew what she'd gone through as a kid, you'd probably be softer on her. Not only is she dishonest, those parasites she calls her daughters are even worse. I know I never let on that I felt this way. I couldn't. It would have killed your mother.

Anyway, I have reason to believe that Agnes has written up another will under pressure from her daughters that will cut you out and take the house from you. I think they're planning on forging my name and hiring that sham of a lawyer, Cheney, to help them.

When your real mother, Sherry, was alive, we took out this insurance policy for you. I kept it up without Agnes knowing because early on, I had an idea she might try to get it away from you when I died. Recently, I realized I had to get it out of the house and put it into the hands of someone I could trust to get it to you. I didn't tell you because there never seemed to be a good time and I didn't want to cause any trouble.

I know the sacrifices you made for me. And I know I wasn't always as good to you as I should have been. I was so caught up in your mother and her problems, I guess I didn't do as much for you as I should have when you were a kid. You just always seemed so strong and capable, like your real ma. Like could take on the world if you had to. Sherry was like that. I wish you'd known her longer.

I know Agnes was hard on you. It was only because she loved you so much. Much more than her own daughters. But they poisoned her against the both of us. I hate those girls. I wish nothing but the worst on them.

I wanted you to know how much I love you and how thankful I am for your great caretaking and help and your great personality. You really have been helping me and Agnes through these really difficult times. I don't know what I would do without you.

I hope this money gets you back on track and helps you get a place to live and maybe helps you get back to your art. You always made such pretty things.

I also hope you find a good man. You deserve the world, baby. And don't let anyone tell you different.

All my love,

Dad

Cynthia flashed on her father, dying in his hospital bed. After being given the Last Rites, he'd gone unconscious. Suddenly, he came to, gripped her hand and stared fiercely into her gaze. She thought he was about to say something nice to her. Maybe say he loved her. He said, "Get the insurance policy, Cinderella, the insurance policy. You, the insurance policy…" then he'd faded out and let go of her. An hour later, without regaining consciousness, he'd died. And she'd been devastated. Not because she'd miss him, because he'd never loved her. She thought he'd been talking about that stupid auto policy.

Cynthia's world turned on its axis. Pain and grief clawed at her stomach. She thought he hadn't loved her. That he was blind to the Stepmonster and the girls. He never told her. He said thank you, but that was it.

He wanted her to be okay. He left her money. He went behind his wife's back to take care of her. His last dying words were about her.

Tears streamed down her cheeks and dripped onto the paper. "I had no idea. I had no bloody idea how he felt."

Jon rubbed her back, took the letter and read it. "My God, Cynthia. The insurance policy. His last words. They *were* about you."

She cried harder. "I know."

"Harry wasn't a dope after all. I thought he was a total moron. He was in there, he just was hiding."

"Damn. I wish I'd known. I thought he was a big patsy."

"So what are you going to do?" Jon said, handing the letter to Butch.

Cynthia grabbed a tissue from the coffee table and blew her nose. "Put off the Gruesome Twosome, cash in this policy and spend the money investigating that forged will. I want to put them behind bars. Including that bastard lawyer."

Jon smiled and squeezed her knee. "You know where a good place to plan the revenge would be? Hawaii. I can help."

She laughed, feeling better than she had in a long time. Hope. She finally had some hope. "Good plan. We'll plan our revenge from Hawaii. Wow. I have five hundred thousand dollars."

Jon's grin lit up the room. "I'm so glad. At least there are a couple positives in all this hell. You now have money and Harry is not the dick we thought he was."

"Sure he was. He had no balls. While this made up for a lot, it didn't make up for him being a complete pussy around Endora. Making me call her Mom when I'd only lost my real mom two years before. Galling, completely galling. But, yes, overall, a chunk of me just healed. Thank God, he wasn't that stupid. Weird."

"Let's have some coffee and plan our trip to Hawaii," Jon said brightly. "Can Butch go?"

"He'd better."

"Oh, goody!" Jon said, clapping his hands together and smiling up at Butch.

Butch stepped closer and crossed his arms across his wide chest. "Great, maybe when we're there you can explain who the hell Kelly and Rex are?" He tilted his triangular-shaped head and seared her with his large, blue eyes.

Cynthia smiled at the tall handsome young man. While he was the only one in the family with an easy inner rhythm—she'd rarely seen him ruffled, even when he was a kid—she wondered how he'd react to the news.

"Sit down," Cynthia said with a sigh. "We have something to tell you."

Butch plopped his large frame down into the recliner. "I can't believe the two of you were actually able to keep something from me this long."

She rubbed her face then massaged her aching head. "Let me just tell you the whole Reader's Digest story of the past three weeks. But I'm ashamed to admit to it. I didn't want you to know about this side of me."

Butch relaxed and sent her one of his killer smiles. "For God's sake, Cyn-a-bun, I know you. Whatever you've done, I'm sure you had a good reason."

"Stupidity and hormones."

He didn't bat an eye. "See? Those are two really good reasons."

First, they dropped the bomb about the fact they'd had a child together. Butch handled it much more calmly than she thought. A yelp, some questions, but he absorbed it quickly. She gave him the rest of the story.

As to be expected, the man didn't react much. Wasn't that alarmed. She wondered if anything ever got him that stirred up.

After she was done, he sat back and cogitated. Finally, he shrugged. "So you liked the guy and fell into bed with him. Pretty normal, Cyn. And I can see why you didn't tell him. But I am surprised after all this time, you're able to discuss it now. Both you and dad are nearly physically incapable of keeping secrets. I can't imagine the mental fortitude it took to keep your mouths shut."

"He's a brat. Isn't he a brat?" Jon said with a mock offended pose.

Butch smirked. "But no, Dad. I'm not making fun of you. I'm just amazed. Took a lot of energy to suppress that." He regarded them both in turn. "You've both been hiding a world of pain from me, haven't you?"

Cynthia nodded and turned to Jon. His gaze troubled, sorrow lines etched deep on his handsome face, he raised an eyebrow and glanced down at the floor.

"Wow." Butch gestured towards her. "But you were right to keep her identity secret from the Gargoyles, Cyn. A Du Charmante? All they see are dollar signs. Ka-ching, baby."

"I know," she said miserably.

Butch sat up on the couch and rested his thick forearms on his tree-trunk sized thighs. "And that Troy creep. What a ghoul. I remember that Christmas when your father had a heart attack and he just stood there with that weird expression on his face. Fascinated by the agony on Harry's face. I've never seen anything spookier. Makes me sick he's becoming a doctor."

Cynthia said, "Well, he won't be a doctor like you. Probably learning how to make people sicker."

Butch made a sympathetic face. "I'm sorry, Cynthia. I was really hoping you'd be on the mend. Been worried about you. You haven't been you in three years."

"Agreed." She took in a deep breath and exhaled through her lips, making them flap. "I still wish I could spontaneously combust. I want out. If this is life, I want a new one."

Butch got up, came over to her and put his large hand on her shoulder. "Cynthia, try not to be so hard on yourself. You've only been out of the Crazy House for a month and a half. Give yourself a break."

She looked up at him, her heart swelling with love for him. "How the hell did you turn out this mature, Butch?"

He leaned down, hugged her and kissed her on the cheek. "Had some good teachers." He broke away. "I'm going to make us some mimosas to celebrate."

Cynthia made a face at him. "Celebrate what?"

He sent her a happy smile. "I have a sister." He disappeared into the kitchen.

Jon and Cynthia turned to each other and laughed.

"Glad there's one adult amongst us," Cynthia cracked.

"Didn't come from me. Has to be genetic."

Thank God for the two boys. They sat in the living room, relaxing with mimosas and making fun of the Gruesome Twosome.

But inside Cynthia, a war raged. While the money made her less paranoid about ending up on the streets, the thought of Sissy getting to Kelly before she did made her head want to explode.

How the hell could she endure two more days of this torture? Why did Rex have to be in Europe?

Chapter Seventeen

"Hello beautiful!" Rex said brightly when she opened the door for him. Before she could even say hi back, he'd taken her in his arms and kissed her.

Everything she wanted to say, all the anticipation regarding the date, every thought in her head evaporated. She melted into him and her knees turned to Silly Putty.

He tasted marvelous and smelled even better. His strong arms around her, his talented tongue playing in her mouth, his warmth, his presence, his heady male scent mixed with cologne, all obliterated her resolve.

He pulled away and beamed like an arc light. She'd forgotten how extraordinarily handsome he was. His sparkling blue gaze, strong jaw and that manly broken nose. She fought for mental clarity.

Running a hand down her arm, igniting the skin as he went, he asked, "Are you ready?"

She shook off the shiver of lust dancing up her spine. "Y-yeah, let me get my purse."

She turned around and had momentarily forgotten that Jon and Butch were standing there. Jon was primping for a photo shoot, fully made-up in a brightly-colored Carmen Miranda outfit—complete with a giant red ruffled neckline and a wild headdress adorned with a

Farmer's Market full of fake fruit. Butch stood behind him, sewing him into his costume.

"Ow!" Jon exclaimed loudly.

"Sorry, Dad, hold still."

Jon nodded towards her. "Aren't you going to introduce us? I mean, last time we met, you forgot my made-up name. Sorry, Rex, I hate lying." He stuck out his hand and walked towards Rex, pulling Butch along with him.

"Dad, stop! God, I almost stabbed you with the needle." Butch smiled at Rex. "Hi, Rex, I'm Butch, Jon's son."

Rex laughed and moved forward to grab Jon's hand. "Hi Butch, and Jon, pleased to meet you both."

"Me, too. Ow!" Jon exclaimed, putting a hand on his lower back where Butch was working. "Sorry, my boy is all thumbs when it comes to sewing."

Butch sent him a glare. "No, I'm fine, you keep moving. And don't insult me or I'll never let you out of this thing. Think shopping at Safeway. Checker would charge you big for all that fruit on your head."

Jon made a huge exaggerated gasp. "You are such a brat. Why do they grow up and turn on you like that? Have you noticed that, Rex? They turn on you as soon as they get old enough to think for themselves."

"Uh, yes, they do," Rex said, laughing delightedly.

"So where are you taking her?" Jon sounded like her father rather than her ex.

Rex didn't miss it. "My intentions are completely honorable."

Jon pointed at the door dramatically. "Well, then, you'd better turn around and walk right out of here, mister."

"We're leaving," Cynthia said. "Come on, Rex, before he subverts you."

Jon sent her a mock upset look. "Did you call me a subvert? Damn, I used to rank high enough to be called a pervert."

"Pervert," she replied.

He shook his head and pursed his red lips. "I fed you that line."

Butch laughed and turned to Rex. "You can't tell they've spent most of their lives together, can you?"

"No. Sound like perfect strangers."

Jon smacked Cynthia on the shoulder. "Did you hear? He called me perfect."

Cynthia rolled her eyes and headed for the door. "Oh, Christ. Okay, Carmen, don't wait up. We're headed to Pescadero."

Jon squealed. "No! We used to camp there, the three of us."

"I told him," Cynthia said.

Jon waved his arms. "Where? Where?"

"Dad, hold still."

Rex stopped at the door and turned back to Jon. "My house. It's on Ranch Road."

Jon's hands flew to his face. "Oh, my God, no! Do you know who owns the pink house? The one with the view? That's Cynthia's favorite. I think it's tacky, personally, but she's dying to get inside."

Rex's lips twitched with a half-smile. "Well, then she's in luck, because I own it. That's my house."

Jon paled. Cynthia and Butch exploded in laughter.

Jon's face turned as red as the apples in his headdress. "And I'm just dying."

"The color *is* tacky, but I kind of like it," Rex said with a cute grin.

Jon cooled his face with his hands. "Ignore me. Christ. Butch when you get done with that seam can you help me get my foot out of my mouth?"

Butch snorted, but didn't move his eyes from his work. "It's so far in there, I think you'll need surgery to remove it."

"We're leaving so you can be contrite alone with your son," Cynthia announced. She took Rex by the arm, led him to the door and opened it.

Jon shook his head and looked heavenwards. "How embarrassing."

"See you later, kids," Cynthia said with a wave as she followed Rex out.

Jon waved back. "Bye. And talk me up to him, will ya? I think he has the wrong impression of me."

She sent him a look. "No, I'd say it's totally accurate."

"Bitch."

She grinned and winked. "Bye, honey."

As she closed the door, Jon broke his "entertainment face" and sent her a worried look. He mouthed the words "Good luck."

God bless the man.

They got into the elevator and Rex burst out laughing. "Is he always like that?"

She gave a slight nod. "Worse, actually." She pushed the button for the lobby.

"Was he always that…?"

"Swishy? No. That came later. When he came out. He was always a bit feminine around the edges, but he wasn't a textbook gay man. He was funny, though. And evil."

Rex's expression softened. "I can see why you fell in love with him."

"He's a great guy. And his son is a doll."

"I noticed. Butch loves you, too."

She smiled. "He's a wonderful man. Going to be a research doctor. He wants to cure AIDS. His dad—his other dad—Malcolm, died from it when he was ten."

"That's rough."

"Yeah, you know that one. Me, too."

He ran his hand down her back in an affectionate gesture, rocking her. "We all have that in common, don't we?"

"I think we have more in common than either of us could ever comprehend."

He grinned, misreading her secret meaning. She was a rat. A giant, two-legged rat.

As they drove down Highway One in Rex's Bentley, Cynthia looked out over the Pacific Ocean. Sun shone off the pristine blue water, waves crashed upon the dark jagged rocks and the golden sand beach. A formation of pelicans in a V shape flew low above the water. Seagulls grouped along the water's edge, foraging.

What a perfect place to drown herself. She could have Rex stop on the pretext of taking a walk on the beach, then hurl herself into the surf. She bit her lip. How badly would it hurt to die from drowning?

Rex kept glancing over at her, sending her concerned looks. It was obvious she was about to explode. She'd ceased all eye contact after the first two miles. Her body tight, she was worried her foot would come off from its ceaseless, violent tapping. She couldn't figure out how to tell him. Maybe she should have confessed when they first got in his car. But she wanted time to explain before he kicked her out of his life.

Once they got to his place, she'd tell him. It was only three miles to Pescadero proper from there. She'd blurt out the truth, let him rail at her, then she could walk to Duarte's Tavern and drink herself into oblivion until Jon and Butch picked her up. Thankfully, Butch had a good car.

But how was she supposed to confess to this amazing, wonderful man that she was his daughter's birth mother? That she'd lied to him? Slept with him knowing how hurt he'd be in the end?

Poor Rex. He didn't deserve any of this crap. Cynthia hated this mirror of her behavior. Hated. It.

No, strike that, she hated herself. More than she ever had.

The mood in the car plummeted.

Think of some polite conversation, you idiot!

"God, I love it here," she said, her voice cracking. She cleared her throat. "I love the walk down below. From Pomponio beach to San Gregorio."

She glanced over at him.

He smirked and nodded at her. "So are you going to tell me what's on your mind?"

Her knotted stomach twisted a bit harder. Great. A psychic. Of course, she had no idea how he could miss her signals. Astronauts on the Space Station were probably picking up on her mood.

"Yes."

"But not now."

"Nope."

"Will I be in danger of driving off the road?"

"Yes," she replied too quickly.

He gave her a sharp look. "Is it that bad?"

To put him at ease, she decided to tell him a white lie. "Look, I'm making a big deal out of this, it'll probably be nothing to you. Don't worry. I have a tendency towards over-dramatizing everything. I'll tell you when we get to your place." She attempted a cheerful smile.

"Okay," he said, frowning.

Was her acting that bad?

Did she really need to ask that question?

They had a calamari appetizer and artichoke soup at Duarte's, a rustic, pine-walled coastal staple. They made small talk, but the air was heavy between them. Cynthia was inwardly beating herself so thoroughly she was sure she must be hemorrhaging.

They drove to the Pink House, as Cynthia knew it, and walked inside. It was musty and cold from disuse, but gorgeous. High ceilings, oak floors, chic three-color paint scheme—copper, off-white and cinnamon—and windows galore. Spacious and light. Not only did the magnificent home afford astonishing views of Pescadero, the ocean and the hills, the walls were filled with extraordinary abstract artwork. Clearly all painted by the same artist.

Immediately drawn to the work, she walked up to a group of paintings to check the signature. *Du Charmante.* She felt clubbed over the head. "You did these? *You did these?* My God, you're a bloody genius. Why the hell are you wasting your time making money when you can paint like this?"

Rex looked between the artwork and her, blinking rapidly, seeming taken aback. "You really like them?"

"More than like, I looove them. Wow, look at you," she said, pushing on his hard shoulder. "An artist, wow." He'd become even more attractive in her eyes. Which in turn made her feel worse.

He broke into a broad smile. "What? You thought I'd paint shit?"

"Yes. You make money, dear. But wow. I was wrong." She turned back to the art. "Magnificent use of color. Bold, exciting work. Very daring, really. Cubism, expressionism and you blend them so well. I mean, two disparate styles and the way you interconnect them, it's genius. I am blown away. You need to show these to the world, Rex, really. You are good."

He blushed and coughed. "Well, I always thought so, but believe me, our views are not shared by my world. This is the only place Elizabeth would let me hang them. And only because she didn't come up here. She hated them."

"You're kidding me. Did she appreciate art?"

"Well, only insofar as decorating. And she needed outside validation on all her choices, she didn't pick from the heart. She didn't understand art nor artists, the whole process bewildered her. It was the part of me she liked the least. She tolerated my endeavor, but it definitely bothered her."

"That's too bad. Because you've got it, boy."

He seemed relieved. His wide shoulders relaxed, his grin turned easy. "Had a teacher in college who thought I had something. He was the last one."

"You stopped showing them after Elizabeth's reaction?"

"Well, yeah." He touched one of his works, running a long finger over the built-up paint. "She was worried about being embarrassed in front of her friends and family. She thought because I'd had little formal training that I was just playing with paints like a child. She didn't want anyone to know what I was doing. She said they'd all lie and say the work was good. She didn't say it to hurt me. She believed it. She thought it would hurt me if people knew. She wasn't mean by any stretch of the imagination, she was a forthright person."

"Wow. Still, I can't imagine squelching someone."

"We lived in a very narrow world. Her world was especially narrow. But that's what I wanted. I bought into it. I chose her specifically for that attribute."

"No, I know you're responsible for half. No one can do anything to you unless you let them."

"True."

"But these are fantastic, Rex, really."

His grin stretched so wide, she thought it might leap off his face.

He showed her the house, then sat her down on a huge brown leather couch in front of a picture window that overlooked the hills and ocean beyond.

He took her by the hand. "I thought I could wait, but whatever you're holding inside you is bothering you to the point where you've barely made eye contact with me since I picked you up. What is it? Just spill it. You'll feel better. I'll feel better."

"You're right." A veil of shame fell over her. Tears welled in her eyes and her body shook. She fought to keep her lunch in her stomach. "First of all, I apologize. This was too important to let it go this long. And I'm ashamed of my behavior."

His expression turned grave.

She stared at her hand in his. This would be the last time. She stifled a sob and sighed heavily. "Remember when I told you that I lost my child?"

"Yes, when you caught Jon in bed with the reverend."

She grimaced. "Well, I wasn't quite truthful when I said I lost her. I had her. I didn't lose her. I gave her up."

He leaned in. "You gave her up for adoption?"

"Yes."

"Was that because of the shock of finding out Jon was gay?"

She rubbed the back of her hand. "Yeah. That was the most horrible part of my life. Thank God for Georgina, my high school buddy. She showed up the day I came home from the hospital and stayed for a week. Without Georgina's help, I would have lost my mind. It was Georgina who suggested surrendering Alice—that was my baby. Has a different name now of course." *Kelly.* She coughed back the tears. "Those last three weeks after Georgey left—when I was alone with the baby..." She shuddered. Rex threw his arm around her and squeezed.

"Horrifying. No sleep, baby's crying, I don't know what to do. I have no one there, no money and no close family to depend on. I couldn't even turn to my pastor because he was part of the betrayal."

"I'm so sorry," he said, rubbing her back.

"Me, too. And I knew I was failing miserably as a mother. Painfully aware of the fact. I couldn't stand it. I knew she deserved better."

"What about Jon? Where was he?"

She let out a long breath through her teeth. "I wouldn't let him near me or the child. I was super prejudiced about the gay thing back then, mainly because it took Jon from me. And I badgered Jon into signing the surrender forms, he didn't want to give her up, he even offered to take her. But all I wanted to do was kill him. I was pretty crazy." *A lot like now.*

"That's nothing to be ashamed of," he said, squeezing her knee. "Your dreams had been shattered. You'd just created *Love Unlimited*, that was how you pictured your life. Not separated with Jon running around discovering his sexuality. Rash decision—I can see why you regret it now—but I don't understand why you'd think I'd have a problem with it. Hell, that's how I got Kelly. If people like you didn't give up their children, I wouldn't have had my little girl."

The phone rang. Cynthia slammed back her tears. She had to keep it together until she told him everything.

Rex put both arms around her and kissed the side of her head. He might as well have punched her. She couldn't handle this. She couldn't.

"Let it ring," he said in a soothing tone. "No one but Jess knows I'm here and she'd only be calling in an emergency. Go on, Cynthia. I don't understand why you're crying. Did something happen to the baby after she was adopted? Did she get into a bad family?"

She wiped some tears from her eyes, but couldn't look at him. She continued rubbing her hands together. "No. A really, really good one."

A voice boomed across the room, coming from the answering machine. "Rex! Pick up the phone, NOW! If you're there, run and catch this. This is Jess and I need to talk to you PRONTO!"

Rex rolled his eyes and shot a disgusted glance towards the phone. "Oh, hell. Cynthia, I'm so sorry, but—"

"Take it, please. This can wait. Believe me, it can wait."

He hugged her and her heart nearly collapsed. Nuzzling her, he said, "I hate to leave you like this."

Tears leaked from her eyes. This was the last time he'd kiss her or hug her.

"Rex! You didn't answer your cell, you must be there." The voice echoed off the tall ceilings and hardwood floors. "I'm sorry if you're busy, but damn it, man, get on the phone!"

She pulled away and gave him a little shove on the shoulder. "I'll be fine. Please, go, she sounds frantic."

"She does."

His expression conflicted, he leapt up and raced to the phone. "Hello? Yes, Jess, I'm here. Wait, what? But I don't have a TV in— there's one in the office. Okay, I'm running." He shrugged at Cynthia and rushed across the room. Covering the receiver, he said, "Jess needs me to see something on TV, I'll be in my office here for a bit. Are you going to be okay?"

She managed a weak smile. "Right as rain, no worries about me."

"Okay, thanks. I'll get rid of her as soon as I can, but this sounds big, whatever it is." He pushed open a door off the expansive living room and hustled inside.

The sounds of a television came out of the room and Rex's muffled voice. She couldn't hear what he was talking about, but he sounded excited.

She collapsed back against the couch and broke into sobs. Shit. Almost got it out. She swallowed hard and got control. The tears stopped. She sat up and shivered. Damn this. It was almost over and now she had to wait. Christ, what torture.

Her nose dripping, she held a finger underneath and searched the room for Kleenex. None on the oak shelves, the knotty pine coffee table or on the tall oak secretary in the corner. A bathroom was off the main living room. She headed there.

Once inside the western-themed restroom, she blew her nose and stared at herself in the barbed-wire trimmed mirror. She looked miserable. Bags under her reddened eyes, a hollow stare behind her gaze. Like a murderer on death row being led to the execution chamber. What was up with that stupid phone call? What horrid timing!

She splashed water on her face and took a deep breath while absently examining the various branding irons adorning the walls. She resisted the urge to pull one off and bash herself over the head with it.

She walked back out into the living room and Vance stood there, hands on his hips. Vance? Her muscles tensed with frustration, her stomach burned with urgency. Now she had to get rid of Vance before she could tell Rex. *Fuck!*

"What are you doing here?" she demanded. "Is Kelly with you?"

Clearly agitated, his face red, he searched the immediate area. "Where's Rex?"

"In his office, something came up, he's on the phone with Jess. What's going on?"

"What's going on?" he hissed. "What's going on? You dare to fucking ask me that when you're here to blow my cover? You lied to me!" he nearly shouted. He glanced towards Rex's office and lowered his voice. "You lied to me."

Her mind a chaotic storm of conflicting thoughts, she couldn't begin to understand him. "About what? What the hell are you talking about?"

His eyes darted between her and the door to Rex's office, his hands twitching. Sweat beaded on his forehead. He looked like he was about to combust. "We can't talk in here, Rex may come back in." He looked around the area and settled on the kitchen. "Follow me, in there, the kitchen. Quickly, I have to know what you told him."

Motioning for her to follow, Vance dashed into the kitchen.

Blazing with irritation, Cynthia followed.

James Miller was on television, his head bowed, his hands manacled, flanked by several police as he was marched past a gauntlet of reporters.

Rex couldn't believe it. He could only stare.

Jess continued her patter into the phone. "...I got the call right after you left. David from James' office called to give us the heads up. James got caught in a sting operation. The asshole was running a Ponzi scheme all these years. You and all his friends were caught in it."

Rex felt like someone had ripped the floorboards from under his feet and beat him over the head with them. Flailing for an anchor, he tried to comprehend the news. "He was running a scheme the whole time?"

"Apparently. All those late-hour trips to Europe were to get money to pay his investors here. He thought the game could go on indefinitely. Guess he was wrong."

His knees turned to liquid and the room canted. "I have to sit down," Rex said, fumbling for a chair.

The betrayal. The amazing betrayal. James had bald-faced lied to him for how long? He collapsed in the large chair behind his desk, his pulse pounding in his ears, his limbs shaking.

He'd married his only daughter off to the fiend's son! Could the humiliation be any worse? He longed to wrap his hands around James' neck and squeeze until his head snapped off.

"I hate to tell you this, but Greg Marx called."

Rex bolted out of his chair and paced across the room. "God, no." He'd been courting Marx for the past two months to come on board Vector. He knew he shouldn't have introduced him to James. *Fuck.*

"God, yes. He was, uh, fairly upset and had some, uh, criticisms."

He clapped his hand to his forehead. "Shit."

"I'd lay low if I were you."

He stalked back to the desk and leaned against it. "I'm going to be stained with this thing. Christ, this couldn't have come at a worse time. I can pay him off, but, oh, God."

"You can't blame yourself. James was your trusted friend for twenty-five years. You married your only daughter off to the man's son. You didn't take that lightly."

"Wonder how many lawyers he paid off. Sure knew how to cook the books, the bastard." He pounded his desk with a fist. "Damn it, I hope we can survive this."

"You weren't the only one, Rex. He took a lot of people down with this one, including everyone in your social circle. I don't know how the guy could sleep at night."

He massaged his forehead, trying to ease the pain. "Well, he hasn't been. He must have known it was all about to crash down around his shoulders. Wonder if Kelly knows yet. Damn it!" He knocked a stack of books to the floor, making a loud thud that echoed off the walls. "Related to the charlatan. Hope I never see him again, I'm mad enough to throttle that jerk. Twenty-five years I've put up with his incessant bragging and showing off. He just bought those houses in Sausalito. Poor Geraldine." He threw his leg up on the desk and half sat on it.

"Don't poor Geraldine her," Jess countered angrily. "She was in on it. She helped him. She got arrested, too, you just didn't see it on the news. Part of his bargain was that he'd allow himself to be showboated in the media if they arrested her more quietly."

"What about Vance?"

"Not enough evidence to implicate him. James is trying to shield him. And not to alarm you, but we were investigated, too. I guess there's been FBI around here, we didn't know it. But you were found innocent. I heard that from a friend down at FBI headquarters, a girl I used to room with in college. I just called her, she gave me the lowdown. Funny, I'd seen her a month ago and she'd been remote. Just now, she apologized. She knew we were under investigation at the time, but couldn't say anything. She wasn't supposed to tell me just now, but she's a good friend."

Rex held his stomach. "I'm going to be sick."

"Sorry to ruin your little homecoming with the Amazon."

"No, thank you. Thanks for tracking me down. God, I'm glad I turned off my cell. Maybe I'll just stay up here for a few weeks until it all calms down." He stroked the tense muscles of his jaw.

"Might as well stay put, at least for the weekend. Let the furor die down. Media's going to be all over you."

"I have to call Marx, at least." He sighed and shook his head. "Shit. Could you put in a call to Horatio and see where our liability is with this?"

"Already did. He's assessing the damage right now. But off the top of his head, he said you did no wrong. The worst is the embarrassment, but legally, you're in the clear. But he is checking to make sure."

"Goddamn him," Rex growled, pounding his fist on the desk again. "Took me for a ride and now my bloody daughter is married to his idiot son."

"Let's just hope Vance is in the clear."

"Christ."

He got off the phone with Jess, stalked over and slammed off the TV. He'd seen enough. Betrayal stung him. Bile crept up his throat. Dizzy, he sat at his desk and put his head in his hands. His whole business could be in jeopardy. What an idiot. He'd smelled something wrong, yet he'd gone ahead and invested anyway. He should have run an investigation on the man the moment he had any suspicion.

Yes, he'd been toying with the idea of leaving Vector, but not this way. With the horror of this being thrust upon him, he realized just how much he loved that business.

Goddamn it!

Tapping his foot angrily, he gazed out the window at the lush, green hills and the fog rolling in over the ocean. At least he had this place to retreat to. Far away from all the mess.

Movement outside caught his attention. Looked like the top of someone's head. He got up from behind the desk to check.

Kelly. *Kelly?* What was she doing there? And why was she creeping by the house with a wary look on her face, like she was expecting to be attacked? She obviously had no idea he stood there. What the hell?

Of course. She probably heard about the arrest and wanted to talk to him, but didn't want to disturb him. Probably thought he and Cynthia were…involved.

He opened the door to the outside. Kelly swung on him, her eyes huge.

"Kelly, what are you doing here?"

"Sshhhh!" she said, making a motion for him to quiet. She looked incredibly upset and ready to explode.

His fatherly senses tingled. Something big was going on and he got the distinct impression it had nothing to do with James Miller. He stepped down the short staircase, allowing the door to close behind him. He walked across the roughly mowed field and up to his daughter. "What's going on?"

"Keep your voice down, Dad, I don't want Vance to know I'm here. I followed him here."

"Why don't you want him to know you followed him? And why is Vance here?"

"Because something's going on with him and Cynthia."

Incomprehensible. Rex couldn't begin to understand what she meant. "Cynthia? How the—"

Kelly waved a hand, the line between her eyes deepening. "I don't know. God, I've had the weirdest day. This morning, in my office, this strange skinny woman with dyed black hair burst in and announced she knew who my birth parents were."

His heart hit his stomach. "*What?*"

She held up her hand, then rubbed her forehead. "Yeah, wait, it gets weirder. She went on to tell me if I really wanted to know, I'd have to pay for the information. A million goddamned dollars. Then —right in the middle of this extortion thing—this tall, weirdly good-looking guy with dark hair and amazing green eyes came flying in and started railing at the skinny woman. He apologized for her and told me that he'd get rid of her and to ignore her. She argued with him and he somehow got her to shut up. Then he stared at me like…" She shrugged her slim shoulders. "I don't know. I was a ghost or something. Then he pushed her out the door and left."

His mind swirled and twisted, trying to make sense of the situation. "What?"

"Yeah," Kelly said, pressing some dirt into a gopher hole with her foot. "So, I was freaking out and wanted to talk to Vance and his cell wasn't on and he was working from home today. So I went home and get this: the same strange skinny woman was there," she said with a large gesture. "And Vance and she were yelling at each other in our living room. Something about an affair and keeping something from me. He ordered her out, she yelled some threats about Cynthia and him—and telling the world something—I didn't hear. So I hid in the alcove near the front door. Vance rushed past me, out the door, and I followed him to this apartment in SoMa, where he pounded on a door and demanded to see Cynthia. I guess it's her apartment."

Adrenaline spiked his heart rate and he crossed his arms. "Are you kidding?"

"No, Dad, wait, just listen. So he yelled at these guys in the apartment—one was dressed like a woman—that was weird, like Carmen Miranda or something, all this fruit on his head—then they shut the door."

His heart sank and his shoulders fell. Cynthia and Jon's place. He'd prayed the story would have taken a different turn. Cynthia's confession. Somehow this all related to what she was about to tell him. His stomach tightened so much it hurt.

Kelly kicked a dirt clod and sent it flying. "So I snuck up and put my ear to the door, but all I heard was your name and Pescadero. Then Vance opened the door, I barely had time to hide on the nearby stairwell. But I saw his face. He was furious, Dad, and ready to kill. I've never seen him so mad. So I followed him here and he just went inside. I think he's been cheating on me, Dad. He hasn't come home a bunch of nights since we got married and with all that yelling about Cynthia and an affair, the only thing I can I think is that Vance is having an affair with Cynthia."

Rex's mind evaporated in a black cloud. His whole body went rubbery, he took a step back, stumbled on a clump of poppies and caught himself. Was this her secret?

But why did she go off on that whole saga about her child? Was she leading up to the part where she was about to confess she was sleeping with his son-in-law? How could the two stories relate? His already nauseous stomach revolted even further. He had to cough to stop himself from puking.

Kelly moved close to him and squeezed his arm. "Sorry to dump that on you, I hope I'm wrong, but that's what I have to find out."

A red-tailed hawk arrowed into the ground not twenty yards from them, nabbing a field mouse. The predator's large brown wings flapped gracefully as it swooped back up over their heads and high into the air, the mouse in its talons squeaking hideously. He knew just how the mouse felt.

She glanced at the bird, then tugged on his sleeve. "Now come on, but stay down," she said, crouching low and dragging him up to the house. She let go, stopped and peeked in a window. "Oh, shit, they're headed to the kitchen." She motioned for him to follow. "Hurry, Dad, and come on!" She sped off around the corner.

He dashed around the edge of the house and caught her hand. "Shouldn't we just confront them?"

She turned to him, her jaw set, her eyes hard. "Vance has been lying to me. Cynthia's lied to you. We can't trust they'll tell us the truth." She jerked her head towards the front of the house. "Come on."

"Good point."

His vision foggy with fear and anger, he tripped on the uneven ground and caught himself before he fell. Cynthia? In an affair with Vance? He thought of that look on her face in the car. In retrospect, it was shame. Damn it. Vance and she? Sleeping together? It would fit. Goddamn it, it would fit! What else could it be?

Ugly dark emotions filled his mind. The weight of the accusation was so heavy, he felt dragged down, like he had anvils attached to his limbs.

Kelly stopped under the main kitchen window.

It was cracked open, Cynthia's voice and Vance's rang out clearly. Kelly motioned for him to get next to her, right underneath the opening to the window. They hunkered down and listened. His heart banged against his ribs and his hands trembled.

"...you were going to tell him about me, weren't you?" Vance demanded.

"No, I wasn't. I told you that. That is between you and Kelly."

"So who was that skinny meth-head dirtbag? You obviously told her. And she demanded money. She's a friend of yours, isn't she? You're trying to bleed me for money and you didn't want me knowing you were behind it."

Cynthia made an exasperated noise. "Oh, for crying out loud, no, I don't want your stupid money. Did she have black hair that looked like it was cut with a weed whacker? Was she missing a couple teeth?"

"So you do know her," Vance replied in an accusatory tone.

Kelly pulled on Rex's arm and whispered. "That was the woman who came to see me."

He nodded and held up a hand to quiet her.

"Yes. Sissy Slaughter. She's my hideous stepsister from hell. She's blackmailing me, too. Guess she decided my money wasn't enough, she was going for the whole lot. God, I hope she hasn't talked to Kelly."

"About me?" Vance demanded.

"About me. And you. Damn it. Her son Troy was following me that night you and I had our little scene at the Tuxedo Club."

Cynthia had seen Vance that night they got together? She hadn't mentioned it.

She continued, sounding upset. "He must have overheard our conversation. I'm sorry. I should have done something sooner. I knew they'd come after you and Kelly, but I thought I'd have a chance to straighten out everything with Rex first. I was telling him who I was just now, right when he got some stupid phone call. As soon as you leave, I'm going in there and I'm telling him everything."

"About me?"

"No, Vance, stop. That's your business. I'm only going to tell him about me, not you. But if Sissy knows you're gay, everyone will know shortly. And I'm sorry."

Kelly gasped and crumpled. He caught her and held her close. Her whole body shook.

"It's okay, Katydid, just hold on," he whispered.

Rage flooded his veins, his jaw clenched. He was going to kill Vance with his bare hands. How dare he marry his daughter when he was gay? This whole James Miller fuckover just got worse and worse. Unimaginable horror.

There was only a slight tinge of relief at Cynthia not being Vance's lover. But what could she be hiding if wasn't about an affair with Vance? And how would Vance know her secret? Something happened that night Rex found her on Polk. She said she'd gotten fired from a stagehand job at the Tuxedo Club. That was where she had a scene with Vance. Was she a drag queen? A drag king? What the hell could it be?

"Goddamn this!" Vance railed. "My life is over! It's ruined. All because of you."

"No, because of you. Because of your dishonesty. You should have told Kelly from the onset about yourself."

Rex had to give Cynthia credit, she was clearly the more lucid of the two.

"I couldn't," Vance said, his voice full of anguish. "I love her. I can't stand the thought of losing her. And I'm not gay, I'm bi."

"Whatever, you're still in a relationship with a man. You should have told her about yourself and broke up with Baldy."

"I can't. I need him, too," Vance whined.

"If you had to pick, could you?"

"Yes, I'd choose Kelly."

Kelly's body stiffened on that line. She punched her fist and her face went red. Rex squeezed her.

"Get your priorities straight," Cynthia ordered. "Come clean with her. It's the only way out. For once, put her ahead of your needs. And do it fast. Because Sissy won't give up."

"Could you stop her?"

"I wish. Once Sissy smells money, she's like an epoxy booger, no way to get her off you. So, today, I tell Rex. And if I were you, I'd tell Kelly. Then those bastards can't get us."

Rex had heard enough. He didn't know why Cynthia needed to come clean or about what, but he didn't care. There had been enough deception, it was time to stop all this bullshit.

He steeled himself and straightened his shoulders. He needed to be strong for his daughter and himself. "Kelly, we need to go in."

Her oval face pale, tears ran down her cheeks. She stared straight ahead, her hazel gaze hollow. "He's gay, Dad. My husband is gay."

His heart tore at the pain creasing his daughter's face. He would do anything to save her this agony.

"And Cynthia apparently knew it. But didn't say anything," he snapped.

Kelly squeezed him. "I don't blame her, like she said, it wasn't her place. It was Vance's. Damn it, I knew something was weird with Mike. He's so possessive of Vance's time. Shit. I'm going to be sick." She held her stomach with both hands.

"Let's go in and confront them. I need to hear the truth from those two people's lips." He took a step towards the house, but Kelly held him back.

"But Dad, we haven't found out Cynthia's secret."

"Direct approach is the best at this point."

Kelly wouldn't budge. "Dad, I don't want to. I can't face him or her. I'm about to fall apart."

He tightened his grip on her. "Come on, Katydid, I'm here for you. Lean on me. We'll get through this. It's best to face these things head on. Even if those two characters are liars and sneaks, we aren't. Hold your head, high, my girl. We've done nothing wrong."

She sighed and nodded. Lifting gaze to his, she said, "You're right, Dad. I feel like I just walked into a nightmare."

"Me, too."

When they walked into the kitchen, the expressions on Cynthia and Vance's faces were priceless. They looked like robbers in a bank vault caught with their arms loaded with cash. Mouths gaped, eyes white with shock. Whatever Cynthia's secret was, it was big.

Vance stepped forward. "Kelly! What are you doing here?"

Kelly wailed, "You bastard! You lied to me! You're gay!" She rushed at him and pounded him on the chest with her fists.

Vance caught her wrists. "Darling, I'm so sorry. I didn't know how to tell you. I—I can't help who I am."

"You should have told me!"

"I didn't want to hurt you."

"Well, I'm more hurt now. *How dare you*?" she sobbed.

Rex would rather cut out his heart and lungs with a can opener than see his daughter hurt like this. It took all his strength not to strangle the boy.

"I want a divorce, I want out, I'm moving out!"

Rex opened his arms to her. "You can move back in with me, Kelly."

"I will, Dad. You're the only one I can count on." She rushed to Rex and flung herself into his embrace.

He wrapped his long arms around her and stroked her head. Her whole body trembled. He hugged her tighter. "You'll be okay, baby, we'll get through this."

Tears streaming down Vance's face, he slumped on a kitchen stool, looking shell-shocked. Cynthia stood back and watched the scene, pain etching her beautiful features. Her focus was on Kelly. She could relate, she'd married a gay man, too.

But what was her bloody secret? He waited for Kelly to calm down.

Quite quickly, his daughter straightened up, stopped her tears and pushed away from him. "I can't give into all this now, it's too big. And there's something that hasn't been settled here for you, Dad. Cynthia has a secret and everyone seems to know it but Dad and me." She faced Cynthia. "Are you going to come clean now? Like you advised my…Vance?"

Cynthia closed her eyes and leaned against the blue-tiled counter. "Oh, the timing here is bloody awful. I'm so sorry, Kelly. I know what you're going through. I married a gay man."

Kelly narrowed her gaze and put her hands on her hips. "Was that true? You've been lying about a lot of stuff. And you've lied to my father, which I don't appreciate. Can you please just tell us what this huge secret is? What? You're married in another state? You're a criminal? You're in the Witness Protection Program, what? I can't take much more of this shit and neither can my father."

"Just tell her, for God's sake," Vance said to Cynthia. "Or I will."

Cynthia's face went stormy and she jabbed a finger his way. "Back off, boy-o. I'm about to beat you for what you've done to her."

"Cynthia, please," Rex said.

She glanced at Rex, then her dark gaze fell to the floor. She looked like she was about to face a firing squad. She ran a shaking hand through her short hair. "Oh, for crying out loud. Okay, okay. It's just so bloody hard." She turned to Kelly and her face became a mask of agony.

Why was she directing her confession to Kelly?

"Kelly, I'm...oh, Christ."

"She's your mother, okay? Your stupid birth mother," Vance blurted out.

Rex's whole world stopped. It was like he was looking at everyone in the room from the end of a long tunnel. Cynthia? Kelly's mother?

He examined her face, every inch of it. Kelly was all over her. The eyes, the chin, the nose. How had he missed the resemblance?

Holy God. He wished she'd confessed to being a murderer. To sleeping with Vance. Anything but Kelly's mother.

The betrayal.

His blood turned to fire, his stomach wrung hard, he had to fight to keep the bile in his gut.

Kelly stared at Cynthia, slack-jawed, her gaze wide. "You? You're my *mother*?"

Cynthia's lower lip trembled. "I'm sorry, kiddo. You should not have found out like this."

Rex couldn't hold himself back any longer. "She sure as shit shouldn't have!" He let go of Kelly to advance on Cynthia. "How dare you use me like this? Just to get to my daughter? How depraved are you, woman? How desperate? You gave her up! You have no right to barge into her life and mine and ruin it. How dare you? I loved you! And you used me!"

"Hey!" Cynthia fired back, her gaze flaming. She pointed at him. "I did not use you! I did not know it was you in the park. I only found out after Jon and I stalked Kelly one day after the accident and there you were in a wheelchair. I had no idea you were her father. No idea. And that's why I ran. I didn't want this to happen."

He sneered at her. "Oh, and that's why you slept with me, because you didn't want that to happen. Don't give me this shit, Cynthia. You knew what you were doing, you used me!" He stabbed at her with a shaking finger.

She jabbed her finger right back at him. "I did not! I lied to you! I made an error in judgment! And I'm sorry, but I had to protect her," she said, gesturing wildly at Kelly. "The only reason I lied was to protect Kelly. Everything I've done, every lie I've told was to protect her from my awful stepsisters." She dropped her arm and her shoulders slumped. "But I didn't use you. I love you too much and have too much respect for you to do that."

Her words slapped him in the face, hard. "Bullshit! Protect her from your evil stepsisters—liar! You don't respect me. You never did. You used me to get to my daughter. *How dare you?* I knew whoever gave up Kelly was an immoral, weak ne'er-do-well. Well, I was right. What I didn't realize was that she was a liar as well," he spat.

Cynthia's jaw clamped and her ears and scalp retreated on her skull. "You're angry and I don't blame you, but I'm neither immoral nor weak and I won't let you disparage me like that, Rex. No matter how much I love you. I did right by Kelly and yes, my judgment was off where you were concerned, but Jesus Christ, man, I did run. I tried to get away from you, but you kept tracking me down."

"And I suppose I *made* you sleep with me. Liar!" He pointed dramatically towards the front door. "Get out of my house! Get out of my life! I never want to see you again!"

Kelly held up her hands and got between them. "Wait! Both of you, shut up and wait. Dad, give me a minute here, this is my mother. Someone I've been searching for my whole life." She turned to Cynthia. "Cynthia, if you're my mother, who's my father?"

At that moment, Jon came rushing into the kitchen in his full Carmen Miranda regalia, Butch right on his heels. "Am I too late?" When he saw Vance, his shoulders fell. "Oh, God, I am. Shit. Vance came to the house, I got here as soon as I could, but I couldn't fit in the car with the headpiece on—practically broke my neck trying to sit— and—what?" He searched everyone's faces, his gaze rested on Kelly, then he turned to Cynthia. "Does she know? Did you tell her?"

Her face grim, Cynthia nodded. "Yeah, but not all of it. Amazing timing as always, Jon." She turned to Kelly and gestured towards Jon. "Kelly, this is your father, Carmen Miranda."

Another gut punch. Rex reeled, so angry he couldn't speak.

Kelly blinked at Jon and gave him an up and down examination. She gestured towards him, seeming blown away. "You're my...my *father*?"

Jon sent her a sheepish smile and shrugged. "Yes, darling. I'm Daddy."

Kelly swung on Cynthia. "So what you told me the other morning is true?"

"Yes. What I didn't tell you was that the baby I lost was you."

Kelly turned to Jon, her brow furrowed deeply. "Did you really sleep with the pastor?"

Jon went slack-jawed, then threw up his hands and made a loud, exasperated huff. "Why is this the first thing that gets out? Why is it always, I was blowing the pastor? Why not, she kicked me out of the house and wouldn't let me in the operating room and forced me into signing the adoption forms?" he said, gesturing wildly. "Huh? Why doesn't that part of the story come up first? No, it's always I was fucking Reverend Gary in our bedroom. It wasn't that sordid. It just happened." Jon sighed and his face drew down with sorrow. "Oh,

God. I'm sorry, kid. I never meant to hurt you or Cynthia. I was in heavy-duty denial. I thought if I ignored my sexuality, it would go away. And then Reverend Gary came over and there were all these hormones and bad judgments and then your mother walked in and whammo, there was her water all over the floor and then all this screaming and she ran out and—oh, God. It wasn't good. But I still wish we'd kept you."

"Jesus." Kelly's face pale, she stared between them.

Rex had enough. He stood tall. "All right, I'm all done with this impromptu family gathering. I want all of you out of my house." He pointed at the front door again. Then he turned on his soon-to-be ex-son-in-law. "And Vance, I seriously hope you go to jail with your father."

"My father?" Vance demanded. His attention darted between Rex and Kelly. "What does he have to do with all this?"

"I'd check your Blackberry if I were you," Rex bit out harshly. "I think you have some important messages. You're going to need a lawyer, a good one."

Vance took a step back, his gaze wide. "What? Why?"

"What happened, Dad?" Kelly asked, putting a hand on Rex's arm.

Glaring at Vance, Rex growled through gritted teeth, "James Miller just got arrested for a Ponzi scheme and I was one of his best patsies and he may have just cost me my business."

"No, no," Vance said, his face turning as white as his polo shirt. He shook his head, held up his hands and backed up until he hit the kitchen counter. "No. No. That's wrong."

Kelly ran her hand down Rex's tense back. "Oh, no. Dad, no."

"God, Rex, I'm so sorry," Cynthia said, taking a few steps towards him, her face full of empathy.

He wanted to leap across the room and slap her. "Your sympathy, I don't need, woman," he snapped. "Now if you're quite through ruining my daughter's life and mine, you can go. And take Carmen Miranda with you." He jerked his head towards the door.

"No need to be rude, Rex," Jon said, seeming offended. "She may have made a mistake, but she never meant to hurt you."

Rex wanted to pound him. "I've heard enough out of both of you today. Never meant to hurt us—you know, that means fuck all right about now. Never meant to hurt me. What bullshit. You should have stayed out of our lives! You're her goddamned birth parents, you knew meeting her would completely disrupt her life and yet you both snuck around like some evil reptiles stalking my poor girl. What the hell were you thinking coming to her wedding and preying upon her and me? What kind of people are you?" He glared between the two of them. "Well, I know that answer to that question."

He let go of Kelly and spun on Cynthia, venom coursing through his veins. "I don't care what shit you told me about your poor upbringing. Oh poor you, your mother died, your stepmother was terrible, your stepsisters were mean to you, blah, blah. Well, it's bloody obvious why, isn't it? It wasn't about them, it was about you. You're the problem, Cynthia, not everyone else in your life. You weren't the victim, you were the abuser. And in my book, you got everything you deserved. And by the way, where would you like that sculpture of yours delivered? I don't want that piece of shit befouling my house any longer. I'll send it to Jon's. Or maybe the city dump where it belongs—with its creator."

Cynthia looked like her entire body drained of blood. She slumped over, clutching the counter for support.

Rex's heart twinged. A voice in the back of his head said he'd gone too far and he'd regret those words someday. But he was so infuriated, he squelched his doubts and let the fires of betrayal billow in his gut.

Jon straightened his shoulders. His mouth tight, he physically put himself between Rex and Cynthia. "That's enough out of you, you leave her alone," he said, pointing up at Rex, his voice deep and commanding. His eyes glittered with fury. "Cynthia, come on and let's leave these people. God, I'm glad you got to see this little window into Mr. Perfect. You deserve someone loving and forgiving, not an abusive asshole like your father." He took her by the hand. "Come on, honey. I'm getting you out of here."

"Good bloody riddance!" Rex spat before he could stop himself.

Jon pulled Cynthia towards the door, she stumbled, he caught her and made sure she was steady before continuing on. As they passed by Rex, she stopped. Tears streamed down her pale cheeks, her lower lip quivered.

The same lip he'd kissed so many times, that lovely chin, her high, rounded cheekbones. His chest hurt like she'd stuffed his heart into a spiked vise.

She wiped her eyes and met his gaze. "Thank you for taking such good care of my little girl," she said, her voice cracking. "You did a great job. I will forever be in your debt for that."

He wanted to stay enraged at her, but dignity in her eyes and the truth of her words derailed him.

She turned back to Kelly. "You know where I live. My door is always open to you. I only have one regret in my life, and that was giving you up. But I'm glad that if I couldn't raise you, you found Elizabeth and Rex." She started towards the door, but turned back to his daughter. "And be careful. My stepsisters *are* evil and will try to destroy you. I'm so sorry for bringing them into your life. I'm sorry for everything. And whether he believes it or not, I never meant to hurt your father. Or you. All I've ever wanted to do was to protect you. I've always loved you with my whole heart. Never doubt that."

She turned back and gave Rex one long, last look. There was no shame in her gaze, no contrition, no deception. Strength radiated from her depths. Strength of character and conviction. Also unspoken rage and pride. Lots of pride in herself.

But mostly pain.

Her intense gaze cleaved his heart in two. "Get out," he ordered harshly, pointing at the door.

Tears pooled in her eyes and her jaw twitched. She turned and walked out.

A part of him wanted to stop her. His gut roiled. His brain twisted. Damn it! She was in the wrong, not him! Why should he feel a shred of sympathy for the witch?

Jon sent him a glare that seared his eyeballs before turning and following Cynthia. Butch took time to glower at him as well as he walked by. The door slammed shut behind them.

Vance and Kelly looked at each other, both clearly devastated. While he didn't even have an ounce of sympathy for Vance, he was Kelly's husband. They needed time alone to end things.

Rex moved towards the door to the entry hall. "Darling, I'll be in my office if you need me."

"Thanks, Dad. I'll be in there soon."

He left the room and didn't remember the walk to his office. Suddenly, he was slumped behind his desk, alone. His stomach hurt so badly, it was like a thousand wild animals were clawing at it. He'd never felt this level of betrayal before. He had no future. No love, no work. Nothing. In the span of a half an hour, he'd lost it all. The only thing he had left was Kelly.

And by God, he'd do all in his power to protect her. From Vance. And from those lousy birth parents.

Why was Cynthia the birth mother? Of all the things she could have admitted to, why was it that?

Would he lose Kelly to them? Would he lose his daughter along with his dreams of a new life with Cynthia? He'd always worried they'd show up and take her away from him. It had been his main objection to the meeting. His most deep-seated fear. He couldn't lose Kelly. He couldn't even stand the thought of sharing her. Especially with a couple of crazy liars. With a man dressed as bloody Carmen Miranda!

Why did Cynthia betray him? Why hadn't she just told him up front? Yes, he would have been shocked, yes, he would have been disturbed, but he wouldn't have felt so used. Would he have dated her? No. How could he? She was the beast that abandoned his sweet daughter.

The thoughts he had about the birth parents. What he'd imagined them to be. Nothing like Cynthia and Jon.

He pounded the desk. "Cynthia, why did you do this to me? I loved you so much. For God's sake, I was going to propose to you this weekend. Goddamn it!" he yelled, hitting the top of his desk again. "I can't get past this. You betrayed me and my daughter. And I can't forgive you for that. Anything else but that."

A large black pit of despair swallowed him whole. He laid his head down on his desk and let loose. The first time since Elizabeth died, he cried. It was over. All over.

His dreams were dead.

Cynthia stared out the window as they drove down Ranch Road, her eyes puffy, her nose stinging, her heart numb from shock. The huge balloon of stress had exploded and only the little shards and slips of her life were left. Welcome to Hell.

And such a familiar place it was.

She reached for her purse to fix her make-up when she realized that she'd left it behind. "Oh, goddamn it, I forgot my purse. I don't want to go back there, but I need it. It's got practically everything I own in it."

Jon looked over at her, irritated. "Shit. We made such a great exit, too. The drama timing is all off if we go back."

Butch laughed from the backseat. "You guys pull up at the door, I'll run in and get it. I think I have the least amount of drama attached to me."

"You do." Jon pulled over in a dirt turnout and headed back.

"Well, that went well," Cynthia said dryly.

"Rex is a dick," Jon replied flatly. "I'm glad you found out before you wasted any more time loving him. What a butthead."

She sighed, flames of pain igniting her insides again. She rubbed her knuckles. "He was hurt, that's all. But I agree with you. He kinda hit below the belt." Tears welled in her eyes and she fought them back.

Jon snorted and made an exaggerated shocked grimace. "Kind of? *Didn't want that piece of shit befouling his house?* Belonged in the city dump with its creator? He may have been angry but that behavior didn't reflect well on him. Okay, here we are. Oh, there goes Vance. He doesn't look very happy, does he?"

Vance's shoulders drooping, his frown extended to his jaw. He kicked the ground with every step as he headed to his car. They pulled up, he shot them a glare, then got into his car, started it and peeled out.

"Yes, he does look rather destroyed," Cynthia observed. "Course, his dad went to jail, he lost Kelly and all he has left is Baldy."

"Not much of a consolation prize," Jon said.

Butch walked to the house and knocked on the door. Kelly answered it. Even from a distance, she looked terrible. Eyes red, hair mussed.

Cynthia's swallowed a sob the size of a bus.

Jon rubbed her shoulder. "It'll be okay, honey. We'll get through this. Maybe we'll get a chance to know her."

"Yeah, I may have lost a potential husband, but we gained a potential daughter today."

"Yeah, baby, we did," Jon said, running a hand over her hair.

Still wasn't much of a comfort.

Shit.

Rex wiped his eyes and blew his nose. He had to shake off this mood. For Kelly's sake and his, he needed to be strong.

The front door slammed shut. He'd better find Kelly and comfort her. At least he had her.

He walked out of his office. Voices drifted from the kitchen. Vance was still there?

He'd better not be worming his way back into Kelly's life. Rex quietly approached the kitchen and stopped just outside the doorway.

It wasn't Vance, it was Jon's son, Butch. Why was he still there?

He strained to listen for Cynthia or Jon, but only Butch spoke.

"…yeah, I know all that, but I want you to know something about your mother. It's important you hear this. My father—my other father—Jon's husband, Malcolm, died from AIDS when I was ten. He died in my dad's—Jon's arms—I was right there, too."

"I'm so sorry."

"Me, too. Anyway, Cynthia dropped everything and came right to our apartment. She was there for us. I mean, *there for us*. She made all the funeral arrangements and since we had no money, she paid for the whole thing."

"Wow."

Yeah, who cared? Kelly was being far too nice. Rex had half a mind to go in there and kick that boy out.

"Two days after Dad's funeral, our landlord kicked us out of our apartment. Neither dad worked for the last six months because Malcolm needed so much care and all their savings went to his treatments and pain meds. Cynthia showed up with a moving van and moved us into her home. She cleared out her art studio and turned it into my room. She even went to Toys R Us and got decorations, new lights and a whole slew of toys for me. And from that day on, for the next six years, she took care of us. Worked in the emergency room at night and was there for me, the next morning, making my lunch for school. She even became my freakin' den mother. I'll never forget what she did for me. And for dad."

"Damn."

Rex's shoulders relaxed, he pictured Cynthia being strong for young Butch. A glimmer of sympathy took hold of him. He tried to distance himself from his reaction. She was a horrible person. No matter what she'd done for the boy, what she did to him spoke to her true character. She was a lying, manipulative abuser.

Butch went on, relating the story about Cynthia giving up all her money to take care of her father and losing the house to the stepsisters. Butch repeated it exactly as Rex had heard it. Didn't mean it was true, it meant Cynthia had constructed her story well.

Although, it probably was the truth.

No, a version of the truth. Cynthia's version. Which had to be jaded. Those stepsisters couldn't be that bad. No one could be that callous. The way Cynthia and Butch described them was a one-dimensional horror picture. Even if she'd told the truth about her stepsisters being raped, they couldn't possibly be as horrible as she said. A family myth. That was all it was. A myth made up by an excellent storyteller.

"I'm just sorry you're meeting her now," Butch continued. "I wish you could have known her before. She hasn't been herself lately. At all. Ever since this last thing, her dad dying, the Gruesome Twosome destroying all her sculptures—horrible stuff—she's off. Really off. She's never lied like this, done anything like this. Nor have I ever seen her this emotional. I'm telling you, this is not the Cynthia I know."

"Do you think she really loves my father?" Kelly asked.

Rex told himself that he didn't care about the answer, but he leaned closer to the door.

"God, yes," Butch replied in a strong tone. "She has it bad for him. I mean, *bad*. I've never seen her this broken up over a dude before. She doesn't fall in love easily. And she's super honorable when she is in a relationship. That's why this was all so out of character for her. She's tweaked right now."

Rex fought the conflicting voices in his head. God, he wanted to believe it. But he couldn't. Besides, she was Kelly's birth mother. Sickening.

"Do you think she really didn't know who he was in the park?"

"No, she had no idea. She found out who he was the first day she saw you and that was two weeks after the accident. I guess Jon tracked you down. And they were spying on you. It was the day she hit Vance's car."

Cynthia hit Vance's car? She was driving the Volkswagen? Rex thought back to that day. His muscles went rigid and his jaw and fists clenched. It *was* them. Damn it. Stalking his poor daughter. Spying on her. He wanted to wring their necks.

"Cynthia's the one who side-swiped Vance's car?" Kelly burst out laughing.

While he was wall-punching mad, the sound of her laughter soothed him.

"Oh, my God, it was her!" Kelly exclaimed, sounding gleeful. "And Jon. I remember, the two people in the Volkswagen. Oh, my God, they almost died! You should have seen that car! I'm sorry. I shouldn't have told you that."

Butch gave a deep, throaty laugh. "No worries. They told me as much. Those guys are a comedy team. Listen, come by sometime. Here's my card. Send me an email and I'll give you their number. They'd love to get to know you. They're very messed up about you. Very torn up. Never seen that much pain on their faces. I think that was part of the problem with Cynthia losing her mind. She can't deal with giving you up. She buried all her feelings and they've been coming out like some volcano erupting. Making her crazy. Not that she's really crazy. Jeez, I'm probably mucking this up worse."

A window of understanding opened in Rex's mind. He slammed it shut. Didn't matter if giving up Kelly tore her up, it should. Throwing away pure gold. Cynthia deserved all her pain. She got all that was coming to her. That's what happens when you make stupid decisions, you pay for them.

Cynthia's haunted expression when she saw Kelly's pictures on his wall now made so much sense. She'd looked like someone had cold-cocked her. No wonder.

Still, he didn't care. She was a weak, horrible, rotten person. Period.

"You're not mucking anything up, Butch," Kelly said. "I appreciate this, I really do. Besides, you're like my…"

"Brother. Weird. Tell me about it. Yeah, but I was adopted, you're the real deal."

"I was adopted too, Butch. Cynthia was right. Rex and Elizabeth are my real parents. Like Malcolm and Jon were yours."

Rex's heart warmed and he sighed. To hear her say those words meant the world to him. She loved him. He was her real dad. Maybe he wouldn't lose her.

"Yeah," Butch said. "And Cynthia's my real mom, too. Look, I should go. They're waiting outside. Don't be a stranger. I'm around for another week, then I go back to school."

"Where?"

"Yale. School of Medicine. I'm going to cure AIDS someday." He laughed. "That's the plan."

"It's a good one." Rex could hear the smile in her voice. "You're a good man. If you're any indication of who they are, I know they're good people."

"They are. Crazy, but a hundred percent. Sorry about that mess with your husband."

"It's okay, I'll get over it. I'm just worried about my dad."

"You'll take good care of him. It's clear he did a good job with you, too."

Butch walked to the door and Rex ditched into the living room. The front door opened and closed. Kelly walked into the room. She stood taller and her face was more relaxed. Butch had helped her. Even though he wished the kid would have stayed away, he'd comforted Kelly. Give him two begrudging points for that.

Rex walked up to her and took her in his arms. She squeezed him hard.

He pulled away and ran a hand down her back. "Are you okay?"

She nodded. "I will be. What about you?"

"Me, too."

She hugged him tight. Rex smelled her hair and remembered a similar moment when she was thirteen and her first boyfriend had dumped her. He'd held her for a long time, just like this. Elizabeth didn't believe in coddling.

Cynthia had missed all of that. Kelly's first tooth. Her first words. Her portrayal of an onion in her kindergarten play.

Damn it, he didn't want to feel any sympathy towards the woman. She was a betrayer. A liar. A weakling who cast aside his wonderful treasure of a daughter.

He couldn't still love her. He couldn't. Yet he couldn't deny that Butch's story had an effect on him.

Damn it. He wished he'd never met her. No matter what good things she'd done in her life, she'd still stuck a knife deep between his shoulder blades. All the way to the hilt.

He'd been a fool before. He wouldn't be a fool again.

Chapter Eighteen

Rex stared at his coffee cup. Half full. Cold. He should get up and get some more, but he couldn't make himself move from his desk. He could call Harrison, but he didn't want to bother him. He'd been home so much lately, he was sure his old faithful butler was sick of him. Oh, that's right, Harrison went to the dentist.

Alone in this gigantic house. Maybe he should get a dog.

He stared at his cup again. He wanted more coffee, but couldn't force his limbs to move. He crumpled up a piece of paper and threw it across the room, missing the wastebasket. The paper ball rolled until it stopped next to the ten other wads on the floor.

He looked at his Blackberry. No messages. Right when he needed distraction the most, there was none. For the first time in thirty years, no one wanted anything from him. Jess was on vacation. Vector was on hold. Three partners quit. Huge shake-up. He and the other founding partner, Jake, decided to take a breather until things settled out.

He thought about going out on his boat, but that took too much effort.

A file folder marked *Cynthia Rella* sat on top of his desk near him, taunting him.

He grabbed it, opened the file drawer of his expansive maple desk and thrust it inside, slamming it shut.

So she hadn't lied about anything but Kelly. So what? Those stepsisters may have a rap sheet a mile long, still didn't mean they were the monsters she portrayed them to be. She was still a liar and a cheat.

He wished he could maintain his level of anger at her. He wished his attraction to her had died and his love for her would fade. But unfortunately, he felt nearly the same for her as he did before he'd found out she was Kelly's birth mother. Only now there was some serious volcanic anger mixed in with that fiery love. A huge tangled pile of conflicting emotions.

Kelly's subtle hints weren't helping. She'd been spending a considerable amount of time with Cynthia and Jon lately and kept trying to tell him about it, even though he made it clear he wasn't interested. Like last night at dinner. She'd attempted to bring Cynthia into the conversation. He hadn't meant to snap at her.

Yeah, he'd better watch that. He didn't want her moving out too soon. Knowing she was sleeping down the hall at night brought him the only comfort he'd found in the past two weeks.

Two weeks. Felt like two years since he'd seen Cynthia.

Cynthia. Her sweet, heart-shaped face, that mole next to her sultry mouth, her perfect rounded bottom. His stomach burned. *Kelly's birth mother.* Still couldn't get past it. Probably never would.

He wadded up another piece of paper and threw it at the waste can.

The doorbell rang. Probably the media wanting a blasted interview. He'd hired a publicist to deal with the Ponzi scheme fallout, but once in a while one of those stupid reporters would find their way to his door. They could go to hell.

The doorbell rang again.

Did Kelly forget her keys? She'd been just as distracted as he lately.

On the off chance it was his daughter, Rex pushed away from his desk and went to answer the door. If it was the media, he'd slam the door in their nosy faces.

He looked through the peephole. All he saw was a big eyeball. Someone checking to see if there was movement inside. Christ.

Pissed off, he flung open the door.

A large woman with a square jaw and a pink beehive hairdo stood there, blinking at him. "Oh, God, it is you, I didn't recognize you at first. Honey, you don't look good. Out late partying?"

Maybelline the Drag Queen.

Rex relaxed and couldn't help but give her a small smile. "Maybelline, what are you doing here?"

She clutched her long, manicured fingers to her chest. "You remembered my name!" She waved a handful of gaudy rings at him. "I love you! Yeah, you weren't easy to find. Luckily—or unluckily —you've kinda been in the news lately. I've been worried about you, honey. You seemed like such a nice guy and this stupid friend takes advantage of you. I figured you could use some good news." Her dark eyes grew bright with excitement. "So I did some digging and found out exactly who bought that pair of shoes and who wears them. Jon Wagner at the Tuxedo Club. He plays Carol Channing and —"

Rex sighed and held up his hand. "I found her."

Maybelline's gaze widened and she pursed her lips. "Uh, oh. That doesn't sound good."

"It's not." Rex looked down and toed the threshold.

"What happened?"

He ran a hand through his hair and rubbed the back of his neck. "God. You want a cup of coffee?"

She jerked back in surprise. She cocked her head slightly. A slow smile grew on her face. "Well, yeah, I'd love one."

"Come on in, then." Rex stood aside and gestured towards his entry hall.

He had no idea why he was inviting her inside, but he was so miserable, any distraction was welcome at this point. And the drag queen had been funny. If he got one laugh out of the exchange it would be worth it. He hadn't laughed in over two weeks.

Cynthia got the cutest look on her face when she told a joke. A sparkle in her hazel eyes, one side of her mouth would twitch with amusement. A storm cloud of fury drenched the memory.

Mentally shaking himself, he led Maybelline into his living room and gestured towards the couch.

Maybelline gasped and rushed right by the sofa to the huge picture window overlooking the City. "Oh, my God! This is unreal! Gorgeous." Then she noticed the drapes and gasped again. Fingering the blue and brown striped window coverings, she said, "Jesus Christ, this is real silk. Do you know how much this costs? Oh, hell, of course you do."

"Don't actually. My late wife was the decorator. I was the checkbook."

Maybelline laughed a deep rumbling laugh, one of the only tells that she was really a man.

"Wait here, I'll get the coffee."

When he returned, Maybelline was luxuriating on the blue couch, running a hand over the material appreciatively. "This material is to die for. Probably costs an entire paycheck of mine to cover one freakin' cushion."

He set the silver coffee tray on the marble-topped table in front of her.

She examined his face carefully. "So it's true, money does not buy happiness."

He smirked and poured two cups of coffee. "Uh, no."

He handed Maybelline a cup and sat near her on an overstuffed, oversized brown chair. He took a sip.

Maybelline sat with her legs tucked tightly together against the front of the sofa, her body turned slightly. Wearing a pink and white suit with a tight skirt, she was more feminine than any of the women in his life. "Okay, so tell me what happened? You found her?"

"Yeah…" Rex gave Maybelline the Reader's Digest version of the saga.

At the point where he revealed that Cynthia was Kelly's birth mother, Maybelline clutched her pearls and gasped. "Oh, my God! This is like a soap opera! Like the plot summary to *General Hospital*. Wow, the birth mother. That's kind of creepy, isn't it? So she was worming her way into your life to get to your daughter?"

"Yeah, that's what I think. She denies it. Kelly believes her."

"Well, of course your daughter does. She wants to. All adopted people make up these elaborate fantasies about their birth parents," she said with a gesture of her arm, her manicured fingers splayed. "But I don't think anyone could come up with that story. That is so strange. I didn't know Jon was straight at one time of his life. Nor that he had a child. I mean, he and his boyfriend raised a son, but, anyway. I've known him for years. I don't want to upset you, but he's a nice man, honey. Of course, who knows what kind of wacko he could have married? This one sounds crazy. And cunning. Is your daughter vulnerable to this invasion? Do you think this Cynthia woman is a real threat?"

"She's already laid the trap. Kelly's probably over there right now."

Maybelline's mouth dropped open in horror. She leaned over and pushed on his knee. "Oh, my God, that's terrible. Here you are raising this girl—putting your heart and soul into it—and this woman comes along and steals her from you. And she betrayed you. The witch. No wonder you're miserable." She clucked a few times in disapproval.

"Thank you. That's what I think." Rex relaxed, glad he invited Maybelline in. "I think she came here to get Kelly away from me. Kelly thinks I'm over-reacting."

Maybelline waved her hand dismissively. "She's a child, what does she know? By the time she's an adult, she'll understand these things. Now how old is the little tyke?" she asked, leaning forward with an expectant look on her heavily made-up face.

Rex coughed and pulled on the collar of his t-shirt. He glanced down at his coffee cup. "Uh, twenty-seven."

"*Twenty-seven?*" she demanded, alarmed.

Rex's face warmed and he pretended to find a flaw in the material of the chair.

She sat back against the couch with a frown. "The way you were talking about her, I thought she was about ten. Twenty-seven? Well, this puts a different spin on things. Oh, that's right, you said the wedding. But the way you spoke…" Her expression softened and she gave him a sympathetic smile. "Rex, darling. She's a grown-up." She chuckled softly. "Cynthia can't take her from you. She's up. And she's living with you." She blinked a few times. "My God, she's twenty-seven and still living with you?"

"Well, that's temporary," Rex said, shifting in his chair.

Maybelline made a graceful sweeping gesture with her arm, her many bracelets jangling. "But she's still here which means she still loves you enough to live with you." She shook her head and took a sip of coffee. Her face went neutral, but her gaze hollowed. Pain lines creased her brow. "I haven't seen my parents in—oh, God." Her voice went deeper and lost some of its affectation. Maybelline still sounded feminine, but Rex finally saw the man inside her. A very wounded man.

Maybelline focused on the coffee service. "Well, they really don't want me. I'm sure they wish I was adopted and that my birth parents would come along and take me back. They barely talk to me." She put her cup down and sat back against the cushions. "I'm their big disappointment. Their big flaming drag queen failure." A hint of a Southern accent came through.

Rex imagined her as a boy on a southern farm feeling like an alien from a distant planet. Yearning for something that everyone said was wrong. How awful that would be.

Maybelline picked some lint from her suit. "They won't even allow me at Christmas unless I wear a suit. No one else has to wear a suit, but I have to wear one if I want to see the family. So I haven't gone in years. I mean, I can't help who I am." She straightened up, held her head up proudly and waved a hand. "But enough about me."

His heart went out to her. No matter what or whom Kelly chose to be, he'd never shut the door on her. She was his daughter. Forever. "I'm so sorry, Maybelline. That's rough."

"Well, I have really good friends, so it makes up for it. I'm not lonely. And I'm fairly happy. Happier than you. So how do you feel about Cynthia?"

Blackness enveloped his mind. His face hardened and his teeth clenched. "Crazy. She—I'm very angry and I just wish she'd go away," he bit out.

"Do you still love her?"

"No."

Maybelline continued to stare at him, clearly seeing through his lie.

"Okay, yes." He sighed heavily, his shoulders drooping. "Insanely. I'm miserable," he said, taking his head in his hands and squeezing. "Can't get past this thing about her being Kelly's birth mother. For years I had all these ideas about who they were and why they'd given her up. I thought they were weak, idiotic, immoral assholes, to be truthful."

She raised a painted-on brow. "Not very judgmental, are you?"

"Yeah, I suppose," he said, chuckling and nodding sheepishly. "I don't know. It's driving me crazy. I'm not sleeping. I'm not eating."

Maybelline watched him for a minute. "Do you want my opinion?"

"Sure, I've heard everyone else's."

"Now please don't take this the wrong way, but you are the biggest idiot I've ever met."

Rex gasped and jerked back in his seat. Anger roared through his veins. How dare she make such a horrible statement! He was innocent and Cynthia was a hundred percent wrong.

Maybelline clearly expected this reaction, she barely reacted to his display. She held up her hand to quiet him. "Now before you go off, hear me out."

He caught himself and sighed, shaking off the rage. God, he was touchy lately.

"Your fear has gotten the better of you, honey. You're afraid you'll lose Kelly. You're afraid of all this emotion you have for Cynthia. It's just fear. No big deal, we all get afraid. And you had all these pre-conceived notions about who Kelly's birth parents were and you totally got caught up in this tornado of fear. This is all really simple. You love her. She loves you. You'll get over this Kelly's birth mother stuff. You need to separate these ideas. Just like with your wife. You had a relationship with her and one with your daughter and they were totally separate. Same thing here. What you have with Cynthia has nothing to do with your daughter. So what if she was the egg donor? You're the girl's father. I mean, she's living with you, what more of a show of loyalty do you want?"

Rex tapped his foot against the leg of the coffee table. "I guess."

"Look, a whole lot of shitty stuff just happened to you, what with your business problems and all. And now I see what you've been trying to maintain, this freakin' palace," Maybelline said, gesturing towards the room, her long pink nails fanning out. "I can only imagine how important your business is to you. So you're having huge problems and I think this woman came in at the wrong time and you're taking out some of your frustration on her. She's just twisted you all up. Which is a good thing. It shows how much you love her. Do you know how hard it is to find someone you love? Who's compatible with you? Sure, she lied. But it sounds like she lied because she thought she was protecting her daughter. Hard to find fault with that motive. And she gave up your wonderful daughter. That can't feel good. She's probably totally screwed up about it. It doesn't excuse her behavior, but it makes it understandable."

Leaning back in his chair and crossing his arms, Rex frowned and shook his head. "I don't know about this whole business with those stepsisters and protecting Kelly from them. I think that's bullshit. Yes, I've seen the women's rap sheets, but that doesn't mean Cynthia's telling the truth there. How could keeping her identity secret protect Kelly? I think she was thinking about herself. She's ashamed of giving up Kelly and didn't want either of us to know who she really was."

Maybelline gave a slight shrug of her broad shoulders. "I had a daughter and once I came out…" Her square face drew down and a haunted look passed behind her dark eyes. "Well, my ex-wife poisoned her against me. I miss her so much…" Her voice broke. She took a deep breath. "…and I grieve for her. From what you said, Cynthia was very conflicted and is still conflicted about her decision. I know how horrible it is to have to walk away from your child for the sake of the child's well-being. It's why I didn't fight for custody, Leticia would have suffered. I'm just hoping by the time she gets to Kelly's age, she'll want me back in her life."

Rex stared at the man in wonderment. A child? He was straight at one time? "Wow, I…"

Maybelline gave him a small smile. "Assumed I always looked like this? Well, my interior did. Finally now, my exterior matches my interior. If I were you, I wouldn't assume what someone else feels until you've walked in their shoes. And protecting your kid sometimes means walking away. My advice is to give Cynthia another shot. Wouldn't hurt to talk to her. See what she thinks. I mean, you guys haven't talked since the big blow up, have you?"

"No."

"So you don't really know what she feels. Talk to her. She won't bite. And from what you've told me, your connection is intense. She's hurting just like you are."

He didn't want to think about that. "Yeah…"

Maybelline examined him, head to toe and worked her red mouth, thinking. "Are you used to getting your way? I mean, has everything gone pretty well for you?"

He shrugged. "Well, I guess. I don't really think about it. Once in a while a deal wouldn't work out the way I wanted, but, uh, I don't know. I mean, Elizabeth dying was horrible, but in business, that's gone great until now. Kelly's been great. I reached all my monetary goals early."

She sent him a warm smile. "I'm telling you, this is all an ego thing. You're a successful guy used to having your way. And all this shit is out of your control. And you freaked." She sat up and her gaze grew intense. "But honey, you have to get past your ego and your fears. I saw real love in your face when you came into the shop. I don't see that very often. That's why I had to come help you. It's rare to find love at this age. Rare to find someone who lights your fire this way. Now," she said, settling back, "was there anything about Cynthia you didn't like, other than her being Kelly's birth mother?"

"Well, she's…uh…no."

"Was she nice to you?"

"God, yes. Well, except for the lies."

"Was the sex good?"

His face went hot. "Er…" He looked at the Oriental carpet.

"Well?"

"Outstanding. The best so far," he muttered with a shrug.

"Wow. Does she believe in you?"

"In ways no one else has. Come to think of it. She really liked my artwork and wants me to pursue it. No one has, well, seen me, the real me like that and liked what they saw. I normally have people like me because of what I own and what money I can make them. But she doesn't care about any of that."

His foundation of logic regarding his rejection of Cynthia was melting beneath him, making him feel unbalanced. He liked hating her, it centered him somehow.

Maybelline twisted her mouth, crossed her legs and sent him a little disapproving stare. "I'm waiting to hear something concrete that's negative about her," she said in a singsong voice.

His mind and gut in turmoil, Rex gestured, searching for a defense. "Well, she lied."

"About something that ruined her life and was the hardest thing she'd ever done. And all because she was trying to protect you and your—her—daughter from her terrible stepsisters."

His back tensed with frustration, he sat up. "But that could all be bullshit," he fired back at her." He got out of his seat and paced the room. "Kelly told me they were bad, but I think they're all exaggerating," he asked with a violent gesture. "Besides, you can't have someone do something to you without you letting them do it. She even, Cynthia, even said that. And she won't take responsibility for what those sisters of hers did to her."

Maybelline held her hands up. "Okay, so she gets involved in dramas with her family. That's a negative. What else? Is she self-centered?"

"No. From what her husband's son says, she's a bloody saint. Saving the world," he spat as he plopped back in his seat.

"Okay."

"You think I'm over-reacting."

"Yes. But, darling, feelings are feelings, you have to honor them. I just want you to ask yourself what's going to net you the better future. Being with Cynthia or being without her. Do you think you can get over her being Kelly's birth mom?"

The question of the day. "I don't know. I just don't know."

"I'd hate to see you throw something so precious away because of a hurt ego," she said, standing. She smoothed out her pink skirt, grabbed her pink and white checked purse and hung it over her long arm. "Well, I've got a date so I must be on my way. Just take my advice. Go find the girl and marry her. You'll get over the part about her being your daughter's mother. You will. And hey, it will make it much more convenient, won't it? You'll all be together like one big, strange weird family," she said with a "voila" gesture.

She made some valid points, but he wasn't convinced. "I'll think about it," he grumbled.

"Good." Maybelline started towards the door, but stopped and turned to him. "And one more thing, if you guys do get together and get married, I'd better be invited to the wedding."

He grinned and his posture softened. "You'll be the first on the list after Kelly, how's that?"

Maybelline's red-lipped smile stretched wide across her slightly stubbly face.

He escorted her to the door and waved good-bye. Returning to his office, he felt shaky. Was she right? Was it his ego? Were his fears out of control? Was he this possessive over his daughter? So afraid he'd lose her that he was shooting himself in the foot where Cynthia was concerned?

When Elizabeth died, he'd clung pretty tightly to his daughter. Was he holding on too tightly to her still?

His mind a muddle, he sat in his chair and stared at the polished surface of his desk.

The doorbell rang.

Maybelline had probably forgotten something.

He chuckled and shook his head. Who would have ever thought he'd befriend a damn drag queen?

He got up and opened the door.

Two of the scariest-looking, fifty-something women stood there: a skinny one and a fat one. All the hair stood up on the back of his neck. His spine stiffened and his limbs readied for a fight.

He placed his handgun: his office. Silent alarm was closer.

He didn't know who they were, but one thing was clear. These women were dangerous. And they wanted something from him.

Chapter Nineteen

The skinny woman looked like a drug addict. Scary-thin, her leathery skin was pocked and scarred. Brown circles around her sunken dark eyes. She looked straight out of a Tim Burton cartoon. On second thought, they both did. The second one was fat with a cow's staring eyes. Her blond bangs shot up like she was in a wind tunnel and she wore a stained yellow t-shirt with kittens on it.

Both had mean stares. Hungry, greedy. And very angry. The epitome of entitled trailer trash scum.

Adrenaline stormed through him and his body went hard. He mentally ran through some defensive scenarios: how he'd take them down and where the nearest phone was.

The scrawny one gave him an up and down appraisal. Her hair looked like it had been cut with a chainsaw, dyed black and smeared with grease. She squinted up at him. "Rex Du Charmante?" she asked. Her voice was gravelly, yet fairly high.

He wished he weren't home alone. "Uh…"

"I know it's you and we gotta talk." She jerked her head towards him. "Inside. It's important. It's about your daughter, her reputation in the community and her future."

His fear vanished and anger blasted through him. "How do you know my daughter?"

"She's my niece," she announced with a little toss of her head.

"Our niece," the fat one added in a smoker's growl.

His thoughts exploded like someone had poured gasoline on them and lit them on fire. Reeling, he fought for mental clarity, putting a hand on the doorframe to steady himself. Who? What possible relation? Did his uncle have a secret set of children? "Who the hell are you?"

The skinny one grinned, showing off a set of rotting yellow teeth with several missing. The stench hit him. Tooth decay and cigarettes. Even more charming.

She stuck out her chin defiantly and put her hands on her bony hips. "We're Cynthia Rella's sisters."

The evil stepsisters. It couldn't be true. These people were more than horrible, they were horror movie villains.

They did look like they'd been in jail. The rap sheet fit. But nothing in their files prepared him for the reality. They were nearly unrecognizable from the pictures he'd been given of them. The fat blonde one had been much thinner with a different haircut. The skinny one had been heavier and much more youthful. He knew they were both in their early forties, but they looked twenty years older.

"Well, I don't know what you—"

Mid-sentence, the skinny one pushed past him and sauntered into the entry hall. She surveyed his house like she owned the place. Shopping more like.

"I didn't invite you in, now turn around and—"

A push from behind knocked him off balance. He caught himself in a few steps, then jerked back around. His body went hot, burning with fury. The fat one had shoved him aside! Oblivious to his reaction, she waddled by him, wheezing and smelling of cigarettes and marijuana.

He stormed past the two nightmares and blocked them from walking any further into his house. "Wait just a goddamned minute. Turn around and get the hell out of my house, you are trespassing. Whatever you want, send it to my lawyer in writing."

Skinny gave a loud guffaw. "Will you listen to him? Send it to my lawyer in writing," she said with a flourish of her pencil-thin arm. "Mr. All High and Mighty in your mansion in the hills." Then her smile vanished and she planted her feet in a wide stance, crossing her arms over her sunken chest. Her face went hard and her gaze darkened. Her mouth got hungrier.

A chill came over him and he fought to keep from shuddering.

She sneered. "Well, let me tell you something, bucko, we're family now. And you're gonna hear what I have to say or you may not like the consequences."

He pulled himself up to his full six six. "Are you threatening me?" he asked in his most deep and commanding tone.

She made an exaggerated face and held up her hands defensively. "No, no, I ain't threatenin'. I just want to have a nice little talk with you, seeing as how we're family now." Her smile broke and she glared up at him. "Okay, fuck it, I'll cut to the chase. I hate fuckin' games, too. Look, I got the dope on ya. You ain't no Mr. Perfect here. I seen you on the news lately. I know you're hurting. And I know you can't afford any…" She tapped her bony finger against her cracked lips. "Let's see how I can put this…" She eyed him with an air of superiority. "Any extra bad publicity. So I'm gonna save your ass. And all I ask in return is something that clearly won't hurt you at all. I'm actually gonna save you money, yes I am. Indeedy do." Her demeanor turned mock friendly. "Belinda and I—my name's Sissy by the way, Rex. Can I call you Rex?"

A surge of hate powered through him. "No."

She didn't miss a beat. "So Rex, the way I figure it, you owe me. I mean, we're *family*," she said like it was all so obvious and natural she was there. She'd clearly thought a lot about this. "Share and share alike. So all you gotta do is share and no one in the world will find out that your little girl is the product of an imposter/liar/loser/moron/*idiot*," she spat in a harsh, hateful tone, "and a no-good faggot/drag queen/fuckin' loser-bait dicksucker. Because I'm just betting that the Enquirer would loooove this. You know they're carrying all the news of your little financial fiasco with the Ponzi scheme." She cocked a hip, and looked at him with contempt. "Like, how dumb are you, anyway? A con artist milks you for twenty-five years and you just bend over and take it?"

The room tilted and his vision blurred. Fury pounded in his ears. He lunged for her, surprising himself. He stopped just as he reached her and forced his arms to his sides.

She leapt back with an exaggerated squeal and ran into the dining room. "Assault! Rape, I'll cry rape!" She grabbed a chair and held it up in front of herself like a lion tamer. "Don't piss me off! You'll regret it! I'm seeing a Hells Angel guy right now and you don't want him and his friends here!"

Rex followed her, pointing at the front door. "Get out," he barked. "Or I will call the police and make sure you spend the next part of your life in jail. I have connections. I will take you down. I'll take you for everything you're worth."

Sissy sneered and laughed, but kept the chair between them. "And get what? I have nothing. Cynthia's stupid house didn't get me anything—the fucker won't even sell in this stupid market—and you're gonna get what from me? Nothing, because I have nothing, you idiot." She gave him another quick evaluation. Apparently deciding he wasn't an imminent threat, she put down the chair and swaggered up to him. "Not all of us are so fucking rich. We're not all lucky and fucking inheriting shit—"

"I made it all myself," he bit out before he could stop himself.

"Well, la di da." She glared up at him. "I don't care what the hell you say, I want the fucking money and you're gonna pay me or I will fucking ruin your life. I've ruined lesser people than you, my friend."

"I'm not your friend."

She snickered. "Well, by the end of this, you will be. You get me, bucko? I got your number," she said, full of bravado. Ambling past him, she headed for the door. "And I'm dialin' it. Fucker all lungin' at me. I'll fuckin' be back." She stopped at the doorway to the entry hall and faced him. "You got one week. I'm comin' back next Friday and you will have two million dollars in cash—"

Belinda, standing behind her, pushed on her shoulder with a chubby hand. "I thought you only wanted a hundred grand."

Baring her teeth, Sissy swung on her. Her face went from gray to beet red. She hissed, "Shut up, you stupid moron! Things changed. I didn't know how rich he was. I mean, I heard, but I didn't believe it. Not until I saw this place. Now I want two million," she said, sounding like she was entitled to it.

Belinda frowned, her jowls hanging lower. "But Jerry only told you to get fifty grand. How much do I get now?"

Sissy pushed her back, furious. "Will you shut up? You are so stupid. You don't talk in front of the mark," she said thumbing over her shoulder towards Rex. "How many times have I told you? Fuck." She turned back to Rex and calmed just as quickly as she'd angered. "Okay, we're outta here. Have the money ready, I don't like being held up."

Rex held himself tall. He sat on his emotions and let none show. "I don't have access to two million cash. I can get you ten thousand," he replied calmly.

Sissy's eyes widened, then narrowed. Her thin lips pursed. "No way. I want two million."

"Well, you won't get it. You'll get ten thousand."

Belinda punched her. "Take it."

"No, I need at least fifty and that's only Jerry's part. No, I have to have a hundred grand at least."

"Ten thousand," Rex said.

Sissy turned back to him, scowling. "I'm not stupid. I know you have more."

He made sure not to flinch even a tiny bit. "If you've been paying attention to the news, you'd realize that I don't. I just lost it all."

She opened her mouth to argue, then shut it fast. She frowned. "Oh. They did say that, didn't they?" She stomped her foot and balled her fists, her face turning red again. "Shit! I was here too late! Fuck! Day late and a dollar short. Okay, okay, ten. Because we're family." She walked up to him, her mouth a firm line, and pointed. "But you gotta understand something, this is only a down payment. You get any more money back and I get some," she said, jabbing a finger into her skeletal chest. "You got that? I'm cutting you this deal this one time. Ain't gonna fly in the future. I'm not stupid."

He kept his expression passive. "I can tell. Next Friday. Here, right?"

She narrowed her gaze and gave him a once over. "Yeah. But don't pull any funny stuff. I'll know if you got a trap set up. And if you fuck with me, you won't like the way I fuck back. I got people. Hells Angel people on my side now."

"I thought Jerry left the Hell's Angels," Belinda said.

"Yeah, he did, because he said they were all pussies. He's tougher than that. And smarter than they are." Sissy examined him for a good long minute. "Okay, ten." She turned towards the door, her shoulders drooping. "Shit, I wanted two million." She walked a few steps and then turned back to him, her expression more hopeful. "You know what? You could take out a loan on this house to pay us."

"Can't. Have a second and a third on it. They won't let me have anymore."

She glowered at him. "Shit. Well, you ain't very good with your finances, are you? See, this isn't fair," she whined, gesturing towards him. "All these rich people and they aren't worth anything. You're like the twentieth poor rich person I've met. Fuck. I gotta pick better." She walked towards the door. "Come on, Belinda."

The blonde one jiggled after her. "So how much do I get?"

Sissy scowled at her. "Nothing. And shut up." She let Belinda go ahead, then followed and slammed the door shut.

Rex was so angry he didn't know what to do. He paced and yelled in the entry hall for a good ten or fifteen minutes. After he calmed down, he called the gate company and ordered a second gate to be installed so no one could get to his front door. After that, he took a shower.

He'd never been more angry in his life. Never. He wanted to murder them.

And unfortunately, it gave him a window into Cynthia's life. He truly hadn't believed her. Of course, he'd never met anyone like these people in his life. And he never wanted to again. But he did have a better understanding of Cynthia's plight. He wasn't happy about it, but he understood better .

Now he just had to decide what to do. Pay them off and risk the future bleed, or set them up and risk the payback when they got out of jail.

He'd take the latter. He had connections. He could take them down. No one did this to him. Threatened Kelly. Threatened him. Those two slimeballs were dead meat.

As Rex walked downstairs after his shower, the doorbell rang. It better not be them again.

He stalked to the door and flung it open, ready to kill.

Kelly jumped back, her eyes big as dinner plates. "Jeez, Dad, you scared me." She walked in and he shut the door behind her. "What's wrong with you? Where's Harrison? Why did you answer the door and why do you look so weird?"

"Sorry, Katydid. I—never mind. Harrison is off today, dental work. Forgot your keys again?"

"Yeah. But I'm glad you're here. I really need to talk to you. I was hoping to find you home."

"Where else would I be?" he asked with a snort.

She gave him a sympathetic look. "Oh, Dad, it'll get better."

"Aren't you supposed to be at work?"

Her face sharpened and her mouth went tight. "I need your help." She pointed towards the back of the house. "Can we talk in your office?"

"This sounds serious."

"It is."

Couldn't be that important. Kelly was a known drama queen. He gestured the other way. "Can't we go into the living room?"

She held her ground. "No, I want this to be a serious conversation. Well, I guess we can have one in there..." she said, frowning.

His stomach tightened, this didn't sound good. Last time she looked this grave, she wanted to go to Iraq to help find homes for the orphans. Took him three weeks to convince her to go after the war stopped. "Okay, Katydid," he replied reluctantly.

He followed her into the living room.

Biting her lip, she indicated that he should sit down. Even worse. Sit down discussions were normally reserved for life-shattering events like that Iraq thing or the first time she wanted to spend the night at a boy's house or her wedding announcement. Sweat broke out on his forehead.

Her expression compounded his worry. Calculating, like the face of a chess master on the final play of the championship. Whatever it was, he wouldn't want to do it. His nerves jittered. This little slip of a girl had twisted his mind and heart and stomach more times than he could count. A smile here, a plea there, and he was writhing in agony. But he was her father. And he would do what it took to protect her.

He steeled himself.

She paced in front of him, gathering her thoughts. So textbook Kelly. He saw her at four, ten, fifteen, twenty-one and now at twenty-seven. The same posture, the same intensity on her face. He half expected her to turn to him and argue the points of buying her a pony.

She shot him a dark look, seeming almost defensive already. "Okay, you're not going to like this."

"I figured that."

"Of course you did. Okay, no bullshit—sorry, I still can't swear in front of you— but anyway, I need your help."

"With what?"

She chewed on her lower lip and stared at him intently.

"Straightforward, what?"

She took a deep breath and launched into her plea. "I need you to help me set up Cynthia's evil stepsisters. They just filed suit against her and she needs that money. I know, I try not to tell you what's going on over there, but damn it, that's the reality. Dad, if you just— no, I'm not going to go off point." She spoke so quickly it sounded like the words were almost blended into one long word. The girl could talk faster than anyone he'd ever met. Amazing downloads.

She took another lungful of air and paced in front of him. "Christ, I feel like I'm ten and trying to get a Barbie doll out of you or something. Damn it, I'm an adult and this is different. Okay, I want to put away those lying, thieving relatives of hers to protect her. She needs that five hundred grand to rebuild her life, get a safe roof over her head and these demons won't leave her alone," she said, working herself into a lather as she paced. "I mean, they took everything and they're horrible! You haven't met them—"

"Uh, I—"

"—you've never met such horrible creatures. They're like gargoyles, freakin' like characters from some bad horror movie, *People Under The Stairs* or something." She stopped and turned to face him. "Anyway, I have a plan. And I have the best ally in the world on my side. You won't like this, but Sissy's son, Troy, came to me to apologize about his mother and I asked him if he'd help me set them up. I knew it was asking a lot, to betray his mom —" She gasped for air.

"Kelly—"

Ignoring him, she paced towards the picture window. "But darn it, it's the right thing to do. They broke the law. They forged a will. After she took care of their mother!" she yelled with a grand gesture as she paced back towards him. "The depths these people will sink to are limitless!" she pronounced, smacking the back of her hand on the upturned palm of her other hand.

"Honey—"

She pointed at him dramatically. "I have this plan, see, and I want to bust them, put them in jail." Her pacing grew more frantic. "And Troy agreed. He wants to protect his mom and he thinks jail is the place where she'll be the least trouble. He's in med school on full scholarship there. He's going to be an anesthesiologist. He's nothing like them. He's a really nice guy. I mean, I can't hold his parents against him and he's going to help me. I just haven't worked out all the details yet. I need to catch them in a scheme and—"

"Kelly—"

She held up her hands in a defensive gesture and kept pacing. "I know you don't want to get involved, but Cynthia's not like that, Dad. She's fine. I mean, she's better than fine, it's why you fell in love with her. I've fallen in love, too, Dad. She's a victim of circumstance—well, she did blow it with you and she fully admits that, it torments her." She stopped to face him. "She is so sorry for hurting you. She's miserable over how it happened. And she misses you and wants you and loves you." She threw up her hands and paced again. "Of course, she won't admit it. Jon told me she cries every night." She turned to him. "Every night she cries, Dad, because of you. I mean, I know you're hurt and she lied and it's weird—her being my mother and everything—but I just wish you'd rethink this whole thing."

"Can I say something?"

She shook her head, her jaw stubborn. "Not if you're going to try to talk me out of this. I'm going to help her, goddamn it, even if the both of you forbid me to. Cynthia actually said that word, she *forbade* me to get involved. Ha. As if she has the power. She doesn't know me that well yet—"

"Kelly! I agree with you! I'll help you!"

"Now, goddamn it, Dad, you have to—wait." She stopped and did a double take, honing in on him. "What?"

He laughed. "Damn, girl, you *have* been holding back, haven't you? I didn't know that was humanly possible. All those words in such a short amount of time. You should be in the Guinness Book of World Records. Look, Kelly, I've been thinking and I—okay, truth. Right before you got here, the two sisters paid me a little visit."

Gasping, her spine stiffened with a jolt and she clutched her hands to her chest. "No!"

"Yes, and I happen to have a perfect plan to trap them and make sure they go to jail for a very long time."

Her jaw on the floor, she stared at him for a long moment, her face frozen in disbelief. Then she burst into a nova of a smile and let out an ear-shredding scream that shook the windows. Jumping up and down, she clapped her hands together.

She ran over and leapt into his arms. "You're the coolest dad in the universe!"

Rex could only laugh and hug his crazy daughter.

She leapt off his lap. "I have to go tell Troy! He's going to be so happy! I mean, not, because he's setting up his own mother, but what that woman has done to him, it's criminal. She's a real criminal." She raced towards the doorway, pointing back at him. "I'll be right back. Don't go anywhere, I have to hear these plans of yours!"

She bounded out of the room. He burst out laughing. Same reaction each time he gave into her. At five, ten, twenty, the same extraordinary explosion of energy. He sighed. Still his little girl.

Her reaction also proved that DNA counted for more than he'd originally thought. It was evident the girl shared genetic material with both Jon and Cynthia. All the questions were answered. She was mostly he and Elizabeth, but it was clear that Jon and Cynthia had a large influence on his sweet daughter.

And as he was coming to realize, it wasn't such a bad thing. It might even be a good thing.

He wasn't sure, he hadn't made any decisions, but his anger towards Cynthia was on the wane. And in its place a very small ray of hope. Nearly microscopic still. But it was there.

Could they work it out? He didn't know. But for the first time in two weeks, his stomach didn't hurt.

He thought of her sweet smile, her laughter and her reaction to his artwork.

Her face when she came.

His cock stirred.

Oh, dear. Maybe life wasn't meant to be neat and tidy. Maybe it needed to be messier and more emotional. She was certainly all that.

Christ, it was still too much to comprehend. For now he'd concentrate on his trap. Then he'd figure out Kelly's mother.

God.

Kelly's mother.

Could he really forgive her?

Chapter Twenty

Cynthia stood in front of her bathroom mirror, practicing looking happy. She smiled. She tried to beam. She laughed at an imaginary joke.

Her face fell and she shook her head, disgusted. None of the happy expressions were authentic. The smile didn't carry to her eyes. The plan wasn't working.

Jon was getting sick of her moping, as was Butch. And it was beginning to affect her new relationship with her daughter. She needed to fake some happiness, so they'd think she was healing from the Rex Thing.

What would she feel like if she were happy? What would make her happy?

A twenty-ton weight of darkness dropped on her head. Rex. He would make her happy.

Christ! She was hopeless. She'd never been this upset over a man before.

What was she thinking? She'd nearly killed Jon.

But this was a totally different break-up. For one, she hadn't caught Rex blowing anybody but her. The timing of that thought made her laugh.

Good Lord, she was laughing!

She quickly checked her expression in the mirror. Happiness had been there for an instant. Could she recreate it?

Gone. The little flicker of joy burnt out. Her mask of misery returned. Damn it. She looked like a sad clown. Like Emmett Kelly.

She practiced a few more smiles in the mirror.

The doorbell rang. Her heart lifted. Kelly was taking her to lunch. The best thing out of this whole ordeal was the newfound relationship with her daughter. Amazing. They got closer with every visit. Kelly was a great person.

Yet Cynthia still had difficulty accepting the twenty-seven-year loss. She'd go along fine, then Kelly would relate a story about a pivotal time of her life and Cynthia would find herself fighting back the tears. She was continually processing the onslaught of emotion.

Another problem: Kelly nearly always reminded her of Rex. She shared many of his mannerisms and sayings. Sometimes she even smelled of his cologne. It sucked. But the more time they spent together, the easier it got.

She opened the door. Kelly's sweet face warmed her.

"Hey Kel, how are you?" Cynthia asked, backing up to allow her inside.

"Great," the girl said, breezing by her.

After a brief, welcoming smile, Kelly got a pensive look on her face. She bit her lip. She then brightened her expression and looked straight into Cynthia's gaze.

If Cynthia didn't know better, she'd think she was about to be worked.

"Um. I hope you're okay with this, there's been a slight change of plans."

Kid was clearly holding back a tidal wave of information. She looked like she was about to burst.

"Okay," Cynthia replied slowly, waiting for the new destination.

Kelly sent her a quick smile, turned and went to the door, motioning for Cynthia to follow. "Good. Come on."

Cynthia stayed put. "Wait, what are the plans?"

Kelly looked away, then met her gaze with a fake smile. "Um. It's a surprise," she tossed off.

Cynthia raised a brow. "A good surprise or a bad surprise?"

"Hopefully good," Kelly replied cheerfully. "Hopefully not a combination of the two or the latter." She tried to sound upbeat, but her worry lines belied her true emotion.

Okay, it was clear. She was being worked. Cynthia blinked at the girl and crossed her arms.

Kelly moved forward, grabbed her arm and tugged on her. "No, it will be good, really. And you have to come with me. I've worked so hard. So have other people."

Cynthia didn't budge. "This isn't a surprise party, is it?"

"No. Well, not for you."

"It's a surprise party?"

Kelly pulled harder. "Just come on. Trust me. I'm your daughter, I wouldn't lead you astray."

Cynthia allowed Kelly to drag her to the door. "I'm not convinced. I do know whose DNA you have. I'm afraid it might be rearing its ugly head about now." She made a stand at the doorway. "Come on, what's up? It looks big."

Kelly twisted her mouth to one side, the line between her eyes deepening. She examined Cynthia carefully, then sighed. She put her hands on her hips. "Will you give me a pass?"

"A pass," Cynthia replied, not understanding.

Kelly bounced in place, looking like she'd just lit the fuse on her rocket engines and Cynthia was preventing her launch. "On explaining this to you. And will you come on now? Or we'll be late and that will definitely be bad."

Without waiting for a reply, Kelly took her by the arm, opened the door and pulled her outside the apartment.

Cynthia dragged her feet a bit, but finally stopped fighting. Let the kid wrap her around her little finger. After all, she had some catching up to do. She'd missed all those pleas for Barbie's Dream House, her own cell phone and a later curfew.

They got in Kelly's Prius and headed up Bush towards Nob Hill. Towards Rex's place.

Her stomach did a flip. There was no way she'd let her daughter con her into seeing him. No bloody way. She'd better not even try. Kelly hadn't seen Cynthia's stubborn side yet. And while she loved the girl, she had her limits.

Cynthia examined her daughter's face, but Kelly wasn't giving anything up. She smiled radiantly. Then when she didn't think Cynthia was looking, she chewed on her lower lip and twitched like she'd drunk a vat of coffee.

Cynthia's pulse jumped. What the hell?

When they turned onto Rex's street, Cynthia started hyperventilating and her heart beat at a crazy pace. She grabbed the door handle, preparing to jump out of the car. "No! Tell me you're not setting me up with your father." She pressed an imaginary brake pedal on the floorboards.

Kelly gasped and appeared horrified at the thought.

Cynthia studied her. Kid wasn't acting.

Her daughter shook her head violently. "God, no. I want you two to get back together, but you are both too damned stubborn for that. No, this isn't what you think. Trust me. This will make you happy. And he helped. But this isn't about him and you. At all. This is only about you. Well, and me. Anyway, trust me."

Not for a second. Kelly was pulling something huge. But she couldn't convict the kid of a crime before she knew what it was.

"Okay," she said reluctantly. She eased back into the seat, but kept her hand on the door handle.

As expected, Kelly drove to Rex's house.

Adrenaline juiced Cynthia's system and she poised to run. Jaw set, she swung on her devious daughter. "I am not seeing your father."

"You won't."

Kelly drove through a different gate to Rex's house. Cynthia's heart pounded harder and she sent her kidnapper a glare.

"This is the service entrance," Kelly explained. "We're going in the back. I'll tell you why once we get in there. But you have to be quiet, okay? Just stay with me and I'll explain once we're inside."

"This is a set-up."

"But not for you." Kelly parked between two large, dark SUVs with tinted windows and got out.

This sounded worse and worse. Cynthia gripped the seat. Kid would have to pry her out. "I don't want to see your father."

"You won't. He's in another part of the house."

"That's still too close. What the hell is this?"

Kelly pursed her lips and motioned for her to follow with an impatient wave. "Just come with me."

Cynthia contemplated locking the doors.

Kelly's face went fiery red. "Cynthia, come on!" She stomped her foot.

Cynthia sighed. Eventually, the kid would win. She opened the door and reluctantly tore herself from the car. "I have a feeling if I'd kept you, I wouldn't be letting you pull this crap on me," she grumbled as she shut the door.

Kelly didn't miss a beat. "Probably not. But you didn't, so come on." She grabbed her arm and dragged her to the service entrance of the mansion.

Cynthia laughed at her daughter's determination. What a tornado. Kid was a freight train.

She followed her daughter inside, her body on alert. They walked down a gray, industrial-looking linoleum floored hallway into an area Cynthia had never seen before. Must be beyond the kitchen. Such a contrast to the other parts of the house.

She followed Kelly around a corner and through another long drab hallway to a flight of stairs that headed downward and ended at a door. Kelly went down the stairs, opened the door and motioned for Cynthia to follow.

By the lack of sounds coming from the room, Cynthia expected it to be empty. Or Rex to be sitting there, waiting to ambush her. She prepared to turn and run.

Cautiously stepping inside, she scanned the area for danger, but Rex wasn't there. The basement room was full of men and women in suits. Several sat at long tables with computers, a few stood. All of them faced a large wall covered in LCD monitors. There were two Asian guys in their thirties; an older woman with short gray hair; a middle-aged black guy; a young, attractive blonde woman about Kelly's age and a tall gangly fiftyish guy with a bushy black mustache. They looked up briefly, then returned their attention to either their computers or the wall of LCD monitors.

With low ceilings and a cement floor, the space was dark, cool and smelled musty. By the half-full racks of wine bottles lining the back wall, Cynthia assumed the room was normally used as a wine cellar. Whatever these people were doing there, it was a temporary operation.

"Come on," Kelly whispered and led her to a back corner where four folding chairs were set up near a group of dusty old barrels. She indicated Cynthia should sit.

Sitting, Cynthia took in the room again. She couldn't make sense of it.

The men and women talked quietly amongst themselves.

It was then Cynthia saw a badge on the young blonde woman. Her breath caught in her throat. The police? What the hell?

Kelly sat on her right.

Cynthia elbowed her. "What is this?"

Kelly pointed at the screens. "Just watch," she whispered. "The show should start soon."

The door opened and Jon and Butch—of all people—walked into the room, smiling like they'd won Oscars.

Her shoulders tight, her brows furrowed to the point of pain. This got weirder and weirder. Especially because Jon was uncharacteristically quiet. He looked like he was bursting at the seams.

Jon rushed over and sat on her left. "This is so exciting," he whispered.

Butch sat next to Kelly.

Cynthia demanded, "What's so exciting? What the hell goes on here?"

Jon frowned and looked startled. "She hasn't told you?" He moved forward to look at Kelly who put her forefinger to her mouth. His mouth went into an O, he sat back and smiled at Cynthia, grabbing her hand and squeezing it while bouncing slightly on his seat. He looked like he did on Christmas morning, ready to jump out of his skin with excitement. He threw his arm around her and hugged her tight. "My lips are sealed except, oh, my God, are you going to loooove this."

"Jon, don't give it away," Kelly whispered harshly.

Cynthia then noticed what was displayed on the screens. Rex in his office. Three different angles.

Her heart launched into triple-time and she put a hand to her chest. He looked so good. Those bluer than blue eyes, his rugged broken nose, yummy jaw and kissable lips. His supple hands. God, how she missed the feel of them on her body. Gloom strangled her mood, a sob caught in her throat and she wrapped her arms around herself.

The tall gangly guy with the mustache pointed at a screen in front of him. "Shit, they're here early."

The screen showed a camera view of the backs of three people standing at the front door. The picture was too small and too far away for Cynthia to make out what they looked like.

"Are we ready?" the older gray-haired woman asked. "Rex? Are you ready? We're going a bit sooner than we thought. Your friends are here early."

"I'm ready. Let's go," came Rex's deep resonant voice over a speaker.

Gray Lady said, "Okay, Bill? Let the butler answer the door."

Cynthia watched transfixed as Rex settled into his chair. She felt like she'd awoken in a weird surreal dream. What was going on? What friends?

Sissy followed by Belinda and Troy appeared on screen in Rex's office. Cynthia let out a yip, then clamped her hand over her mouth. Light-headed, she nearly keeled over. Her pulse pumping in her ears, she clutched Jon.

He held her tight and whispered, "Watch this."

Sissy strutted up to Rex's desk.

Rex didn't get up. His hands were folded together on top of the desk, his forefingers steepled.

Sissy gestured at him, then cocked a hip and sneered. "Well, look at you behind your big desk." She snorted. "Big man, can't even come up with two million. My boy looked into your finances, you know. He's smart. You think I'm stupid, well maybe I don't have a good education, but my boy, Troy, does. You're lucky you didn't lie to me. Now where's my money, I got a date." She tapped his desk.

Sissy blackmailed Rex? Cynthia's jaw on her lap, a tanker-load of adrenaline dumped into her system, and she nearly leapt from her seat. This was a sting operation! Really? Could this be true? Was this really happening?

Rex gave a short nod. "Right here." With one small movement, he pushed an envelope across the desk.

Sissy pounced on it. "Finally. Fuck. Finally getting some money," she said, holding up the envelope in triumph. "Your old girlfriend is so lame. She's worth nothing. But you, my friend, you may make this all worthwhile. Not to gloat here. Okay, we're out of here." She turned and swaggered towards the door.

"Aren't you going to count it?" Rex asked calmly.

She turned back, a smug look on her overly lined face. "Don't need to. You wouldn't mess with me. I got too much over you."

"Mom, count the money," Troy said in his usual emotionless tone. "He's not that trustworthy."

She swung on him and stroked her chin. She nodded and smiled. "You're right, boy. Makin' me glad I didn't abort ya."

Jesus, what a cold bitch. But Troy barely reacted, only raised his brows a bit.

Sissy turned away from both Troy and Sissy and counted the money. She gave a quick nod. "It's all here."

Belinda pushed on Sissy's shoulder. "What do I get?"

"Nothing, yet," Sissy snapped. She let out an exasperated breath. "Oh, hell, I'll give you something. I always do. Lame-o. You need to come up with some plans for making money. Why do I have to do all the thinking in this family?"

Troy nodded towards Rex. "Make sure he understands what this payment covers, mother. Make it crystal clear."

Wow, Troy was playing right into the cops' hands. What an idiot! Cynthia's mood soared and her interior bubbled with anticipation and joy. Her wildest fantasy come true.

"You're right." Sissy stalked over to Rex's desk and struck a regal pose, clearly glorying in her victory. She pointed at him. "Listen, mister, this only covers keeping my mouth shut about those idiot parents of your daughter's. And for only a set amount of time. Like, let's say six months. In six months, I'll expect more. My due. You know, another ten grand, say. No, make it twenty. Then I'll keep my mouth shut for longer."

Rex didn't move one muscle of his face. Remarkable poise. Amazing control. Cynthia would have had Sissy on the floor by now and would have been bashing her head into the carpet. He just sat there, impassive.

"Do we understand each other?" Troy asked Rex.

After another long moment, a slight nod. "Yes."

Troy's shoulders relaxed. "Good. Mother? Shall we?" He gestured towards the door.

"We got 'em," Gray Lady said. "That's it, Rex, that's a wrap. Let them get out the door, we'll arrest them as they walk out."

Cynthia wanted to scream with joy and dance all over the room. They had them. Finally, the bitches would get their due. All of them, in jail. With Sissy and Belinda's criminal records, this should put them away for a long time. It couldn't be true.

Rex held up his hand. "Sissy, I've been thinking," he drawled. "I may be able to use someone like you. You know, to take care of business that I can't, well, be seen participating in."

The mustached cop turned partially towards Gray Lady, but didn't take his eyes off the screen. "What's he doing?"

Cynthia's stomach clenched, her back and arms went tight. *God, Rex, please don't blow it. Please don't. Let them go down. Let them go to jail now.*

Troy stared at Rex, seeming a bit alarmed. Belinda had lost interest and picked at a scab on her forearm.

Sissy smiled like she was about to feast on a succulent steak, showing off her missing teeth. "Keep talking, Rex." She ambled back to his desk.

Mustache hissed to the young blonde, "This wasn't part of the deal. What's he doing?"

Blondie shrugged. "I hope he doesn't wreck it."

The cops worrying worried Cynthia. She nearly crushed herself in an embrace and jiggled her leg.

"There are many things a man like me needs doing," Rex said, his voice and tone even. "Just don't have the right contacts. I think you might be able to help me with those. Maybe do a job yourself. I need smart people like you on my team. I mean, you got me to pay up. And I'm good."

"Yeah, I did, didn't I?" Sissy puffed out her bony chest proudly. "So what's the deal? What kind of jobs?"

"First, I want a bit more information. How good are you at revenge?"

She laughed harshly. "Real good. Who's the target?"

Rex's jaw twitched. "Someone you know. Someone who hurt me. Humiliated me." His gaze went hard and his face turned to granite. "Cynthia Rella."

Cynthia's stomach dropped. She was sure he was lying, but that anger in his gaze frightened her. What the hell was he up to?

Sissy went slack-jawed. She stared at him like she couldn't believe what she was hearing. "*Cynthia*? You want me to help you get Cynthia?"

"Depends. On how good you are."

"Oh, I'm good. Really?" She lit up like someone had given her the crown jewels of England. She burst into a huge, toothless smile. "Holy fuck, a dream come true! You're kidding me."

"No. I'm not," he replied coldly. "I want her to suffer."

Sissy let out a gleeful yelp. "Cool. Me, too!" She bounced in place. "Okay, what should I do?" She started pacing and snapping her fingers. "Think, think. I know! We can get her nurse's license taken away! Then she couldn't earn any money!" She stopped and pointed at Rex. "No, I can get Jon fired! That would really hurt her." She gasped and clutched her Jack Daniels t-shirt. "No, I got it! We kidnap her daughter—oh, she's your daughter, too. Never mind. Too bad, that would really get her."

"Kelly is obviously off limits," he replied smoothly.

Cynthia relaxed a smidgen. She knew Rex well enough to realize he was playing Sissy. Dude was an amazing actor. But what was he after? What did he want from them?

Sissy waved a hand and continued pacing. "No, course not." She stopped again and turned to Rex. "I could do something to that idiot son of that fag husband of hers," she asked in a hopeful tone.

Cynthia checked quickly for Jon's reaction. He tensed and his eyes went cold. She looked at Butch. He chuckled. Could care less.

"I'd rather hit her directly," Rex said, leaning back in his chair. "But I'm not sure with what. Tell me what you've done to her already. Inspire me."

Cynthia's body knotted, her heart knocked against her ribs and she clutched the seat of her chair. She didn't know if she could handle this.

Sissy burst out in delighted cackles. "God, you name it, I've done it. Haven't we, Belinda?"

Belinda's eyes shone, a huge stupid grin spread on her rotund face. She waddled up to Rex's desk, waving her chunky arms, excited. The last time Cynthia had seen that joyful of an expression on her face was when five pizzas got accidentally delivered to the house.

The Human Cow nodded, her several chins jiggling. "We got her real good. Real good. Hee! You want the list?"

Rex cracked a small smile. "Might be amusing."

"Okay, jeez, where to start?" Sissy said, her dark eyes shining.

"Hold on, baby," Jon whispered, tightening his grip on her. She leaned into him.

Belinda pointed at her sister. "Tell him about that stupid school of hers, that was the best, she almost killed herself!" She snorted with laughter.

Cynthia's body froze. No. *Tell me they didn't have anything to do with that. Tell me they didn't.*

Sissy's gaze alive, she grinned at Rex. "Okay, get this. Cindy—Cynthia—we always called her Cindy because she hated it—anyway, Cindy was this real snob artist brat when she was a teenager. Everyone made over her, she got in these stupid magazines, for all this crap she made. You should have seen it, hideous shit. Could have been made by a monkey. Anyway, my mom was so impressed Cindy got in these stupid galleries she lost her mind. What there was of it. She was a fuckin' moron—God rest her soul. Well, there was this super hoity-toity art school that Cindy really wanted in. I mean, bad. Everyone was sure she'd get in, Mom and Dad were all bragging to their friends. Well, she got into the school. But she never knew that." Sissy exploded in evil laughter.

It was like a skyscraper toppled over and flattened Cynthia to the floor. No air in her lungs, her insides crushed and bile rose in her throat. She grabbed her middle and started breathing hard, trying to control her nausea.

Jon hugged her tightly. "Stay tough, kid. I'm here."

Belinda howled and slapped her thick thigh. "Sissy found the acceptance letter and burned it!" she cried. "It was so funny!" After laughing hard for a bit, she calmed so she could talk. She was so excited, she began panting and wheezing. "Then, Sissy was so smart. She made up some letterhead."

While overwhelming and horrifying, there was something strangely satisfying about hearing this truth. Finally, the unvarnished story from the two predators. Finally, the real dope. The real emotion. Nothing held back.

They were even worse than Cynthia had thought. Just when she thought she understood the depths of their depravity, they surprised her. Whatever low they reached, they could beat. There was no limit to their hatred, their evil.

Sissy got in front of her sister, eager to tell the story. "I copied the original letter, it was so good. I was so good. And I wrote this rejection letter. Well, I copied one of mine from a college Mom applied for. She wanted me to go to school for some stupid reason. Like I would waste my time at some lousy school. Well, I copied a rejection letter—all nicely typed up—and freakin' put it in our mail box."

Belinda roared with laughter.

Cynthia shuddered and dry sobs choked her. Kelly joined Jon and hugged her. But even with two sets of arms around her, Cynthia felt hollow and alone. She flashed on her hot attic bedroom when she was a teenager. Curled up in a ball on her tear-stained bed with that letter in her hand, howling.

Sissy could barely talk she was laughing so hard. "Then I called the school and impersonated Cindy and told them to fuck off, that I wouldn't lower myself by attending their retarded school. They were so pissed! Oh, man, that was so good. Mom was so mad. She turned on Cindy, big time. That was the funniest, freakin' best thing I ever pulled."

Unreal. They'd taken her life from her. They'd destroyed her. And they thought it was funny.

Sorrow turned to rage and her body flooded with heat. Fists clenched, arms hard, teeth gritted, hungry for blood, she wanted to kill them. Beat them until they were both dead. How dare they do that to her!

Belinda made her normal hideous snarfling laughing sounds. "It was so funny! Cindy cried for weeks! Oh, that was good." Tears ran down her cheeks, she wiped them and fanned her face. "So funny."

Rex didn't react much besides a slight smile. "What else?"

Sissy stopped and screwed her face up like she was thinking hard. "Hell, what else? Well, if you want to talk real crime, I'm really good at crime." She got a cocky look on her gaunt face. "Get this: I forged a new will of my parents, paid off this slimy lawyer— well, I blew him and gave him some meth—and he filed it in court and we're gonna split the profits." She grinned widely.

Belinda giggled. "Yeah, Cindy was all pickin' out her dad's casket and when she got home, we showed her the fake will and told her to get out, that all of it was ours. Oh, man—" She frowned. "Well, that was actually bad, she beat me up."

Sissy's face went hard. "And me, too, the fuckin' bitch." She narrowed her eyes and smirked. "But we got her. Good. We got her put in jail for assault and then the will held up in court and we got everything. I mean *everything*. Her clothes, her TV, all her junk. Her mom's jewelry—well, we sold that. Didn't get much for that crap."

Another wallop of pain hit Cynthia's gut and she let out a muffled cry. Jon held her tighter while Kelly rubbed her back.

Belinda burst out in mean laughter. "And we busted a bunch of her retarded sculptures right in front of her. Man, she went nuts. That was great. Well, getting beat wasn't, but getting that house was cool. Wish we could sell the fucker."

Rex nodded slowly. "So you girls actually forged a new will? Pretty clever."

Sissy postured. "Yeah, we are good. I mean, *good*. And besides, it wasn't fair. That first will only gave us a few thousand. Cynthia got the whole house. I mean, so what if she spent all her money taking care of my parents and their stupid medical bills? That was because she was an idiot. I shouldn't have had to pay for her stupidity. They didn't ask for it, you know. That was her decision. They weren't that bad off. Their cancer wasn't that bad. They would have done fine without her interfering. Fucking bitch. That was my house," she said, jabbing a thumb towards her chest. "And I got it back. I just had to pull some shit."

Belinda gestured towards her. "And blow that skanky lawyer."

"He gave me a tip," Sissy offered.

"You girls certainly are smarter than I thought you were."

Sissy stood taller. "Oh, I got lots more stories like that. Like smearing dog shit on her prom dress—"

"That was so funny!" Belinda exclaimed, bending over and screeching with laughter.

Sissy slapped her sister on the back. "Ex-lax in her brownies."

Belinda laughed so hard, she had to gasp for air. Clapping her hands, she finally choked out, "I keyed her new car!"

Sissy waved her hand and sent her sister a smug grin. "Fuck that, I sliced her tires. And that was when she was at work, so she couldn't know it was me. Man, we've done all kinds of shit to her." She put her hands on her hips and tilted her head thoughtfully. "Gotta give her credit, she doesn't crack easy." She turned to Rex. "It'll be tough to break her, if that's what you want to do. God knows I tried."

"We tried hard. She's tough." Belinda nodded emphatically.

Rex let out a long breath. "Well, you've got me convinced. Tell you what. Let me think a bit and I'll get back to you. Leave me your number, okay?"

Sissy reached in her back pocket and took out a card case. She flicked it open and withdrew a card. She set it on his desk and pushed it over to him. "My cell's on the card."

He took it and gave a slight nod. "Professional."

"Well, that's for my side business," she explained like she was talking about a multi-million dollar corporation.

"Side business?"

"Yeah, I deal meth," she announced proudly. "If you want any or know anyone who needs any, the stuff is killer. Day or night, I deliver. I have some on me, if you want to try it."

He gave his head a quick shake. "Not right now." He narrowed his gaze. A slight shrug. "Well, maybe."

She sent him a knowing grin. She dug in her front pocket and withdrew a small white packet. "Here, I'll give you a bag on the house." She tossed it on his desk.

Rex didn't touch it. But he sent her a pleased smile. "Thanks."

"No problem. Seeing as we're going into business together." She gave him a flirty smile. "You know, I think I'm gonna like this arrangement, Rex, old boy."

Troy cleared his throat. "Mom, I have a class, can we go?"

Sissy seemed startled. "You still here? Good for you. Finally figuring out when you need to shut up." She turned back to Rex. "Troy's a good boy, but he's a bit uppity. Goes to school, gonna be a doctor. Me, I hate school, never challenged me, really. Troy takes after his father. His father had six degrees. Got 'em all in prison. Loved school. I'll have to tell you about his father someday. You might remember him. They called him the Rope Killer. Such lies. He only killed one woman and that was because she deserved it. They pinned all these others on him and he got a lethal injection, but he was a sweetheart. I mean, once you got past the facial tattoos. And that weird lump on his forehead—"

"Mother," Troy said, sounding impatient.

She nodded and waved him off. "Okay, boy, okay." She turned to Rex. "Pleasure doing business with you. Until next time." She turned and walked out the door on Troy's heels.

Belinda went to the door, then turned back and waved at Rex. "Bye, Rex, this was fun!" she said with a huge, stupid grin on her empty face.

She left, closing the door behind her.

Rex slumped in his chair.

Mustache said, "And go Unit Two, they're on their way to you."

On the small screen, Sissy and Belinda walked out the front door and were immediately surrounded by police. No sound, but it was clear they were screaming from their open mouths. Both were forced to the ground. A few minutes later, they were cuffed and taken away.

Cynthia finally breathed. But couldn't take her eyes off the screen. She couldn't believe it.

In a corner of the screen, Troy stood, talking to a uniformed policewoman.

"Why aren't they arresting Troy?" She looked around the room for answers.

Kelly touched her arm. "He helped us, Cynthia. He was in on it."

Cynthia's attention snapped to her. "*Troy* was in on it?"

Kelly nodded. "Uh-huh. He's sick of his mom's drama. He thinks she'll be out of trouble in jail. And she'll stop bothering him."

Cynthia didn't know whether to laugh or cry. She was completely blown away.

Gray Lady whistled. "Man, Rex knew a goldmine when he saw one, didn't he? Can we hire him? Jeez, what a cool customer."

Kelly sighed and beamed. "He was fantastic."

"Did you get all that?" Rex asked, looking into a camera.

"Boy did we," Mustache replied.

"Are they arrested and off my blasted property yet?"

Gray Lady laughed. "Almost."

"Thank God. Someone get the staff up here to clean the carpets. I need a shower."

Cynthia turned to Kelly and threw her arms around her. "Thank you, honey." She kissed her on the cheek.

"I couldn't let them hurt you anymore, Mom. I mean, Cynthia. I mean, Mom."

Cynthia's heart expanded like a hot air balloon. Tears rolling down her cheeks, she hugged Kelly harder. *Mom.* She called her Mom. "Love you, kid."

"Love you, too." Kelly pushed away. "Dad helped me plan this. I didn't push him into it. He came up with this plan on his own."

Taking several deep breaths, Cynthia couldn't begin to process that aspect of the scene. "You guys are one in a million," she said, a sob nearly choking her.

"You gotta tell Dad that," Kelly said.

Rex. Her heart and guts ripped apart like someone had thrown them into a blender and hit puree. She cried harder. Why did he veer off plan and dig until he got them to confess all they'd done to her? Why did he do that? To see if Cynthia had told the truth about them? Did this mean he wanted her back? Did it mean he still loved her?

Kelly. Of course. Kelly had begged him to do it. He wouldn't have done it on his own. He did it for his daughter, not Cynthia. She had to get hold of her wild thoughts. This did not mean he wanted her, it meant he hated injustice. He'd told her that.

She forced her tears away. She had to hold it together. She'd give into her feelings later, when she was alone. She'd thank Rex and then get the hell out of there.

Oh, God. She had to see him. Face to face. She'd rather swim through the shark-infested waters of the Bay covered in bloody dead fish.

Maybe she could fake a heart attack. Talk about a perfect time for a brain aneurysm. Damn this. Short of spontaneously combusting or dying, there was no way out.

How in God's name could she handle seeing him?

Chapter Twenty-One

Cynthia hung out with Jon, Butch and Kelly in Rex's living room, drinking wine and eating cheese and crackers, waiting for Rex to finish with the police.

Holding back her emotions was taking superhuman effort. Her body was a powder keg of suppressed grief, the fuse had been lit and she was on the brink of exploding. While she was thrilled the gargoyles were finally put away, she still couldn't begin to comprehend the amazing amount of abuse she'd suffered.

But even that turmoil paled in comparison to the Rex Thing. Thankfully, their earlier exchange had only lasted a few seconds—a brief glance across the entry hall as he escorted the police to his office. He had smiled at her, his sweet energy stabbing her heart like he'd pierced it with a thick metal spike.

She reached for her wine glass, smacked into it and barely caught it. A bit of red wine splashed on the marble-topped coffee table. Kelly rushed to clean it up.

Cynthia barely stopped an avalanche of tears. She was two seconds away from imploding.

She got up. "I'm going to go find the restroom."

As she passed Kelly, heading for the doorway, the girl grabbed her arm. "You know where it is?"

She forced a smile. "Yeah, thanks."

She walked purposefully towards the bathroom. But when she arrived there, she gave a quick check around. Seeing no one, she dashed out a side exit to a private little garden space with a small fountain surrounded by a marble bench. The area was concealed by a large hedge. No one could see her from there.

She collapsed on the bench and her emotional floodgates burst open. She pounded her palm with her fist until she couldn't take the pain, then took off her sweatshirt, balled it up and screamed into it. She bellowed and yelled and howled, trying to release all the sorrow and rage from her gut.

Her screams became cries and she broke down, wracking with sobs.

A hand on her back made her yelp and leap from the bench. Her gaze bleary with tears, the person was fuzzy and out-of-focus, but it was clear from their height who it was.

Rex. Goddamn it. She wiped her eyes and tried to maintain.

"Cynthia?" he asked with a sympathetic look on his handsome face.

Exploding in a cloud of agony, she held up her trembling hands. "Go back in the house! I can't take it, okay? I can't take any more rejection right now! I love you too much and this is killing me! I need some time," she said, crumpling to the bench. She dissolved into sobs.

He swept her off the bench and into his arms. She tried to push him away, but he held on tightly and wouldn't let go.

"No, I won't let you push me away. For God's sake, they destroyed you. It has to hurt. Just get it out. Let me be here for you."

Sobbing, she pushed on him harder. "You hate me, I don't blame you. Stop lying to me and let me go!"

"I'm not lying, I love you. I was wrong. All you did was try to protect Kelly, I get that now. I love you, Cynthia."

He just felt sorry for her, that was all. "Please let me go," she said, pulling back, hard.

He crushed her to him. "No. Not until you listen to me. Not until you let me hold you."

The logic of this statement stopped her. Instantly, her tears ceased, she met his gaze. "So wait. You won't let me go until I let you hold me. So how would you know exactly when I was letting you hold me?" She started laughing, surprising herself.

He chuckled and pulled away, his mouth open with shock. "Are you laughing?"

"It's funny."

"No, you're funny."

Wait. She had to have this wrong. The tears returned with a fury. "Tell me you're not fucking with me," she said with a sob. "Tell me you meant what you just said."

"I mean it," he said, his expression softening. "I love you. With my whole heart. It's why I went so wacko on you, I haven't felt like this ever, Cynthia. Ever. Not even with Elizabeth. She didn't understand me like you do. You and I click. On so many levels."

"God, Rex. Are you sure?"

"Never been more sure of anything, ever."

She blinked at him, wiping the tears to study his face carefully. No hidden words on his sexy lips. No doubt on the rugged creases of his forehead. No deception, only clear, pure love in his eyes. He wanted her. He was hers.

She threw her arms around him and buried her face in his chest.

He wrapped his long arms around her and nuzzled the top of her head. She reveled in the feel of his warmth, his familiar musky scent and the love pouring from his heart.

She cried again, only this time with tears of joy. He held onto her like he'd never let her go.

When she calmed, he pulled away and took her by the hands. "I think the biggest issue—the reason I didn't call you—is hard for me to admit. But I really thought that when Kelly met her birth parents I was going to lose her. And when I found out you were her mother, I was sure you would take her from me."

She gaped at him. "I'd *what*?"

He shook his head, reddened and grinned sheepishly. "I know. It makes no sense. I've just lost too many damn people in my life. A good—yes, a good friend recently got through to me. He or she said —"

"He or she?" she asked, cocking her head in confusion.

He laughed, pulled her tightly to him and kissed her on the cheek. A rush went through her. His twinkling blue eyes, his gorgeous face, the way he tilted his head to one side when he laughed, she'd missed every single bit of this man.

"He's a drag queen. Met her when I was hunting you down with Jon's platform shoe."

"You have a good friend who's a drag queen?"

He grinned, meeting her gaze, sending another thrill through her. "There's lots you don't know about me. Anyway, she said that love like ours doesn't come along very often. And that I was being a total idiot. That true love can conquer any obstacle. She nailed me on my fears about losing Kelly, too. She made me see how ridiculous I was being. She really got through to me. Took me a while to process, but she was right."

"Wow." She giggled. Then small storm of guilt attacked her gut.

He frowned and worry lines appeared on his handsome face. "Uh, oh. What?"

She sent him an easy grin. "Don't worry. I just…" She heaved a sigh and her frown returned. "I have to say some things to you. I blew it with you. Sleeping with you before telling you who I was is an entirely new low for me."

He gripped her arm. "Don't, I—"

She held up her hand to silence him. "Let me say this. I have to. I'm so sorry. I lied to you and put myself ahead of your needs that night, Rex. You were right when you accused me of that and I'm ashamed of my behavior. But I needed you so badly, everything else went out the window. Still, it was ethically, morally wrong."

He rubbed her back. "I get it, honey. Believe me, I get it. Please stop apologizing." He sent her a grin. "I didn't exactly make it easy on you to avoid me. And you did a damn good job of trying."

"But you were better."

He gave her a serious look. "Damn straight."

A surge of lust went through her loins. He was so deliciously Alpha.

He broke into a huge smile, pulled her closer and ran a hand down the side of her face. She leaned into his palm, relishing the warmth of his touch. He kissed her on the forehead, zapping her skin, giving her goosebumps and a wonderful tingle down her spine.

"Damn it, Cynthia. I've been such an ass. I took all this shit out on you and you didn't deserve it."

"Now don't you start apologizing."

He pulled away and sent her a stern look. "You had your say, let me have mine."

She laughed. "You're so good at negotiating and we've only just started."

"Damn right. Now listen to me. I finally got it. Got you. I can be thick some times. Like with James. But you. I can't imagine your suffering. You'd just lost your father, your home, all your best sculptures, everything you owned. You saw your daughter for the first time. Pretty easy to see why your judgment was off. And mine? I don't have as much of an excuse. I've been kicking myself for the crap I said to you—"

She rubbed his ripped upper arms. "You thought I was using you to get to Kelly, to take her away from you. You'd just lost your business, your best friend, your son-in-law—the thought of losing Kelly was just too much. And I betrayed you in the worst way, you lost me, too. You were grief-stricken."

His mouth became a grim line. "Didn't excuse the behavior."

"Yes, it does," she said, running her arms around his waist. "You and I are a lot alike. We hold ourselves to impossible standards."

He lifted his brow and nodded slowly. "Yes, we do."

"And I have to thank you from the bottom of my heart for what you did for me earlier," she said, giving him a squeeze. "You have no idea how much it means to me."

The planes of his face grew severe, his jaw clamped. "I'm so sorry you had to hear that. I had no idea. I would have done something different if I'd known. All I meant to do was get them to confess to forging the will. I couldn't believe the shit that came out of their mouths. Horrid bitches. I had to work hard to keep from diving across the desk and killing them with my bare hands. They're beyond anything I've ever been exposed to. I think this was part of my problem. I'd never met such evil. And just because they were victimized doesn't excuse their behavior. They're career criminals."

Cynthia snorted. "They wish. Amateurs. Which is why they're in jail. But Troy helping—I can't believe that. At all. That's the weirdest. I swear, that kid is the creepiest human on the planet, why the hell would he turn like that?"

"Kelly."

"Oh. Yeah. She's somethin', isn't she? Damn, that kid can have you wrapped around her finger and you don't even get it until after you've done what she wants."

He smiled knowingly. "Uh, yeah. She's a force of nature, that one. Been like that from Day One. In your face, throwing so much logic at you so fast, it makes your head spin. I told her she should be a trial lawyer with her astounding ability, but she won't listen."

"Stubborn. Immovable as a mule in cement."

He grinned down at her. "So nice to have someone else love her as much as I do. I've missed that since Elizabeth was gone. She was a little hard on Kelly, but she loved her fiercely."

"I'll bet. And Kelly doesn't seem any worse for wear. Got a solid foundation underneath her." A stab of longing for Kelly's childhood speared her heart. She sighed.

He ran a hand down her back and the edge went off her pain. "I wish you'd been there, too, Cynthia."

It didn't surprise her that he'd read her mind. Tears threatened and she fanned her face. "I don't wanna cry. This has been so overwhelming."

He brought her closer and gave her a full body hug that rocked her. A sob of gratitude caught in her throat. She swallowed. She'd missed his steely arms around her. He made her feel so safe. She relaxed into him, taking in his scent, his love. "You know, I was thinking, if the Gruesome Twosome hadn't ruined my chances for that art academy, I wouldn't have met Jon or had Kelly. And I wouldn't have met you."

He squeezed her. "Good things always come out of tragedies. I have to remember that, too," he said, more to himself.

She pulled away to look at him. "I'm so sorry about James."

A brief raise of his eyebrows and a haunted look appeared behind his gaze. "Me, too. But thanks."

After a moment, his expression brightened. His attention dropped to her mouth, he leaned in and kissed her. A bolt of heat rose from her feet and blasted out through her heart. Her body cried out for him. She gripped him hard.

He took her face in his large hands. His warmth sent waves of lusty energy pulsing through her. He deepened the kiss, commanding her mouth and she groaned with longing.

Some part of her centered. He grounded her. Their love, it was real. She could feel it. He was supposed to be there.

Her future stretched out before her. And it looked really good. Better than good. The best.

"Stay with me, the best is yet to be," she whispered when they pulled away. She caught herself. "I said that aloud, didn't I?"

He beamed down at her and nuzzled her neck. "God, I love you, lady."

"I love you, too, Rex." She looked deep into his azure gaze and her feet tingled.

He kissed her even more deeply and she melted into him.

Shot to the stratosphere, his love filled her heart, thawing the last bits of the icy barrier. Hot energy pulsed through her body. She ran her hands over his hard muscles, loving his chest, his shoulders and his neck. She couldn't wait to make love to him. Be with him again. Feel that delicious smooth skin next to hers.

He pulled away, ran a hand over her hair and grinned down at her.

She sighed, her cheeks sore from smiling so hard. "So where do we go from here?"

"Where do you want to go?"

Bed. "I know you have a plan."

He made a face like he was thinking. "Um. Okay. Date for the next minute. Then you move in. Preferably this afternoon. We get married in the spring. You do your art, I do my art and we spend time on my boat. Oh, and sex. Lots of sex. Mainly sex," he said to her mouth. He kissed her a long, wonderful luxurious one, making her ache with want.

When he ended the kiss, his smile lit the foggy afternoon like sunshine at noon. He took her by the hand and pulled her towards the house. "Come. I want to show you something."

"I've seen it and it's awesome, but those guys would miss us."

He laughed, his blue eyes dancing, his crow's feet deep. "You are bad. You are a very bad woman," he said, taking her in his arms and kissing her hard. Smiling, he pulled away. "No, I want to show you something I think you'll like."

He led her through the house and down a hallway off the entry hall, past the dining room. He sent her sweet little glances, his face alight with expectation.

What the hell?

He opened a door to a huge room, an atrium almost. She walked inside, wondering why he was showing it to her. High, floor-to-ceiling windows lined one wall showcasing a magnificent view of San Francisco and the bay beyond. In the room were some oddly shaped furniture—she stopped and stared. A potter's wheel. It was a potter's wheel. Not only that, a huge worktable lined the center of the room, with containers of sculpting tools sitting on top. Against the far wall were shelves that held clay, paints and glazes.

This wasn't what she thought it was, was it? Her heart banged hard against her ribs.

He pointed to an empty corner. "A kiln is going right there, it's on back order. Already got the wiring done for it. There's an old shop next to the basement I'm having converted to a foundry so you can do your metal work again."

Her mouth dropped open and she could only stare. She lightly slapped her face. "I am asleep. I am about to wake up. This is not real."

He grinned, threw an arm around her and kissed the side of her head. "It's real, Cynthia. It's time things turned around for you. It's time your life settled out. You deserve this. And I love you. With my whole heart. And I want you to be happy."

Her thoughts vaporized in a cloud of overwhelm. She clutched her hands to her chest and suppressed a sob. "I can't take this all in. It doesn't compute. Things have been so crappy for so long, I can't believe this."

"Believe it," he said, tightening his arm around her.

A shriek from behind them made them jump apart with a start. Heart thumping painfully, she turned towards the source of the noise.

Jon, waving his arms. "I'm going to cry! You're back together and look at this studio he built for you! I'm going to die! Will you look at this?"

She cracked up and Rex joined her.

"Yes, Jon."

Behind Jon, Kelly and Butch came into the room, their sweet faces shining.

Jon circled the room, gesturing dramatically. "Oh, my God! Look at this place! I'm so happy for you," he gushed, hugging himself. "Tears, I've got tears, actual tears, see?" he said, rushing up to her.

He pointed at the corner of his eye to show her. Then he hugged her, almost breaking her in half.

Kelly looked in wonderment at the room. "Dad, you did this? When?"

"Last week. After your magnificent speech."

Cynthia turned to Kelly and sent her a teasing smile. "You made a magnificent speech?"

Kelly flushed, then smiled and glanced at her feet. "Sorta."

Rex burst out laughing. "You should have heard her."

"Dad," she said, reproachfully. Then she shrugged. "Even though I meant it."

Cynthia looked at each person in turn. Unreal. Harmony on a scale she couldn't even comprehend. *Was it really over? Had her life finally turned around?* "I am living in a dream world."

"It's all so sweet," Jon said, gazing at the group. His eyes nearly had cartoon hearts for pupils.

Butch came up and hugged her. She swore he got taller and bigger every day. "So happy for you, Cyn-a-bun." Smiling, he pulled away and went to stand near Kelly.

"It will register someday," she said wryly.

Rex put his long arms around her and formed her to his body. "When you wake up with me enough times, you'll get it."

"I love the sound of that."

"I love the sound of Mrs. Cynthia Du Charmante."

She pushed on his chest, raising a brow. "Don't even be proposing to me in front of all these people," she said, waggling her finger at him.

He got the cutest look on his face and promptly got down on one knee. He took her hand. "Cynthia Rella, will you be my wife?"

His proposal hit her like a fully loaded semi-truck. Reeling, she laid a hand on his broad shoulder to steady herself. This was all too much! Her head swam, her feet tingled and she wanted leap in the air and prance around the room.

He looked around his immediate area. "Oh, shit, I don't have a ring." He reached in his hip pocket and pulled out some Rolaids. He ripped off some foil, then put the antacids back in his pocket. He quickly folded the foil into a ring. With a happy smile, he offered it to her.

She burst out laughing and so did everyone else.

She allowed him to put in on her finger. "Yes, of course, I'll accept this foil Rolaids wrapper as a token of your affection and commitment." She helped him up, he gave her a huge hug and a kiss.

Jon, Butch and Kelly exploded in applause, cheers and whistles.

Her heart roaring with love, her entire body on fire, she still couldn't get her head around the extreme turn of events.

Mrs. Cynthia Du Charmante. Had such a great ring to it. Now where was she going to find that peach silk number from the thirties and those lilies?

She didn't know. But she knew Rex was going to look great in that grey tux.

Epilogue

"Mmmmm," Cynthia said, nibbling on Rex's neck. She pulled away to adjust the silk sheets and plump up the pillow behind her head.

He stroked her bare belly, gently cupping a breast. "God, I love you."

While mesmerized by his touch, the faces of her family popped into her mind. Followed closely by the Christmas tree and the roast in the oven. "We have to get up."

"No."

"Yes. People will be here."

"We need a cook again. Then you wouldn't have to go slave over the meal."

"It's not a big deal. The roast should be done soon. I planned an easy dinner."

He pulled away and lifted up the sheet over her body. Closing in on a breast with his mouth, he said, "It's a big deal if it takes you away from me. I wish you'd let me hire a cook again."

She laughed as he sucked on her nipple. He chuckled deep in his throat. "I will someday. Helga's only been retired for a month. And I love cooking. So nice to have that kitchen all to myself. I've been driving her nuts for the past few years, barging in there to cook my own recipes—stop that, you're making me horny."

He popped up from under the sheets, a huge grin on his face. "You're an amazing cook. One of your hidden talents." He moved up and kissed her, dropping a hand to her sex.

She giggled into his mouth and pushed his hand away.

He pulled back with a smirk.

"Come down with me and help," she said, running a hand through his hair.

He sent her a wicked, dark grin. "I want to help here," he said, stroking between her legs.

Her sex argued with her as she moved his hand again. "We can't start that all over. I'm finally satisfied."

"Why not? It's Christmas, I want my presents early. I loved unwrapping you…" He kissed her.

She got lost in him, his taste and what he was doing with his amazing tongue. Jon's face smiled at her. She pushed Rex back. "Kelly and Mark and Butch and Jon and Colin plus—erg, Troy—will be here in forty-five minutes. Oh and Beauty, too. Her dad's not feeling well and insisted she go somewhere fun for Christmas. I have to get up. I don't want to look like I just had sex."

"What's wrong with that?" He nipped her neck and ran his hand up her thigh.

She grabbed his wrist to stop him. "No one wants to picture old people having sex."

He sucked her earlobe, then chewed on it lightly. She shivered. "I do. As long as the old people are us. I still can't get enough of you." He ripped out of her grip and his hands roamed her body. He leaned in and nibbled at her lips, then licked all around her mouth.

Hot sensations rocked her clit and waves of pleasure pulsed through her, making her nipples hard. Damn it, she had to get going.

"Flatterer. Really, I have to go cook."

He stopped and fell back against his pillow. "Maybe so. I should get the bar set up. I promised Jon and Beauty I'd make my special rum punch." He chuckled. "Last time Beauty was here, I didn't stop laughing once. She's a joy. Hope she finds a good man someday."

"Poor thing. Best interior but damn, saddled with her father's looks."

"Right guy will see past her plain features—the worthy guy. She'll find him. I've no doubt."

"She could use a makeover. Maybelline could help her. Speaking of which, is she stopping by?"

He sat up, shaking his head. He stroked her arms. Shivers of delight prickled her skin and she craved more. Stupid Christmas!

"No, Maybelline won't be here this year," he said. "A niece invited her. And she doesn't have to wear a suit."

"I'm sorry she lost her parents, but damn. Maybe there'll be some healing in that family."

"There sure needs to be." He raised a brow at her and his mouth tightened. "This family could use some healing as well. Please don't call him Erg Troy when he arrives."

She made a face, lay back, and sighed. "I'm trying." A small black cloud formed over her head. She wished the kid would stay away. But he and Kelly were friends and had been since Troy helped her set up Sissy and Belinda.

Rex propped himself up on an elbow and moved a wisp of hair off her brow. "Troy isn't his mother."

"I know," she said, frowning.

"I don't really like the boy, either. But for Kelly's sake and the sake of what's left of your family, just tolerate him. His mother's still in jail, his aunt is living in a halfway house and he's all alone."

"I will. Haven't I been?" she asked, a bit defensive.

"You weren't exactly warm the first couple years."

"I know. I tried. He strangled my cat."

"I know. He denies it, you know."

She waved her hand dismissively. "Heard that story. Suffice to say he's welcome here, but I don't really have to completely like it, do I?"

"No. You don't have to do anything you don't want." He wrapped his long arms around her and held her close. "Like leave this bed."

She kissed his slightly scratchy, but very warm cheek, fully enjoying his scent. "You are so bad."

"It is Christmas..." He stroked her breasts, then ran his hand down her belly and gently toyed with her clit.

Her toes curled and her sex screamed for release. She checked the clock. They had forty-five minutes before the guests arrived, an hour before the roast was done.

Oh, why the hell not? She sent him a half-smile and "the look."

His eyes dilated and his cock surged against her leg.

"Merry Christmas, baby," he said, climbing on top.

She lay back, her body hungry for him. "Joy to the World, I'm going to come," she sang.

He stopped and laughed, shaking his head at her. "What am I going to do with you?"

She took his rear in both hands and pulled him deep inside. "I thought that had been decided."

He groaned and closed his mouth on hers.

The End

About Periat's Fables

After writing *Cinderolda*, I got to thinking. Why not do a twisted Janet take on all the big stories? While I didn't want any paranormal or magical elements in the books, I loved the framework of the fairy tales. I also love series with common characters. And thus, Periat's Fables was born.

The second book in the series, *Deadly Dreams* (*Sleeping Beauty*), will feature Kelly DuCharmante, Butch Wagner and Troy Slaughter, with Cynthia, Rex and Jon in supporting roles. *Beauty and Mr. B* will be third, with Beauty White—Kelly DuCharmante's best friend—who we'll meet in *Deadly Dreams*. The fourth book will be *Snow White and the Seven Dorks,* featuring Beauty White's cousin Snow, owner of a computer software firm.

Look for *Deadly Dreams* in early 2013.

The following was the winner of the First Page Contest at SV-RWA's Authors Conference, 2010.

Deadly Dreams

The victim exhaled his last breath and his body went still. He fit in so nicely among the presents laid out around the bottom of the Christmas tree. Blue, yellow, green and red twinkling lights reflected in his sightless, staring eyes, his gray skin bathed in soft hues of the ever-changing light show.

A surge of energy welled in the killer's body. Stronger this time. Unexpected, but wonderful. Closing his eyes, he took a deep breath of air. He imagined taking in the essence of the life he'd just extinguished. He felt stronger, invincible, omnipotent.

Outside on the street, carolers meandered by singing *Joy To The World*. Perfect background music for the occasion. One more rival gone.

Aside from the victory, killing itself had been so fun. More fun than almost anything. Well, anything but capturing her. Being with her. Owning her.

If she didn't wake up and come to him soon, he may have to put her to sleep.

He wouldn't kill her.

But he would keep her.

Forever.

Look For *Deadly Dreams* in early 2013

www.janetperiat.com

www.ingramcontent.com/pod-product-compliance
Lightning Source LLC
Chambersburg PA
CBHW020225260626
47156CB00002B/542